Stella Quinn has had a love affair with books since she first discovered the alphabet. She lives in sunny Queensland now but has lived in England, Hong Kong and Papua New Guinea. Boarding school in a Queensland country town left her with a love of small towns and heritage buildings (and a fear of chenille bedspreads and meatloaf!) and that is why she loves writing rural romance. Stella is a keen Scrabble player, she's very partial to her four kids and anything with four furry feet, and she is a mediocre grower of orchids. An active member of Romance Writers of Australia, Stella has won their Emerald, Sapphire and Valerie Parv awards and has twice been a finalist in their Romantic Book of the Year award.

You can find and follow Stella Quinn at stellaquinnauthor.com.

Also by Stella Quinn

The Vet From Snowy River
A Town Like Clarence
A Home Among the Snow Gums
Down the Track

A SNOWY RIVER
Summer

STELLA QUINN

A SNOWY RIVER SUMMER
© 2025 by Stella Quinn
ISBN 9781038903938

First published on Gadigal Country in Australia in 2025
by HQ Fiction
an imprint of HQBooks (ABN 47 001 180 918), a subsidiary of HarperCollins Publishers Australia Pty Limited (ABN 36 009 913 517).

HarperCollins acknowledges the Traditional Custodians of the lands upon which we live and work, and pays respect to Elders past and present.

The right of Stella Quinn to be identified as the author of this work has been asserted in accordance with the *Copyright Amendment (Moral Rights) Act 2000*.

This work is copyright. Apart from any use as permitted under the *Copyright Act 1968*, no part may be reproduced, copied, scanned, stored in a retrieval system, recorded, or transmitted, in any form or by any means, without the prior written permission of the publisher. Without limiting the author's and publisher's exclusive rights, any unauthorised use of this publication to train generative artificial intelligence (AI) technologies is expressly prohibited.

This is a work of fiction. Names, characters, places, and incidents are either the product of the author's imagination or are used fictitiously, and any resemblance to actual persons, living or dead, business establishments, events, or locales is entirely coincidental.

A catalogue record for this book is available from the National Library of Australia
www.librariesaustralia.nla.gov.au

Printed and bound in Australia by McPherson's Printing Group

*For my readers. Thank you for your support.
My books would be very lonely without you in their lives.*

CHAPTER 1

Damon Johns' life imploded in a red-brick archway of a building that had once housed convicts. He might've recalled more specifics about the building's history if he could think, but thinking wasn't happening.

Nor, and this was the problematic thing, was breathing.

The voice in his head that had been plaguing him these last few months started up. Always an expert witness, always an emotionless tone no matter how horrendous the topic, and always a grim outcome. Sometimes, like now, the expert was focused solely on Damon. *When I conducted an autopsy of the man found collapsed in a brick archway within Sydney's historical Hyde Park Barracks, I found evidence of asphyxia including submucosal haemorrhagic petechiae and displacement of the—*

Damon pressed his forehead into the dull brick and willed the expert witness, who he'd nicknamed Dr Gloom, to do him and the world a favour and piss right off. Rude, yes. Necessary, also yes. He felt dizzy. Sick. His heart was pounding like it had grown legs and a tail and turned into a racehorse. His lungs were made of barnacles and his hands, when he brought them up to rub his face, had developed a tremor that no-one—*no-one*—could ever see.

He forced hot Sydney summer air into the pain pit where his lungs used to be, then just as urgently forced it out. He had only a few minutes to pull himself together and sort out this new and unwelcome physical development. Dr Gloom was annoying, but he'd been ignoring him (mostly) for months; Damon was blessed—or cursed, depending on the context—with a memory that refused to forget anything at all, so having a running commentary in his head of the many, *many*, grim cases he'd worked on hadn't seemed *too* nuts. But this new thing? This heart-racing, barnacle-in-the-lungs thing? He could barely *stand*, let alone ignore it, which was kind of a major deal problem, on account of the fact that on the eleventh floor of the blockish, beige concrete-and-glass high rise behind him, a judge and jury and witnesses and court officials and corrections services officers and spectators were right this very minute gathering for the verdict of a trial, and everyone was expecting to see Damon Johns stride on in there like he was confidence incarnate.

Because, of course, that's what he'd been for some years now: a barrister to be reckoned with. A force. A powerhouse. A legend at the bar, even, if he read some of the tripe dished up by the court reporters in the daily news. Which he did. Avidly.

So what had changed? Why *this* case? Why *now*?

He didn't want to think of the accused's testimony and the Crown's cross-examination, but there they were, in his head, memorised perfectly.

You were jealous, in fact.

No.

Your mother—in your own words—abandoned you, so you bought a weapon—
No, I—
You drove to her home—
It wasn't her home, it was her boyfriend's place, and—
And you bludgeoned her with—
Objection!

Damon lifted his head from the bricks of the archway, and then wished he hadn't. He was clammy, and he did not feel well at all, and how on earth was he going to get himself back to court in this state?

The scratch of a match made its way through the rushing in his ears and the stink of nicotine fouled up what little oxygen he was getting. 'You look like you need to put your head between your knees,' said a voice behind him. A voice which, unfortunately, he knew.

'I'm fine, Judge,' he said. Or tried to say; gritted teeth and an undiagnosed lung condition were quite the impediment. Also, showing weakness? In front of anyone, let alone a *judge*? Not an option. Barristers weren't weak. Ever. It was the unwritten code and a barrister with ambition like Damon's—limitless, unbounded; arrogant, even—had helped write that unwritten code.

'I'm leaving,' said the voice behind him. 'Pretend I wasn't here. But if you've got a brain hiding under that cocky facade, you'll get your head between your knees the second I'm gone.'

A little less than thirteen minutes later, Damon was in the corridor outside a courtroom in the blocky Law Courts building he'd escaped from a scant hour ago. He'd returned via a cursory visit to the men's loo, where he'd wiped his face down with damp paper. He'd then adjusted his robes and donned his ancient wig, which resembled a grubby little animal rather than a symbol of justice, and both actions helped settle him. He could do this.

He *had* to be able to do this.

The head-between-knee thing had worked and his lungs had seen sense and decided to cooperate. Good. Excellent. That attack downstairs had been a one-off and no need to dwell. Every need, in fact, to soldier on as normal, so what would normal Damon be doing at the end of a trial?

Celebrating, that's what. He pulled his phone out of his pocket totally casually. Flicked an equally casual text to the latest in a long string of short-term girlfriends: *Up for a drink? I'll be free shortly after four o'clock.*

Good. Excellent. *Normal.*

'Free for a drink?' said his friend and law clerk, Sean, who'd pounced on him like a mother hen when Damon had emerged from the elevator and was now reading over Damon's shoulder as they joined the crowd forming to re-enter the courtroom.

Sean was one of Damon's oldest friends and—to use his own words, but no-one disagreed—the administrative heart of their chambers, Johns & Wickramasinghe. Warunya, Damon's other oldest friend, was the other barrister. She was calm and unflappable. Damon didn't care about being calm, or about administration, or even about having a heart. When he put on a good show for the jury, the jury voted his way, and Damon always, *always*, put on a good show.

Even if, like today, the show resulted in some sort of existential ... wobble.

Abandonment trauma can result in emotional disconnection, feelings of inadequacy, self-sabotaging acts, an inability to—

Was Dr Gloom implying this case was a trigger? Ridiculous to think so. Ridiculous to compare his own feelings of being abandoned by his mother and brother to the defendant's.

Trigger or not, Damon was winning the case today. He knew it. He had a gut feeling. He took a deep breath into lungs that felt almost normal. A win was a win, and money in the bank, a notch on the board for their chambers and a long, obsequious queue of solicitors wanting to brief him for work.

'Even if the jury comes through with a verdict,' Sean continued, clearly not done, 'you've got six crates of paperwork to take back to the office. Don't think I'm lugging it away for you by myself.'

Damon watched the thumbs-up emoji flicker onto his screen, then turned his phone off. 'Relax, mate. Those jurors were all on Team Damon, I'll bet you ten bucks.'

'The jury will believe anything you tell them. There's something wrong about that. Something unjust. Especially when your client's a total psycho who we both know clobbered the hell out of his mother.'

'I'm his barrister, Sean. Convincing the jury that my words are spun gold and my client is not guilty is what I'm paid to do.' Did that make him sound shallow? So what? He was shallow and successful, which was enough ... most of the time.

When his lungs worked.

When the expert witness in his head shut up.

'Spun bullshit more like.' Sean had dropped his voice to a whisper; personal conversation was frowned upon in court, which was a compelling clue as to how ticked off he was. Sean was a by-the-book kind of guy and normally wouldn't so much as rustle a notepad. 'I'm telling you, Damon—as your friend—it's making me uneasy. The facts are what ought to convince a judge and jury, not your theatrics. You've been over the top lately. Reckless. Something's going on with you and it is not a good something, mate.'

Suggesting Damon's work in court was even vaguely like theatre work was a low blow and Sean was one of the few people who should know that. 'Me winning cases is paying your wages,' he said, frowning. Was it obvious to everyone around him that he'd been off lately? Or just to Sean?

He didn't want to think about the answer to that question, so he changed the subject. Another thing he was good at. When stuff—life, he supposed was the correct word—popped up that he didn't want to deal with, he took on a new case, the trickier the better, and got busy. As a strategy it had been a total winner. Up until recently.

Alex Hancock, the solicitor who'd given him the case, was looking back at him from the bar table and tapping her watch.

'Why are you even here, anyway, Sean? Don't you have cases of Warunya's to get all sanctimonious about?' Damon said.

'She can look after herself. You? I'm not so sure.'

To prove how little he cared about what those words implied, Damon grinned. He might be shallow, and he might let Sean do most of the legwork, but he had his pride. He was also very accomplished at lying. 'Relax, Seano. I'm totally fine.'

'Cancel your drink plans. We've got a chambers' dinner tonight, seven o'clock, remember? Maybe your date can take a back seat.'

'I'll be sure to suggest that to her.'

Sean wasn't amused. 'Don't play your word games on me, mate. I've been listening to them since you were that cocky little shit of a sixteen-year-old who I was forced to include in my senior school debating team, and I know all your tricks.'

Damon bit back his cocky-little-shit answer because the court official had come into the room. Judge McMary must be on her way.

'Here we go,' he muttered instead and strode to the bar table. He didn't bother taking his seat, and the words 'All rise' from the court official had everyone standing as the judge entered from the side door at the front of the room and took her seat at the high bench. Her associate followed in her wake, taking a seat at the table between Damon's and the judge's. Everyone in the room did the nod-type bow that was expected, and then sat and waited while the jury filed back into the courtroom from their jurors' room.

The court was silent. Damon tucked his six-foot-one frame in behind the glossy, engineered-plywood desk with which the state of New South Wales had furnished its criminal courtrooms sometime in the last decade. He noticed a smear of red-brick dust riding the knife-crease his dry-cleaning service had pressed into his charcoal suit pants and he flicked it off with a finger that did not—ha!—tremor at all.

Maybe he was cured. Probably he *was* cured.

The judge was rifling through paperwork, but Damon was happy to avoid meeting her eye by concentrating on the jury members as they formed a line in front of the jury box. They weren't as skilled at maintaining a poker face as Judge McMary and the telltale signs were all there: no eye contact with Adrienne Khoo, representing the Crown; furtive glances at their watches; posture a mix of relief and self-consciousness; looks of approval coming his way. Oh, yeah, he was getting his client acquitted all right.

Tonight's dinner was probably so Sean and Warunya could present him with some hideous pen or monogrammed tie. Wins in court for one of them brought work into chambers for both of them. Good, high calibre work. Stuff more interesting than the traffic violations and low-level white collar cases that most early career barristers got lumped with.

Sean was wrong; everything was going *great*.

The solicitor beside him gave Damon's shoe a nudge with her three-inch stiletto heel and Damon snapped out of his daydream to realise the courtroom had grown silent and the judge had replaced her poker face with a look of deep irritation.

Oops.

'Are we boring you, Mr Johns?'

Whatever she'd said to him, he'd totally missed. That wasn't like him—he was a venus flytrap in the courtroom, not a word or a nuance passed unnoticed. Usually.

He cleared his throat. 'Thank you, Your Honour,' he said, hoping he was guessing correctly. 'Yes, the defence is ready to hear the verdict.'

The judge frowned at him for a long period before nodding to her associate, who stood and faced the jury. 'Members of the jury,' the associate said in a monotone. 'Are you agreed upon a verdict?'

'Yes,' said the foreman.

'How do you find the defendant, Paul Wilson? Guilty or not guilty of the charge of assault causing bodily harm? So says your speaker, so say you all.'

'We find the defendant not guilty.'

Damon flicked his eyes to the clock on the courtroom wall. Oh yeah, he'd be out of here by four. He turned to the row behind him where his client, Paul, was flanked by corrective services officers and nodded. Nailed it. As expected.

He tuned out the murmurs from Alex beside him, and from the prosecution, and even the announcements from the judge as he gathered up the papers before him on the bar table, but then looked up when he heard Judge McMary say his name.

'Court is adjourned for everyone except Mr Johns ... A word, if you please. My chambers, now.'

Damon turned slightly in his chair to raise his eyebrows at Sean, then stood with the courtroom to perform the perfunctory bow as Judge McMary disappeared through her private door. 'Wonder what the dragon wants?' he said, as Sean came over. He knew. Of course he knew. But was he going to be sharing that with Sean?

No way.

'Whatever it is, you'd better listen. All week, she's looked less than impressed with your antics.'

'She didn't stop me though, did she?' This was perfect. If Damon had conducted himself like a vanilla ice-cream sandwich all week, like Sean would obviously prefer, then he'd have to explain why he'd been called in to see the judge. Allowing Sean to think he was about to get a bollocking allowed him to keep his secret.

'"Good fame and character", mate.'

Damon chuckled to hide how pissed off he was to have words from the New South Wales Bar Association's disclosure obligations quoted at him. The tight feeling in his chest returned and he willed it away. 'Looks like you get to drag all this lot back to chambers on your own after all, Seano. I have judges to schmooze, women to woo.'

Sean's hand settled briefly on his arm. 'Seven o'clock. Don't be late.'

Damon slapped him on the back and headed across the courtroom. When was he ever late?

At seven oh three pm exactly, just as Damon did a rat run through Bass Lane to avoid the snarl of traffic blocking Fox and Stanley, a uniformed cop stepped out from behind a parked police car, held up his hand and motioned Damon to halt.

Crap. A serve from a judge who thought he was treating her courtroom with disrespect—'more tricks than a Kings Cross sex worker' was the phrase she'd used—had thrown his schedule. Fobbing her off about why she'd found him clutching a brick wall during court recess having what she considered to be—but surely not!—a panic attack, had taken even more time. He'd eaten a dodgy chicken salad. Late onset asthma. Or perhaps he'd been subjected to freon gas leakage from an overworked aircon unit … the excuses he'd offered up had been barely plausible and largely laughable, and she'd listened to him with narrowed eyes.

Damon wound down the window of his car. 'Can I help you, officer? Kinda in a hurry here.'

'There some reason why you're avoiding the RBT checkpoint?'

'Uh …' A random breath testing unit at this hour, when the whole of the Sydney CBD was trying to get home? Did they have all the side streets covered to catch RBT evaders? No wonder the traffic had been a snarl-up. 'Sorry. I'm running late for a meeting. I was just ducking traffic to get to a restaurant—didn't even see the checkpoint.'

The police officer turned to nod at his offsider in the police car holed up in a loading zone. 'Licence, please.'

Damon sighed. His wallet was on the passenger seat, buried somewhere amidst the files he was taking home to brief for whatever case might be next on his list. He dug around until he found it, then extracted his driver's licence and handed it over.

The officer inspected it. 'All right, Mr Johns. I'll be needing you to blow into the tube for a count of ten.'

'Seriously? Look, I wasn't evading anything. See that restaurant up there on the corner? Nyom Nyom? That's where I'm going. My journey's practically over, mate.'

'You'll be taking a journey with me to the station, *mate*, if you don't blow into the tube. Here or the station, take your pick.'

Damon rolled his eyes. 'All right, keep your shirt on.' He was about to acquiesce without any more fuss and backchat, but then a thought struck him. An unwelcome thought.

Was he over the limit? There'd been the beer at the Duke of Clarence while he waited for Melita to show up. Then, after she breezed in full of news about her promotion at work, he'd splashed out on a bottle of Taittinger. Showing off, obviously. Nothing at all to do with Sean hitting a nerve in the courtroom earlier, Judge McMary's ticking off, or that insane moment of sweat and choking lungs …

How much of it had he drunk? Not more than a glass. Or two …

He leant forward and blew into the tube the cop was holding.

'You right, Damo?'

Oh, great. Sean and Warunya just had to be walking past as he was being breath tested. Why couldn't they have been on time for a change, safely inside the restaurant and out of sight?

'It's nothing,' he said. 'You go on ahead and order me the red duck special. This is sorted.'

The police officer crossed his arms. 'In charge of a motorised vehicle under the influence of alcohol is not nothing in this city, Mr Johns,' he said. 'Nor is anything sorted. Step out of the car.'

Damon looked up. 'What was the reading?'

'Point oh five oh two.'

Every DUI case he'd heard back when he was a junior barrister replayed in his mind in triple time; having a near-perfect memory had some perks, after all. 'Do another reading,' he said. 'That could be a false positive.'

'You had anything to drink in the last twenty-four hours?'

Crap. 'Yes, but—'

'Then it's not a false reading.'

'I want a blood test.' Oh five oh two was barely over. He'd seen low-range readings challenged in the courts, and if any old barrister could argue the point and win, then he sure as hell could, too. Would he even need to disclose this to the Bar Association? A low reading, a first offence, no conviction …

It was the police officer's turn to roll his eyes. 'How are you going to manage a blood test, sunshine? You've got a two-hour window to get it done, and I don't see a nurse standing nearby, do you? If you're a first-time offender, you cop a fine now and a three-month licence disqualification. No conviction.'

Yeah. Damon knew all that. Cold comfort.

'That's not my only option.'

The cop had clearly heard every argument a thousand times and had every answer ready. 'You want to argue it out in court? Well, you can do that too. Your choice. What you're not doing is driving that car again tonight. Out you get, sir.'

'A DUI charge? Damon, are you shitting me?' Sean looked like the buttons on his business shirt were about to pop off. He and Warunya were standing on either side of the officer now, like sentries on duty.

'Settle down, Sean. I don't have to accept the disqualification. I can challenge it.'

Science will support the low-range DUI charge challenge because blood alcohol content, or BAC as we describe it in the report provided to the court, discriminates between age, gender, body mass and liver quality, rattled off Dr Gloom, trying to be helpful for a change.

'You want to go in front of a magistrate on this?' said Warunya. 'Bandy your name around in a room full of flappy-eared lawyers who'd just love to spread some scurrilous gossip about you? This could jeopardise our chambers.'

'Three lawyers. Just my frigging luck,' said the police officer.

'Two,' said Damon, and could have kicked himself. Sean's eye roll felt worse than a good kicking would have done. Worse, even, than a lung malfunction.

'Whatever. If the two of you who *haven't* been pulled over would like to step back,' said the officer, 'me and Mr Johns can conclude our business.'

The fine was a pain in the arse, but he could afford it. A three-month disqualification? Embarrassing and a total inconvenience that he could do without. But the expressions of disapproval on his colleagues' faces? Yeah, that hurt.

And how had this come about? Bloody champagne. Which he didn't even like. Come to think of it, he didn't much like Melita either.

Damon scrabbled around on the passenger seat until he had the essentials stuffed into his briefcase—file notes, phone charger, wallet—then got out and held his car keys up. Warunya walked to work from a swanky two-bedder on Elizabeth Street that he knew for a fact had an empty car space. 'Can you take my car, Runya? Park it at your place tonight?'

Warunya's eyes narrowed. 'I'll take it,' she said. 'But when you're done here and join us at Nyom Nyom, we're going to be having a long overdue chat.'

Yeah. Whatever. Damon snorted at the smirk on the police officer's face as his friends walked off and he began parroting the details of his life. The smirk stung, but Damon could deal with it. That's what being awesome did for you; it gave you the confidence to push through these social stings.

A tepid rain began to fall, and he drew his awesomeness around him like a cloak.

Nyom Nyom was a modern shack tucked into a narrow alley between two old sandstone buildings that dated back to a time when Sydney was just a colonial settlement, and displaced landowners raged in the country beyond the range of musket fire. Nyom Nyom's owner didn't bother throwing out lures to passersby in the form of arm-waving gold cats or chef's specials. She didn't need to. The restaurant's six tiny tables were always full, despite the fact customers had to weave through towers of rice sacks and cartons of bottled water to find them. The whine and clatter of delivery mopeds arriving and departing in a steady stream was the venue's background music, and the menu consisted of a sticky, laminated A3 sheet taped to a wall. Behind a thin counter, three cooks worked their magic under a massive rangehood.

At the door sat the matriarch of the enterprise. Mrs Dao could wield two phones, a cash register, an eftpos machine, a calculator and concurrent conversations in two languages without any apparent effort.

'My darling Damon, one minute please,' she said. 'Two panang chicken one pad thai prawn one special fried rice two ginger beef ninety-six dollars forty cents no Amex.' This last was directed at whoever she was speaking to on the phone through the headset clamped to her face. 'Your friends are here. Very cranky faces.'

Damon leant to the side to avoid being clobbered in the head by an order being handed by one of the chefs to a tiny woman in a very large motorcycle helmet who'd come up beside him. Mrs Dao wasn't wrong about the cranky faces. The dull surge of ... *something* that had tightened his chest as the police officer had booked him grew.

'Go, sit. They ordered the usual for you, okay?'

He managed to nod. Totally casually. He was fine. And if he wasn't? Well, if it wasn't dodgy chicken or late onset asthma, he probably had some virus. Pleurisy. Lungworm. Anything would be acceptable so long as it wasn't what Judge McMary thought it was. 'Thanks, Mrs Dao.'

Sean got straight into it just as a plastic platter of fishcakes was plonked on the table. 'Warunya and I have talked.'

'You're always talking. We're always talking. We're talkative people.'

'About you, Damon.'

Okay, that shut him up.

'Specifically, we're worried about you.'

'I am totally fine,' he said for what felt like the tenth time that day. He was not at all fine and the sharp, oyster-shell feeling rolling over in his chest knew it. But the thing about being a barrister was that your one and only emotional response at all times had to be unbridled confidence. *Had* to be. And both Sean and Runya knew that; at least, they ought to.

'For your sake—and this is going to be hard on us, too, Damon—we've decided you need some time out.'

Damon laughed. It came out as a croak, like he had undiagnosed emphysema. 'Time out? What is this, kindergarten?' Time out was the last thing he needed, especially now. There were some good cases in the cab rank—career-building cases—and he had an excellent chance of scoring them. Success was in reach. *His* place in the world as the successful one was in reach.

He stopped with the fake laugh when he saw that their grim faces were unmoved.

'We've checked your case load. Wilson's case has wound up sooner than you'd allowed for and Runya's agreed she can take on Cooper. Whatever's after that, we pass—personal reasons. You're a train crash waiting to happen, Damon. We'd been going to talk to you tonight about slowing the pace a little, but called into judge's chambers today for a bollocking? What is that, the second time this month? And now a DUI? Consider this an intervention. You have an excellent career ahead of you, but not if you don't tone down some of this, I don't know, deranged hyperfocus we've been seeing lately.'

'*What?*' Deranged hyperfocus was hardly a medical term. He should know, he'd heard enough medical witnesses in his court describe medical terms, in literally microscopic detail, from blood pooling patterns in a corpse to subcutaneous bruising. He had his own personal expert witness living in his bloody head, constantly spouting medical drivel at him that he couldn't get rid of. 'Come on, guys, that cop was overly officious and the judge—'

'Forget the cop,' said Warunya. 'Forget the judge. Sean and I have been worried about you for a while. You've been a little, I don't know … wired, lately. On edge. Reckless.'

'You've been running back-to-back cases—emotionally fraught cases—and you've been peacocking about like the facts can't touch you,' said Sean.

'Peacocking? I think you mean winning, mate.' Wasn't that what his job was? To be confident, to show no emotion, to dig deep into the darkness at the heart of the crime, to be a weapon of freaking justice. And keeping the facts from touching him … well, if Sean and Runya thought he was managing that, then he was better at hiding his inner demons than he'd been giving himself credit for.

'We have to think about the reputation of the chambers, and that means you taking a break and rethinking just how cocky you think it is appropriate to be in court when you're supposed to be acting on behalf of a client, not putting on some theatrical performance to satisfy our egos.'

Theatrical? Again? Had the two of them been workshopping their intervention script?

'I'm not cocky, Runya.' Okay, he was cocky, but he knew how to put a spin on it. He could put a spin on anything. 'I'm competitive, which is why I'm an excellent barrister.'

'Humble, too. Another thing you and Nick have in com—'

'We have nothing in fucking common.'

Forks stopped scraping plates; ginger and shallots stopped tossing in woks.

He hadn't meant to say that quite so loud. He swallowed, but nope, that thing—knot—*something* latched onto his lungs was now scraping and clawing up his throat. He could feel sweat on his back. One random episode in a brick archway he could brush off, but what in heck was happening now?

This was bad. Bad, bad, bad. And he had a horrible feeling that Dr Gloom was not wrong about what had turned the stress that had dogged him the last few months into this insanity-of-the-lungs problem. It had been when he was questioning the psychologist who'd been treating Wilson.

So if I were abandoned as a child, it's possible that could leave me with trauma? Trauma that would carry through into adulthood?

And the psychologist's answer: *Yes. And you may not even have been abandoned. It would be enough that you, as a child, felt abandoned.*

Ridiculous to feel an affinity with the Paul Wilson case. Personalising a question was a very typical style of address; it was what barristers did. *If I were to suffer from a fatal arrhythmia, Dr Mack, would there be some physical manifestation? If I pulled this trigger, Officer Gambino, would you expect to find gun residue on my fingers, on my palm, or both?* Ridiculous, too, to compare his slightly abandoned eighteen-year-old self, who'd had all the benefits of a good education, and options, and a share house with other uni students to sleep in safely each night, and life bloody *goals*, with a drug-addled and impulse control–challenged defendant in an assault case who'd grown up in and out of juvie.

'Take some leave,' said Warunya. 'You've not had a holiday that didn't involve booze and a legal conference in forever. And that is not a suggestion, Damon. We'll call it a sabbatical if anyone asks. It starts now.' And then she made the mistake of being kind to him, which was way, *way* worse than having her go all courtroom-cold-face on him. 'We're your oldest friends, Damon. We care about you.'

It was so much to take in but he couldn't even get *air*. He was the rising star. The silver tongue that was getting their chambers noticed. The go-getter.

'You can't make me take leave,' he said. 'I don't work for you and I pay my own rent.'

'We're in chambers together, Damon. You want to keep your name on our nameplate? Live the life the three of us have been dreaming of since school? Then you do as we say. It's two against one and good luck affording rental space on your own, or finding anyone else who'll put up with you showponying around in court all day and doing none of the grunt work.'

'You're both overreacting.' He sounded desperate and he *hated* that. But he needed to work. He *was* his work. Pride and the drive to be a success was all he had.

Sean took a fishcake and dipped it in sauce. 'See? The husky voice, the woe-is-me face, the dramatic eyes ... just more theatrics, mate. This is exactly the sort of bullshit you pull in court.'

'Three months,' Warunya said like an annoying echo. 'We don't want to see your handsome face again until you've grown a conscience that's bigger than your dick.'

Sean coughed. 'Bigger than his ego, I think we were going to say, Runya.'

Warunya rolled her eyes. 'Same difference. One day you'll thank us, Damon. Now, stop looking like a thundercloud and have one of these before Sean hogs them all. They're delicious.'

She was waving a platter in front of him but the barnacle-knot-lump was now impeding his lungs and throat and chest. A conscience was a liability; didn't she get that? Something to be suppressed, turned off, ignored. He sucked in air but all there was in the restaurant was steam and garlic and failure.

And this wasn't theatrics. This wasn't him bullshitting them. Couldn't they see that? His two best friends in the world?

This, he realised with a shock, was *fear*.

Him. Damon Johns. Afraid of *himself*.

'I've ... got to go,' he said.

'Oh, come on, man,' said Sean. 'Don't storm off. At least let Mrs Dao box up your curry. We ordered the red duck special. Your favourite.'

No, nope, no to both, any, all. He couldn't talk to anyone, not this second, because the barnacle that had clawed its way up out of some deep part of him was dangerously close to ripping its way to the surface.

He pushed past a crate of potatoes and hit the street. The rain was heavier now, great fat drops of it falling onto the dark cloth of his suit, wetting his hair, finding the crevice between collar and neck. He closed his eyes when rain landed on his face but he couldn't tell where rain ended and sweat began, and if he could only ... just ... breathe ...

CHAPTER
2

Vintage tractor enthusiasts were treated to a display of old-school furrowing techniques at the Dirranbandi Show, involving a deep-digging single-furrow mouldboard plough attached to an Ursus C 360 powered by a 4-cylinder diesel, made in Poland in the 1960s and imported to Australia by Gladys and Bill Spooner of Blue Pines Station in 1973. One enthusiast recalled using a similar setup to plant potatoes in Scotland in the 1950s.

Australian Vintage Tractors Digest, *May 1986*

Kylie Summer was fond of old issues of classic tractor magazines the way some people were fond of chocolate. Her bookshelf housed dozens of the things—tatty, grease-stained copies that she'd picked up at garage sales over the years—which was lucky, because the classics collection at Hanrahan Library had been digitised onto microfiche and where was the fun in scrolling through that? Nowhere. No fun at all. And the library certainly wouldn't have welcomed her at sunrise, clad as she was in her fluffy pink dressing gown, holding a mug of tea, her feet ensconced in ridiculous slippers with koala faces on them.

A little light tractor reading was a comforting way to start the day. Particularly at the moment, when her normal sunny optimism was a little, well, unsunny. Not that she felt low, as such—Kylie didn't believe in feeling low—but there *was* the small matter of the cashflow crisis. The imminent finance repayment due on her secondhand hoist. The three cancelled vehicle services she'd been counting on this week, and probably best not to think about the spike of invoices on her workshop bench that was enough to wallpaper her living room.

Kylie scraped the blunt curve of a butter knife around the squared-off base of the almost empty jar of Vegemite. Tractors were so much lovelier to think about than unpaid invoices, so she turned the page to read an article on the origin of the term 'horsepower'. Tractors represented all that was good in the world. They were strong. They were reliable and (mostly, if you omitted the early models that needed cranking and pre-warming with eyebrow-singing blow torches—looking at you, Lanz Bulldog 1949) uncomplicated. Tractors had a cheerful work ethic that endured mud, rain, snow and anything else the world might like to throw at them. Even the passage of time.

Tractors were like a good bloke, in fact. If only she had one of those to share her morning slippers and Vegemite ritual with.

Thinking about the passage of time made her look at her watch. She'd make yoga if she ate her toast on the run; another start-of-the-day routine she was fond of, although one she didn't indulge in as often. There was only so much well-meaning small-town meddling in her life she could laugh along with and pretend to appreciate, and yoga seemed to attract the most meddlesome of the Hanrahan locals. They, too, had noticed the absence of tractor-like blokes in her life and were full of advice on the topic.

She swirled the stingy lump of Vegemite through the butter melting on her toast, then turned to the washing basket taking up half of her sofa. *See?* she thought, in an only slightly defensive way. *There is method to my laundry madness.* If she'd folded her clothes and put them away in actual drawers, then she'd have been late for yoga. A mental image of Wendy Summer frowning over this slovenly attitude was dismissed. Her mum did so much frowning over Kylie's choices, what did one more frown matter?

She flung her pink fluffy dressing gown over a corner of the bookcase, stripped out of her flannel pyjamas (because even though it was mid-summer, when you lived in the lee of the Snowy Mountains, nights were cold) and checked the colour of her nail polish before wrestling her way into a sports bra (blue), clean knickers (also blue) and neck-to-ankle lycra (burnt orange). Just because a girl had left behind a career as a beautician to become a mechanic did not mean a girl had to sacrifice her fashion sense or her colour-matched underwear and nails habit.

Her sneakers were outside on the world's smallest balcony, propped up against a plant pot where a rosemary shrub had once thrived before it came to live with her. She pulled them on, wrapped her hair into a messy but cute ponytail, and was out the door, toast and handbag in hand, exercise mat under an arm, a bare minute later. Marigold Jones, the town matriarch who ran dawn yoga classes summer and winter, autumn and spring, had a particularly grim way of dealing with tardy yoga attendees that involved balance and calf muscles. *Been there, done that,* Kylie thought. *Lesson learned.*

She had her mat unrolled and was jogging lightly on the spot to keep warm, nodding at the usual cluster of locals who'd fronted up to the patch of grass on the lake foreshore, when Kev spoke.

'Any takers this week, pet?'

A year ago, when she'd finally decided to join an online dating app after realising that the quota of unmarried, eligible males who farmed the arable land on the outskirts of Hanrahan appeared to be zero, she'd not thought that her online profile would become a joint venture between her and the yoga crew. *For singles looking for love in the country*, the app marketed itself. *Live rural? Looking for romance? Let RuRo match you with your dream farmer!*

Unfortunately, RuRo's efforts on her behalf had not amounted to much, and the yoga crew liked to entertain themselves amidst their poses by dreaming up catchy phrases for her online profile. They'd long since exhausted wishful ones like *Lady mechanic committed to country life looking for meaningful long-term relationship with adorable farmer.*

'Sadly not, Kev,' she said, dropping into a lunge and wincing. She'd spent yesterday morning on a farm, overhauling a ride-on mower and she'd pulled a muscle or a tendon or something, dragging the darn thing out of its shed. Ibuprofen, she thought. If she had any. Hopefully she did, because she was pretty sure her bank balance was sitting below the five dollar mark.

'I've been thinking we try a new strategy,' he said.

'Yes?' Kylie was only half listening, because Marigold had assumed her position at the front of the group and had begun her warming up moves. Kev, of course, would not be told off if he didn't pay attention, unlike Kylie. He was not officially a yoga participant, but he was always there on the park bench, looking benignly on as Marigold barked out instructions like 'Utkatasana!' or 'Tadasana!' He was also the apple of his wife's eye, as the saying went, which granted him immunity from one-legged balancing torture.

'What say we give farmers a miss and think about blokes who work in town?'

'Um, that's a hard no,' said Kylie. 'You're forgetting my endgame: little kids in gumboots feeding chooks, Kev. A paddock of sheep. Sun shining over canola fields and the comforting throb of a lovely old tractor.'

'All right, then,' he grumbled. 'If you're going to be a fusspot, you might be interested in the way fellas found their brides in the 1890s.'

'I'm intrigued. Tell me.'

'I've been reading old newspapers.' Kev was involved with the running of the local community group and spent his days at the Hanrahan Community Hall, either in the archives room, where the historical society kept its records, or outside, tending the roses. 'Quite eye-opening they were. Did you know people used to advertise for partners then, too?'

Kylie was twisted like a bread-bag wire tie so she huffed out a grunt in response.

'Yes, indeed. Here, I copied out a few for you.'

'Lucky you, Kylie,' said Janine, town librarian and red hair–dye addict, from two mats over.

Kylie shot her a grin. 'Let's hear it then, Kev.'

Kev cleared his throat. 'Wanted, a man not so old as to be lame of leg or toothless, but not so young as to be without means, for husband.'

'Not old and not young,' said Kylie. 'Okay, a good start.' She could have done without the whole lame and toothless image in her head, but whatever.

'He must be well acquainted with the necessary accomplishments—' continued Kev.

'Huh. I can't wait to hear what these are,' said Mrs Northam drily. Mr Northam was currently sleeping on the sofa, according to town gossip.

'—being boning a fowl, broiling a fish, receiving amorous advances without coldness and roasting beef; and he must be absent of frowns and caprice, and must not be in the habit of using taunting language.'

Kylie laughed. 'No way an actual advertisement says that.'

'Hand on heart, love,' said Kev. 'I had to look up "caprice" in the dictionary. I might have switched up the hes and shes a little.'

Of course he'd switched the misogyny of yesteryear around for her and replaced the word 'husband' for 'wife'. If only Kev were sixty years younger and not besotted with the incredibly bossy Mrs Jones, Kylie would have invited him to pop on over to her apartment to broil a fish.

'That might exceed the word length, Kev, but I like your thinking.'

'Yoga now, Kylie,' barked Marigold. 'Romance later.'

Hmm. Truer words …

Kylie had been telling herself a similar thing for a while—career now, romance later—only later had never arrived. What with the business taking up all of her time and the shortage of suitable farmers, she was beginning to wonder if later might never happen.

She was still wondering at the end of the day, which she'd spent in the mechanic's workshop she rented on Bogong Street, when a drop of oil fell onto her face. She was under a car—a boxy, mustard-yellow, 1996 Volvo station wagon to be precise—and oil was leaking from its undercarriage the way rain leaked from clouds. The Brutnalls were good people—the best—but they needed to cough up some cash for new wheels. Preferably a vehicle built in the current century.

When had romance in her life come to a grinding halt, anyway? There'd seemed to be guys aplenty in her early twenties. Young ones, handsome ones, fun ones—dickhead ones—but they'd mainly been the ski season worker types: here for the winter then disappearing off to work the lifts in Canada or Europe in the off season. Not reliable types.

Not *tractor* types, she thought with a grin. 'Not like you, Trev,' she yelled from under the car. Not that Trev had ears or could respond—Trev wasn't just her vintage tractor and workshop mascot, he was also the love of Kylie's life. The 1960s Massey Ferguson tractor was missing all four tyres and lived on the concrete pad out front beside the obsolete fuel bowser. Kylie loved Trev despite the fact that she did not yet have enough money to restore him to his former glory.

She clamped a pencil torch between her teeth. Craning her head a little to encourage the light to travel where she needed it, she worked her spanner at the ruined hex head bolt that was just one of the many problems in view in the station wagon's undercarriage, see-sawing it until the bolt started to turn.

'Boss?'

She answered around the torch. 'Yes, Braydon? Shouldn't you have gone home already?'

'Phone call. It's Dave Ryan from Hanrahan Trekkers.'

Dave Ryan? Dave Ryan was calling *her*?

Kylie scooted herself out from under the car on her wheeled dolly and lay looking up at the high school student who, since Term One started just a few weeks ago, was now spending one afternoon a week doing vocational training with her. Knock-off time was five o'clock and it was well past that. She'd have liked to believe she was employing him as a trainee apprentice out of the goodness of her heart. The reality was, he came with a government cash incentive that had helped pay last month's rent. He was also her distant cousin, so when his mum, Kelly, asked her to find him a job, Kylie was too chicken to say no. Kelly was scary.

'But Dave dislikes me,' she said, wondering if Braydon was hoping she'd pay him overtime. He was an operator that way.

'Yep.'

'He's of the same school of thought as my mother, which thinks women who wear overalls and tinker with engines are one grasshopper plague away from bringing on the apocalypse.'

Braydon grinned. 'Yeah. Well, if it's any consolation, he did sound desperate. Let's make him wait some more before you take the call.'

'Tempting, but giving in to feel-good, petty impulses is no way to run a business. Pass me the phone.' Kylie held out her hand.

Braydon leant his hip against the workbench, clearly hoping to be entertained.

'Go clean something. Go buff Trevor ... Actually, go home,' she said, before turning her attention to the phone and trying to channel a calm authority she wasn't at all feeling. 'Dave. This is Kylie Summer, Hanrahan Mechanic. How can I help?'

'What do you know about diesel engines?'

'Plenty,' Kylie said, her mind whirring. Dave used the highway mechanic from down near Cooma for his fleet of tourist vehicles—her nemesis, Nigel Woods, to be precise. A total dick of a man who had done nothing but badmouth her to anyone who'd listen since she took over the lease of this workshop from old George Juggins. Just thinking about Nigel Woods made ominous orchestral music start playing in her head. So why was Dave calling her? 'You've got truck trouble?'

'I've got boat trouble.'

Huh. That might be a problem ... but suggesting she wasn't mechanically competent to Hanrahan's most successful business owner was not an option. 'If it's the engine, and if it's easy access, then I can fix whatever's wrong.' She hoped. 'If it's component parts that are marine specific like bilge pumps or gimballed bearings I can take a look but no promises.'

She held her breath, awaiting his response, unsure whether she wanted him to book her for a job or not. Snagging some work from the district's biggest tourist operator was just what her low bank balance needed and she'd be a fool not to jump at the opportunity. But snagging some work that usually went to Nigel Woods? He'd be pissed. *Super* pissed. Even more pissed than when he'd come by her workshop last month and spat—*spat*, as in full footy-player hawk and gack—on her roller door. Ew.

'Can I ask why you're not calling Nigel?'

'I have called him. He's in bloody Melbourne, taking his wife to some musical.'

Oh, yes. Pam Woods: big hair and weekly gel coat nails. 'I see.' This would be a one-off, then. Maybe Nigel wouldn't take it too badly and she'd be able to pay Braydon's wages and have enough left over to replace her Vegemite.

Dave huffed. Clearly the claims of a wife wanting to see a musical weren't a suitable reason to leave him and his diesel engines in the lurch. 'So? Are you gonna come fix my boat or what?'

His voice blasting out of the phone made her jump. She blinked. 'Of course I'm coming to fix your boat,' she said, dropping her voice an octave, as though having a deep voice made anyone a reliable expert on anything, let alone whatever diesel problem was afflicting one of Dave's boats. But she was taking the job.

Braydon, whose efforts to clean Trev had so far consisted of picking up an oily rag and tossing it from hand to hand, raised his eyebrows at her. 'A *boat*?' he whispered incredulously. 'For *Dave Ryan*?'

She drew a finger across her mouth in the age-old zip-it-or-cop-my-wrath manoeuvre. Dave Ryan may be a grumpy old codger, but he was also loaded and he paid his bills.

'See you at the dock,' the man in question said in her ear.

'What, now?'

'In the morning. Seven o'clock.'

'I'll be there. Wait … which boat is it?' The little putt-putt barbecue pontoons Dave's company hired out to summer tourists had outboard motors and so did the fishing tinnies, but there was a cabin cruiser that might have a diesel in it, or—

'The *Moana*.'

'The paddlewheeler?' No longer a steam engine, even Kylie knew that, so a diesel replacement engine to power the massive wheels on either side of the boat made sense. But crikey!

She took a breath and reminded herself she was an awesome mechanic. Drive shafts, moving parts, pistons … how different could those wheels be to a tractor's, really? And tractors had always been a passion project of hers, so no need to feel doubtful. Or gulp uselessly, which was what she seemed to be doing.

'That's right. And she's the love of my life, so if you so much as scratch her paint, you'll be answering to me.'

'Dave, I promise you, I wo—'

The phone went dead in her ear.

Braydon was all adolescent hairy eyebrows and picked spots and bulging eyes. 'For real? You're going to do a job for Dave Ryan?'

She took a breath and held it until she felt herself going dizzy. 'For real.'

'OMG. Mr Woods is going to be *so* pissed off.'

Yeah. He was. But that was a problem for another day. Right now, she had to get on the internet and read everything she could find about marine diesel engines in restored historic paddlewheelers.

CHAPTER 3

Damon took off down the narrow lane, purposefully moving in the opposite direction from where his car was parked. The rain was pelting down by the time he reached the corner and the commuters queued up at the lights had their windscreen wipers at a frenetic tick-tock. A slurry of cigarette butts, water and fuel smut was filling the gutters at his feet as it pooled around a dysfunctional city drain.

He focused on his lungs. Or, to be more precise, he could *only* focus on his lungs. Bronchitis! Maybe that's what he had. That had to explain the way he couldn't breathe. Could barely stand.

Or was he having a heart attack?

Aortic stenosis can present as pressure in the chest even when inactive, Mr Johns. Blood may be present when you cough.

Yeah, thanks for that, Dr Gloom.

His heart was a drum in his chest and he would have clawed his way out of his clothes if he hadn't been trapped by *people* and *bustle* and *traffic*. All things he normally loved, thrived on, even, but now?

The city didn't seem to understand that Damon had lost his tether. The footpath was clogged with people hurrying from here to there, clutching umbrellas, black ones mostly. Everywhere he looked was business as usual, brisk and brash, and those drivers behind the windscreen wipers, those strangers under their umbrellas, all had places to go, people to see, projects to promote. Everyone but him, who'd just been shunned by his closest friends.

Abandoned.

No, that was too strong a word, and he'd be able to think of another if it wasn't for all these headlights. Horns blaring. That *rain*. He put a hand to the closest upright thing he could find so he didn't fall, and a pedestrian crossing button bleated by his side, the sound filling his brain.

Don't walk was an unnecessary caution, he thought inanely. He didn't know if he could even crawl.

'You right, mate?' said a stranger from beneath a curved beak of umbrella fabric.

Fine, he tried to say. A lie. He was not fine.

If he could get just one breath in, he could go to his chambers. Stage a protest. Draft an argument. Get the locks changed, drum his heels on the carpet, smash some shit up ... But the thing in his chest was bigger now, and heavier, and he had a horrible, horrible feeling that he'd passed some sort of no-turning-back point and if he went to the office, or to his home, or to anywhere that would remind him that he was supposed to be Damon freaking Johns, success story, then this tuberculosis or whatever the hell this thing was would *explode*.

A cab skidded into the kerb, spraying water up in an arc so high its VACANCY sign blurred. Damon didn't even think, he just threw himself into its back seat.

'Where to, mate?'

An emergency department or away. They were his only two choices.

Away. Four points on a compass; which would be easier to say? 'West.'

'Western suburbs? What, Parramatta? Ryde? Penrith?'

'West,' he wheezed again. 'Go, for fuck's sake.'

The driver moved out into the stream of traffic and the anonymity of it, the ordinariness, helped. So, too, did Damon shoving his head between his knees, which had always seemed a super dumb thing to need to do until, like now, you needed to do it. For the second time in a day. He closed his eyes and breathed in and out and in.

What was wrong with him?

After what might have been a minute in the cab or an hour—he'd kind of lost track—he pulled out his wallet. He had a debit card, a personal credit card and a business one, but he also had cash. He fanned the notes out like they were a poker hand and the recklessness of the gambling motif spoke to his mood. 'I've got three hundred and sixty in notes,' he said, thrusting them through the gap between the driver's and passenger's seats. 'How far will that get me?'

A set of eyes in a lined face topped by a bald-as-a-cueball head met his in the rear-vision mirror. 'Depends what you're running from. I can get you someplace else if that's what you're wanting.'

Damon didn't know what he wanted. Or why he was losing the plot. But going someplace else sounded like a start.

Three hours and just less than three hundred kilometres later, the cab driver—Steve—let him out in the carpark of a roadside motel then frowned up at him through his open window. 'It doesn't seem right, leaving you here. I can take you back to the city, man, free of charge. You wanna ride up front?'

Oh, Damon wasn't going back. Not yet. Fear had turned to rage had turned to bitterness, and now he'd decided they'd need to beg him on bended knee. If they thought he was competitive in court, they hadn't seen anything yet. He could win anything, even sulking, and that's what he planned on doing.

Besides, at some point on the taxi ride, he'd realised he couldn't go back until he'd dealt with this barnacle in his chest. What if this happened in *court*? No. Nope. Not happening. His career would be over.

'Thanks for the ride,' he said.

'At least take a sandwich. My Loretta, she makes a cheese and chutney sandwich that'd make Maggie Beer jealous. Swipe of mustard, some fancy bread, and she makes the chutney herself. It's the raisins that lift it, you know what I'm saying?'

Damon looked down at the brown paper bag that was being handed out the window to him. He'd give his left nut for a cheese and chutney sandwich but he hesitated. 'You sure?'

The cabbie nodded. 'You take it, son. I hope you find whatever it is you came out here to find.'

Damon looked around the dimly lit carpark of a rundown roadside motel somewhere between Canberra and Kaliabah, then at the brown paper bag in his hand. The bag was folded neatly at the top, a smiley face drawn on the fold with a marker, and the words *love you Steve xx*.

The cabbie picked up a business card from a clip on his dashboard and handed it through the window. 'Here's my number, just in case this place turns out to be one of those old movie–style motels where they come at you with knives in the shower.'

'Appreciate it.'

Three minutes and a conversation with a bored motel desk clerk later, Damon was alone in Room 6. The bedspread was the colour of sewage. So was the carpet and the walls, and the battered lamp by the bed drooped as though it had witnessed one too many lonely motel guests.

He made a pyramid of the lettuce-leaf-thin pillows, then stretched out on the bed.

Lonely.

Where had *that* thought come from? He wasn't lonely. He was out five nights a week: meeting clients; having dinner; playing touch footy in the social competition at the fields near his home; speed-reading case notes before a trial.

He was also—he breathed in and out and stale motel-room air moved easily and airily through his lungs—totally cured. Not pleurisy, then. Or TB or lungworm.

He could do a search for panic attacks on his phone but that'd be an admission he had no interest in making. Panic attacks were for other people. He didn't understand them, he didn't believe in them, and he certainly didn't have them. Jeez.

But …

He looked at the lamp again. It was definitely drooping.

See what time to think did to a guy? It made him nuts, that's what it did. He wasn't lonely, he didn't have reckless-cocky-whatever issues to reflect upon, he could totally cope with his high-octane lifestyle, and he sure as hell didn't need a three-month time out.

But the back alley. The barnacle in his chest. The switching off in the courtroom, the decision to drink and bloody *drive*.

Damon dug his phone charger out of his briefcase, attached it to his phone then plugged it into the grimy little slot next to the droopy lamp's plug. The silence in the room was hideous now that he could think. Where was the traffic noise? The blare of a fire truck? The sounds of an argument from next door, the doosh-doosh music of the slouchy teenager across the road?

The silence started to fill with questions he didn't want to think about and answers he *definitely* didn't want to consider.

He wiped the dubiously sticky front of the TV remote on the sewage-green bedspread as case facts from the endless list in his head jockeyed for position. (Was it sticky with spilled juice? Donut sugar? Chip grease? *Semen?*)

Of course, Dr Gloom had to weigh in: *Microscopic examination can determine semen maturity and identify the presence, or lack thereof, of epithelial cells and dust.*

Ugh. Anything had to be better than his own company, so he switched the TV on and arrowed through the channels. A pollie causing a scene on the lawn outside of Parliament House; a race record by an Australian woman in a solo row across the Atlantic; another cyclone forming in the Pacific ... He kept scrolling through screens of news and sports and infomercials, his finger pausing when a familiar name caught his ear.

'—and rumours of trouble on set for none other than Australia's singing boy wonder turned TV celebrity, Nick Johns! Stay tuned for all the details and—'

He tried to feel something, but didn't. Nick was in the news again. So freaking what.

Damon stared upwards, so keen to obliterate his own thoughts he concentrated instead on wondering which architect had brainstormed the idea of putting lumpy paint on ceilings.

He ate the cheese and chutney sandwich (Thanks, Steve and Loretta), then he went for a wander through the carpark and ate his way through every letter and number combo that the vending machine had on offer: nuts, jerky, lollies, muesli bars, chocolate.

He washed his socks and jocks in the manky sink and hung them over the towel rail to dry. Sometime around the seven-hour mark of his self-imposed purgatory in the sewage-coloured motel room, he finally managed to fall asleep.

❦

The bleat of his phone woke him—startled him awake, in fact—and he rolled onto his back with a groan. Dull light showed through the old curtains—not the harsh lighting of the fluorescents lining the carpark, but morning light. A new day.

He rubbed his hands over his face, feeling and hearing the bristle of his beard growing in.

His phone blipped again. Sean, probably. Or Warunya. Boo hoo.

He'd ignored the texts he'd received from both of them last night, but what if one of his cases had blown up and they needed him and only him to swoop in and fix it? Even though it was Saturday and the courthouses were all closed for the weekend so teams of janitors could vacuum the carpet and polish the linoleum.

Even better, what if it was that Sydney cop? *So sorry, our breathalyser units have all been recalled; you're actually a model citizen and no-one could ever accuse you of being one of those barristers who let the pressure of the job turn them into dysfunctional crackpots.*

Either option and Damon's world could settle back onto its axis.

He checked the screen and blew out a breath. Not salvation, then, but not somebody he was in the habit of ghosting. Much.

'Hey, Mum.'

'Damon. Hello, darling.'

He looked at his watch, tried to work out what time it was in New Zealand where his mother lived with husband number three, and gave up. Later than here, wherever here was.

'What's up?'

'Nothing's up. Can't a mother call her favourite son?'

A couple of grenades in that sentence. For starters, his mother always called for a reason. And the favourite son thing? In his current mood, an argument best left alone.

'Sorry,' he said. He was not at all sorry. 'How are you? How's Murray?'

'He's fine. Why are you sounding like a wet week?'

That was one way to describe it. Another would be to say he'd managed to get himself stuck in the most dreary motel room in New South Wales, where a drooping lamp had convinced him that there might actually be something in what Sean and Warunya had said.

Was this what burnout looked like? And now he'd had some get-out-of-Sydney tantrum and was going to be stuck in this sewage room for the next three months because, for the first time in what felt like forever, he did not have a thing to do.

'Finished a long trial yesterda—' he began.

'I won't be making it to Sydney this week after all,' his mother said, cutting him off. 'Something's come up.'

He frowned. 'Did I know you were coming to Sydney?'

'Surely I told you.'

Surely she hadn't. Or was his memory turning fallible along with everything else?

'Anyway, you remember Tina?'

'Er … of course.' Tina was a cat. Or his mother's nail artist. Maybe a stepdaughter from husband number two?

'She was so kind to me when I first moved to Melbourne.'

Damon rolled his eyes. Oh. That Tina. Some woman his mother had befriended the year his brother had stopped being a regular brother and became a teen idol to everyone in the country, and a pain in the arse to the people he lived with. The autumn of Damon's eighteenth year. Fun times.

The barnacle in his chest gave a twist so he reached out and tipped the lamp on its side. *Piss off*, he thought in its direction.

'She's over here on a driving holiday and wants to pop in. I've had to rearrange things.'

He tried to recall what things his mother might have to rearrange. She didn't work—hadn't for years. She lunched, she golfed; she was on the board of some theatre. A glimmer of memory shone through. 'You were going on a country retreat, or something.'

His mother laughed. Gaily. It filled him with suspicion. 'Nothing so glamorous, Damon. No, I was flying over to inspect that property I told you about.'

'Property?'

'Yes, you know—in the Snowy Mountains. My half-brother passed away and somehow or other, his assets have come down to me in the will. You explained what probate meant, don't you remember? Well, it's all going ahead and the estate's been transferred to me now.'

Oh, yes. The relative that his mother had mentioned maybe once in their whole lives and who they had never met. Not atypical for Deirdre. She wasn't a woman you could describe as warm. He did remember. 'A few acres and an old cottage, wasn't it?'

'Mmm,' his mother said vaguely. 'I think the term is hobby farm. Grapes, did I read? Or was it apples? One of the emails might have mentioned cool climate pinot noir. I'm supposed to be meeting a lawyer in the town nearby to sort things. There's a caretaker looking after the place, I understand, but somebody needs to collect the keys, inspect the house, get a realtor over to value the land and whatever structures are on it, then put it on the market.'

'You're selling it, then.'

'Well, of course, darling. Can you picture me tromping about a frosty paddock in gumboots? How horrid.'

Nope. His mum was a city person just like he was—one of the few things they had in common. Tromping, paddocks and gumboots were a hard pass.

'I don't suppose …'

Here it came. The favour she apparently hadn't called for.

'Tina's visit means I won't get over to Australia for a few weeks. I wondered if you'd fancy a little getaway to sort things out. You still have power of attorney for me, right? You could sign everything on my behalf and I'd love to treat you to a few days in the country as a little thank you gift.'

Classic Deirdre. Asking for outrageous favours and dressing them up as a thoughtful act of generosity.

But … Damon cast a glance around the depressing motel room and listened to the ominous silence. Even the highway five metres from the thin plywood door didn't offer much more than the occasional roar of a passing semitrailer. He needed a bolthole. Some old cottage surrounded by grape vines and/or apple trees didn't sound at all like his sort of place, but it'd have to be better than here.

'How far is this house from the town you mentioned?' he said. Silence wasn't good for him. He'd need people. Coffee. Distraction.

'Um … Do you know, I haven't the faintest idea.'

Which could be true, or it could be that the place was isolated from all humanity but his mother didn't want him to know that. But isolated versus sewage?

'I'll go,' he said.

There was silence from his mother's end of the phone.

'Mum?'

'I heard you, Damon. I was just staring in amazement at my phone. You understand you need to go in person? Out of Sydney? To the far-off mountains?'

'Yeah, yeah. I understand.' He wasn't doing her a favour. He was taking on a banal and no doubt tedious chore because anything, even tedium, would be something better to think about than this barnacle business. Maybe it would go dormant with lack of attention ... kinda the same way his and Deirdre's mother–son bond had.

She sounded doubtful as well as amused. 'Well, fabulous! The lawyer up there has been sending me a swag of emails, which I haven't read properly yet. Something about irrigation and schedules and Alfie's problem.'

He sighed. His mother's attention to life admin was notoriously abstract. 'Text me the lawyer's address,' he said. 'I'll make my way there.'

Somehow. With no wheels, no licence, and no real clue exactly where he was.

CHAPTER 4

The secondhand diesel engine that powered the heritage paddle-wheeler *Moana* was purring like a kitten. Kylie slipped off the ear-protection muffs and climbed the narrow metal rungs up from the shallow cavity where the engine was housed. A very large kitten; the rungs beneath her feet throbbed.

Dave Ryan, local tourism industry legend and boss of Hanrahan Trekkers, stood beside the hatch, looking down at the spin of the crankshaft with a tear in his eye. 'That's my darling,' he said to his boat.

'Those new seals will hold for the time being, but I'll have to order in the proper ones. Should have them here within the week,' she said as she stood beside him. 'Busted seals were what was causing your engine to overheat, and they were behind all that water you've been having to pump from the bilge.'

A diesel engine that sucked in water from Lake Bogong to act as its cooling system had been quite a stretch from the trucks and tractors and cars and lawnmowers she was used to. Imagine if the old girl had still run on steam! It had taken her all morning to pull the water pump off the engine and take it back to her workshop to disassemble, diagnose the problem and come up with a solution. The fact she had a bunch of random seals in her storeroom, which had (sort of, with some swearing and jiggery-pokery) fit, had come down to blind luck rather than any mechanical skill on her part, but no need to share that with Dave.

Tractors had run on steam too, once, and she'd seen one, oh, a good few years ago now, at some museum in Melbourne whose name she couldn't remember, but she remembered every detail about that tractor and its locomotive-style multitubular boiler. A Cliff & Bunting, it had been, circa 1912. Single cylinder, two-speed, eight horsepower ... well, nominal horsepower, that is. Not to be confused with belt horsepower or take-off horsepower or—

But she was getting distracted. 'I'd like to let her run for a while before I head off,' she said to Dave before he could ask her what she was daydreaming about. 'Check she's got no other gremlins lurking.'

'She'd better not. We've two dozen passengers booked for a cruise around the lake at two o'clock today and tomorrow, and I'll be bloody upset if I have to refund tickets.'

No pressure, then.

'Walk with me,' he ordered, then, without waiting for her response, he took off through the timber-lined passenger cabin and a narrow doorway out to the aft deck of the paddlewheeler.

A kid in a red shirt was wheeling a trolley stacked with boxes across the narrow gangplank from the dock; he nearly toppled himself and his trolley into the lake when he saw Dave bearing down on him.

'Almost finished, boss,' the kid said, scrambling to clear out of Dave's way.

'Are they my new flyers? About bloody time.'

'Um. Dunno, boss.'

'Put 'em here so I can have a look, then you can get these rope coils tidied up.'

'Yes, boss.'

Dave grunted, which the kid must have interpreted as a sign to get moving, because he scampered off.

Dave had ripped open the top box from the pile on the trolley and was perusing its contents when the phone in his pocket started up a shrill racket. He held a flyer out to Kylie. 'Hold this for a tick, will you? What's up, Sue?' he said into the phone, before walking over to lean on the deck's rail.

The leaflets were glossy and full of warm colours, just the sort of thing Kylie would like to have printed for her workshop if her advertising budget wasn't limited to the dodgy black and white handouts spat out by a printer she'd bought at the post office, which were then carefully guillotined into three equal-ish strips of paper by her admin staff, also known as her high school vocational ed student, Braydon.

'What's that? Speak up.' Dave must treat everyone like a soldier in his personal army, not just her. 'Wait on, it's these bloody hearing aids of mine. I'll put you on speaker.'

Kylie had no problem with eavesdropping, but just in case Dave did, she engrossed herself in the flyer.

Come for a ride on one of Australia's heritage paddlewheelers, PW Moana. *Built in 1894 by Wilson & Burkett as a paddlesteamer, the* Moana *has a colourful history! She's carvel planked in red gum and her flat hull allowed her to work the Murray River's shallow tributaries as a 'bottle-o' and firewood boat. (Don't worry, we'll fill you in on that story when you're aboard!) The* Moana *was converted to diesel in the 1950s and used as a tourist cruising vessel before falling into disrepair and being left to rot on the banks of the Murray. Dave Ryan and Hanrahan Trekkers purchased the* Moana *in 2020. Inspired by the cross-country relocation of the* Pride of the Murray *to Longreach for use as a tourist vessel on the Thomson River, Dave decided the* Moana*'s new home could be Lake Bogong, right here in Hanrahan at the foot of the Snowy Mountains. Now, after a heroic effort by Dave, his team of experts and the history buffs of the Hanrahan and District Community Association, the* Moana *has been restored to her former glory. See below for tours and packages and …*

'Say that again!'

She looked up as Dave thumped his fist onto the polished handrail.

'We might have a problem with the Picnic in a Vineyard cruises.' The disembodied voice at the other end of the phone call sounded stressed.

Dave's straggly grey eyebrows joined into one straggly grey line. 'Well? Spill it, girlie.'

Spill it, *girlie*? Oh, that was so not okay. *You're about to send him a big invoice*, Kylie reminded herself. *Broke mechanics need to put profit ahead of political correctness.*

'What's the problem now?' said Dave.

'Maureen Plover. Again.'

'That woman.' Dave said it like a swear word and Kylie totally got why. Maureen Plover had worked at the Hanrahan Pharmacy for years—*years*—traumatising locals with her habit of announcing, loudly, every product she was ringing up on the till: 'Tampons, two packets. Haemorrhoid cream. Nit comb.'

You'd have thought retiring would have been the end of the judgement, but oh, no. Maureen had appointed herself editor of The Hanrahan Chatter, the local page in the *Snowy River Star*, and, to borrow one of Braydon's phrases, gone berko. The woman had a talent for gossip that lived in the grey area between public interest and downright malice, dressed up as community interest stories. A fascinating way to spend your retirement.

Maybe Maureen had had a go at one of Dave's tourism businesses in her local news column. Maybe that's what the problem was, and Kylie just hadn't read that edition of The Chatter.

Unlikely. She was as addicted to the gossip in The Hanrahan Chatter as she was addicted to the sourdough butterscotch donuts from The Billy Button Café. Did that make her a hypocrite? Totally. Did she feel bad about it? Nope.

'Maureen's threatening to go on strike because she's been handling everything since Frank died—burning herself to the socket to keep the business running, she says—and now she's found out that the other owner's coming to town to put the property on the market.'

On strike from what? What property? And which of the town's Franks had died, and why was Kylie just hearing about it now?

The business was why. Working flat strap to get Hanrahan Mechanics into the black was why.

Ears very much a-flap, Kylie pretended to be engrossed in picking grease from under her only slightly chipped jacaranda blue acrylic nails so Dave would forget she was there.

'She says it's all too much for her,' said whatever employee in Dave's office had been tasked with calling him with the bad news. 'She'll do this arvo's vineyard picnic and then—hang on, I wrote it down—"That'll be the last scone I bake until hell freezes over".'

'The picnic cruise has been our top seller this season,' said Dave.

Vineyard. A brain cell twanged and she had it: the Frank they were talking about was Frank Silva. Older guy. Sweet. Steel wool hair kept very short, owned a smudge of land on the far side of the lake. Recently deceased, not a regular at anywhere she hung out (the café; the pizza place; the specials aisle at the supermarket; the borrowing counter of the Hanrahan Library) but often to be seen at the community hall, chatting with Kev over the rose bushes. That's all Kylie knew about him. He'd been in business with *Maureen*? Like, willingly?

'You want me to try to track down the new owner?'

'No. I'll be on the *Moana* for this afternoon's cruise and I'll speak to Maureen myself. I'll remind her of the penalty clauses for effing up my bloody summer season. No-one stuffs up business for Hanrahan Trekkers and gets away with it.'

Kylie sucked in a breath. No pressure on her engine fix, then, and those almost-the-right-size seals …

Fortunately the rumble of the diesel motor was still pulsating comfortably through the hull into her steel-capped boots. So far, so good.

'Right,' said Dave. He must have ended the call because those grey eyebrows swung in her direction. 'You. Kylie. I've twenty-four passengers booked for our cruise over to Snowy River Vineyard today, same again tomorrow. Is my boat going to be functional?'

'She's running like a dream,' said Kylie, injecting her voice with a swagger she wasn't totally feeling.

'We get into trouble in the middle of the lake, it's not going to do my reviews any good.'

Well, it wouldn't be doing the future of Hanrahan Mechanics any good either. If that water pump hadn't been fitted correctly? Yeah. A sunken heritage paddlewheeler in the middle of Lake Bogong was not the sort of advertising she needed. Dave wouldn't pay her invoice—he'd probably sue her for all her worldly assets, humble though they were—and her nemesis from the highway would bag her mechanic skills to anyone who'd listen. She'd lose the few customers she'd won.

She had more riding on the cruise than Dave did.

'Why don't I come out with you?' she said. 'Both days, today and tomorrow. Keep an eye on things.' It'd delay returning the

Brutnalls' car and delay the $370 she'd be charging them from hitting her bank account, but the greater good and all that.

Dave grunted. Assuming the kid in the red shirt knew his stuff, she took the grunt to mean the discussion was done. Also, Dave wasn't frowning anymore; he was staring back along the length of the paddlewheeler. Kylie turned to look at it with him.

The *Moana*'s cabin structure gleamed with white paint and polished brass. The railings of the upper deck were picked out in black to match the boat's name on the hull and little coloured triangles of canvas flew from wire stays. There were fairy lights along those stays, too; not much to see now, but Kylie had seen them at night, pretty as baubles and reflecting in the still waters of the lake. The *Moana* wasn't graceful—her lines made Kylie think of a children's book tug boat, sturdy and sweet—but the chunky structures on either side of the boat where the paddlewheels lived behind decorated panels gave her character. Charm.

A flag snapped lazily from a pole on the upper deck in a breeze that carried with it the warmth of a Snowy Mountains late summer afternoon. A warmth Kylie had felt every summer of her life.

She got it. Dave might be a grumpy old codger but he loved his boat. And while a rented workshop with her beloved antique tractor parked out front, a secondhand hoist and an ancient fuel bowser that was no longer operational couldn't compare in beauty to a historic paddlewheeler, she loved her workshop with that same starry-eyed fervour.

Her workshop stood for something. Hard work and possible failure, yes, but so much more than that. It stood for success. Pride. Independence.

It stood for everything Kylie Summer believed in.

CHAPTER
5

Damon Johns stared at the folded piece of fabric being handed to him by the tiny, grey-haired woman he'd met exactly one minute ago on a gravelled drive beside a sign that said SNOWY RIVER VINEYARD. It had taken him a day and a half to get here and this was not his idea of an appropriate welcome to the country.

'It's a *what*?'

'An apron. When we serve up scones and cups of tea, we need to look the part, pet. The *Moana* is due to dock at our—excuse me, *your*—itty-bitty wharf at two pm, and there'll be tourists on board who'll attach themselves to your picnic tables like ticks on a cow's ear.'

His brain cells had shorted out on the words 'when we serve up scones', but his ears were still transmitting messages … Ticks? Cows? And what was docking where?

The woman waggled the floral apron at him again, and he wondered if the pub manager who'd given him a ride out here from the tinpot town of Hanrahan had taken a wrong turn. Maybe he'd arrived at an asylum for deranged cooks instead of the country block his mum had inherited.

'Hang on a second,' he said, attempting to bat away the apron before the woman strapped him into it. Maybe she was just *saying* it was an apron. Maybe straightjackets came in a trendy range of fabrics these days so lunatics with lung delusions didn't feel like they were missing out. 'There's been some sort of misunderstanding.'

The woman crossed her arms. She reminded him of his terrifying third grade teacher, Mrs Schmidt, only with more hair, less bosom and way, *way*, less green eye shadow.

'I made it clear in my emails. All seven of them. And clarity of expression, young man, is one of the many astounding skills on which I pride myself, so do not dare talk to me about misunderstandings. I've been running this operation on my own since the summer season started and I'm done. *Done*. My column is suffering and that man—*that man*—has pushed my buttons one too many times. You young people aren't the only ones who can lay claim to having a life, you know.'

Point of order, he thought. He'd *had* a life—past tense—up until the day before yesterday, and frankly he was busy enough moping over his own fall from grace to evince any interest at all in the problems of the pinch-lipped senior citizen who'd bailed him up. But Damon kept the correction to himself. Also, what emails?

'Perhaps we could start by you telling me who you are and why you're here?' He used the tone he'd perfected on hostile witnesses in court, the one that had brought him fame—or infamy—and won him a cult following from Sydney's jaded mob of court reporters.

The woman let out a sigh. 'Just my luck. Another nincompoop in a suit. Come on, the paddlewheeler will be here any minute. Let's walk and talk.'

The old-fashioned insult did what a taxi tantrum and a shitty motel and two lengthy, poorly connecting bus trips to the foothills of the Snowy Mountains had not: it made him laugh. Resigning himself to the fact that he'd stumbled into some small-town comedy caper and an explanation was not likely to be forthcoming if he stayed here on the gravel by himself clutching his briefcase while stewing in two-day-old barely washed jocks—or was it three?—he set off after the woman.

She set a cracker of a pace along the gravelled drive around the side of a stone house with a steeply pitched roof and dormer windows and a wide, wraparound timber verandah. The place looked nothing like the ramshackle fibro house and man shed he'd been imagining. Flowers were everywhere, in pots, in flower beds, in hanging baskets, none of which Damon could name. The mysterious Frank must have been quite the gardener.

Damon snatched a quick look up the gently sloping hill to where vines were staked out in neat rows, and where dirt tracks were thick with mud and stamped with the rolling tread of tractor tyres. Beyond the vines, overshadowing the land, were the steep, rocky crags of the Snowy Mountains. Benevolent today, but he'd seen the movie: one foray too far away from civilisation and next minute you'd be on a narrow ledge on a vertical cliff face in pouring rain, hoping for a passing local to ride by and rescue you with a leather whip.

'This *is* Frank's place, I take it,' he said as the woman opened up a heavy wooden gate at the side of the house. He was still unable to shake the feeling that he was the wrong guy, in the wrong place, at the wrong time. 'Frank Silva?'

Damon had been given keys. He had a business card stapled to a yellow A3 envelope with some local lawyer's name on it—Tom Somebody-or-other—who'd handled the estate while it was being transferred into his mother's name, but the lawyer in question hadn't been in when Damon had fronted up to the address Deirdre had given him. A pub, as it happened, with a law office renting space in a back room. Weird, but whatever.

'Of course it is,' the woman said, waiting for him to fall into step beside her. 'Why else would I be here wasting a perfectly good afternoon? Foolish man,' she added, before bursting into noisy sobs.

Damon was well aware that everybody he knew, including himself, would describe him as having been absent from the womb the day the DNA strands for empathy were switched on, but even he could connect the dots here. The woman was grieving.

He offered her the apron she'd handed him, but she hunched a shoulder and pulled a neatly folded tissue from some secret location under the neckline of her dress. Okay, not *so* secret. She pulled it out from under a bra strap; of course he knew that was where women kept such things. But he tried not to think about the bra straps of senior citizens and what lay within. Was that shallow and ageist? Yes. Was it true? Also yes.

His mind was wandering. Perhaps that's what came of being forced onto sabbatical from the barristers' chambers you had co-founded: your brain cells began to atrophy. Maybe he should answer one of the calls he'd been ignoring from Sean and Warunya and let them know he'd be virtually useless in three months' time if his brain continued this descent into mush.

He ordered his mind to get its shit together and concentrate on what was actually happening: crying woman; emails of clarity; Frank and the acreage, which was not, as he'd assumed, a rural block with a few chooks and a ride-on mower, but an actual agricultural enterprise.

'I'm sorry for your loss,' he said. 'Were you and Frank, um, together?' How old had Frank been, anyhow? And if Frank and this old bird had been a couple, why hadn't she inherited the vineyard instead of a half-sister who'd not bothered to keep Frank in her life?

'Frank is—was—my friend,' she said, putting her tissue away. The other bra strap, this time; perhaps there was a system in place, clean on the left and used on the right. Another senior citizen bra moment he had not wanted to have. 'And business partner. *Legally binding* business partner, apparently.'

This last was said with a huffy emphasis and a return to the pinch-lipped facial expression of before. Contemplating the joy he was going to find in wringing his mother's neck, metaphorically speaking, for sending him out here to deal with factors unknown, he decided introductions were in order.

'Damon Johns,' he said, holding his hand out. 'My mother was related to Frank.'

The woman looked at his hand for a second before shaking it. 'Maureen Plover. Your mother's Deirdre, I take it?'

'You've heard of her?'

'Of course. Frank was always rabbiting on about his childhood. Riding the pony to school, milking the cow at dawn, climbing the gum trees, mimicking the kookaburras and the currawongs ... you'd have thought he'd grown up in a May Gibbs story book, to listen to him.'

Damon blinked. This was like hearing of a parallel universe in which his mother had once got her hands dirty. Milking a *cow*?

Enough. He could come back to Frank's story later. For now, he needed to know about the present. 'What's this legally binding business arrangement you mentioned?'

Maureen raised her eyebrows. 'The picnic business, of course. The one I have emailed about. At length, with astou—'

'With astounding clarity. Yes.'

Damon resisted the urge to pull his phone out of his pocket and hack into his mother's email account. What else hadn't she bothered to tell him?

Maureen looked expressively at the apron he was still holding. 'I don't have time to fill you in on the details now. It's showtime. Which means, Damon, you're going to want to put that on.'

'Showtime?'

'You hear that?'

He did hear that. Anyone within a thousand kilometres of Mt Kosciuszko would have heard that. A horn, deep and loud. What in blazes—?

'That's our cue,' said Maureen. 'Come on, handsome, you can learn the business on the job. I'll be with you today, but next week the *Moana* docks Wednesday, Friday, Saturday and Sunday and you'll be on your own, because, I, as I have told you—'

'Are done,' he said. Yep. He'd got that one, loud and clear as that horn.

'I hope you can bake.'

Ominous words.

They rounded the corner of the house to find a lawn dotted with more shrubs (flowery ones, no surprise) but here and there were gravel patches turned into seating areas with bleached timber chairs. A handsome outdoor fireplace made of stone sat beyond a trellis covered in what he could only assume was some grape variety. Beyond the lawn stretched a lake whose surface was a collection of ripples and whitewash as an old—like, *really* old—but restored boat edged up to a wooden dock. A nimble kid in a bright red shirt leapt off its stern and looped a rope around a bollard.

PW *Moana*, read the raised black lettering adorning the white-painted hull of the paddlewheeler. And crowded on its fore and aft decks, and leaning out the windows of its central cabin, were two or three dozen hungry-looking tourists.

'A picnic business,' he said weakly.

Maureen's shoulder nudged his. Perhaps she'd misinterpreted his mutterings as admiration instead of horror. 'Pretty as a picture, isn't she? Dave Ryan might be a pain in the arse to deal with, but he did a good thing when he rescued the *Moana*. Frank helped, of course. She became a real community project.'

Damon's earlier feeling that he'd been dropped into the middle of a comedy caper without a script intensified, but now it was a historical comedy caper. He hadn't the foggiest who Dave Ryan was—although he suspected the guy's other name might be 'That Man'—and while the boat was kinda sweet if you were into that sort of thing, he wasn't sure what it had to with him or Deirdre.

'Now, stop being such a baby about that apron, Damon Johns, we've a picnic to host.'

'But—'

'I'll do the tea and coffee, you do the scones. There's jam and cream and let them put their own on, for god's sake, because everyone's got an opinion on which goes first and I don't have enough life span left to waste a minute more listening to that idiotic debate.'

'I don't—'

Maureen silenced him with a look. A scary, Mrs Schmidt, third-grade tyrant look. 'This isn't rocket science, young man, this is the hospitality business. A business your mother is now a fifty per cent owner of, ever since Frank decided to be so bloody selfish and die on me. Now, we'll have the tourists here any second, and they get obstreperous when they're made to wait.'

More obstreperous than Maureen Plover? Was that even possible?

Yielding to the inevitable, Damon pulled the loop of the apron over his head, strapped its ties around his hips and surveyed the basket of scones, the bowls of jam and cream, and the tower of china plates and napkins spread out over a colourful tablecloth.

A cluster of tourists was emerging from the boat and wandering along the dock to the grass of the foreshore, and once the first of the tourists managed to help himself to the food on offer without incident and without need of assistance beyond a 'G'day' and a 'Help yourself, mate', and agreement that yes, it was, indeed, a top day for a lake cruise, Damon relaxed. His role was clearly supervisory. No problem.

After a rush that lasted about a half-hour, the scone basket was nearly empty and Damon was able to take a moment to appreciate the irony of how quickly a life could change. In the past forty-eight hours, he'd been on a graffiti-tagged street in downtown Sydney, getting his arse handed to him by a cop; in a dingy motel room; on a bus with striped velour seating that had smelled very much like armpits and now here he was in a floral apron, breathing in mountain air and strawberry jam smells.

He was also breathing freely in an easy-breezy, totally non-sweaty way. Who knew leaving the city would be so—

'I hope there's a scone left for me.'

Damon looked up from the tabletop carnage left behind by twenty-five tourists keen to get their money's worth of the goods on offer. His gaze fell on the grease stains first, so his brain wasted a minute trying to marry the work-stained overalls with the sunny female voice. But then he noticed how the overalls were stretching and clinging in interesting places, and his eyes travelled upwards to the face of the woman.

Wow.

No, he hadn't thought that with enough amazement, so he thought it again, but with feeling: *Wow.* So much to see and notice, and was it *possible* for hair to be so blonde and caramel and honey and tousled all at once? The woman was smiling, and the sun grew dim in comparison. Her eyes ... was there even a name for that colour? Forest moss or deep ocean, or ... He shook his head. Was he a freaking poet now, as well as a loser drunk driver with leprosy of the lung?

But still ... wow. Even with the smudge of dirt across one cheekbone and the tideline of sweat darkening the neck of the T-shirt he could see in the unbuttoned V of her overalls.

Her eyebrow quirked as she looked at him, and he realised he was staring.

'You are filthy,' he said. What he meant was: *You are beautiful!*

She grinned. And everything he'd noticed about her, yet struggled to find enough superlatives to describe, amplified by a factor of a thousand.

'You okay, mate?'

Yes. He was more than okay. He'd just figured out that being chucked out of his own life and sent up here to the Snowy Mountains for a three-month prison sentence might have some perks.

CHAPTER
6

'Stop the clock,' said Kylie. 'Who's the helper?' If she'd known the scones were being dished up by a drop-dead hottie, she wouldn't have stayed aboard yesterday when the paddlewheeler docked, no matter how much mucky water had collected in the bilge.

Maureen Plover, the poison-pen, pharmacy-shaming retiree herself, looked up from the hot water urn she was refilling and snorted. 'Turned up just before the *Moana* docked. Totally clueless. He's the son of the new owner of the vineyard and he's here to see the place sold.'

Kylie raised her eyebrows. 'Doesn't look much like a man of the land, does he? A pin-striped suit, here in Hanrahan. On a Sunday, no less. When did we last see one of those?'

Maureen was dabbing at her eyes with the corner of a tissue so Kylie slung her arm around the older woman's shoulders. Were pin-striped suits so awful? What in the world—

'In a coffin,' Maureen sobbed. 'I had to choose, and it didn't seem right to bury him in corduroy trousers. And where was Mr Fancypants *then*?'

Oh. Frank had been buried in a suit and Mr Fancypants, Kylie assumed, was the one looking into a bowl of depleted whipped cream as though it was a conundrum that could never be solved.

'I'm sorry,' she said. 'I know how fond you were of Frank.' A lie; she'd had no clue at all that Maureen was fond of anything other than sowing discord. Wait. Had Maureen and Frank been an item? As in, together? Loved up? In a *relationship*? Karma could be a kick in the teeth sometimes, couldn't it? Not that she was jealous. Much. But—

'*And* Dave's been a heartless beast about the whole picnic business. You should have heard what he said to me yesterday when he came ashore.'

Yeah. No leap of imagination required there. Two days in Dave Ryan's company and Kylie had learned a new definition for what it meant to be a ruthless business operator. Insisting a dead man and his grieving friend honour a contract to supply scones and tea to tourists? Not surprising. Not at all.

Her gaze drifted back to the stranger standing behind the food table. The suit. The close-cut hair. The aura of arrogance that hung over him the way the aura of diesel fumes was no doubt hanging over her. But there was that apron wrapped around his waist. She grinned. Not so arrogant he didn't mind a joke.

'I didn't know you were in business with Dave,' she said. 'When did all this—' she gestured around at the lawn, the picnic benches, the tourists, '—start?'

'Picnic in a Vineyard was Frank's idea. When Dave first brought the *Moana* up to Hanrahan to begin its restoration project, Frank got himself a little attached and sentimental about the old girl.' Maureen inclined her head in the direction of the paddlewheeler. 'He started to see a synergy, he said.'

'Um … why?'

'Frank's dock and garden, my scones and homemade jam, Dave's boat full of tourists all coming together. Even a new book. Dave liked the idea. He had a contract drawn up, which we all signed. He reckoned he was the one with all the risk because he was the one doing all the advertising, so the contract meant we had to commit to the full summer season no matter what.'

Including death, apparently. Tough terms. No wonder Maureen was looking frazzled. And what was that about a book? Some history pamphlet for the community association, perhaps.

'Frank had the business sense of a numbat, mind you, but he and Dave were friends of sorts. He was happy to sign the contract. Besides, it gave him a push to get his easel out again.'

His easel?

Maureen gave a sad little smile. 'I signed the contract, too, of course. Frank and I celebrated over a frittata and a bottle of wine from his cellar. A bit of fun for us, a bit of income, it was win-win, we reckoned.'

'Was he ill for long?' Kylie said. 'Frank? I'm sorry, I don't think he and I ever officially met.'

'Dropped dead among the pinot noir vines, a pair of secateurs in his hand. An aneurism, apparently. Happened in seconds.'

Kylie stood beside Maureen, feeling guilty for all the many (many!) times she'd considered Maureen to be the villain of Hanrahan. Did that make her a bad person? Was this why her mechanics business was not the happy success she had assumed it would be when she painted her sign over the workshop roller door? Karma really *was* putting the boot in.

Maureen sighed. 'Frank would have loved this. See how happy everyone is? Wandering through his garden, inspecting the vines. He used to say that wine brought people together and made the world a wonderful place. Almost makes me feel guilty.'

A slightly *elitist* view, Kylie thought. There were plenty of people around (her, for instance) who didn't have room in their weekly budget for wine or picnics, but still hoped their world could be wonderful and full of people. But she understood the sentiment. Snowy River Vineyard was beautiful.

The rest of Maureen's words finally hit home and Kylie turned to face her. 'Wait. Guilty about what?'

Maureen smirked—villainously, Kylie was relieved to note, so take that, karma—as she looked over at the food table. 'About our clueless young friend,' she said, before picking up a tray of used cups and saucers and marching off in the direction of the house.

Kylie looked over to the food table where the man had fallen into conversation with one of the *Moana*'s passengers. Was he single? Was he eligible? Was he the sort of drop-dead hottie who moved to a country town to realise their dream of farming the land, and was looking for long walks by the lakeshore and a forever friend?

Clueless wasn't a word she'd have used to describe him. Easy on the eye? Yep, she'd have said that. Tall, dark and dangerous? Totally all of the above. As she walked closer, she could see he was older than she'd first thought, and the short cut hadn't quite tamed the curl of his hair. He held himself like someone who was used to being in charge, despite the fact he was looking faintly ludicrous with that apron tied around a business suit.

A *crumpled* business suit. *Billionaire or homeless person?* she would have demanded of her friend Hannah if they'd spied him on a girls' night out.

She slipped between a woman in a hibiscus print dress and an older gentleman whose walking cane was giving him a little trouble on the thick grass, being careful to not brush her grease-stained overalls against anyone, then approached the table.

'Hello,' she said. 'I hope there's a scone left for me.'

The man's eyes locked onto her like a spanner onto a locknut. Woah, where was Hannah when she needed her? Her fingers itched to start texting: *Hot bloke alert. Eye contact established. Hold my beer.*

His eyes were impossibly dark blue she could see now she was up close. Like navy, only darker. He was tanned, like he'd spent the summer jogging along wild coastal walking tracks in snug running shorts and no shirt, and he had a day's worth of stubble—the good sort, the I'm-too-busy-adventuring-and-running-shirtless-to-shave sort, not the manscaped sort—and a quizzical look on his face that was almost a grin. The look was also, unless her dating skills had been so long in storage they'd gone as rusty as the Brutnalls' exhaust pipe, flirty.

'You are *filthy*.' He delivered it like a line. A win-on line. Definitely flirty. And that voice? Rumbly. Deep. Smoky. The good sort of smoky, too, as in campfires and brick chimneys and snuggling up, not the carcinogenic, lose-your-toes sort.

She should probably be saying something back rather than standing dumbstruck in her grubby gear, but she needed a moment. She'd spent a long dark winter of discontent (okay, other people would call it a long green winter of jealousy) reading novels in a doona-nest on her sofa or upgrading her online profile with the yoga crew, wondering where all the good men had gone, and why her bestie Hannah had managed to find love when she hadn't even been *looking*. But maybe Kylie's days of discontent were over! Here, on a scrap of foreshore on the northwestern edge of Lake Bogong, was an in-the-flesh reminder that good things could happen to a girl.

Even when that girl was wearing overalls.

She was not the only one doing some high-octane staring, she noticed, when the silence between them had grown so tight it felt like a fan belt about to snap.

'You okay, mate?' she said, because it was the first thing that came into her head.

He grinned. 'I'm Damon.'

Not an answer, but definitely a fact she was glad to acquire. He loaded a scone onto a plate and handed it to her and she decided, what the heck, why not find out the other pertinent facts?

'Please tell me you're single and nice and you're planning on owning a farm with chooks and you live nearby.'

He was surprised into a laugh and she laughed, too, so she could pretend she'd been joking if he turned out to be married or gay or disinterested in women who wore overalls, but it came out all weak and fluttery, like she was some bogong moth blinded by a blaze of torchlight.

Not a moth. A woman. Slightly love starved, but fully functional, she told herself. And one who might need to kick herself in the butt to remind herself of all the dangers of hot guys who were all charm but no substance.

'One out of four. You want to guess which one?'

An enigmatic answer, but with that same flirty delivery. Oh, yes, he was dangerous, which her libido thought was a big tick. Only problem: he looked totally out of place here in Hanrahan, which her life plan knew was a very big cross.

'Um,' she said, unsure why she felt flustered. She was hardly shy. Or secretive about being single. She had a profile up on RuRo, for Pete's sake, which anyone could find and read: *single, nice, owns a farm, lives nearby.* Wait, that wasn't her profile—that's what she'd hoped his might be.

Her brain had turned to custard.

'Help yourself to jam,' he said. 'There might be more cream, but if there is, no-one's told me where.'

'I like them plain,' she said. A lie, but the zipper on her overalls had told her just that morning that it was time to lay off the fun food. She tore the scone in half and sank her teeth into the softness of the bottom section. Paddlewheeling across a postcard-perfect lake two afternoons in a row, with a robustly thumping engine and an expertly sealed water pump testament to her mad mechanical skills, had given her an appetite.

The man—Damon—looked around the lawn before wafting one tea towel over the last few scones and another over the condiments. Food service was over? Or he wanted to chat? Either was fine with her. Dave was happy—she'd be drafting him up a hefty invoice when she got back to the workshop—the sun was that perfect mix of summer warmth and mountain cool, and, for the next little while until the *Moana*'s horn blew, there was nothing she needed to be doing except stand here and find out if Mr Fancypants was going to be the remedy to her winter of discontent.

Be a crime not to. And even if he wasn't, it had been a long time since she'd enjoyed a good flirt. Every tool needed sharpening, right?

She perched a hip on one corner of the food table while she finished her scone, noting that there was nothing at fault with Damon's profile. Nose just the right size, eyelashes dark but tipped at the end with gold, like her favourite makeup brush, only manlier.

And those cheekbones. Also ... manly.

Damn it, she *was* out of practice. She had snappy conversation, so where was it?

She pulled her spare rag from the back pocket of her overalls and wiped her hands. 'Nice scone,' she said, amazing herself with her own ineptness. Maybe she should just go back to the engine room and talk to the timing gears.

He nodded. 'Since you're not guessing, yes to the single ... although it does seem a little early in our acquaintance to be divulging such things.'

Which meant ... *not* nice? And not here to stay? And—bummer—no farm. Those little children in gumboots were getting further away by the day.

'You're a four out of four, I'm guessing,' he said.

She shrugged. 'Three. No farm, sadly. I live in town,' she said. She waved her rag in the loose direction of home.

That grin again. It was working its way down her collar and tickling the back of her neck like a Snowy Mountains breeze.

'Hanrahan? Would you call that a town?'

From here, Hanrahan was a smudge of pastel on the far side of the lake that, as soon as she was back on the *Moana* and making her way south over the water, would reshape itself into a cluster of Federation-style buildings and a foreshore of walking paths and parks and rickety old docks. Her home, and home to a thousand or so people. None of them the right age, male, single and easy on the eye.

'Oh. You're a city type,' she said. The suit had been a clue but a girl could hope. Would it be too much to hope that this particular city type had decided to ditch the fast lane for the slow? 'Always so dismissive of what you don't know.'

'What, did my suit give me away?'

She grinned. 'Suit, hair, the fact I don't recognise you, and also Maureen's given me the lowdown on why you're here.'

'The tea lady?' he said.

'Oh, Maureen is so much more than a tea lady,' she said. 'I hope you've not got her offside.'

'Getting people offside is one of my special skills,' he said. 'But then, I don't know much about you, yet. Maybe you're prone to exaggeration. One senior citizen pouring cups of tea can't be that scary, can she?'

She laughed. 'Just you wait.'

'And ... are you?'

'Am I what?'

'Prone to exaggeration?'

'The only thing I'm prone to is romantic entanglements that don't end well.' Crap, had she actually just blurted that out? '*Used to be* prone to, I should say. Those days are over.'

'What a pity. I'm quite fond of a romantic entanglement.'

She cleared her throat.

'As for Maureen,' he continued, as though he hadn't just lobbed a heatwave down her collar, 'she and I have barely spoken. I introduced myself, she bullied me into an apron, and here we are.'

'Yes,' she said. 'Here we are.'

He came around to her side of the table and leant against it so the two of them were shoulder to shoulder, the pretty garden and lake laid out before them. 'You ever going to tell me your name?'

'Kylie,' she said. 'Kylie Summer. I wish I could say I was happy to meet you.'

CHAPTER 7

The blast from the horn as the paddlewheeler eased away from the dock was as decisive a cue as the bang of a gavel. Damon shrugged his way out of the apron and headed for the house, where Maureen, carrying a large floral teapot, had disappeared through a side door only moments earlier. Inside, he found himself in a corridor where wide-planked hardwood flooring was dotted with thick rugs, house plants thrived in brass pots, and the walls were full—as in, *full*—of art. Watercolour landscapes, mostly, with a bright acrylic here and there, and the occasional whimsical country scene: a windmill with eyes and a face; an old-fashioned ute filled with hay bales; a hefty black dog lying alongside a barbed wire fenceline with a stick in its mouth.

Hmm. Cluttered, not what he was used to, but … charming, he supposed, in a fussy way that would require someone with a lot of spare time to maintain it all. A large plus was that he couldn't see a sewage colour or a droopy lamp anywhere.

A wide staircase sat to the side, turning mid-flight to head up to an upper storey, and he could see milled timber archways leading off to who knew what. The Secret History of Half-Brother Frank.

But first, it was time for Maureen to stop brushing him off with despotic utterances and jam jars. He followed the sound of running water into a kitchen almost as large as his inner-city terrace house in Sydney. Maureen stood at the sink, emptying tea leaves into a sieve, and at her feet lay the fattest dog he'd ever seen.

'Maybe we could leave the tea for a minute and talk,' Damon said, 'because I for one have no idea what is going on.'

The dog huffed out a series of deep grunts as it see-sawed its way to its feet and lumbered over to sniff Damon's black shoes. 'I wouldn't, mate,' he said. 'I've been wearing these socks since Friday.'

Maureen turned to him, wiping her hands on a tea towel. 'Don't leave them where he can reach them or he'll eat them. Alfie is on a diet.'

'He should be. What do you feed him, wild brumbies?'

Maureen's pursed-lip expression almost, but not quite, softened. 'You're cute, I'll give you that. His food's in the laundry, in a tin which has a really big sign on it, saying, *Do Not Leave The Lid Off This Tin*.'

Oh, he did not like where this was going. 'And the dog's food would be in Frank's laundry because?'

Maureen took a seat at the scrubbed pine table. 'The dog belonged to Frank, so he's now the responsibility of whoever inherited his estate. Your mother would know all about Alfie and his complex dietary and veterinary needs if she ever read her emails.'

Alfie took a seat by Damon's feet and looked up at him with wide, hopeful eyes. 'It's pointless looking at me, buddy,' he said. 'A) I have no idea what's going on, and B) I can't be trusted with animal management.'

'No need to worry that he'll be alarmed by you being a stranger, Alfie loves everyone. That's his "feed me" look he's giving you. He's working out if you're going to be as big a pushover as Frank.'

Damon was no pushover. And he'd be telling his mother that any minute now, adding it to the list he was compiling in his head. He was also totally ill-suited to taking responsibility for a dog—he was a workaholic with unfettered ambition, no interest in changing and no time or inclination to be responsible for anyone but himself. At least, that's what he hoped he still was.

'The pantry is stocked with some staples that'll see you through a week or so while you get yourself sorted. Don't thank me—Frank's lawyer insisted. Now, take a seat,' Marjorie said. 'Better still, have a look in that rack above the fridge; I think that's a Snowy River Vineyard pinot noir.'

Above the fridge, Damon found a bottle bearing a quaint little label in sepia tones that sported a sketch of a dog that looked remarkably like the dog now sprawled belly down on the floor. Maureen busied herself gathering glasses from an overhead cupboard and arranging crackers and half a wheel of brie on a plate with some grapes.

He poured her a glass when she'd stopped fussing and sat back in his chair. Silence had a way of asking the best questions, so he took his time pouring a scant inch into his glass. It was barely past three o'clock and that did seem a little early—a comforting thought that only someone with a healthy relationship with booze, not a drunk driver, would have, surely.

He held the pinot noir up to the light and swirled it. He knew nothing about the finer points of wine: tannins; chocolate notes; hints of elderberry and bullshit ... It all sounded like marketing spiel to him. But he'd attended enough swanky legal lunches in his day to know that swirling—allegedly—mattered.

Alfie didn't appear to care much for the finer points of pinot noir, either. The brie, though ... the dog had come to sit beside Damon, his bum fat spreading over Damon's shoe, blocking most if not all of the blood supply past his ankle, and his massive chest was practically on Damon's lap. The dog's muzzle was at table height, and he had it pointed in the direction of the cheese plate. He was breathing in with such vigour and hope, it sounded like he had a snorkel stuffed up his snout, and his tail thumped against the floorboards like he was spelling out *P L E A S E*.

Maureen took a sip and grimaced. 'Not one of Frank's finer years. Why don't you tell me what you do know.'

'My mother was supposed to come up here this week and collect the keys, look the place over and find a realtor to handle the sale, but she's had something come up. I'm, er ...' On time out? An undiagnosed asthmatic on a health retreat? Having a crisis? He wasn't sure what he was, but the terms that sprang to mind sounded neither complimentary nor shareable. Time, perhaps, to gloss up his situation with his own notes of elderberry and bullshit.

'My work schedule had an unexpected gap, so I volunteered to come up. I have authority to act on her behalf in all things.'

Maureen nodded. 'In all things? Well, that is indeed excellent, and all I needed to hear.' She tossed down the rest of her wine like a woman performing a duty, stood up, then untied her apron. 'You're in charge now, so my caretaking role is over.'

'Wait, in charge? Oh no, I'm just here to see what needs to be done to sell the place.'

If Damon hadn't spent years in court charming—or pissing off, depending on where you were seated in the courtroom—witnesses, jurors, judges and defendants, he might have missed the glassy sheen in Maureen's eyes. The rigid set of her neck. Assessing people's emotional responses and using them to his advantage was a skill he'd honed, so how should he play this?

She barrelled on like he hadn't spoken. 'The dog you know about. I've been minding him here since Frank died, because his dog bed and toy boxes and food tins were more than I could carry, so no need to worry that he won't be settled.'

'Bu—'

'Now, the vineyard's a little overgrown, what with it being the end of summer and all, and the weeds are starting to encroach on the flower beds around the house. I've been paying a kid up the road to mow the lawn near the dock—which is not at all in our business arrangement and I'll expect a *full* reimbursement from the bank account—but that mowing arrangement can now, obviously, cease.'

Nothing was obvious. Not the dog, not the mowing, not the bank account.

'You'll need to get the ride-on mower started up; it's in the shed. Frank apparently had to trick it into starting somehow but the workings of spark plugs are beyond me. I know nothing about the vines, but there's books in his study, so you'll maybe want to start there.'

Getting a word in and turning this monologue to his advantage was proving difficult. 'Maureen, there's been some miscommuni—'

'I can ask Kev to pop in and walk you through the irrigation system. It's rained on and off through December but we're into a dry spell now and no doubt Frank would be fussing about the vines' water intake if he were still with us. The cellar's not too full. Frank takes his harvest over to a winery in Barradine to have his wine bottled—it's never much, and he only ever sells a few barrels to the local wineshop in town, but he was fond of his "vintages", as he called them. The bottles he does have here are stored within a certain temperature range, so you'll need to check the cellar's gauge from time to time and take appropriate action. Frank had it hooked up to his phone with some app but I don't know anything about that, either. The vineyard you can tend or let fall into ruin; that's on you. The picnic business, on the other hand, must, according to the most obnoxious letter and talking-to I was given yesterday afternoon, honour its commitment to the paddlewheeler until the close of the Easter holidays, or we will be sued.'

Damon's impatience was building, but his ears pricked with the one word in that endless spiel that sounded useful. Sued? Now, this was something he could work with. The possibility of being sued was the nicest thing he'd heard since he got here. 'Can I see that letter?' he said.

But Maureen held up her hand in the time-honoured signal that meant I-am-so-far-from-being-done-you-had-better-hold-your-tongue-or-else. She struck him as a woman who had been waiting some time to have her say, and she was at full voice now. What a pity there was no judge present to order her to silence.

'It's best if there's two people to work the picnic tables, but I've managed it this season so far on my own. Scone recipe's written on the blackboard in the pantry, jam supplies are on the shelves ready to go, but tea and coffee, milk and cream, et cetera, will need to be restocked each week. That man—Dave Ryan—may try to push you into an evening wine and chamber music event, but that's not in the contract, so you can say no to that one if you're not up to it.'

Okay, now he did need to interrupt. 'Maureen, I'm listening to what you're saying, but you need to understand something off the bat. I'm not running some inconsequential picnic business.'

'*Inconsequential?*' Maureen turned to the large dresser from where she'd plucked the wine glasses, opened a drawer and pulled out a plastic sleeve stuffed with papers. She slapped it on the table with a violence quite at odds with her birdlike frame. 'This contract says you are. Well, to be precise, this contract says your mother is. This top letter is the one I received yesterday, hand delivered by Dave, but written by some twerp in Cooma. You and he might get along well.'

Ouch. Damon hesitated before putting his hand on the sleeve, wondering if it was akin to a poisoned chalice.

'Contracts can be broken,' he said soothingly. 'Especially contracts written by twerps.' A term he'd never heard himself described by before. Reckless, cocky and career-destroying, yes, but Maureen didn't need to know that.

Maureen sniffed. 'I may not be some city slicker in a suit and two-day-old socks with "gaps" in my "work schedule", young man, but I am not dim-witted. I've read this, cover to cover, and our lawyer here in town, Tom, has read it too. There's no backing out of it without a fight with Dave Ryan.'

'Who is this Ryan bloke everyone seems to be running scared from?'

'He's the owner of that paddlewheeler that was just here. He owns half the mountain, in fact. His pockets are deep.'

Fair point. Deep pockets often did convey a winning hand in petty legal disputes, but … 'Frank's dead,' Damon said, trying not to state it too baldly in case the waterworks began again. 'Even a man who owns half a mountain can't sue a dead man.'

'Frank's shares though. In the business. They haven't died.'

He groaned. 'You set up a company?'

She nodded. 'Picnic in a Vineyard Pty Ltd.'

'And my mother is now half owner, I'm guessing.'

She splashed another inch of wine into her glass. 'You catch on quick. Your mother, of course, would know all this, if—'

'If she bothered to read her emails.'

CHAPTER 8

Kylie was not squeamish, not at all, but the horror lurking within the nappy of her best friend's baby was making her rethink her stance. Especially since she was starving and she'd been planning on celebrating having not sunk the PW *Moana* by treating herself to a takeout lasagne from The Billy Button Café. Graeme, one of the owners, was another of her besties, and understood her need for a generous slice.

'What are you feeding that kid?' she said, pulling wipes at breakneck speed out of the backpack still strapped to her friend's back. She'd been hefting her toolbox down the dock from the paddlewheeler to where her ute was parked when she'd come across Hannah and baby Eva taking a stroll along the foreshore.

'Milk. From out of my boobs. I feel like a freaking dairy cow, so it's time to girl up, Kylie, stop with the look of horror and help me.'

Kylie looked at the fat little arms and legs thrashing about within the boxy confines of the pram Hannah had been pushing. The thrashing was like yoga, only faster, and with a lot—a *lot*—more stinky sludge. 'We're going to need a hose. Hazmat suits. A toxic waste disposal bin. I am so not qualified for this.' Maybe her little gumboot kiddies could do her a favour and arrive fully formed at the age of three. *Note to self: Did I tick the single dad box on my RuRo profile? A single dad farmer would be acceptable.*

Hannah snapped her fingers in front of Kylie's nose. 'Just grab her ankles, would you, and stop your whingeing. There, my lovely, who's a smoochy little sweetheart? Who's been a very good baby for Uncle Joshy while Mummy pulled ticks off a sad abandoned doggie? Who's got a fully functioning digestive tract?'

Assuming only the first bit of this nonsense was aimed at her, Kylie grabbed both fat little ankles and averted her gaze. The sour baby-poop smell wafting into her nostrils was eroding all her lustful lasagne thoughts.

But … perhaps this afternoon's rare sighting of Hannah was serendipitous. Babies, it turns out, were selfish little hogs of their mothers' time. 'Han,' she said, 'I've been missing you.'

Hannah looked up from cooing at the selfish little hog in question. 'I've been missing me, too.' Her eyes narrowed. 'Is something up? Do we need to talk? Has something happened in your life that I don't know about?'

Yes, Kylie wanted to say. Everything. Nothing. Stuff that was making her feel a little down. But that wasn't her role in the Hannah–Kylie friendship. She was the upbeat chatty one and Hannah was the moody one. Nostalgia for the good old days before adulthood got all messed up had her saying, 'Remember when we used to come skinny dipping down here with the boys from school on New Year's Eve?'

'That was once, and I blame the vodka Cruisers you made me drink, and don't change the subject.'

'Simpler times,' said Kylie.

'With terrible hangovers,' said Hannah. 'Now quit with the long-ago-when-we-were-young stuff and tell me what's bothering you.'

Where to start?

'Wendy been on your case again?'

'No more than usual.' Kylie found her eyes following the rise and fall of the low, patchwork hills on the far side of the lake. Wendy Summer didn't approve of Kylie's life choices. Especially the ones that had included taking herself back to school and earning herself a couple of Cert IIIs in diesel engine and light vehicle tech. She didn't approve of them in a sad, woeful voice, quietly but often.

She put her mother out of mind. 'Han, has Tom said anything to you about a new bloke in town?'

'Yes. No. Maybe. Dunno. Why?'

Helpful. 'In the last week,' she prodded. 'To do with a property over the far side of Lake Bogong.'

Hannah had rolled the nappy into a noxious football and was busy stuffing it into one of the council dog-poop bags that hung on posts in the carpark. Nappy disposal was possibly not a purpose intended by Mayor Barry O'Malley for public funds, but whatever. A new nappy was slapped into place, sticky tabs fitted and the fat ankles Kylie was holding were taken from her and stuffed into an adorable little onesie covered in dinosaur and fern frond prints and little speech bubbles saying, 'ROAR!'

'Did I buy this?' she said, distracted, as always, by excellent fashion, as she helped tuck the top inch of the onesie's zip into place.

'If I'd had more than three hours' sleep last night, I'd be able to tell you,' said Hannah.

'It's adorable. I must have bought it; my taste in clothing is so much better than yours.'

'Agreed,' said Hannah. 'Here, hold her for a sec.'

Kylie accepted the baby that was being proffered and felt the heavy, velvety head flop into the crook of her neck. The sour-poop smell was gone and she breathed in a great big waft of delicious baby. 'Does it matter if your first born is sucking on my collar?' she said as her neck grew damp. 'Because you may not have noticed, but I'm in my work gear. I checked oil and crawled around a diesel engine in this thing.' And she'd flirted, but she wasn't up to that part of the story yet.

Hannah had shrugged out of her backpack to stuff various mother paraphernalia away, and now that she was no longer in mother-on-duty mode, she was giving Kylie a critical inspection.

'What?' Kylie said.

'You're looking a little tousled, Kyles. Not your usual glam self.'

'Yes, well, we don't all have dainty little jobs pulling ticks off shih-tzus with surgically sterilised tweezers. I've been out on the lake guarding an engine all afternoon in a totally badass way. It tousles a girl.'

Hannah also looked a mess, but that was situation normal for Hannah Cody. She looked tired, but she was smiling, and layered over the tiredness was a glow of contentment that only made Kylie a teensy (and by teensy, she meant a lot) jealous.

'Want to take a walk with me and the rugrat along the lakeshore before my boobs start leaking again?'

Kylie chuckled. 'Who could say no to that? Take your baby back while I lock my toolbox in the ute.'

A minute or so later, the three of them were walking in the last of the sun along the foreshore of Lake Bogong. 'So,' Hannah said after a bit. 'What's all this about a new bloke in town that Tom may or may not have told me about?'

Kylie tucked her arm into Hannah's. 'The best looking one I've seen in a long time,' she said. 'And that includes online, TV shows, billboards, the odd questionable R-rated movie on SBS, and your husband.'

Hannah smirked. 'You wouldn't be saying that if you'd seen Tom in an R-rated setting.'

'Quit boasting. I was over at Snowy River Vineyard earlier this arvo. The boat I was on docks for an hour or so while the tourists have afternoon tea and wander about the garden, sniffing flowers or grapes or whatever. That's where I saw him.'

'The *Moana*? Doesn't the misogynist from the highway look after Hanrahan Trekkers' mechanical needs?'

There was that ominous orchestral music again. 'I'm hoping Nigel won't find out.'

'In this town? I'm betting he already knows. I'm betting he's doodling pictures of you right this minute, adding devil horns and a noose.'

Kylie narrowed her eyes at her best friend since forever. 'You know how to cheer a girl up, Han.'

'Okay, sorry. Forget Nigel Woods and tell me more about this bloke you saw.'

'Tall, dark, dangerously attractive.'

Hannah grinned. 'Just the way you like them. How dangerous, exactly?'

Dangerous enough to make Kylie forget her plan to only date farmers. To forget her commitment to her business. To forget everything but—

'Very,' she said. But now she'd acknowledged it, she could regroup. Rash behaviour was last year's Kylie, not this year's. 'You know I'm not interested in flings anymore, Han,' she said, as much to remind herself as to remind her friend. 'I'm a business owner now.'

'That would explain the face of doom,' said Hannah. 'This tall, dark and dangerous person ... was he a tourist on the paddle-wheeler, just here on a day trip?'

'Not exactly. Maureen Plover had him in an apron behind a picnic table, dishing out scones with jam and cream.'

'*Maureen Plover?*'

Kylie chuckled. 'I know, right? Apparently the winery owner who passed away recently was in—'

'Wait, Frank? Frank *died*? Bloody hell. What else have I missed? You have one little baby and, blink, three months flash by.'

'Um ... yes,' said Kylie. Hannah had been notably absent lately, but she didn't want to get all pointy-fingered about it. 'Did you know him?'

'Frank Silva. Owns a labrador with a butter and sock addiction. Fattest thing you've ever seen on four legs but Frank was too much of a softie to limit the old boy's food no matter what I said. I wonder who's looking after Alfie? Maybe I should drive over and do a welfare check—it's what any concerned, professional veterinarian would do.'

'You just want to do a tall, dark and dangerous check.'

'Damn right I do.'

The conversation was drifting away from where Kylie wanted it: she wanted to vent about almost meeting someone at last but then finding out they were totally unsuitable, and she needed Hannah to say, *There, there, Kylie, you'll be right, chin up.*

'Forget the dog with the butter problem for a minute.'

'Sorry. Where were we? You met a dangerously attractive guy, you must have chatted with him, I'm assuming, long enough to work out that he's not sticking around to be the man you deserve to have in your life now that you're all grown up and a businesswoman and all.'

'Huh. Considering you're so sleep deprived and sore boobed, you've summarised my predicament pretty well.'

The sun was long gone by the time Kylie let herself back into her apartment. She stripped off her overalls and left them in a stinky puddle by the front door, and decided her singlet and underwear were totally appropriate evening wear to enjoy lasagne on her tiny balcony. She collected a fork from the drying rack by the sink and took a long whiff of the meaty, cheesy smell wafting out of the catering box Graeme had given her. She sat down at the small table, then lifted the lid.

Heaven's above, the lasagne looked sensational, and Graeme, the lamb, had not stinted on the serving size. She was nearly through wolfing it down, ruminating on the miracle properties of layered pasta, cheese and tomato to make a crazy old world seem a place of wonder for a few lovely moments, when her phone rang.

Her mother. Crap. There went the lovely moment.

'Hi, Mum,' she said.

The phone call went the way phone calls with her mother always went: Wendy Summer could do passive-aggression like it was a recipe she'd concocted in her own kitchen. Despite the fact the two of them were communicating via phone towers or satellite or cables dug into culverts, Kylie could tell that her mother was spinning her wedding ring on her finger and looking as sorrowful as a four-member boyband singing about their shallow, broken hearts.

As expected, after the usual dissertation on the humiliations to be borne when running an ironing business from your home, the gentle regret didn't take long to appear. 'Pearl Harper showed me her engagement ring this week when she picked up her basket.

Slacks and blouses, Kylie, and a smart linen dress; not an ugly, greasy garment to be seen. She's marrying the Pappadapalous boy from down near Dalgety.'

'Mum, Pearl's onto her third husband since high school, and that "boy" from Dalgety must be pushing fifty.' Also, who said 'slacks' these days? Her mother was living in some 1950s world, where women welcomed their husbands home from a day at the office with slippers and a pipe, despite the fact Wendy Summer had been born in 1968. This, Kylie thought, was what came of being escorted by a young man to the Cootamundra Debutante Ball in a white gown and a tiara (tiara!) and getting married to that same young man a year later. Your notions—her mother's notions—were archaic.

'But such a nice man, Kylie,' the former debutante was saying. 'A provider.'

It was pointless arguing, it really was, but she couldn't help herself. 'Mum, some women want more for themselves than being provided for.' Like an income from work they loved. Like pride. Like independence and self-sufficiency and all those other things that Wendy pretended didn't exist because the role of bitter widow was now the sum total of her personality. 'Did you know windscreen wipers were invented by a woman, Mum? Think about that next time it's pouring down and you're trying to drive home. If that woman had sat around at home waiting for a bloke, where would you be? In a ditch.'

'Your father would roll in his grave to hear you talk such nonsense, Kylie.'

Not more wisdom from the virtuous dead. Kylie had memories of her father, cherished ones, of being driven down the mountain to Cooma on a Saturday morning to visit the ag equipment store her father had managed, of being allowed to hold the torch when he was changing the oil in the Holden Kingswood that had been his pride and joy, but it was hard to hold onto those in the face of all the stories her mother had recounted since. He'd passed away long ago, but Wendy liked to quote verbatim his many, *many* sayings. At least, his sayings according to Wendy, but which actually sounded like some garbage printed in a 1950s guide to being a good housewife.

'"A man works hard ..."' her mother began.

'Don't say it, Mum. Even thinking it sets the women's movement back a hundred years. It's like hate speech. Hate speech against *us*. Women. A group which includes you.'

'"... and a loving wife is his reward."'

'Women are no-one's reward.'

'Show some respect, Kylie.'

'If Dad spouted nonsense like that, I don't think he and I would have liked each other.'

'Why, Kylie? Why do you have to punish me?' A little sniff punctuated her mother's words. 'At least tell me you're not spending every minute in that horrible little workshop. You're a beautiful girl. If you just made a little effort, there's no reason why some nice man wouldn't ask you out.'

'An effort? Like not wear overalls?' she said dangerously. 'Let me tell you, Mum, that not every man in the world thinks a woman in overalls is an abomination. And it's not about what some man wants. It's what *I* want. Who *I* find suitable. Who *I* ask out.' Her thoughts skittered to the hot look the man in the vineyard had dragged down her faded, oil-stained front. The look that had burned the whole way down. He would have asked her out, she was sure of it; he practically had. But guess what? *He* didn't meet up with *her* expectations. Take that, Wendy Summer.

The fact she'd felt sad and bitter and just a little defeated ever since wasn't something she needed to share with her mother.

'But Kylie. You're *thirty-one*.' Wendy whispered it like she'd just discovered her only child was wanted for aggravated burglary in three states and the police were at the door. 'Overalls, online dating, driving around the countryside attending breakdowns … I don't know where I went wrong.'

Kylie concentrated on breathing in very slowly and then breathing out. She would not lose her temper. Or feel bitter. She would *not*. 'Overalls are practical,' she said, through gritted teeth. 'Online dating is practical. Attending breakdowns is how I earn a living.'

'*Practical?* But what about romance, Kylie? The more I hear about this dating app of yours, the less I like it.'

The conversation hadn't started on a high note, and it plummeted a few octaves as Kylie tried to reiterate how meeting people online was the new normal and Wendy bleated on about perverts and daughters and blighted hopes. Kylie reeled herself in eventually; she was too tired for this. Too demoralised by constantly having to stand up for her choices and justify her every breath.

'Luckily, Mum, I don't care what you think, because today I met someone who *loved* my overalls.' Sort of true. Sort of false. Nothing whatsoever to do with RuRo and said (she justified to herself) to shut her mother up. Pride had nothing whatsoever to do with it. Okay, it had a lot.

'Oh, Kylie, who?'

'A newcomer to town, here on family business.' Vague but plausible. 'We adored each other on sight.' Had she actually just said that? Nothing true and everything false and she'd better get off this phone call before she said something even more dumb.

'You met somewhere public, I hope. What if he's a predator? What if he—'

'Oh, Mum,' Kylie said crossly, suddenly aware how ridiculous she was being. Arguing with Wendy was always ridiculous because Wendy never, ever accepted anything Kylie had to say.

She hung up. Then she chucked the cold lasagne in the bin. And then she did what she had promised herself she would never, ever do—

She cried herself to sleep.

CHAPTER 9

On the evening of his arrival at Snowy River Vineyard, and after Maureen had run out of spleen and let herself out the back door of Frank's house, Damon sat in the kitchen with the pile of papers she'd left him. A wet swipe across his ankle startled him momentarily before he remembered the giant lump of fur he'd also been saddled with. He leant down and looked under the table, where two great, placid eyes stared up at him lovingly.

'No licking,' he said. 'That's rule number one.'

The dog woofed.

'Rule number two: Don't get attached to me. I am not here to stay.'

Those eyes. Still placid. Still loving.

'What's your name again, big guy? Alfie?'

The dog made a growly sort of mumble and rested his head on Damon's lap.

He hardened his heart. A man who could listen to, question, and dissect the most heinous acts mankind could dream up could certainly withstand one overweight, overly needy animal. At least, he had, up until last week, been able to listen, question and dissect. 'Up you get, fatso. We have a house to inspect, clean socks to find and a contractual agreement to crush between now and Wednesday.'

Baking scones to earn, what? Minimum wage? As if. He didn't get out of bed for less than two thousand dollars a day. 'Also, we have to organise a realtor. Talk to the lawyer who handled the estate to see where he's at with the transfer of assets. Make Sean and Warunya suffer some more. It's a lot, but you look to be a robust sidekick.' Understatement. The dog looked like he had energy reserves to outlast a second ice age. 'You coming?'

Alfie didn't need to be asked twice. He lumbered to his feet and moved to the doorway, the floorboards creaking under his weight.

As Damon wandered from room to room, the house felt oddly welcoming, considering it had been owned by some dead guy he'd never known. A living room off the kitchen had the last arrows of evening sun shafting golden points across its rugs and timbered floor. A double fireplace—nice!—of old convict brick shared itself between the living room and a more formal room that might once have been a dining room, but had been set up as a study. Those thick rugs Damon had noticed earlier were in here, too, in reds and blues, and books were everywhere—everywhere!—on topics ranging from viticulture to beekeeping to henhouse construction. Maureen hadn't mentioned anything about bloody chooks.

Alfie bumped his snout into a giant leather recliner by a bay window in the study and gave a mournful, if slightly muffled, sigh.

'Don't be like that,' Damon said.

The dog's rib cage huffed in and out like bellows.

Scone baker. Drunk driver. Grief counsellor for an obese dog. What next? The wires of fate had gotten themselves totally crossed if they thought Damon Johns cared one hoot about doing anything beyond signing a contract to sell this place. He had his own shit to deal with. He added a mental note to his list: the dog would have to go.

'It's pointless trying to guilt trip me, Alfie. Hard heart, emotionally disconnected, and ruthless, remember?'

Upstairs, three bedrooms were tucked under dormer ceilings, all of them stuffed to the gunnels with antique furniture, homemade quilts, more books, more art. Damon felt like he'd stepped into the set of some olden day Australian movie, only there was neither cast nor crew around to give him advice on where to find things like a towel. Or clean sheets. Or something to wear that wasn't his on-the-nose, wool, pin-striped suit. He stopped at a display of watercolours hung on the landing: cattle, a herd of them, were dark smudges against silvered grass; and a series of sketches of a bright orange tractor which had been given eyes and a mouth in the same style as the artwork he'd seen on the lower floor. But this time he noticed the signature in the bottom right-hand corner: the initials F.D.S. in dark red. Frank Silva, he had to presume.

He heard a tail thwacking at something soft, like curtains, and turned away.

'Alfie? Where are you, buddy?'

He followed the noise and found the great lump in a corner room overlooking the vineyard, flopped into a heap by the side of the bed.

'Frank's room, I take it,' Damon said. He'd pick a different one to make his own for the time he spent here, but …

He strode to the cupboard doors and flung them open. His eyebrows raised as he took in velvet jackets in plum tones, a silk dressing gown, cherry red–striped business shirts, a rack of short-sleeved shirts that favoured cartoonish prints like pineapples or hibiscus or palm trees. Hmm. Not quite his style.

His roving eyes fell at last on a flannel shirt, washed so often its plaid had faded into a sepia version of itself. Jeans he found in a drawer, okayish in size and not at all the daggy wide-leg version he'd have expected from some old bloke of his mother's vintage. He gave them a sniff, and they smelled cleaner than clean, like they'd spent a sunny afternoon on a washing line in a strong mountain breeze. They'd do.

'What do you reckon, Alfie? Would Frank mind if I borrowed some clothing?'

Alfie didn't seem to have an opinion on the matter, so Damon kept rifling until he'd found a couple of plain T-shirts, a forest green sweater that still had its sale tag attached and corduroy pants that'd stay up if he used his belt. Of socks, there was a drawer full, but at jocks, he drew the line. He could wash his own—in a machine, hopefully, and not in a chipped motel sink—and go commando while they dried. A shower. A meal of whatever he could find. But first, he had a call to make.

He called his mother in New Zealand as he wandered downstairs and back to the study. The bay windows had matchstick blinds drawn down, so he pulled on the cords until he could see out to the garden. The sky above was a deepening blue as the evening turned into night; not a plane to be heard, not a streetlight to be seen, nothing but the spindly limbs of a massive old gum tree reaching up like a giant hand.

No answer. *Call me*, he texted. He debated adding *ASAP*. Deirdre was self-absorbed and unreliable and incapable of self-reflection, but she was never far from her phone. Also, she loved to talk. But give a hint that the phone call might involve some onerous task and she'd ghost him.

The way you're ghosting Sean and Warunya?

He ignored the pesky voice of his conscience—so easy to do—left the text message as it was, then tried to hit on a plan. No point calling realtors or lawyers now—it was Sunday, and late. What, then? Because as much as he was unused to being the helpful house packer upperer, busy was good. Busy was awesome.

Tackle the desk? The bulky timber piece was the only thing in the house that was a cluttered mess. Unopened envelopes tottered in a deep pile in the in tray, and open books lay haphazardly on the desk's surface like birds shot from the sky. Damon picked them up to close them and inspected the titles: *Setting Up Your Own Micro Vineyard*; *A History of Paddlewheelers on the Murray*; *Illustrating Children's Books*. Hmm. A far cry from the case law and financial newspapers Damon read in the little downtime he allowed himself.

Shrugging out of his jacket, he rolled up his sleeves and took a seat behind the old-fashioned desk. The chair creaked in a homely way, and the dark bulk of the dog bulldozed in past his legs and collapsed onto the thick rug beneath the desk with a heartfelt sigh.

'That your spot, is it?'

A thump-thump of tail was his only answer.

Not the wildest Sunday evening he'd ever spent, Damon thought, contemplating the total absence of people and noise and clamour. Surely this amount of silence wasn't normal?

His phone trilled, thank god. He held it to his ear. 'Hi, Mum.'

'It's not Mum.'

Nick? His first urge was to hang up. His second urge was to vomit, which was crazy, *crazy*. He closed his eyes and told himself to breathe in, breathe out, and calm the hell down. Maureen flinging umpteen chores at him and Frank's farm sale turning out to be a major undertaking and not a minor one hadn't freaked out his newly acquired disorder, so why now?

Why with Nick?

Of course he knew. He just didn't want to admit that he knew. But he found he could talk again, so he cut off whatever Nick was waffling on about with: 'What are you doing with Mum's phone?'

Foolish question. Nick and Deirdre were tight. What was it to him if Nick was over there in New Zealand, all cosied up in the bosom of the family?

'Hello to you, too, little brother.'

'Put me on to Deirdre, will you?'

'She's upstairs. I saw your message, and thought I'd—'

Damon didn't much care what Nick thought. About anything. 'I'll call back later.'

'Wait. Don't hang up, I—'

The pause was unlike Nick. He was as chatty as Deirdre was. As Damon was.

'Why can't I hang up?' Damon said impatiently. 'You having a bad hair day, Nick, and need to whinge about it? Try whingeing to someone who cares.'

There was a long silence. 'You haven't heard, then.'

'Heard what? If you think I spend my days following your every social media post, you are way off.' Although, there had been that TV item he'd scrolled over.

The silence stretched out again, and this time it had a quality to it that set Damon's teeth on edge. Something was up. Something he ought to care about but couldn't bring himself to.

'I'll tell Mum to call you,' his brother said, finally, in a voice that held none of the Logie-nominated charm that had won him fans and fame and did nothing but irritate his brother.

Curiosity almost had Damon asking what the matter was.

Almost, but not quite. 'You do that,' he said, ending the call.

He rounded the night out in a stinker of a mood, hating the silence, hating the inky blackness of the night sky visible through every window, hating himself and this weakness he'd developed. He was only slightly assuaged by a shower in Frank's swanky bathroom, and the discovery of a stash of frozen meals in a chest freezer in the pantry off the kitchen. They had neat little labels on them marked THE BILLY BUTTON CAFÉ and promised such delights as shepherd's pie and boeuf bourguignon.

While the boeuf was spinning around in the microwave, the dog reminded him he had other duties. Dog kibble duties. Duties that didn't give a flying frisbee about Damon's sibling dramas and panic issues.

There. He'd allowed the word to come up out of his subconscious and settle where he could see it. Panic. *Him*. It couldn't be true ... could it?

First thing Monday morning, he was on the phone to the office of the local lawyer.

'Tom, is it?' he said. 'Damon Johns. I'm the one who collected the keys for the Silva property. Was wondering if we could have a meeting.'

'Sure. I've got someone in at nine but then I'm free. Why don't you come in, say, ten o'clock?'

'You couldn't come here, could you?' said Damon. 'Be good to walk the property over with someone who knows more about it than I do.'

There was a sound of rifling papers, then: 'Sure. I'll see you about half ten or thereabo—'

'Wait. Does Hanrahan have a coffee shop?' His hopes weren't high—he'd walked from the bus stop to the pub and then been driven out of town, but his impression hadn't registered much beyond a lake, a park with a handful of old buildings clustered around it and the absence of anything remotely like a thriving café culture. At this point, he'd have looked forward to a cup of hot weak froth from a self-serve vending machine—anything had to be better than the sachets of instant coffee that were stockpiled in the pantry for the picnic guests.

'Sure, we do. The Billy Button Café.'

Why did that ring a bell? Oh, yes. The freezer meal he'd helped himself to, which had been phenomenal. Was it possible that a coffee in the country could be phenomenal, also?

'You want to meet there, instead?'

'No, let's meet here. But if you wanted to bring me a takeaway cappuccino, as large as they've got, I can promise you I'll be a lot nicer to deal with.'

⁂

Tom Krauss, who ran his law firm from an office in the back of the grand old pub in Hanrahan, turned up as promised, but was quite the surprise. For starters, he wasn't old or short. Or sporting a bowtie, which, for some reason, Damon had stereotyped all country lawyers with.

Damon ushered him into the study where he planned on nitpicking Frank and Maureen's contract line by line, but then he'd fallen on the proffered takeaway cup of coffee with the same sort of enthusiasm with which Alfie had fallen onto his meagre scoop of kibble last night, which gave Tom an opportunity to kickstart their meeting with a shot across the bows.

Turns out, the country lawyer wasn't pudgy or dozy or sluggish on the finer points of contract law, either, another assumption Damon had made. In fact, the man looked like a stern-faced diplomat ready to upbraid the United Nations on climate change. At least, he did until Damon noticed the splodge of something— poached fruit? Porridge? Baby food, maybe?—on a shirt sleeve.

'You won't get out of this contract, not without a fight that'll last longer than the rest of the season, so I'd have to advise you not to bother.'

'I don't mind a fight.' Damon's response came out a little distracted, the coffee was so good. Not just good—it was fantastic. His brain cells had never felt so alive. Who knew that was even possible this far from Sydney?

'Nor does Dave Ryan, owner of Hanrahan Trekkers, with whom your mother is now in business. What's the problem with seeing out the summer season? Even if you were to put Snowy River Vineyard on the market today, it might take that long to find a buyer or to settle. Easter weekend is when the commitment ends, and that's less than three months away.'

'Three months of arguing contractual obligations sounds a lot more enjoyable than the alternative.'

'Come on, welcoming a boat in, chatting with tourists, keeping the grass mowed. How hard can it be?'

Damon snorted. 'Easy for you to say. You know Maureen Plover?'

Tom chuckled and the fierce diplomat vibe softened. 'Everyone around here knows Maureen.'

'Right. Well, she was here when I arrived, but she's gone off in a tantrum and left me a scone recipe, a page of instructions on preparing afternoon tea and an obese dog.'

Where *was* Alfie? Not underfoot, like he usually was. Had the lid been put back on the food container last night? Had the fridge door been left ajar? The great beast hadn't left Damon's side since they'd been introduced in the kitchen, and now he was just ... gone.

'Hold that thought,' he said, frowning, and bolted for the pantry. He'd had recalcitrant clients who'd not been this much of a nuisance. 'Alfie! ALFIE!'

The dog was not lying dead beside an empty cannister amid a pile of kibble dust. So far, so good. He wasn't upstairs looking mournfully at Frank's bed, nor was he snacking on the contents of the sock drawer.

The three loos of the house, which even a few hours *in loco parentis* had been long enough to teach him that Alfie viewed these household necessities as high-end water bowls provided for his convenience, were also dogless, and … the back door of the house was ajar.

Crap.

He went back to the study, where Tom was entertaining himself with a book on viticulture that had been on Frank's desk. 'Mate, you reckon we can walk and talk? The dog's done a runner and I'm not sure if he's allowed out unsupervised.'

'This dog. Would he be an old black labrador the size of an aircraft carrier?'

'You know your dogs.'

Tom smiled. 'My wife is one of the local vets. There was a dog heading off into the vineyard when I pulled up.'

'Awesome. Let's go. You can give me the short version of where the estate is at while we walk.'

'Your mother's been emailed copies of everything *and* been sent certified paper copies. She answers about one in ten emails.'

'Oh, I'm not doubting your work here, Tom. Mum's inbox can be a dark void when she's wanting to avoid dealing with something, and what she's told me about this place would fit on a thumbtack. I hold power of attorney for her—I can email you a copy and have a certified copy couriered from Sydney if she's not sent you one—and the one thing she *did* tell me was to get the place sold and the estate wound up.'

'We've been working pretty swiftly to get through the bequests.'

Damon nodded. Tom hadn't mucked around. Just getting probate could take months, let alone collating bank accounts and superannuation and life insurance and all the other endless chores a deceased estate entailed. The guy must be as efficient as Sean.

Who Damon didn't miss. Not at all. Sean would have this place packed up in a week.

'Frank's death might have been unexpected, but he had a will naming me as executor, his tax affairs were up to date and his accountant knew where all his assets were at, and nobody stepped up to contest the will. As estates go, it's been hassle free, other than the picnic contract.'

They were outside now, going up the rise to where the vines were laid out. The morning sun was warming the air and butterflies flitted about and flowers were abeaming and bees were abuzzing and all that country crap that Damon had no interest in being distracted by. 'Not sure I've seen a legal practice set up in a country pub before,' he said. 'Particularly not an effective one.'

Tom grinned. 'The publican lawyer, my mate Josh calls me. I hadn't planned on setting up a practice as a country lawyer, but life got a little crazy a while back and that's where I've ended up. Also, the pub has an office on the ground floor and a pie warmer. The arrangement suits.'

The limp hadn't been obvious before, but now they were walking uphill, the lawyer's gait had a pull to it.

'Old war wound.' Tom answered Damon's unasked question.

'Not literally?'

Tom shrugged. 'Afraid so. But we're not here to talk shrapnel, so let's get started.' They'd reached the hilltop, and from here they could see over the roof of Frank's house to where neighbouring houses dotted the lake's edge in a curve arcing back to the north, and across to Hanrahan on the far side of the water. 'Okay. Here's the lowdown. Frank's property, along with all plant and equipment, his super balance, his personal effects including pets and furniture, a handful of shares in blue chips, all goes to your mother, his half-sister born Deirdre Drummond, now Deirdre Parata, being his only surviving relative. The transfer of property and shares has occurred, but his bank balances and super payout are sitting in my trust account. We're needing to get an estate tax return lodged. It's done, but unsigned. Also, I've asked your mother for a bank account so I can make a distribution, but she's not provided one as yet. Funeral costs were met by the funds in trust, and household costs since then, of course, but there are no other debts other than whatever time on WIP I've not yet billed.'

'I can sort an account number for you when we get back to the study.'

'Thanks. It's a pain in the butt having it in my trust account, so that'd be good. Royalties from Frank's published works are to be divided evenly between the Hanrahan Library and the Hanrahan and District Community Association. That's a bit of a palaver to administer, but won't involve your mother at all, and Frank's collection of writing material—drafts and so on—are to be donated to the community association archives. That's been on hold until we had your mother here. We wanted a family member on hand to supervise which of Frank's documents and so forth left the house.'

'Royalties and published work. I noticed a fair bit of art that had Frank's initials on it. Was he a commercial artist?'

Tom smiled. 'Frank wrote and illustrated children's books before he retired. Don't be thinking your mother's missing out on the big bucks, however. I don't think he's published anything in years and the only royalty amounts I've seen coming in are from public lending rights. You know, from libraries. Some of his books must still be in circulation.'

'Who should I call from this community organisation to collect the writing material? I'd like to get that wrapped up before I turf the contents of the study.'

'Marigold and Kev Jones,' Tom said.

'Kev Jones? Maureen mentioned his name yesterday. Something about being able to help with irrigation.'

'Kev's a local legend around here and can turn his hand to just about anything. If you need help with the vineyard operation, he'd be a good start. He and his wife are both on the community association committee, so you can hand any of Frank's writing material over to them and consider the bequest fulfilled, legally speaking. Speaking of ... I ran your name on an internet search before I drove out here this morning.'

Damon smirked. 'Learn anything interesting?'

Tom chuckled. 'I'm glad I'm not coming up against you in court, Damon.'

'I'm not here as a lawyer, I'm here as a son.' A comment that surprised him even as he said it. 'I'd like to keep it that way.' Which might even be true, he realised. Maybe he *did* need a time out. 'But this picnic palaver ...' He rolled his eyes. Getting into a legal wrangle and potentially triggering some lung attack, as hideous as that felt, might be preferable to the alternative. 'I'm not baking bloody scones.'

'It's an irritation, agreed. But I think you'll find Hanrahan Trekkers have every right to expect the picnic company to honour the terms of their joint venture.'

'Until Easter. That's a lifetime away.' An exaggeration, but still. It got his point across.

Tom grinned. 'With an option to renew, of course, for next summer, if the terms are agreeable to all parties.'

'Not a chance in hell.' Damon's words hung in the cool air off the mountain, and with no city noise or chatter or traffic to disperse them, he had enough time to reflect that he'd sounded a little harsh. Rather than dig deeper into self-reflection, he switched topics.

'Frank was your client. Did he tell you anything about his relationship with my mother? She never said much about him.' Which wasn't odd for Deidre, considering she had a habit of never looking in the rear-view mirror, but to then inherit Frank's estate? There must have been a bond at some time between them.

His relationship with his own brother crossed his mind, and he quashed it. Really, this self-reflection stuff sucked, as did having the time for it to surface. There was no comparison; none.

'Not really. Frank liked to say his childhood was wonderful all the time except when it wasn't. Cryptic, I know, but it's all I've got.'

A sentiment shared by many, no doubt, Damon included. 'It's a pity he didn't think to leave his shares in Picnic in a Vineyard Pty Ltd to Maureen. She seemed a little ticked about that the other day when we met.'

'Agreed. An oversight on my part, perhaps.'

'Why don't I sign the shares over to her? Then she can have all the profits and all the bother.'

'Yeah. Great idea. But if your plan, as it seems to be, is to sell the property, then she's got no way of running the business once it sells. I can't imagine any new owners agreeing to a condition of sale allowing use of their grounds four times a week in the summer. Maureen doesn't have a dock on her property.' Tom nodded in the direction of the cluster of houses ringing the lake shore.

'Maureen lives nearby?'

'Yep. Next door. A bit of a slog uphill and down by road, but I imagine there's a well-worn track along the edge of the lake by now. Frank and Maureen have been friends for years.'

Help was close. Good to know. Maybe Maureen was over her snit and he could pop over and charm her back into an apron. He had until two o'clock on Wednesday, according to the schedule typed up in the pantry above the sachets of undrinkable coffee.

'Frank might have been Maureen's only friend, come to think of it,' Tom mused.

'Yeah? Why's that?'

'Oh, you know. Some people have a knack for pissing everyone off.'

Hmm. He had a feeling if Sean and Warunya were here, they'd both be giving him the hairy eyeball right about now. Well, to hell with them. And yes, he could see the irony of being annoyed with Maureen about the snit she was in with him while at the same time feeling totally justified about the snit of his own that he was in with his colleagues.

'No sign of your dog up here,' said Tom.

'He's not my dog.' He paused. 'Legally speaking.' Only, he wasn't sure Alfie had read that particular clause in Frank's will.

'You want some free advice?' Tom said as they walked between the rows of vines back towards the house. Damon eyed the heavy-looking clusters of fruit with a sense of foreboding. Grapes, he was pretty certain, did not pick themselves. Would a vineyard full of unmanaged fruit put off a potential buyer? Another problem to add to his list.

'Sure,' he said. 'I'll take all I can get.'

'Call the café in town. Put a batch order in for scones, and maybe see if they can hire out one of their waitstaff to you to serve the tea whenever the boat's due in. Vera and Graeme, who run The Billy Button Café, could have this picnic problem of yours handled in a heartbeat. It'll cost you, but cost can be relative, can't it?'

The man wasn't wrong.

CHAPTER 10

Country girl with a passion for old motors and lazy Sundays looking for love and commitment.

Kylie reviewed the update while her finger hovered over the submit button. Not the yoga crew's best work, and she hadn't had a lazy Sunday in years, but she'd *enjoy* a lazy Sunday if the opportunity arose, so it wasn't a total porkie. Of late, it had seemed like she continued to pay for the dating app more for the yoga crew's benefit than for hers, but a week had passed since she'd met the unsuitable hottie on the far side of the lake, and she'd been feeling a little ... fretful ... ever since.

Not that she had any real hope that RuRo would find her a match, but she had to do something to get Tall, Dark and Dangerous off her mind, and this was all she had time for. She hit submit, then switched to her banking app. She'd been hoping the overnight deposit she was expecting from the Brutnalls had miraculously appeared in her account, but nope.

Bummer. She shifted on the stool she was perched on at the bench in her workshop and reached for a pen. A large piece of butcher's paper was spread out on the bench, spanners and screwdrivers and hose clamps pushed to the side, and she was ready to brainstorm solutions for the hole her business had fallen into.

First she drew exactly that: a black hole in the centre of the page. Then she started doodling, because the ideas weren't coming. *What?* she wrote. *What, what, what?*

There *must* be something she could do to inject life into Hanrahan Mechanics. And by life she meant clients, car owners, hot rod enthusiasts, tractor drivers and even lawnmower owners, all of them keen-as to bring their clogged fuel filters and leaky hydraulic lines and defunct spark plugs into her workshop for some good old-fashioned service. Her love life was a joke, her family life was a soap opera, so it was absolutely not okay for her business to be anything other than a success.

She jumped when she heard a loud, metallic tap, tap, tap from out front of the workshop, and her pen—which for some reason had been doodling a bloke in an apron on the deck of a sturdy little paddlewheeler—dug its nib into the paper. She twisted on her stool, seeing through the roller door that someone was standing beside Trevor, whacking a tool against the tractor's old engine housing. What the hell? Who would—

Oh. Nigel Woods.

Now he'd stepped forward to stand at the threshold of the workshop, the sun turning him into a silhouette. A beefy, boot-clad, pissed-off silhouette. One of his hands held a wrench. Not a huge one. Not an I'm-here-to-smash-stuff-up one. But an unsettling one, nonetheless. Who entered someone else's business premises carrying a wrench?

As she watched, he gave the chain that held up her roller door a tap. Then another, and another: tap, tap, tap. The chain shivered and rattled and she totally got it—she felt a little rattled and shivery herself.

'Your chain's rusted,' he said. His voice was rough, like road base laid with not enough bitumen, and something about his bulk looming there, blocking the outside world from view, sent goosebumps over her skin despite the thick cloth of her overalls. 'Workplace accident waiting to happen when this roller door lands on someone. Hope you've got real good insurance.'

'Thanks for the tip,' she said, and feared her morning coffee was suddenly, urgently, about to run down her leg. This was not the first time he'd visited her workshop. It was, however, the first time he'd visited in the early morning quiet when she'd been alone. The psychopaths her mother was always warning her against felt a whole lot more real.

'What do you want, Nigel?' Brave words. She wished they'd been bravely said.

He moved closer, so his silhouette resolved itself into a three-dimensional man. She could see lines on his face. The mean set of his mouth. He was big in every sense—tall, solid, bulky—and she knew he'd been in the heavy transport industry before he'd bought the servo and workshop down on the highway. He had a gap in his teeth where a canine tooth should have been and it made him look like the sort of bloke who'd pick a fight in a pub for the fun of it.

He was also bald. Shiny bald. Tough guy, tattooed-neck bald.

She had nothing against bald guys, mind you. Bald could be hot the way dark and dangerous in a pin-striped suit could be hot ...

This bald guy, however? He was giving her the willies. Not that she would be giving him the satisfaction of showing him.

'Looks busy in here.'

Her car hoist was empty and her workbench was, besides the brainstorming paper and assorted tools, full of unpaid bills. A ride-on lawnmower of uncertain vintage was spread out in pieces across a tarp on the floor, but that was the only sign that she had any work on at all. His observation grated, but she took a breath, ordered her bladder not to be a scaredy cat, and got off her stool. If her nemesis wanted to stand there and look intimidating, then she'd stand, too. Kick her elbows out a bit, roll her shoulders, get her gorilla stance on. *Note to self: maybe switch up yoga to karate.*

'I'm guessing you've not come by to borrow a cup of coolant.'

His eyes narrowed. 'Yeah, I've heard that about you. You're chatty. Jokey.' He said that like it was an insult. 'All talk, no work.'

Okay, now that definitely was an insult.

'Did you come here and try to bully George Juggins when he was the Hanrahan Mechanic, Nigel?' she said. 'Or is it just women you like to bully?'

'George,' Nigel said with a snort. 'He barely serviced a car the last five years he ran this place and you know it. Coming here and tinkering with his tools was the way he got away from the missus. Me and him had a deal.'

This was the first she'd heard of a deal. 'George signed the lease over to me.'

'Yeah. He did. But he was supposed to sign it over to me. I don't like competition.'

Yeah, well, Kylie didn't like mayonnaise, but she didn't go around with a wrench in hand to every business in the district who served it on their sandwiches.

'Your beef is with George, then, Nigel, not with me.' She felt slightly bad about throwing the frail, eighty-year-old widower under the bus. George hadn't mentioned any of this to her when she'd taken over the workshop, but ... she had been very keen. Persuasive. Chatty, even, to use Nigel's term. And George had been grieving the loss of that very same missus. Maybe the old dear had just taken the path of least resistance.

Nigel was walking around the car bay as though he was sizing up where he'd be fitting his tool racks and his collection of hunting knives and his fridge full of VB, and it pissed her off. He ran a fabulous business on the highway, with not only passing traffic pulling in to fuel up, but also all the highway breakdowns and a customer base that stretched from Crackenback to the west, Dalgety to the south and Cooma to the east.

She didn't want that; she'd be content with earning a steady income from the Hanrahan town and farming community and knowing her clients, each and every one. Time and funds enough to work on Trevor in her spare time would be icing on the cake. Nigel didn't need her to disappear and he didn't need her workshop.

He just wanted it.

This was what came of generations of women delivering slippers to the man of the house at the front door. She wanted to say to her mother, *See? You're part of the problem, Mum. We give, and some men just take, take, take.*

'If that's all you've got to say, then we're done here,' she said firmly.

'Oh, we're not done, girlie.'

Girlie. That word. She had no problem with it when it was delivered by sweethearts like Kev Jones, or even old bulldogs like Dave Ryan, who managed to infuse it with a kind of bluff ignorance that the world had moved on, but Nigel Woods? He managed to say it in the most belittling, confidence-crushing way.

He was scanning her workbench now, and he'd seen the assortment of flyers she had scattered among the wrenches and alligator clips and loose nuts and bolts. He picked up the glossy PW *Moana* flyer that Dave had given her and her innards quaked. Now they'd be getting to it: the real reason Nigel was here.

He opened the flyer and took his time reading it, then closed it and held it with one hand, tapping it against the palm of his other hand. Tap, tap, tap …

She hated herself for it, but she couldn't help with the self-justification. 'He was desperate. *He* called *me*.'

Nigel nodded, like he totally understood, but also like he totally knew where to stash a dead body. 'You should have said no.'

The urgency to wee ramped up a notch.

'I've replaced those seals,' he said. 'The ones you installed. A miracle the boat didn't sink; at least, that's what I told Dave when I ripped them out and put in new ones.'

She sucked in a breath. 'Those seals were fine. I told him they were a temporary measure, and he okayed the installation.' Why was she justifying herself to this ape? *And* she'd ordered a prop shaft seal kit from her supplier that'd arrive any day. She'd like to think a wasted twenty-two bucks wouldn't break the bank, but …

'You like stories?' he said conversationally.

'What?' Who wanted to hear stories at a time like this? And Dave. Had Nigel managed to convince him she'd done a dodgy job and put his paddlewheeler at risk? Dave's word carried weight in this town. Dave could ruin her fledgling business in a *heartbeat*.

'I like stories.' Three innocuous little words made utterly creepy.

'I don't have time just this minute for whatever it is you're trying to say, Nigel, so—'

'I've got a story for you. You ever heard of Boggo Road?'

'No.' She shot a glance out to the street. Please, someone, anyone, walk by.

'Division Two. Place shut down in 1989, it was getting so notorious.'

'I have no idea what you're telling me.'

'Got myself a little souvenir while I was there. Picture tells a thousand words, doesn't it? Consider this your thousand-word story.'

He dropped the flyer and Kylie was glad the incessant tapping was done with, but then he pushed up one of his sleeves so she could see more of his arm. A tattoo—and not a professional-looking one—of a spider web in deeply inked lines. A bulky, many-eyed spider flexed at the centre of the web.

'Messy work,' she said faintly, as her bladder upped its urgency. 'You might want to get that tidied up.' The small portion of Hanrahan she could see through her roller door was like a ghost town. Where were the meddlesome locals when she needed them?

'Did it myself. Here's the short version: you don't want to get caught up in my web, Kylie Summer.'

'Is that a *threat*?' Was he nuts? He'd delivered that line like they were in some TV police drama in which he was the villain and she was clueless blonde female #3.

He'd picked up his wrench and was slipping it into the top pocket of his coat the way a doctor might slip in a pen. Professionally.

'Think of it as a warning.'

Kylie's hands were shaking. She waited until she heard Nigel's ute drive off then closed the roller door, deadbolted the walk-in door, and ran to the tiny loo so she could have the freak-out pee that had been threatening to wet her overalls.

He'd come here to scare her.

Don't be ridiculous.

Tap, tap, tap ...

Take a breath, girlfriend.

Can't. Too busy freaking out.

She pulled her phone out of her overalls while she sat there on the loo and tried to ignore the way her hands with their sunshine yellow nails were shaking as she typed a search string into Google: *Where is Boggo Road?*

Pages and pages of results popped up, and front and centre were the words *Brisbane's most notorious prison, known for its riots. Condemned as inadequate for prisoners' needs and its infamous Division Two was closed in 1989.*

Holy shit.

After a few minutes of staring blankly at the cruddy door a foot in front of her nose, Kylie decided sitting on a loo for the rest of her life was not going to achieve anything. So what should she do? Call the police? Get back to work? Fall in a heap?

She imagined herself picking up the phone and calling the local copper, Meg. A police car would rock up out front. Meg would be spotted walking into the workshop. She'd go interview Nigel Woods, who'd say who knew what, who knew how loudly, and three minutes later, Wendy Summer would be knocking on Kylie's door with a casserole and an I-told-you-so face. She'd pull out a pair of pinking shears with which she'd want to chop up anything in Kylie's wardrobe that looked like tradie workwear.

Nope. Couldn't do it. Which left only one choice.

If Nigel Woods thought she was going to fall into a heap just because he was a prize arse ... Well. Clearly, he didn't know that Kylie had a lot of practice standing up for herself in the face of unswerving opposition. Take a bow, Wendy.

She'd been brainstorming ideas to save her business when Nigel had turned up, and now? Well, now he'd just given her more incentive. The days when women could get bullied into doing what men wanted were over, and—

Oh.

The thought was a good one. A great one, in fact. So good, it gave her the energy to get up off the loo and haul her overalls back into place and stop shaking.

She wasn't the only woman in business in Hanrahan, and surely other women would have faced some pushback from idiots like Nigel Woods. If there was a local women's business group, she'd know about it, which meant there wasn't one.

Yet.

Somewhere to share advice. Get support. Bounce marketing ideas around. Trash talk chauvinist dickheads. What could be more wholesome than that?

The inaugural meeting would have to be a frugal affair, though, as her eftpos card was an embarrassing 'declined' moment waiting to happen.

Women in business breakfast, she typed into a new text message. The cheapest meal of the day. *Inaugural meeting Tuesday 7.30 am at The Billy Button Café.* Who to send it to? Vera, the owner of the café, of course. Hannah. Val from the supermarket, Penny from the boutique, the lady with the dalmation who sold honey and firewood from a stall out front of her property on the road to Crackenback, whose name Kylie would remember any minute now. Barb Smart. Who else? Her old boss from the salon, Tina. As little as she had any interest in sharing one of Vera's delicious muffins with Maureen Plover, she supposed (grudgingly) that Maureen did qualify as a business owner.

She added a suggestion for everyone to think of other women in the area who were in business and invite them, asked Marigold to forward the invite on to Barb and Maureen whose numbers she didn't have, then hit send on her phone.

She felt like a suffragette. *Take that, Nigel Woods. Kylie Summer is not going anywhere.*

She went back into the workshop to prove how brave she was feeling and put the roller door back up. The *Moana*'s flyer was lying face down on the stained concrete and Kylie picked it up, wiping it on her overalls to get rid of any nemesis germs. It wasn't enough. She was feeling *energised*. She was setting the flyer back on her workbench when she paused. Dave Ryan might be a cranky old fart who would never require her services again, but he paid his bills and he ran a heck of a business. Maybe she should use his flyer as inspiration for updating hers, instead of just chucking it among the junk littering the workbench.

Sure, she'd run a few ads in the local paper when she'd taken up the lease on the workshop. *Hanrahan local Kylie Summer is reopening the doors of Hanrahan Mechanics! Come on down and say g'day: she does servicing, wheel alignments and more!* But newspaper space, even in a small country newspaper, didn't come cheap. Maybe her new women in business group could share business cards and flyers and promo material with each other to hand out to their clients; in which case now was the perfect time to do up a new flyer. In colour. With a discount. If only she knew someone with graphic design skills who could create something as fancy as the *Moana*'s flyer. She could letterbox drop flyers, too, distribute them around town …

Oh yes, she was on a roll now. Of course, this project was dependent on her knowing someone rich enough to be able to afford printer ink in any colour more exciting than budget black, but that was step two of the problem.

Step one was finding someone who could design her something on the cheap.

Braydon, she texted. *Best boss ever Kylie here.*

Wassup?

Straight to the point. *You're a teenager, right?*

Last time I checked.

You study graphic design at school? If so (and even if not) can you rustle me up a flyer that's an improvement on my efforts? Something I can drive around and give out to potential customers? A bit fancy schmancy so we look successful ...

His reply came as quickly as expected from a kid who'd grown up texting from toddlerhood; it was all in the thumb dexterity, apparently. *You know I'm at school, right? Weirdly, my teachers think I'm here to do economics, general maths, history ...*

The kid was cheeky but he had a point. *Sorry. My bad.*

I've got a spare next will rustle something up :) I'm getting paid for this right? Because I'm saving up for a new hutch for Peanut and I've just spent 43 minutes listening to Mrs Gatnich in Economics lecturing on wage theft and industrial relations law ...

Braydon clearly had a much better business brain than she did, and yet the kid was barely old enough to grow stubble (but still sweet enough to dote on his guinea pig). *Don't spend more than an hour*, she texted. *Offer a 10% discount on the labour component of regular service prices if they bring in the flyer.* Then she put her phone aside.

Assuming he came up with something decent, there'd be the printing issue. Maybe Hannah would take pity on her and let her use the vet clinic printer in return for a discount oil change. Then all that would be left would be distribution. Unless some work came in, Kylie's days ahead were looking as exciting as a bald tyre so there was nothing stopping her driving around, in a totally confident and not at all desperate way, to drum up a little business.

CHAPTER 11

Damon took to the lake at the bottom of Frank's garden like the proverbial duck, which appeared to please the beast he'd been saddled with.

He developed the habit of throwing himself into the ink-dark water at the break of dawn and the shock of the chill must have been efficacious for his lungs.

Had to be, because he'd been here at the vineyard for a week and he'd not felt even a twinge from his lung barnacle since hanging up on Nick.

He swam in past the old dock, emerged from the lake, and stood for a moment on the shingled shore beside the upturned hull of an old clinker rowboat. He closed his eyes. The heat from the sun warmed the drops of lake water clinging to his skin. He could smell the dog, Alfie, who'd grown tired of swimming after a stick and was now looking for something dead to roll in on the foreshore. Grass. Something sweet and floral that might have been jasmine but could as easily have been one of the many other flowers growing about the garden.

Blood spatter has a distinctive smell, said the expert in his head. *As does a meth lab, a burnt body and ejaculate on a motel carpet.*

'Go away,' he said, but mildly. Dr Gloom he could deal with; he was, after all, just a collation of all the many testimonies he'd heard and remembered from court. So long as the other issue didn't present itself, Dr Gloom could do as he pleased.

He breathed in and in and in, and guess what? The air was lovely here in the lee of the mountains, beside the smooth silver of the lake. He held in the breath until all the forensic detail just melted away.

Breathe in, breathe out. Easy peasy.

The lung-busting tension that had blown itself up into an unmanageable mess during his last case was, simply, gone.

Or hiding. But, hopefully, gone.

Here, in this sunny patch of foreshore, he felt … what was the word? He had to hunt through his extensive memory to find the elusive little bugger.

That was it. He felt calm.

But there was only so long Alfie was willing to be left to his own devices, and pretty soon Damon felt his moment interrupted by a whiskery muzzle snuffling at his hand.

'All right, mate,' he said. 'You've earned a piece of toast, I suppose.' He opened his eyes to see if the calm he was feeling would stick around once he reconnected with the actual world, and was nonplussed to discover he wasn't alone in the back garden: an elderly couple was seated at one of the tables where the paddlewheeler picnickers had their afternoon tea.

He put on his most aloof courtroom face. 'Can I help you?' he said. Possibly he should have bothered to go swimming in more than a pair of red plaid boxer shorts with slightly too loose elastication but, in his defence, he'd thought it was just him and the dog.

He blamed the country quiet for his clothing choice. The lack of noise was so very not what he was used to, that it was easy to believe the actual world had ended and now it was just him and Alfie.

'A cup of tea would go down a treat, son,' said the man. He was thin and small-boned like a jockey, and he had a face like an old prune. He wore a felt cap that Damon had seen aged cabbies in Sydney wear in winter, and he had a woolly scarf around his neck that looked like it had been found in an op shop bargain bin in about 1960.

Alfie had spotted the new arrivals and bounded—well, bounded wasn't quite the right word; barrelled, perhaps—over to the couple and was busy pressing his snout into their pockets and laps, no doubt hoping they were carrying sustenance.

'Alfie, stop begging,' said the woman in a masterful tone. She was tall and as large-boned as the man was small. Her hair was a halo of grey and her outfit was a retina-smacking budgerigar green. 'Hello, Damon.'

She eyed him up and down with no subtlety at all, and with the ghost of a grin. He pictured the tracky daks lying across the end of the bed upstairs that he'd not bothered to put on when the dog had started headbutting the door. The warm shirt. The towel from the bathroom rail that he could so easily have brought outside with him, but hadn't.

What with some strange elderly woman giving him the once-over, and the cold damp of the grass's pre-dawn dewfall rising up and shrinking his pride and joy, he felt slightly at a disadvantage.

But only slightly. He was Damon Johns, after all. At least, he was on a good day.

He ambled over to the table and Alfie rewarded him by rolling in the wet grass, then lumbering to his feet and having a good shake, so that dew and grass bits now covered Damon from collarbone to boxer. This country life was not for the faint-hearted.

'Have we met?'

The man stood up and held out his hand. 'Kev Jones. This is my wife, Marigold. Maureen Plover told me you were needing a hand with your irrigation.'

'Uh, yeah. Thanks.' What time was it, anyway? A little early to drop in unannounced, Damon would have thought, but perhaps he'd swum for longer than he'd—

He dropped a discreet look at his watch and blinked. It wasn't even *seven*.

'Well, come on, the day's a wasting,' said Marigold, as though she'd seen him look at the time but chosen to put a totally different spin on their intrusion. 'There's nothing like yoga at sunup for getting a head start on your chores. Why don't you go find yourself some clothes, pet, and I'll pop the kettle on.'

'I'm not set up for visitors just yet,' he said. Or ever.

Silence met his words. Silence, and a charged glance from big-hair elderly woman to felt-cap elderly man. What? They couldn't seriously be expecting to come *in*? At this hour? With him not even dressed?

'Oh, dear,' said Marigold.

'Yes, pet,' said Kev. 'But he's young, yet. Let's not write him off just because he's clueless.'

'Clueless and freezing to death,' said Damon with a bit of snark. 'I seem to have disappointed you both in some way, but here's the thing. I wasn't expecting you. The pantry is one tin of sardines away from being bare. And while I'd be very happy to pay someone—you, Kev, for instance—for some advice on keeping the vines watered, it's a little early. Why don't we make a plan to get together later on? Today? Tomorrow? Shall we say ten o'clock? Two o'clock? Any o'clock that's not before breakfast?'

A phone was ringing somewhere inside the house. His mobile. Great. His mother had been ghosting him for days and now he was trapped outside in some inane conversation with two oldies.

Kev was looking at Marigold and Marigold was looking at Kev and some sort of unspoken decision must have been made, because Kev dropped the hand he was—still—holding out for Damon to shake and said carefully, 'Ten o'clock it is, lad.'

'Awesome. Great. See you then.'

After the pair had disappeared around the side of the house to whatever vehicle they'd arrived in, and silence had settled back over the garden, Alfie looked at Damon.

'What?' he said crankily. 'You think I was a little unfriendly?'

The dog sighed, lifted his leg to pee on one of the imprints Marigold's shoes had left in the wet grass, then wandered back to the house.

A dog's disapproval was more of a wound than Damon would have thought.

The phone call hadn't been from his mother. He stared at the missed call information on his mobile screen for some time. Had a shower thinking about it. Dressed in more of Frank's borrowed clothing while thinking about it. Drank a disgusting cup of instant coffee still thinking about it. His conclusion? There was something very awkward about, on the one hand, being pissed off about someone not calling *you* back, while, on the other hand, actively not picking up the phone to the people who wanted you to call *them* back. *Avoidance is one of the mechanisms for escape that a person coping with pain or trauma will employ.* Yeah. Thanks for that. But pain and trauma were wildly dramatic terms that in no way described whatever minor—and fleeting—ailment Damon was having.

'Shut up, Alfie,' he said to the dog, who hadn't said anything but was still looking at him. To prove his point—which he wasn't totally clear on, but whatever—he picked up his mobile phone, scrolled through until he found Sean's number and hit the icon for a video call.

'Finally,' came Sean's voice after a minute or two. 'Wait, Runya's chopping up an avocado.'

Damon waited while Sean's phone camera showed him the collar of a business shirt and a dizzy run of ceiling tiles before squaring off into a view of his colleagues seated at the tiny table in the chamber's kitchen. His vantage point told him that Sean had propped his phone against the microwave. Warunya was eating a slice of avo toast with feta crumble and tiny little tomatoes chopped into delicious peppered rings that reminded Damon he needed to find a grocery delivery service as a matter of urgency. If he holed up at Frank's much longer he'd be forced to share Alfie's kibble.

'Where on earth are you?' Runya said. 'And what's with not answering our calls all week?'

'Long story.'

'I've got court in twenty-seven minutes so give me the precis.'

'I'm on a farm. Well, more of a vineyard. Prepping it for sale.'

Sean and Warunya looked at each other and Damon was reminded of the look his early morning visitors had shared with each other. What was it about his pronouncements that made people think he didn't mean what he said? Or that there was subtext to what he said? He was beginning to think fondly of Maureen Plover's assertion that she was known for her astounding clarity. *He* spoke with clarity. *He* was astounding. At least, he'd grown accustomed over recent years to thinking he was.

'And, er, when did this crop up? I didn't know you knew anyone west of Parramatta.'

'Very funny,' he said. 'It's my mum's place. She inherited it, I'm selling it; it was somewhere to come after you both gave me the boot.'

Warunya sighed. 'Not the boot, Damon. A loving kick up the arse. Come on, you've had some time to think—were we wrong to be worried about you?'

The knee jerk was to say yes, of course, they were totally wrong and he was outraged and how dare they, yada yada yada. But the truth was, now he'd stopped, he'd realised that, actually, he had been very, very wired.

'I'm prepared to admit, without prejudice, that a break has not been totally unwelcome.'

Sean grinned. 'Did you hear that, Runya? I'm interpreting that wordy, show-off sentence as an admission that we were right.'

'I heard it,' she said, frowning at her watch. 'Running off like that. You gave us a fright, Damon, and I'd like to dig into that a bit deeper but I do have to go. Promise me you'll stop ghosting us.'

'I promise.'

'And what is that hideous noise?'

Damon turned the phone so they'd have an eyeful of the dog, who was sitting beside the fridge, making a subdued howling sort of noise. No doubt this was a plea that had worked on Frank, because the dog put on this performance a couple of times a day, but Damon was made of sterner stuff. Also, the fridge was a barren wasteland.

'A dog! Do you even like animals, Damon?'

'Not at all,' he said, turning the phone back. 'Especially ones who make a racket at the fridge door.' He frowned at Alfie, who took the hint and lay down with a grunt. 'Petulance will get you nowhere.'

'Um,' said Sean, 'were you speaking to the dog or to me? Runya's taken off.'

'Sorry. Dog minding is more labour intensive than you might think. Hey, Seano, I'd better go,' Damon said. 'I've got an irrigation guy coming round soon and I've already put him off once today.'

Sean wasn't done. 'You know, it's a tough profession, Damon. Plenty of barristers get overly wired and lose the plot.'

Was that what it had looked like, his performance in the restaurant? Him losing the plot?

'Burnout is not something you should think only happens to other people. You've been working too hard and too recklessly. We've been telling you for months. This quest for glory you seem to be on, all these back-to-back court wins, has a dark side.'

Burnout? Could that be what was causing the pleurisy? The leprosy of the lungs? No way, not him. 'I'm a little young for burnout, Sean.'

'I'll send you some information. Barrister wellbeing is a hot topic amongst us law clerks, you know, and there's a pattern we all see: working your arse off in a profession that demands you to be confident and unaffected by the drama you're dealing with every day so you become exceptionally good at avoiding emotions, even your own, but then becoming totally disconnected and apathetic.'

'I've never had an apathetic day in my life.' Even as he said it, he was envisioning himself in that sewage-coloured motel room with the drooping lamp and his total lack of will to do anything at all besides mope and eat cheese and chutney sandwiches.

'Well, stress doesn't follow a rule book, does it? I'll send you some literature. By email. And I'll be putting a read receipt on it so I know you've actually looked.'

'Thank you, mother hen.'

'See that, there? Mocking me for trying to help you? That is you disconnecting yourself from the fact that, actually, you might very much need help.'

Sean looked at him and Damon looked back for a long minute.

'Okay,' he said at last. 'I'll read what you send me.' Was he lying? Maybe. It was hard to tell these days what was his truth and what was his nuanced phrasing designed to get an appropriate response from the other person.

'Good. Now that we're over that hurdle, don't get too comfortable up there, mate. We do really need you down here. When your head is in the right space.'

'There's no chance of me getting comfortable in the country, Sean.'

CHAPTER
12

The kid might be an operator, but he came through. When Braydon arrived for his next shift, he brought his laptop with him. Kylie scrolled his screen up and down and side to side to review his work. 'This is epic, Braydon. You have skills. Who knew?'

Her young cousin began ticking off his fingers. 'My mum, my teachers, my basketball coach, my guinea pig.' He winked. 'My girlfriends, obviously.'

She flicked an oily rag at him. 'Ew. Too much information. And what do you mean, girlfriends, plural?'

'Hey, what can I say? I'm popular.'

She snorted. 'Forget I asked. But thank you. And I thought you had the hots for Poppy Cody?'

He sighed theatrically. 'Long-distance relationships make the adolescent heart grow weak, Kylie. She's in Sydney—I'm here. What's a guy with burgeoning hormones to do?'

'You are so shallow.'

'I know,' he said comfortingly. 'About this flyer—you want me to tweak anything?'

She viewed his design again. *Hanrahan Mechanics, your one-stop mechanic shop for engines large and small. Farm machinery welcome.* The discount was typed up in huge red writing and below it, the terms, and it was a massive leap ahead of her own typed-up efforts. 'It's great.'

He scratched his head. 'Maybe something about the mobile service? You do callouts anyway, so why not advertise it as though it's a special thing we do? "Your trusted mechanic is one phone call away", something like that?'

'Oh, that sounds awesome,' said Kylie.

Braydon swivelled his laptop around to face him and his fingers tippety-tapped over the keyboard. 'In bold font,' he muttered. 'Mask layer, a shadow of a spanner in the background and ... Okay, we're done. These are the cut lines, here, so you'll get three to a sheet. Not as fancy as Hanrahan Trekkers, but it'll save on paper, meaning you get more to hand out. What do you think?'

He turned the screen back and her new flyer shone up at her. 'I love it.'

'Enough to give me a raise?'

She ruffled his hair. 'Enough to give you a big kiss,' she said, smooshing up his cheek and planting a big noisy one on it.

He leant away. 'That is so gross, Kylie. And probably illegal.'

'That was a thank-you-skilled-cousin kiss, not an employer kiss, so don't start quoting your economics teacher at me again.'

'You want me to stick some flyers under the windscreens of the teachers' cars at school? Because I will do, if you promise to never slobber all over me again.'

She laughed. 'It's a deal. Now save it onto a memory stick for me, so I can take it over to the vet clinic while you get started cleaning up these lawnmower parts; the Codys have said I can use their good printer.'

Once Braydon had been taught the joys of restringing the pull cord of a lawnmower and changing out a spark plug, Kylie sent him home early then hung her OUT ON A JOB sign over the door of the workshop. She forwarded the landline to her mobile, gave Trevor a pat and told him he'd been promoted from workshop mascot to security guard, then hit the road. On foot, at first.

The laundromat had a community noticeboard, as did Vera and Graeme's café. The guy behind the counter at the retro clothing shop below her flat said he couldn't support more paper waste and why didn't she have a good hard think about carbon emissions from vehicles. Thanks for nothing, Pete. Her yoga buddy Janine, who was on the loans desk at Hanrahan Library, said she couldn't stick anything up without council branding due to some new rule Barry O'Malley, the mayor, had brought in, but she could sneak a few flyers in as bookmarks if any of their regulars came in, wink wink. The darling. Kylie borrowed a book she'd ordered in for her while she was there, *A Short History of Tractors in Ukrainian*, and nobly hid her disappointment when she realised it was fiction.

An hour later her feet were sore and the sun had dipped behind the mountains, causing the temperature to plummet, so she decided it was time to letterbox drop from the comfort of her ute. Hanrahan didn't have a large population, so it didn't take long to work her way up and down the streets.

Going home for a bath and a glass of wine and a binge watch of some crime show on television was tempting, but she was on a roll, and the Codys had been generous with their ink and paper. She took her ute along the road that followed the lake west then north, to where land parcels were larger and agricultural machinery was just as important to the residents as vehicles. Cattle, horses, a few small mixed farms, retirees enjoying the peace and space of the country, a small piggery ... Families of all shapes and sizes lived out here, nestled in the foothills of the Snowies. A lot of empty houses, of course, short-term rentals that were busy in snow season but uselessly empty the rest of the year, but still, plenty of the land was being worked, and all those properties had letterboxes at the start of their driveways. Fun letterboxes, most of them, made from old kero or milk tins and resembling emus or pigs or wombats. At the curve of the lake, where the last of the farmable land lay, before Mt Creel pushed upwards a thousand steep feet from the waters of Lake Bogong to the source of the Snowy River herself, was Snowy River Vineyard.

Kylie took her foot off the accelerator and let the diesel engine idle while she contemplated what she was about to do. The evening mountain breeze coming in through the open windows was making the last few leaflets on the passenger seat flutter as wildly as her thoughts.

It was time for a reality check.

Unless the weeks ahead brought in new work, then she was not going to make her hoist finance payment. She was, as her mother had so thoughtfully reminded her, thirty-one. She had no resources beyond rent paid up for another month on her flat and about three weeks' worth at the workshop. She had her trade, of course, if the workshop failed ... but the closest mechanics were the ones on the highway employed by Nigel Woods. No salvation waiting for her there. Cooma, maybe, but that'd be a long commute. Doable, but only when desperate.

Leave Hanrahan and move elsewhere? No. She couldn't. She'd been born into this country and every dream she'd ever had for her future featured her here, in a sunny paddock, preferably with little gumboots and a burly farmer within cooee. This was the country into which she wanted to be buried and she was as wedded to that idea as her mother was wedded to wringing her hands.

There was her other trade, of course. The one she'd left school for at the start of Year Eleven when her mother was crook. The trade she hated. She could walk into the hair salon near the park in town tomorrow, probably, and Tina would give her a job doing nails or eyebrows or wedding makeup. Wendy Summer would probably throw a party.

Kylie sat there in the twilight, wondering if she was nuts to pin her hopes on a women's business group for ideas to help with marketing, and on a handful of updated flyers.

Nuts or hopeful. She liked to think she was hopeful.

In the same spirit of optimism, she considered the decision she was facing now at the start of the gravel track leading to the vineyard. Do a U-turn or drive in? Good decision or bad decision? Nuts or hopeful?

Or maybe there was some level of decision between good and bad, hopeful and nuts, and she just didn't know about it yet.

As she was dithering, a shiny new SUV pulled out of the driveway, the words *Monaro Realty* plastered all over its glossy sides. It seemed Damon wasn't mucking about getting the place on the market, and after that? Well, he'd be gone. He was not a keeper, which she already knew, so why was she still lurking here at the top of the driveway?

In the end, after a bit more finger-drumming on the steering wheel, she drove in. Vineyards had machinery, didn't they? Utes and ride-on mowers and grape-crushing equipment ... Popping in to see if the newbie in town required mechanic services for equipment that a new owner would need to see freshly oiled and greased was a prudent business decision.

And yes, okay, she had another motive. She'd not had the easiest week—or month, or year. When had she last done something a bit foolish and fun? Her bestie Hannah had been caught up in Tomland and then babyland. She hadn't had a night out with a guy in months (and *that* had been a total fail, RuRo!); her dreams of being someone who could run her life her way and prosper were kinda maybe imploding no matter how much of an optimistic slant she put on everything; she'd been threatened by an ex-con with a prison tatt and nearly peed her sunshine yellow knickers; and—as per usual—she was totally ticked off with her mother.

She had no-one to talk to, and she dearly loved to talk.

Gravel crunched as she navigated the narrow track. Snow gums grew sparsely to the left, trunks twisted and bark lying in shreds at their base. Granite boulders too large to clear put some weave into the track, and the summer wildflowers lent prettiness to the rough ground. The land began to incline downwards to the lake and she came through a small stand of young pine to arrive at the house.

A bore must have been dug somewhere. No-one could irrigate the vines spreading up the hillside to the north of the house with the lacklustre rain that marked most summers in the Snowies. That meant a lot of irrigation pipes, which meant a lot of pumps. Maybe she should stock them at the workshop for the local farmers who didn't have time to drive into Cooma?

Of course, she'd need cashflow for that. Which she would have. Any week now. Hope, remember?

The gardens that flanked the house were greener than the countryside, too. She might have noticed a bit of colour and whatever when she'd come in via the dock, but her mind had been on other things: water in the bilge on the first day and the new bloke on the second. Show her an antique motor and she'd have remembered it in detail a week later; a fine set of tyres mounted on heavy duty cast steel rims with phenomenal ground grip? Oh yes, she could wax lyrical about that to anyone within earshot. But show her a shrubbery? Yeah, nah, as Braydon would say.

A deep woof sounded just as she lifted her hand to the brass knocker on the front door and a huge black animal bounded around the corner of the house. For the second it took to realise the beast was a dog with a wagging tail, not a grizzly bear (which didn't even exist in this hemisphere), her heart rate punched into overdrive. It stayed there as Tall, Dark and Dangerous came into view behind the dog.

Saying hi would have been her first word, but the dog got in the way of that, leaping up to plant two huge, muddy paws front and centre on her overalls. 'Ooof,' she managed instead.

'Get down, you idiot,' Damon said. To the dog, she assumed, because he followed the words with a wide smile that she very much wanted to believe was for her.

Damon hadn't grown any less newsworthy in the days since she'd last seen him. He'd lost the apron and replaced it with a scruffy pair of jeans and a faded navy T-shirt. He looked relaxed, too, as though he'd spent his time snoozing in a hammock under the pale mountain sun, with an overfed dog snoring, tractor like, by his side.

'Remember me?' she said.

He grinned. 'Plain scone no jam or cream, blue fingernails, handy with a spanner. There's no forgetting you, Kylie Summer. A little surprised to see you, though; I thought we parted ways with you saying you weren't pleased to meet me.'

Oh, this was good. Banter. Teasing. This was just how she liked a conversation to unravel. The burden of her day fell away as she smiled back. He was interesting and he was looking at her as though she was someone special. This was *fun*.

'Well, that's your fault for being so unsuitable. To make amends, I've got a little something for you.'

One of his eyebrows ticked upwards. A neat trick. It said *Oh?* and *Tell me more* and *I'm fascinated by your every word* all at the same time.

She swallowed. Perhaps she hadn't needed to phrase it quite so ambiguously. 'It's, um, a flyer. For my business. Which I guess I've left in my ute.' Wow, this was getting lamer and lamer by the second. 'Just in case any of the machinery out here needs a, um, service.' Could she sound any more desperate or crazy? Clearly, she *had* been driven nuts by debt and being an endless disappointment to her mother, and she should get back in her ute and hightail it back to Hanrahan, hope be damned.

The look Damon gave her was so thorough and lasted for so long, she couldn't decide whether her heart rate went up because she was flustered or flattered. Or both.

'I was just about to take fatso here for his evening waddle through the vineyard. Why don't you join us? You can tell me all about your services in person.'

Why did that sound salacious? *Because you're a man-deprived woman and he's a total hottie*, her rational self whispered frantically in her ear. *Drive away now, girlfriend. Life goals, remember? Good decisions only! Blokes who only pass one of your four rules are bad decisions!*

'Fatso?' she said, falling into step beside Damon. Apparently, her rational self wasn't in charge this evening. 'Is that a politically correct way to refer to your overweight dog?'

'Point of order: he's not my dog.'

She blinked. 'Point of order? What does that mean?'

He chuckled. 'Sorry. Old debating term from school. It's the sort of fatuous phrase that sticks.'

'Riiight,' she said. Meaning: wrooong. Debating? Seriously? What was he, some product of private school and privilege, who had pricey lakefront properties dropping into his family's lap every week? She and this man had nothing in common and the more they talked, the more that would become clear. To both of them. Mr Point of Order versus Miss No Senior Certificate.

'Point of order number two,' he carried on blithely, 'Alfie doesn't seem to mind what I call him. Does he look offended to you?'

She stared down at the dog, who was practically standing on her boots and looking up at her as though she was his saviour because he hadn't eaten in six months and was about to expire, any second now, if she didn't immediately produce a stuffed and trussed roasted turkey. A long and disgusting string of drool was dangling mournfully from his lower lip.

'I see what you mean,' she said.

Damon went up a narrow lane between two fields that bore the telltale gouges in the ground that put a skip in her step: tractor tyres had trundled this way. No wonder she felt so relaxed.

'His name's Alfie,' he said. 'That is one of the few things my Picnic in a Vineyard partner told me before she flounced off in high dudgeon last weekend.'

'Maureen's not been back? What about the *Moana*? I thought it picnicked here four days a week.' Dave would be frothing at the gills!

He smiled. 'You are very well informed about its schedule. Don't worry, the contract's being honoured—for the time being, at any rate. The lawyer in town gave me the name of a caterer who could handle the vineyard's end of the arrangement.'

'This lawyer. Was his name Tom?'

'Yeah. Tom Krauss. You know him?'

She chuckled. 'Of course I know him. I'm godmother of his new baby.'

'Everyone really does know everyone here, don't they? I don't know how you stand it. Everyone with their noses in your private business, even at ungodly hours of the day.'

That was oddly specific. She shrugged. 'Maybe us country types are better at hiding stuff than you city people.'

'You reckon?' His tone had switched from easygoing to dry. From friendly to distant.

'Sorry. Did I touch a nerve?'

He looked at her. 'I guess my nerves are a little closer to the surface than they usually are. I'm blaming it on all this space.' He waved an arm to indicate the view, and she realised they'd climbed quite high since they'd left the house. The dog was barely a black dot in the distance below them.

'Too quiet for a city boy to sleep, is it?' she said. She'd spent time in cities, of course. Melbourne, Canberra, Sydney, even a wild week at the Gold Coast back when she was twenty-three that had been awesome. But stay there? Long term? No way.

'You've clearly never shared a room with an obese dog. Alfie's snoring is equivalent to sharing your bedroom with three buses, a high-speed train and a six-lane highway.'

She laughed. 'Can't you put him in the kitchen? Or laundry?'

'I tried that. He howled so loudly the foundations cracked.'

They turned down a narrow track between vines that looked nothing like their verdant neighbours; these were barely more than foot-long roots, staked beneath a three-string arrangement of wire, and they seemed years away from growing leaves, let alone fruit. This vineyard business—and dog ownership, now she thought about it—was not a turn-up, sort-out, bugger-off-again style of enterprise. She wondered if Damon, or his mother, understood that.

'That's the country for you,' she said.

'What? Animals keeping you awake all night?'

She smiled. 'No. Sorry, I'd backtracked a little to what you said earlier. The country gives you space to think ... even when you'd rather not.'

'You're not wrong,' said Damon. 'So tell me, what is it you'd rather not be thinking about?'

She looked up at him. He was one of those people who had the knack of making you feel like they were totally focused on every word you had to say. It was unnerving. And kinda wonderful. If she could believe it. Which she couldn't.

'That's a very personal question, considering we've known each other for about six minutes.'

'A stranger in a vineyard,' he said, almost to himself. 'Who better to unburden yourself to? And you know, if I were to guess, I'd say your business flyer isn't the real reason you came out here.'

She cleared her throat. 'Yeah. Okay. Busted.'

He laughed and she felt absurdly happier than she'd felt in weeks. When his hand tucked itself under her arm as they started walking back down the slope to the possibly hyperventilating dog, her heart flipped over like a pikelet in a frying pan.

'Tell me everything, and don't stint on the details. I *love* details. Although, I'm having a break from hardcore details, so better keep them on the bland side.'

Another odd thing to say, but okay. 'Here goes with reason number one. Mind you, this would have more credibility if I'd remembered to grab one of the flyers out of my truck. I'm running a business promotion, ten per cent off a regular service when you bring in the flyer.'

'Uh-huh. Perhaps I should have mentioned this when I was helping you to a plain scone, but I don't have my car with me.'

They were nearing the side of the house closest to the fields, and not only could she see more tractor tyre ruts disappearing behind a sturdy shed, but she could also see ordinary tyre tracks; Frank *must* have had a vehicle. And no way was anyone mowing all the lawn down to the lake on a push mower. 'You know how a vet in the city pretty much just does dogs and cats? But a vet in the country delivers calves and vaccinates pigs and trims the hooves of goats and horses?'

'Um … yes?'

'I'm a country mechanic. Tractors, irrigation pumps, anything. Anything farm or vineyard related. Especially vineyards that are about to get sold in tip-top working order. Although, if I'm honest, tractors are my specialty.'

'Really? What's so special about tractors?'

She grinned. 'Don't get me started. They're all muscle and no show off. They're reliable. They can be heroes rescuing cars from bogs and cattle from floodwater. They have a history dating back to the 1890s and they're—' She stopped. *They're my ideal guy.* As in … nothing like Damon. 'Sorry. People who know me well just tell me to shut up when I start in on a tractor monologue.'

'I was incredibly interested,' he said.

'You're an incredibly bad liar,' she said, matching his grin.

'Hmm. People who know me better might not agree with you.'

She frowned. Did that mean he *was* a liar?

An awkward pause followed but then Damon filled it. 'There may well be equipment here in need of a service but I'm still working out what goes where. You don't happen to know how to maintain a vineyard, do you?'

She laughed. 'Um, no.'

'Frank has quite a library on the topic and I'm working my way through his books.'

'Irrigation has to be the most important thing at the moment,' she said. 'We've not had much rain.'

'Yeah. That's what Kev said.'

'You've met Kev already? Gosh, you're almost a local now.'

'Apparently I must be very obtuse when it comes to farming logistics because he seems to have taken me on as a pity project.'

'Kev's a sweetheart and he loves a project. His wife is my yoga instructor.'

'Marigold. I met her, too.'

They'd reached the dog, who'd found something interesting to snuffle in the grass clumped at the base of a post supporting a row of trellised vine.

'What's the other reason?' said Damon.

Oh. Kylie had almost forgotten she'd admitted to having dropped by with a nefarious purpose. 'You know what a nemesis is?'

'Of course. An agent of destruction fixed solely on you. You have one? Huh, maybe the country is more interesting than I'd thought.'

She stumbled on a patch of scree and Damon grabbed a handful of her overall pocket to keep her from slipping.

'You okay?'

'Sorry,' she said, a little flustered. 'You rattling off a definition like that. I think I prefer my term, it's a little more ...'

'Vague?'

'Yes. Vague. Less destruction and fixed solely on me.'

'I've got a thing for definitions.'

'What are you, a teacher?'

He grinned. 'No way.'

'Dictionary writer?'

'No again.'

She waited for him to jump in with what he did actually do when he wasn't strolling through lakeside vineyards at sunset, but nothing was forthcoming.

'I'll guess eventually,' she said.

'I look forward to it. But back to your nemesis; who is this person who's got it in for you?'

'Another mechanic. He's been badmouthing me ever since I opened up shop, and then he came over when I was alone in the workshop and—'

Scared me, she'd been about to say. She cleared her throat. Just because Damon lived out here with a dog for company didn't mean he was outside of the bush telegraph that Wendy was tapped into.

'Put it this way. He thinks he's the only mechanic the area needs. Some fresh air is helping me get him out of my head.'

Damon was frowning slightly, but as they resumed their ramble down the hill, he said, 'Sounds like you were leaving out a big chunk of that story.'

What was he, psychic? 'Yeah. Maybe.'

Minutes passed and she wondered how it was that some personalities were totally fine with the stoic silence but hers ...

'It's my mother,' she said.

'Oh, yes.' Damon's voice sounded resigned and she glanced at him.

'I haven't told you the bad part yet.'

'No, it's just ... my mother has been causing me a few problems lately, so I totally get where you're coming from.'

'Right. My mother, Wendy, is a traditional sort. You know, bakes pavlova, hangs her laundry items up on the line with matching pegs, wears stockings, goes to church, thinks thongs are a symbol of everything that's wrong with society and is constantly bemoaning why things can't go back to the way they used to be.'

'By thongs, I'm guessing you're not talking about Australia's favourite footwear.'

'Your guess would be correct. When I lived at home, whenever she found clothing of mine in the laundry that she deemed unsuitable, she'd chuck it in the wheelie bin.'

'Really? Come on, Kylie, this is no time to stint on details. Give me an example of something she threw out.'

She nudged his shoulder with hers. 'Idiot,' she said.

He chuckled. 'All right. I'll just have to use my imagination.'

'She's been wringing her hands and weeping gently ever since I switched careers to become a mechanic.'

'You weren't always a mechanic?'

'Nope,' she said. 'And she thinks my switching from a white tunic as the in-house beautician at the hair salon in town to wearing overalls in a workshop is the reason I don't have a husband to fawn over and she doesn't have grandbabies to knit booties for.'

'Oh, I see. A rabid feminist.'

This surprised Kylie into a laugh. He got it. He understood.

'We had a blue a few months back when she found out I was using an online dating site, and it began this whole downward spiralling saga about what a disappointment I was, and if I was only different I wouldn't need to be "online" where "perverts hang out" and so on, and the usual routine of why had I ruined my life, and why wasn't I—' No need to get into the whole cashflow saga as well. 'Long story short, last time we spoke, she was going on as usual and things have been ... well. She told me I was thirty-one like it meant I had one foot in the grave already.'

Damon raised his eyebrow. 'And ... you told her she was living in the dark ages? To get a life? To butt the hell out?'

Kylie could feel a blush rising, which was very unlike her; she was so not a blusher. Maybe it was from the climb up and down the hill while wearing a pair of fire-retardant overalls. Maybe it was embarrassment at having to admit she was a grown woman who had Mummy issues.

But, actually, maybe it was about the big fat porkie she'd told her mother.

'Um, no. You remember I said I have a profile on a dating app?'

'Yes. My brain has filed that away for later conjecture.'

She looked at him. He was smiling down at her with what could only be described as affection. *Why*, she thought bitterly, *why, why, why, couldn't he have been here for some other reason than to get the hell out as quickly as he'd arrived?*

'How'd she find out you were on an app?' he said.

'Oh, one of the yoga crew must have mentioned it.' In answer to the question on his face, she said, 'I do yoga a few mornings a week with a whole heap of Hanrahan locals. You know, I said Marigold was the instructor. Somehow, they've fallen into the habit of helping me update my profile when I don't get any likes. It's become a bit of fun, to be honest.'

'I find it hard to believe you're not getting any likes.'

She snorted. 'Damon, the population out here is *tiny*. Strip out every guy who's married, or gay, or underage or in an aged care facility, and there's not a lot of scope left for finding a meaningful relationship. The last time a potential match popped up on RuRo, it turned out to be an auditor from the tax office who'd lied about being a farmer and was out here to check people weren't pocketing the cash from their tills. He wasn't bad looking, mind you, he just had the personality of a broad-toothed rat.'

'You have a thing for farmers?'

'Absolutely. Who wouldn't want to bring their kids up in the fresh air, with animals to play with, paddocks to frolic in? It's kind of a vow I made to myself when I turned thirty: no more flings, only keepers from now on. I'm very clear about that in my profile.'

'What a shame. If only your vow was to save yourself for charming visitors from Sydney.'

Had he just said that in a flirty way?

Flustered, she hurried through an answer. 'Too far for me. I'm the Hanrahan Mechanic, remember?' Maybe for not much longer, but that didn't mean she had any interest in leaving her home town. 'Anyway, back to Mum. She said the only men I would ever meet online would be horrible people with no personality who had probably lied about their age and used a false photo. I said she was old-fashioned and prejudiced and *I* was online, did that make me a horrible person with no personality? It got a bit heated.' Well, Kylie had got heated. Very heated. Her mother didn't do heated emotion, she just got prim and let her lips tremble and her eyes well, as though she was the true victim and her daughter was a heartless, loud-mouthed bully.

'She was pushing all my buttons so I may have said I'd met someone recently who wasn't a loser.'

Damon didn't say anything, but he didn't say it in a way that had her face heating up again. Why, oh, why had she begun this inane conversation?

'Someone in town on family business.'

Damon wasn't stupid. 'Family business, huh?'

She cleared her throat. 'Yep.'

'And ... not a loser.'

Was he poking fun at her? It was hard to tell. He had this way of delivering lines so they could be interpreted in a multitude of ways: he could be being sarcastic, being thoughtful, being kind, being a dick ...

The silence lasted long enough for her to start mentally cringing. She was an idiot. A woman driven over the edge by a diet of two-minute noodles, a passive-aggressive mother and an ex-con with a habit of stopping by her workshop to intimidate her.

The sun had fallen so low behind the mountain ranges that it was just a halo of burnt orange. She risked another glance. Damon had stopped to lean against a large chunk of granite and his face was too shadowed for her to read.

'You know I'm not here to stay,' he said. A statement, not a question.

She frowned. 'Did I say it was time to start imprisoning doves in a wedding cake, Damon?'

He chuckled. 'Noted. I just … think we might have a problem here.'

Crap. He was right. Ridiculous to assume, from one five-minute lakeside conversation, that there was anything between them beyond scone crumbs and a momentary spark.

'I'm sorry,' she said. 'I shouldn't have lied and I certainly shouldn't have inferred anything about you to my mother when you and I don't even know each other. I shouldn't have come by this evening, either. I was …' *Lonely and a little wretched.* 'Being an idiot,' she finished.

'The lie doesn't bother me,' he said. 'The thing is … I think you and me … well. To put it bluntly, I think we fancy each other.'

She blinked. That *was* putting it bluntly. She knew there'd been a spark!

'But you have your vow.'

She did? Oh, yes. *That* vow. Farmers and little gumboots.

'And I …'

'Yes?' she said, when the pause lengthened.

'I'm not a farmer and I'm not sticking around. No matter what.'

No matter what. Unfortunately for the sanctity of her vow, her mind was able to think up a dozen 'what' scenarios. What if this spark he'd admitted to feeling turned out to be more than momentary? What if Frank's vineyard took months and months to sell? What if fate was real and not just some kooky concept and it had brought her and Damon together for a reason? Were those all the scenarios Damon was saying he wouldn't stick around for?

'Understood.'

'I should probably warn you that I, myself, have made no vow.'

There was that hot flush again. 'Luckily I have endless reserves of self-discipline.'

'Excellent,' said Damon. 'So it won't matter if we spend time together while I'm here, with me being as charming and flirty as I like.'

The heat that curled her toes was involuntary. Perhaps lusty thoughts could get more fuel than they needed the same way engines could. Fuel that resulted in a monumental backfire. *Your vow*, she reminded herself.

'Why would we want to spend time together?' she said. Again, a dozen scenarios came to mind. She pulled her overalls away from her neck a little to let some cool air in.

Damon chuckled and her engine might have backfired again because … *that sound*. Warm, deep, naughty. Almost as much of a turn-on as tall, dark and dangerous. Was he going to sugge—

'I need a driver.'

Her toes uncurled, her pipe blew out its exhaust without drama, her shoulders would have drooped if she hadn't forbidden them. 'As in … a person who drives?' Did that sound as dumb out loud as it did in her head? She should be relieved, not disappointed.

'Yep. A small misunderstanding with an RBT checkpoint in Sydney.'

Far out. No job, too charming for his own good, no interest in staying in Hanrahan and a drunk to boot. Her hormones sure could pick 'em.

'You've lost your licence,' she said flatly.

'Yep.'

How did he think it was okay to say that in such a cocky, yeah, whatever way?

'So, now my licence has been suspended for three months, I'm stuck here at Snowy River Vineyard unless I can find a driver. Pinching scones from the tourists will only keep me alive so long.

The pantry was thin on supplies when I arrived and now it is tragically bare, I need clothes, my need for decent coffee and a meal that isn't out of a can or a freezer is intense, and I have a property to prepare for sale that's going to involve trips to the dump, trips to an op shop to offload clothes, countless tasks all requiring me needing available wheels.'

She closed her eyes for a second. *Don't make a bad decision, Kylie.*

She took a breath. 'I'm sorry. No deal. I have a business to run.' There, her vow wouldn't be challenged if she kept well away.

'What if poor old Alfie gets a wombat stuck down his throat and needs a vet? You'd not be available then?'

'The vets do callouts. Josh and Hannah. Lovely people and you don't need to guilt trip them to get them here.'

He winced. 'Okay. Perhaps I haven't been totally clear. I intend to pay you your hourly mechanic rate: you clock on when you leave your workspace; you clock off when you get back to it.'

A paying job! Might just be a hundred bucks, of course, but every dollar mattered. But ... 'Can you afford to pay me?'

'Of course I can afford to pay you,' he said, sounding affronted.

'You promise there'll be no haggling or bad debts or ...' She tried to think up any other possible complications but wasn't coming up with any. A paying job! And just in the nick of time, too. She wondered if it was appropriate to put in a clause, like *No flirting with the weak-willed driver.* 'No late nights, either,' she said. 'I'm a morning person, and I do yoga at dawn a couple of times a week.'

'No late nights, no missing dawn yoga, got it. Any other conditions?'

'No. Yes. Wait ...' Hanrahan was a small town and pretty much everyone knew her. The yoga crew, especially, knew her. If they saw her driving a good-looking guy around town, they'd be scurrying up like ants to a picnic.

'Um,' she said. 'People may make assumptions.'

'About why I can't drive? Why would I care? I'll be out of here in a few weeks.'

She cleared her throat. 'No. About why you're in a car with me.'

'Oh.'

'Small-town gossip. It's an actual thing, not just a cliché in novels and TV shows. People will talk. And stare. And wonder.'

'You say that like I'm going to get paraded about like a stud bull at a country show. How about tomorrow? Are you free? Shall we say two o'clock so we can both get some chores done first?'

She made a noncommittal noise, because his facetious remark was actually spot on. The second she rocked up in Hanrahan with Damon Johns in the same vehicle, word was going to spread like bushfire through drought-stricken brush that Kylie had a bloke in tow. Heaven only knew how Wendy would react, especially since Kylie had been driven to inferring she'd met someone in their last phone call.

'Do we have a deal?'

Damon held out his hand and she stared at it. Her cautious inner self wasn't quite sounding the alarm bells. She had a new paying client, that was all. A distracting one, sure, but that was on her to manage. She could do this. Earn some money—enough to keep her bills paid—while she worked on growing her business.

She put her hand in his to acknowledge they did, indeed, have a deal, and suffered one of those fateful knocks to the heart. The knocks that come with goosebumps and funny breathing and hairs standing up at the back of your neck …

Oh crap, her cautious inner self said. Maybe that fate thing was real.

CHAPTER
13

Damon woke before dawn on Tuesday, a week and two days exactly since he'd arrived at Frank's vineyard, unable to breathe. He was—or he'd just been—trapped in a courtroom with the psychologist who'd been a witness in the Wilson case, whose voice had now morphed into Dr Gloom's. *In its extreme, and by extreme I mean at the abusive end of the abandonment scale, the loss of parental care can lead to Abandoned Child Syndrome, a behavioural or psychological condition which—*

Worse than the breathlessness were the other effects. His adrenalin was up, up, *up*, and a bedsheet clung to sweat on his back. His lungs burned with effort, his ears pounded.

He struggled, arms and legs pushing at the bedding covering him, and it wasn't until the chill air coming in from the open window hit his face and torso that he could hold onto a coherent thought.

I'm not in court.

Well, thank fuck for that, he thought, as the symptoms started to recede. But he wasn't totally thankful; he'd hoped being here, at the vineyard, had dealt with the horror movie that had taken up residence in his lungs.

It hadn't.

He breathed in more of the cool mountain air, and through it, got a whiff of Alfie's rotten-possum breath wafting over his face.

'You'd better not be on this bed,' he said.

A large, furry head settled itself across his ankles and let out a little sigh.

His arms and legs felt like lead, but he raised his head, frowned, then gave the dog a shove with his foot. 'Boundaries,' he said, pointlessly, as Alfie had none. 'It's a simple concept. The bed is mine. The floor is yours. Preferably the floor of the downstairs part of the house. Off you go, mate.'

Alfie looked at him lovingly, letting his tongue loll so long it hit the bedspread. Good. Maybe it would act like a lint roller and collect some of the hair the great lump left behind him everywhere he went.

'I'm not getting up,' Damon said. 'I'm on a time out from work. Nobody cares where I am or what I'm doing and you don't need to be fed at dawn.' A mopey thought, but a panicky awakening, turns out, when he'd hoped all that stuff was behind him, made him feel quite mopey.

He blamed Sean for the onset. Not that he'd clicked into or read any of the so-called wellness guff Sean had dropped into his inbox late last night, but he'd read the names of the attachments: *When Pressure Becomes Chronic*; *Escaping The Perfectionism Trap: A Guide For Lawyers To Find Balance and Success*; blah blah blah.

Alfie cocked his head and made another of the odd noises Damon was used to now, but had at first thought meant the dog had eaten a bag of marbles and was drowning in his own drool. A sort of growl-moan-plea-warble.

'Emotional blackmail won't work on me, dog. I watch people get fined or sent to prison without a qualm.' Untrue, but it ought to be true. Being the best *demanded* it be true. Qualms, he suspected, were the cocoon stage of full-blown lungworm.

Alfie warbled again, but this time he put some lung power into it and the whole bed rocked. Damon cursed and rolled to his feet.

'All right, I'm up already. Remind me to shut my door tonight, will you?'

The dog capered about as Damon made his way down the stairs and into the laundry. Fresh scratch marks dinted the tin holding the dog's kibble.

'You've given it a solid go. It's a pity you don't have thumbs, Alf. Here you are,' he said, as he scooped out a pile of the bone-shaped dry food.

Alfie fell on it like a starving man onto a rump steak and Damon left him to it.

Coffee, he thought, before remembering the sachets of freeze-dried muck for the picnic goers were all that was on hand. Thank heavens he had an arrangement with a don't-flirt-with-me driver to restock supplies later that day.

Thinking about Kylie made him think about her vow. His issues. And the thing she hadn't said when she'd been telling him about the guy who was giving her a hard time. Then he thought about her fingernails, and how they'd been blue, and then sunshine yellow, and then he found himself smiling vaguely as he remembered how she filled out a set of overalls in totally fabulous ways. Her smile. Her laugh. She had a dimple, too, and—

Enough. Life was already complicated. And one of the things he had to do to uncomplicate it was get this house sorted, so it was time to stop procrastinating.

A few hours of clutter sorting at Frank's desk had him thinking longingly of the good old days back at the chambers when Sean did all this sort of humdrum crap for him. He yawned, then picked up a book at random from one of the as yet unsorted piles.

Cool climate grapes will typically be harvested in late February or early March and is best done early in the morning. That was a worry: it meant harvest time was only a month or two away. Damon turned the page and found the writer had become quite impassioned on the subject of hand harvesting versus machine harvesting and the perils of oxidation from grape skin damage. Yeah, whatever. Forget oxidation. What he wanted to know was who picked the grapes? And what happened then? Were they sold? Stomped on by seasonal workers? Pressed by some machine that was in a shed on the farm that he had yet to come across?

He set the book aside in a new pile he christened 'Come back to' and grabbed the next item on the stack in front of him. It was a torn-out page of a newspaper. *The Snowy River Star* was written in small font on the uppermost border, and *The Hanrahan Chatter* in bold black type as a header. *By Maureen Plover*, read the byline. *Submissions to PO Box 711 Hanrahan NSW 2630.* He scanned the page. A local choir was looking for a piano player, there were a few snide comments about some local councillor who'd not approved a grant to house historical archives, and, along the bottom, an advertisement for the PW *Moana*'s Picnic in a Vineyard cruise: *Cruise aboard one of Australia's oldest surviving paddlewheelers. Afternoon tea at a vineyard on the shores of Lake Bogong and bird spotting from the deck!*

Damon looked for a date but it had been torn off. Frank must have been the last person to sit here at the desk, unless the lawyer had visited while the funeral arrangements were being made and the estate was in limbo prior to probate being granted.

A thick stack of invoices for assorted items like fertiliser and wire coils and mulch was next, thankfully all stamped PAID so they could go in a 'Dealt with' pile, and below that was a tatty copy of a kids' book. The front was torn off—or eaten off, perhaps. Damon had been minding a labrador for barely the blink of an eye, but already he'd developed a keen eye for recognising drool-edged destruction. The book was mid-air, being tossed to the 'Chuck it out' pile, when he noticed the words on the exposed title page: *The Enormous Dog. Story and illustrations by F.D. Silva.* He snatched the book back and flipped it open to a full colour, two-page spread sporting a massive black dog towering over a pond or creek in which, under rippled water, swam a tiny brown thing that might've been a platypus. The simple artwork on the house's upper landing was all making sense now.

'Alfie?' he called, and heard the click, click, click of dog paws making their way towards him. A muzzle pushed the door wide and the dog wandered in. 'Is this you?'

Alfie sniffed at the torn book Damon was holding out, then gave it an exploratory lick.

'Definitely you. We'll start a pile for the community group, and we need to do an inventory of the vineyard,' he said. 'Grab pen and paper. We'll make a start on the sheds. What's that? You don't write? That'll be that thumb shortage again, mate. All right, I'll be the scribe, you be the guide. Let's go.'

He was at the back door, wrestling his way into gumboots, when his phone rang somewhere on the upper floor. Deirdre. It had to be. He took the stairs two at a time and pounced on it.

'Damon, darling boy. How are you getting on?'

He let the word 'darling' flow over him and out the open window. In his mother's vocabulary, it was a figure of speech.

'Slowly,' he said. 'Hampered by being totally in the dark about this person whose life's collection of assets you have inherited. What gives, Mum? Why didn't you keep in touch with him?'

'I barely knew him.'

'Why is that? And which side is, *was*, he your half-brother on?'

'Darling, do we really have to get into this? Tell me what the realtor said. What's it worth, this little farmlet I've inherited? How soon can they get the place listed? Can the furniture be sold with it so all you have to clear out are the cupboards?'

Was farmlet a word? 'There are a lot of cupboards here, Mum. And … it's really very lovely. Are you sure you don't want to come over and see it in person before it goes on the market?'

'I'm sure. Just get it done, Damon.'

Deirdre wasn't short of a buck, despite the fact she'd not had a job since she moved to Melbourne with Nick when he won the TV contest. Damon doubted money was what was motivating his mother's desire for a quick sale. Husband number one—Nick and Damon's father—had provided well for the family. For a time. Until the family split up when the boys were little and his father moved overseas to Thailand and started a new family. Husbands two (deceased) and three (current) had both been chosen for their lifestyles as much as their personalities.

No, it wasn't money his mother wanted. She did this. Avoided things. Ask her a question she didn't want to answer and suddenly she *had* to tell you the most *darling* story about something *completely* different.

The truth about her relationship with her half-brother could wait, so Damon turned back to the topic that couldn't: her half-brother's property. Frank's place was many things, but a farmlet wasn't one of them.

'Mum, you really need to start paying attention to your emails.'

'Oh, Damon. You know I don't like paperwork.'

He frowned. Why did that line sound so familiar? Oh, right—that was what he was always saying to Sean and Warunya. He wondered if it ticked them off as much as it was ticking him off now.

'This place is not some patch of dirt with a chicken coop, Mum.' The swipe of a revoltingly wet tongue up his ankle reminded him of the long list of other things she was now responsible for but had foisted off onto him. 'For starters, you are now the owner of a morbidly obese black dog called Alfie.'

'A dog? But I live in New Zealand. There are quarantine laws. Rehome him, darling. Find him somewhere lovely with a nice garden so he doesn't have to get the little prick in the paw.'

Alfie rolled over so he was on his back, all four of those defenceless paws waving like furry flags. If this was his I'm-too-lovable-to-be-rehomed-or-euthanised look, it was working.

Damon dragged his mind back to the now. 'You're also a part owner of a hospitality business which provides afternoon tea and vineyard tours to day trippers on a historic paddlewheeler that operates here in Lake Bogong.'

'Oh, dear.'

'So I'm assuming it's just a matter of time before you front up here and start baking. Scones, they like. Mountains of scones. There are spare aprons in the pantry and the hot water urns for the tea and coffee are only slightly very incredibly heavy. Lucky you go to the gym so often. But don't worry, you only need to be baking four days every week—that's *every* week—until Easter.'

'Damon, I—'

'And have I mentioned the vineyard, yet? Because, apparently, it's going to be harvest time soon. According to your mystery half-brother's copious notes, his grape vines are needier than premature babies. They need to be irrigated, fertilised, sung to when they wilt. Their vigorous shoots need training, their basal buds need supervising and god only knows what any of that means.'

His mother made a noise that sounded suspiciously like laughter.

'This is so not funny.'

'I know, darling. It's just—I don't ever recall hearing you so passionate about something. I always thought Nick was the emotional one.'

His chest knotted up into the same hard, immovable mass that he'd woken with, and Alfie, who seemed to be some sort of empath as well as a dog, gave his foot another lick. The *unfairness* of her comment, given the fact she'd *abandoned* him when he was eighteen. When would she have had a chance to hear him talk passionately about anything? Never, because she'd gone. With his brother. Whose claim upon their only parent who maybe gave a shit about them apparently outweighed his own.

Ah yes, resentment. Known to be a subconscious protective mechanism. Also known to be negative and self-destructive when clung to.

Oh, shut up, thought Damon, blithely ignoring Dr Gloom to focus on Deirdre's words. 'You really want to go there, Mum? Rehash the past? Who did what and who left who? And who—despite *everything*—actually earned himself a successful career without any help at all?'

Silence. Too much of it. Silence long enough for him to hear how plaintive his words were, but also long enough for him to wonder if rehashing the past was, actually, what he *did* need to do.

'I guess I always thought …'

Her pause dragged out.

'What did you always think, Mum?'

'I always thought I *was* part of your success too, darling. As well as Nick's. You are my son, after all. You're so like me, Damon. We're selfish people, you and I. Cold, in our own way.'

He took a breath. Losing his temper never ended well, and he wasn't losing his today over this. A gene pool counted for diddly squat compared with actual parental involvement.

'Maybe you should fly over when your friend whatsherface leaves, Mum.'

He could hear her exhalation through the phone. 'Look, Damon. I'm sorry this inheritance has turned out to be such a headache. Just do what you think is best, all right? We both know I've got no interest in moving to some country backwater to sing to wilting grapevines.'

'So, the whole estate is up to me?' he said. 'Deal with it all? The picnic business? The vineyard, the house, the dog? Do what I want?'

'Yes, yes, whatever you please.'

He tapped his finger on the desk and willed the dark knotty mass that was now lungs, heart and head to go away. 'Put it in writing,' he said shortly. 'Email it to me. ASAP, okay?'

Fuck the picnic business. And the contract. And the whole world, while he was at it. He was here, so he'd sell up for his mother, but he'd be damned if he'd feel responsible for a boatload of tourists or pluckable bloody grapes.

'Or you,' he told the dog, covering the mouthpiece of the phone. 'Yes, I'm a heartless prick. Tell me something I don't know.'

His mother sounded a little too smug when she responded: 'I'll do better than that, son, I'll courier it to you. My permission to do as you see fit regarding my inheritance. The courier can be on their way in minutes.'

CHAPTER
14

On Tuesday morning, Kylie walked into The Billy Button Café and saw that Vera and Graeme had done a lot more than plonk a Reserved sign on the big table in the back room. Pens and little notepads were grouped at either end, the flowers the café had been named after bobbed their sunny heads in small glass jars, and a plate of delicious, fruit-studded biscottini sat pride of place in the centre of the table. Kylie eyed them with approval. She'd know them anywhere: almond and dried fig from Vera's Italian cookbook. She leant down to give them a sniff.

'I wanted to mark the occasion of Hanrahan's first women in business breakfast meeting with a little fanfare,' said a voice behind her.

Kylie turned to see Vera, as dark haired and pale skinned and serene as Kylie was blonde and suntanned and all-over-the-place, smiling at her.

'I *love* fanfare. Especially when it involves your biscottini.'

'Graeme did point out that giving away biscuits was likely to shrink our breakfast orders, and was that what a wise businesswoman would do?'

'Where is he? I'll take him out the back and shoot him.'

Vera chuckled. 'He's off duty today. Besides, if you hadn't suggested this women in business breakfast, I'd not have been so inspired, so thank you for the prompt. Here, see what else I've done.' She gestured to a little stack of printed postcards that Kylie hadn't noticed. On it was a catering menu and phone number, and the card was fancied up with the chocolate brown and gilt lettering to match the café's sign. The back was like a postcard with space for a stamp and address and message. 'Everyone this morning eats one of my biscuits, takes a card away with them to stick up at work, and when they need a catering job done for a funeral or christening or mothers' group or whatever, The Billy Button Café will be front of mind.'

'You don't need more business, surely? You're always neck deep in customers.'

'In ski season we are, but summer can have its lulls, so some more catering jobs wouldn't be unwelcome. Just last week we picked up a gig on the far side of the lake catering for the *Moana*'s picnics.'

'Mmm,' said Kylie blandly. 'Have you been over there yourself?'

Vera grinned. 'I've not laid eyes on Hanrahan's newest hottie, if that's what you're asking.'

'I can fill you in,' said a new voice.

Kylie and Vera turned to greet Marigold, who was clad in a floaty, colourful dress with enough fabric in it to cover half-a-dozen picnic tables. Her keen-eyed gaze raked Kylie and Vera from head to toe.

'My word, Marigold,' Kylie said, not without admiration. 'You're sneaking into conversations very stealthily these days.'

Marigold smiled serenely. She looked like a swarthy Madonna painting, only with way more attitude and dangly, feathery earrings. 'Now, now, don't be snarky, Kylie. Where were you, this morning? Yoga is a way of life that requires your devotion, not infrequent attention.'

'I overslept.' Because she'd spent most of the night overthinking, but telling Marigold that would be like putting a match to petrol.

'Is this a business meeting or a yoga recruitment drive?' said a stroppy voice. Hannah, of course. With baby Eva strapped to her front.

'Oh, pet,' said Marigold, her face wreathed in smiles. 'Pass me that baby this instant. I keep looking for you at craft group. Motherhood will soften your views on knitwear, darling girl, mark my words. I have some *dear* little bootie patterns somewhere and—'

Kylie snorted. 'The look of horror on your face, Han.'

Hannah muttered something dark that sounded rather like 'Sore freaking boobs, parvovirus in the litter, no sleep, and now this'.

Time to bring this convo back to the matter at hand. Kylie pulled the sleeping infant out of the contraption Hannah had attached to her front and passed her to Marigold. 'Shall we take a seat? Now, I have apologies from Val. She was on open this morning at the IGA but she'll be able to come to the next meeting if we give her a little more notice. Hannah, sit down and have a biscottini.'

Her friend might be all nappies and snarky sunshine now, but it wasn't so long ago she'd been all antisocial and snarky grump. Best to get her sat down and fed.

But Hannah had other ideas. 'Spill the beans on the hottie, Marigold.'

Marigold was cooing at the baby, but at this command, she settled her bulk next to Kylie, passed the baby back to her mother, and leant in. A promising start. Leaning in meant hushed voice, and hushed voice meant scurrilous gossip, and scurrilous gossip offered almost as much sustenance as the plate of almond and fig delicacies Marigold's bosom was threatening to flatten.

'Kev,' Marigold said, 'has been called in to help the hottie understand the irrigation system.'

'And?' said Kylie.

'He's quite chuffed. He and Frank grew quite close when they were researching the *Moana*.'

'Forget Kev for the minute, Marigold. The gossip. Let's concentrate on that.'

'It's not gossip, as such, but when Kev and I popped into the vineyard the other day after yoga, we were not made to feel welcome.'

'In what way?' said Kylie. She'd felt very welcome. Too welcome, in fact, both times she'd been at the vineyard.

'Damon informed us he'd prefer we schedule an appointment rather than just drop in. Very formal and unfriendly he was. Well, other than the fact that he had just emerged from the lake clad in the thinnest boxer shorts I have ever, *ever* seen.' Marigold lifted the menu and gave her decolletage a fanning.

Hannah perked up at this. 'Did you take a photo?'

Marigold ignored this interruption. 'And Maureen says—' Marigold lowered her voice even further and did a quick shoulder to shoulder pan of the café to check they weren't being overheard. Kylie's neck felt like it would snap if she leant in any closer.

'What does she say?'

'He arrived with no luggage. In two-day-old socks.'

'And a crumpled suit,' said Kylie. 'He told me last night—'

Three sets of eyes were suddenly staring at her intently. Four, if you counted baby Eva's.

'Yes? What exactly did he tell you, Kylie Summer? And last night? What does that mean, precisely? Why is it you've been having cosy conversations with a single man and not reported back to me *immediately*?' said Hannah.

Kylie blinked. 'Um.' Would it be wrong to mention Hannah had moved from fellow-single bestie to married-with-a-baby bestie and the dynamic had shifted? That she'd had no-one to confide her day-to-day dramas in for months? That the adjustment had been *hard*? 'We're doing some business together.'

'What sort of business?'

'Er.' How to say this without starting a barrage of questions? 'He needs a driver. Hanrahan Mechanics needs a paying customer.'

'Old socks, unfriendly to Marigold and Kev, and he doesn't *drive*? I don't know if I approve of this arrangement, Kyles. Your hottie sounds like a loser.'

'Oh, goodie, look, here's Maureen Plover.' A sentence Kylie never thought she'd hear herself saying. 'Maybe we can give me the third degree later and start talking about business tips now that she's here. As much as I love you guys getting totally involved in my love life, what I really need this morning is business advice.'

'Right, business,' said Marigold, once Maureen had taken a seat and placed an order with the waitstaff for a cup of tea. She pulled a notepad and pen from her capacious leather handbag and opened it to a page she must have, as the saying went, prepared earlier. 'Kylie, why don't you start our inaugural meeting—which is an excellent idea by the way, pet, bravo—with what prompted you to gather us businesswomen together?'

Where to start and what to reveal? Pride was telling her to keep her financial woes to herself, and no way was she going to reveal the extent of Nigel's threatening behaviour, but … she could share a little.

'Okay. You know I took over the workshop from George Juggins?'

'Yes,' the others said, jointly and severally, with some head nodding thrown in for good measure.

'It has recently been brought to my attention that George and Nigel Woods had talked about Nigel taking over the lease. Nigel has been a little testy about the fact George signed it over to me.' Understatement. 'I'd hoped he would realise my business wouldn't be a threat to his, because he has more than enough going on down there on the highway, but I'm worried he's going to cause trouble for me. Have any of you dealt with that? A competitor who resents you for being in business?'

Vera nodded. 'When Graeme and I introduced an evening menu and started serving wine, we stepped on a few toes. We were able to come to an arrangement with the local wine bar where we would source our local wines through them. It's a little pricier, but we can offer cheaper wine to customers from elsewhere in Australia, so it was a doable solution.'

'The Cooma vet was thrilled when I started up my clinic,' said Hannah. 'We can share nights on call, help each other out when we have a complicated surgery. I have better X-ray equipment; he has specialist training in pathology.'

Kylie tried to imagine herself calling Nigel to consult on a particularly vexing hydraulic leak. Nope. No way. 'I can't see diplomacy helping me with Nigel.'

Maureen spoke up for the first time. 'You need to find a point of difference, Kylie. It's like the picnic business across the lake. Scones and tea you can find anywhere. Scones and tea in a vineyard after a cruise in an historic paddlewheeler? That's something special that people will pay good money for.'

Good money. That's what she needed. But scones and lake cruises were not at all comparable to a car service or an oil change in a tractor, so what on earth could her point of difference be?

CHAPTER 15

The tyres of Kylie's sturdy work ute weren't due to crunch their way onto the gravel out front of Frank's house until the afternoon, which was a long wait when you were desperate for a barista-made coffee, but Damon was managing to fill his time. After his morning's work, he had a notebook filled with lists of Frank's possessions, and he'd found a business down in Cooma willing to deliver a skip bin the next day, into which he could chuck anything that seemed like junk. The easy part was done. Next up, the storage areas.

He went out of the gravel forecourt at the back of the house to where the manicured garden beds ended and Frank's property became distinctly agricultural. A newish shed with a massive roller door threw a shadow over water tanks. A small door was cut into one side of it and Damon let himself in and hit a green button that made the roller door rumble its way up, up, up into a great aluminium sausage over his head.

Where to start? He barely recognised any of this stuff. He should have asked the rural property realtor to send someone up to help with this aspect of the property sale.

'Sorry I'm early,' called a voice from the work yard. Damon turned, and there was Kylie, striding towards him from the direction of the house.

The contrast between the overalls she usually wore and today's pink silky blouse, tight, *tight* jeans, floral perfume, lashings of lipstick and dusty, dancefloor boots—he breathed in and out and told his dick to settle the hell down—was quite something.

'You look different,' he said, feeling his mood even out into the peaceful rhythm he'd only found lately while swimming in the lake.

She cleared her throat. 'Um, yeah. A minor argument with a wheel bearing this morning after my women in business breakfast. I was covered in grease by the end of it so figured I'd better change.'

'That colour looks great on you.' Total understatement. She looked incredible.

She grinned. 'I thought you liked my overalls.'

'Oh, I do,' he said, and he wasn't lying. He *really* liked the overalls. He shot a look at her fingernails, hoping for something outlandish, and was not disappointed. Hot rosy pink, the same colour as her blouse and his lusty thoughts. Crikey. Kylie in overalls was quite something. Kylie in woman clothes was another matter entirely.

'You ready to go?' she said. 'I can sit on the dock for a bit if you're in the middle of something.'

'I wish I was in the middle of something. I'm supposed to be doing an inventory of the farm for the sale documents, but I am clueless about this stuff.' He gestured into the dimness of the shed. 'My list so far just says useful things like, *Large orange metal contraption, function unknown.*'

She brightened like he'd offered her a box of chocolates. 'A shed full of mystery farming stuff to explore? Sounds like my ideal afternoon.'

She was grinning, and it was infectious enough that he found himself grinning back. 'Can I tempt you to take a few steps closer, then?' he said. And yeah, okay, he said it in a flirty way. *He* hadn't made any foolish vow.

Her eyebrows raised, but the smile hadn't dimmed. 'Excuse me?'

'In your professional capacity as the Hanrahan Mechanic, of course.'

'That's what I thought you meant,' she said.

'That's what I thought you'd think I meant,' he said, parroting her defensive tone for the fun of it.

A pause while they both narrowed their eyes and then grinned at each other like idiots.

'There's stuff in here I don't even know how to describe, let alone value. You think you can help?'

Kylie was rolling up those silky sleeves. 'I'm on the clock, right?'

His sweet little mercenary. 'You are totally on the clock.'

'Ride-on mower, good model, you'd be looking at over seven grand new for one this size, maybe two-thirds that for a secondhand one in this condition.' She moved to the next chunk of metal. 'This is a tractor attachment. Some sort of mechanical weeder, maybe? I can look it up. This is another tractor attachment—see that lethal-looking row of hooks hanging down?'

He looked. 'Furrows for planting?'

'Damon, you're fitting in out here in the country already. Yes. This one will drag a field, loosen it and it'll even spit seeds out. Not sure why Frank's got one, though. Some farmers will plant a field up with rye or barley for sileage when it's not in use—a crop that can be turned back into the soil to improve its quality—but I can't imagine the hills about here are good for any crops other than grapes or cattle. Let's see, what else do we have here. Power tools, hand tools, workbenches, storage racks,' she listed, pointing to the walls. 'There's a lot of money in setting up this sort of workshop, but I don't know that you'd get its value selling it piece by piece. And farms? They tend to get sold with their working equipment included. You might not want to strip the shed of stuff that the new owner might need.'

'Helps me get the farm valued, though,' he said. 'Having this gear itemised.'

'Yeah. I'm not sure that Frank would have made a living off a micro vineyard. But it's a magic place to live, isn't it? If you could afford it.' She sounded wistful.

'You like the idea of living on land out of town?'

'Sure. I'm looking for a farmer, remember?'

He remembered, all right. Why he kept thinking about it was the real question at hand. What was it to him if Kylie had been clear about what she wanted in life, and there was no room there for some feckless barrister from Sydney who'd suddenly developed a tuberculosis problem?

'Look at this place, Damon. It's peaceful, and beautiful, and the mountains are like *right there*. Hanrahan's less than half an hour away, Cooma's just two hours away for the other stuff like hospitals and department stores. And I've not been inside that house, but it looks fabulous.'

'I should get you to write up the sale ad.'

She laughed. 'I wouldn't. My writing skills are a long way behind my talking skills.' She turned away to review the contents of the shed, her hands on her hips. 'The weird thing, though …'

'What weird thing?'

'Well, where's the tractor? You've got all these attachments, and you can see marks from tractor tyres out there in the yard where the mud's dried after rain, but where is it?'

'Oh, yeah. The back wall of this shed has a little lean-to structure. The tractor's there, but it's a piece of junk, so you can dial down that look of expectation I can see on your face.'

'Tractors are never junk. Sometimes they just need a little loving to bring them back to their best. Show me.'

He went into the work yard and around to the back of the shed. A slanted roof of galvanised iron was propped up against the shed on one long edge, with two rough timber posts on the other long edge. The tractor parked within its confines was huge, ugly and orange. How it still worked—*if* it still worked—was a mystery.

He heard a faint noise from Kylie, and was expecting to see a laugh, hear ready agreement about it being nothing more than an eyesore. Instead, her eyes were bright, her mouth was stuck in an 'oh' shape, and her hands were reaching out to lay themselves upon the scratched and dinted surface of the engine housing as though within it was the secret to the meaning of life.

'Um …' he said.

'A Champion 9G,' she breathed. 'Sixty-two horsepower, manufactured by Chamberlain right here in Australia in the 1950s. Still its original orange! Oh, Damon. This is *wonderful*.'

He grinned. 'Honey, it's a tractor.'

'It's *history*. And it's gorgeous. Can I start her up?'

He held his hands wide. 'By all means, if you think that's possible.'

Kylie must have forgotten she was dressed for pretty not practical today, because she was tinkering with caps (oil? fuel?), lifting part of the engine hood and making little noises that were not totally different from the noises Alfie made when he thought he'd been overlooked when morning toast was being buttered, and then she was fiddling with something that even Damon could see looked like a crank handle.

'You, er, need a hand?' he said.

She grinned at him. 'No need to sound so enthusiastic. I'm good.' Then she swung herself up into the seat up behind the massive motor and gave the gear stick a firm waggle that sent a rush of blood from his brain to his—elsewhere.

'The key's in the ignition,' she said.

Like anyone would be stealing this heap of junk.

'Choke, gear in neutral, clutch … clutch … where's the freaking clutch? Oh, here …' A clunk, a sputter and then the great beast between her knees roared into life.

'What an absolute beauty!' Kylie yelled.

True, he thought. Though he did not mean the chunk of rusted orange metal.

Kylie had the beast in gear and it started to trundle forward. 'I'll just do a loop?' she yelled, holding her hands in the universal palms-together fashion that women—was that sexist? Some women, anyway—used when they really wanted something. He nodded and she gave a whoop, then she and the tractor rolled out of the lean-to.

When she'd parked it again a couple of minutes later and jumped off, she was flushed in the cheeks and her eyes were sparkling. 'I cannot believe this has been here at Snowy River Vineyard this whole time and I never knew.'

'Frank wasn't one of your customers, I take it.'

She grimaced. 'He probably used my nemesis.'

Damon was surprised into a chuckle. 'Don't worry. You can look after it from now until it's sold.'

'Thank you, but let's not ruin a special moment talking about dickface. And Frank's tractor is not junk. There are collectors out there who adore these early models.' She was looking wistfully at the battered metal.

'Collectors like you?' he said.

She laughed. 'Gosh, no. The closest I come to being a tractor collector is owning a skeleton of a Massey Ferguson. It had been stripped of parts when I bought it years ago. Back when I had an income.'

He frowned. 'You don't have an income now?'

She cleared her throat. 'Sorry. *More* of an income. Hanrahan Mechanics has a temporary cashflow problem, hence why I am giving up my valuable time to drive you around. I bought Trevor when I didn't have small business owner responsibilities like superannuation and finance repayments and workcover insurance to pay.'

'Trevor being your skeleton?'

'Trevor being the love of my life.' She grinned. 'Now, as fun as this shed business is, we better get going if we want the shops to still be open when we hit town. The closed signs will be up and the workers on their way home on the dot of five.'

'Let's go then.'

They set off for the front of the house, where he assumed she'd parked.

'What's the plan?'

'Food,' he said. 'I need groceries.' He looked down. 'I don't suppose there's a place in Hanrahan that sells clothes? Frank was way more partial to plum-coloured velvet than I will ever be, and I've just about exhausted his stock of jeans and T-shirts.'

Kylie looked him over from head to toe and if he was vain, he would have winced when she noticed the work shoes he'd had to wear with the jeans and T-shirt he'd commandeered. Okay, whatever, yeah, he was vain. Add it to the list.

'You never did tell me why it is you turned up here for a lengthy stay with no baggage.'

He grimaced. 'Long and boring story.'

'Okaaay,' she said.

'What does that mean?'

'It means, note to self: Damon's touchy about personal questions.'

'Huh. Well, yes, but that's because even though I have no clothes of my own, I brought plenty of emotional baggage with me.'

Her eyebrows rose. 'Is everything okay?'

He'd said too much so he shrugged. 'Another long and boring story.'

She was silent for a moment, then: 'Okay. We're looking for groceries, clothes and you might want to add some work boots if you're going to be dragging equipment around in sheds. I thought, if we have time, I could give you a tour of the town so you know what's what. You ready to go?'

'Just let me find the dog and put him in the fenced part of the garden.'

A few minutes later, Alfie had been locked into the fenced yard on one side of the house and they were out the long gravel drive and trundling along a minor road that looped up and down the foothills of the mountain range as it traversed the western rim of the lake.

'It's a pretty drive,' he said.

'Yes. A pity you can't drive it yourself.'

He rolled his window down a few inches so the wind whipped at his hair. She'd just been making conversation—or, now he thought about it, she may well have been asking a question in the sort of sneaky way he asked questions—but that didn't make it sting any less.

'Sorry,' she said, after a good kilometre of silence. 'Is that a sensitive topic? Part of that emotional baggage you mentioned?'

'Part of the long story,' he said. Long, awful, shitty.

'We've got another ten k to go,' she said. 'If you want to unburden, I feel obliged to let you know that our driving arrangement covers confidentiality.'

He was tempted. He barely knew Kylie, but she was fun. Practical. Grounded. How many women of his acquaintance could claim those three attributes? None.

But still, some shit ran so deep, you ran the risk of drowning in it just by bringing it up. So he trimmed his backstory down to a few palatable facts.

'I've been working hard lately. Too hard, perhaps. Losing my licence was a low point.'

She didn't say anything. If this was also a tactic, it was a good one and not one he was well practised in turning to his advantage, because A) it was usually him in charge of the tactics; B) he was a talker; and C) in court, if no-one said anything, the judge got all huffy and started barking out instructions like: 'The defendant will answer the question or be held in contempt.'

He relented. 'I left Sydney in a snit, if you must know.'

She chuckled, which was kind of deflating, in that his snit had felt totally justified. He had been wounded. His closest friends had given him the boot. He'd disgraced himself in the most personally shameful way possible. But it was also—surprisingly—as much of a mood soother as dawn swims in the lake and Kylie's smile had been. Now that he had some distance, he could see that he had, after all, run away from a perfectly delectable Thai dinner. He'd leapt into a cab and gone full drama in front of the cabbie: *Take my money and keep driving until it runs out.*

He had, as much as it galled him to admit, not been thinking rationally.

'A snit,' Kylie said. 'Let me try to picture this. You're in some fancy office building in downtown Sydney in your pin-striped suit, doing whatever mysterious job you refuse to admit to, and you had some—snit—and somehow, boom, you're in an apron on the shores of Lake Bogong, unemployed and handing out scones.'

'Pretty much. You've missed a few details, like there was a cab. And a motel. And a bus to Hanrahan with fuzzy grey seats that smelled *rank*.' Not to mention a workplace intervention. 'And after the cab, but before the bus, my mother rang. She couldn't make it to a handover meeting with the lawyer up here who handled Frank's estate—your mate Tom—so I offered to come up for her.'

'A handover meeting?'

'Uh-huh. No mention of the dog, the picnic business, the vineyard that seems imminently close to harvest nor the disgruntled neighbour who's been left high and dry by Frank's will.'

'She dropped you right in it.'

'I told you that you weren't the only one with mother trouble.'

She grinned. 'Maybe not. Hey, we're getting close to Hanrahan so let's make a plan, okay? There's a boutique you can—'

'A *what*?'

'A boutique. That's what us country business owners like to call our clothing stores. Penny's Boutique. It's ninety per cent ladies' wear because the men round here buy a good shirt once a decade, but there is a men's rack. The ag store might be your best bet for some boots, so long as you're okay with function being more important than fashion.'

'Totally okay.'

'I can drop you at the boutique and point out the ag store. There's an IGA up by the bus depot where you probably arrived, and we can do a grocery shop last to grab whatever else you need.'

'Clothing, ag store, groceries.'

'I'll drop you off then go tidy up a few things at the workshop.'

'It's a plan. Also ... is now a good time to confess that I have been having lustful thoughts about beer and pizza?'

She flicked him a glance. 'Lust no more. We have one of the finest old pubs in the country that runs a bottle-o out back, and we have a pizza place just near the town park.'

'Maybe we could share one for dinner.'

She frowned slightly, and he took a breath. Yeah, where had that question come from?

'You're the only person I know in town,' he said. 'It's been a long week with just an obese labrador for company.' He wasn't sure why he was pushing this. He was here for a few weeks more, tops, and he and Kylie weren't ever going to be a thing—she had made that clear. But Kylie was ... distracting. Fun. When he was with her it was oh so easy to forget all the things he very much wanted to forget.

She tapped a finger on the wheel. 'I have a loose plan to meet up with Hannah and Tom for a drink at the pub after work. I suppose ...' she hesitated. 'Do you want to join us? They won't stay long as they'll have a baby with them, then we can go pick up a pizza before I drive you home.'

'A sharing pizza,' he said. A question, but delivered as a statement, because as a strategy to get your own way, it was a winner. One of his many tricks, no doubt, according to Sean.

'Would it be double cheese and pepperoni?'

Maybe his day was looking up. 'Is there any other kind?'

CHAPTER 16

A dud battery was waiting for Kylie back at the workshop, along with its owner, Janine, her favourite librarian.

'Sorry to pop in without calling,' Janine said. 'My car radio has been playing up for a couple of days and then I was leaving work and it took me ages to get the engine going. I've been slipping your business flyers into books all day, so I knew just where to come.'

'I'm glad to see they're working.' Kylie was just as glad that she had a suitable model ready to go. After testing the old battery and determining, yes, it was cactus (to use a technical term), she tucked a clean rag into her blouse neckline like a bib to save her good clothes, then switched out the old battery for the new.

'How's that tractor book going that we ordered in for you, love?' said Janine.

Oops. She'd dumped it on her bedside table when she'd brought it home and not given it a thought since. 'I've been a little flat out for reading, sorry.' Then she had a thought. 'Hey, you reckon the library has any books on business coaching? Or small business tips, that sort of thing? A few of us in town have started a women in business group and we could do with some discussion topics.'

'What a great idea. Why don't I put together a list for you? Better yet, why not have one of your meetings at the library and we can have a display of books up for you. It'll give us a chance to dust off the hot water urn and crack open a pack of Iced VoVos.'

'Sounds like a plan. You paying cash or card?'

The workshop tidy, her bank balance a little healthier, but no messages on the answering machine requiring her to hotfoot it anywhere to save anyone's day—mechanically speaking—Kylie made herself a cup of tea and took it outside to sit with Trev.

'How are you, my darling boy?' she asked her tractor. No response, but she didn't need one. All told, her day had been pretty good. The creepy feeling her nemesis had left in his wake was fading, and the afternoon was mellowing into the golden hue of a long summer evening. An evening which was going to include company. Conversation. A handsome man.

Life was okay. Not wonderful, like it should be, like she deserved ... but okay.

Her phone blipped from her jeans pocket. Thinking it would be Damon, she pulled it out to see where he was at with his chores, but it was a message from Hannah.

Cranky baby. Might need to cancel our drinky plan. Can we do Friday instead?

Hmm. Baby Eva was turning into quite the party pooper.

No worries.

Sorry!!! I still love you I promise.

Pity was not what Kylie wanted, so she set her thumbs to the keyboard. *It's fine. I'm meeting a client at the pub, anyway, so no need for sorries.*

What client meets you at the pub??

Kylie rolled her eyes. *The one I'm driving around.*

The answer was slightly longer in coming. *New plan. We're coming to the pub.*

Before Kylie could give her own view on Hannah's desire to have a gander at the man she was driving around, a new text was blipping.

Come meet us at the clinic and we can walk up together.

'Don't hate me,' said Hannah, when Kylie let herself in the back door of the vet clinic and sang out a hello. 'The phone rang just when I'd finished messaging you and now I'm behind schedule. What time are you meeting this so-called "client" of yours?'

'Not a so-called client. A paying client. The Hanrahan Mechanic has branched out to include chauffeur duties, remember? And I have plenty of time.'

'All right, no need to get defensive. I've got sixteen inches of blocked intestine to incinerate before I'm free, so you get to chat with Tom and play with Eva for a bit before we head up.'

'We've talked about this, Han. I'm on a need-to-know-only basis for animal surgery.'

Hannah grinned. 'They're in the back office. Sandy has chocolate biscuits hidden somewhere in there and I've nearly torn the cupboards off the walls looking for them, so feel free to have a snoop around.'

Kylie's nose twitched as she made her way through to the back office. Wet dog. Antiseptic. Some sort of casserole with wine and rosemary, which had to be coming from Vera and Josh's apartment upstairs, and had to mean Vera was home. Josh could barely pour corn flakes into a bowl.

In the back office, the baby was awake in her pram, grizzling a little and sucking her fist in a noisy fashion. 'How's my precious lamb?' Kylie said, tweaking the little socked feet. 'Do you know what your mummy is doing outside? Something noxious.'

'Hello,' said a deep voice from an old and dumpy sofa.

'Oh, hey, Tom,' she said. Hannah's husband was reading a newspaper. 'How's daddy life?'

'Exhausting. Eva may look sweet, but she's as temperamental as her mother and has now decided she only likes to sleep in the car. Speaking of, how's your car business?'

'Great!' she said brightly. Tom's father had owned half the buildings in town, and since Bruno had now passed away, that made Tom a little intimidating when it came to admitting anything less than financial amazingness. The fake brightness took a little more out of her than she'd expected.

'Nigel Woods still being a killjoy?'

She would have liked to mention the intimidation tactics Nigel had used the other day at her workshop, because Tom could be a total badass when he wanted to be. But if she told him Nigel had threatened her, he would probably get all alpha about it and go and sort Nigel out. And then Hannah would know, and then Josh and Vera and Graeme would know, and then Wendy and the pinking shears and the I-told-you-so face would be at her door.

'He's been away, I hear,' she said mildly. 'Maybe a getaway to Melbourne with his wife has turned him into a nicer bloke.' She'd been feeling mellow and looking forward to an evening not thinking about her current life dramas, but for some reason, Tom was managing to ask every question she didn't want to answer.

'Yeah, I wouldn't be taking bets on that.'

'Me either.' A change of topic was required. Urgently. Kylie was feeling weak and she *hated* feeling weak. 'You know what your wife's up to outside?'

He grinned. 'I try not to ask.'

Hannah's voice spoke up from the door. 'For better or worse, Tom. My worse just happens to be a lot worse than your worse.'

Tom chuckled. 'No argument from me there, brat.'

I'm not jealous, Kylie thought. *Not for one, green-eyed second. Or broke, or lonely, or worried.* 'Stop your bickering,' she said, totally intending it to come out as a joke, but then, for some out-of-the-blue and insane reason, she discovered she was crying.

Ugly crying.

'Um ... what the fruit?' said Hannah.

'This is where you hug your friend,' Tom said gently.

Kylie had some sort of face-leak-voiceless-gulp event going on, which rendered her incapable of both stopping crying and telling them she was totally okay and to just ignore her for a minute and carry on with their domestic bliss. They wouldn't have listened or believed her anyway, and then she didn't care. Hannah was shorter than she was, but Tom was taller, and he came in too for a group hug, because he actually *was* an affectionate person, as opposed to Hannah, who normally expressed affection by insulting someone. Tom's head was on Kylie's head which was on Hannah's head and it was all so very unexpected—but nice.

'Sorry,' Kylie managed to blurt when the emotion of the moment was tapering. 'I don't know what came over me.' The smells—the truly noxious smells—coming off Hannah's work scrubs started to heat up in the warmth generated by a three-person hug. 'Also, you stink, Han.'

Hannah chuckled, and then Kylie started to laugh at the same time as cry, and the baby joined in with a shriek of disapproval that she wasn't the centre of attention.

Tom unclicked Eva and picked her up so she could join in. 'You want to talk about it?'

Kylie looked at Hannah. This was the complicated thing about your best friend getting herself hitched: your two-person BFF code of thirty years was suddenly being reviewed by a third party.

'This might be a girl thing,' Hannah said mildly, but Kylie didn't miss the look she shot her husband. 'All righty, give me three minutes to shower and change and then we can go to the pub and meet Kylie's hottie.'

'Far out, Han, he is not my hottie.'

Hannah gave her arm a squeeze and whisked herself and her intestinal-tract stink from the room.

The Hanrahan Pub was a two-storeyed, twin-chimneyed grand old lady situated at the eastern end of the town's lake frontage and had become a social hub since its recent renovation. Winter tourists enjoyed a mulled wine by a roaring fire after a long day skiing, and the locals were kept entertained by trivia nights, live music sessions in the garden out back on a Sunday afternoon and in the main bar on a Friday night, and a classic pub-food menu. Kylie wasn't a regular—mechanics on budgets didn't splash their cash around on booze and steak sandwiches—but she was at the pub often enough to be on a first-name basis with the manager, Greg.

Tom went to the bar while Kylie and Hannah found a table in a quiet corner where Eva's pram wasn't in the way, and once they were seated, Hannah gave Kylie a spill-the-beans-or-else look.

Kylie cleared her throat. 'I don't know what came over me.'

'I will be very, very sad if you think that I don't have time in my life to love you just as much now as I did before I got together with Tom. I'm the person you can tell anything to. You know that, don't you?'

Wow, she really must have freaked Hannah out if her friend was making declarations of affection. With actual words. In public. Hannah was, or had been, she supposed, the most emotionally repressed person in the Snowy Monaro district.

She put her hand on Hannah's. 'I don't think that. It's just ... well. I haven't liked to bother you with my dramas lately, mainly because you're incredibly cranky when you're short on sleep—'

'Rubbish,' Hannah said with zero conviction.

'—but I have been stressed lately. And that's new for me. I'm not usually a "getting stressed" kind of person.'

Hannah lifted up her hand and ticked off her fingers. 'Wendy. Business. Love life. Which one is getting you down?'

'You've not touched finger number four: all of the above.'

'Oh, Kylie.'

'Yeah.' Kylie let the pleasing hubbub of pub noise soothe her. 'And Nigel's standover tactics shook me up a little more than I realised—'

'What do you mean, standover tactics?'

'Um.' She hadn't meant to go there. 'You know. Undercutting my pricing, that sort of thing.' She was saved from going into the nitty-gritty of just how awful Nigel had been by the arrival of Tom, who was carrying a tray of drinks and had Damon with him.

She'd have said hello, but she found herself distracted by Damon's change of outfit. Not that what he'd worn to town had made him look bad or anything, it just hadn't been particularly well sized. But now? Those jeans were inky blue, and smart, and the sort of denim that hugged all the bits that should be hugged. The plaid shirt was what half the guys in the bar were wearing, but Damon wore it *well*. Slim fit, collar open, white T-shirt visible beneath. And the padded jacket in navy corduroy was awesome, too, and just a tiny bit funny. It gave him a lumberjack vibe that was totally working. For him and for her. Who knew she had a secret fetish for lumberjacks?

'Nice,' she said, after giving him a frank—and leisurely—up-and-down. She twirled her finger.

He smirked, then spoke low enough so only she would hear. 'I am so not spinning around so you can check out my arse.'

She bit her lip and replied in an equally low voice. 'I have no interest in your arse, remember?'

Hannah chose that moment to bulldoze her way into the conversation. 'You must be Damon. Kylie's not told us anywhere near enough about you. Have a seat.'

Jeepers. She hoped Damon was up for this. She caught his eye and gave a little apologetic shrug, but he didn't look bothered. The opposite; he gave her the ghost of a wink.

'First things first, how's that dog doing?'

'Alfie?'

'Yes. Fattest dog on my books, and that's saying something. Is he still taking his meds? Fish oil for the arthritis, ear drops after he goes in the lake, tick and flea monthly, heart worm—'

'Have a glass of chardy, Dr Cody,' said Tom, cutting off the inquest. 'The clinic is closed for the day and you, my sweet, are not on call.' He passed Kylie the schooner of zero beer she'd asked for and raised his own glass of beer in a toast. 'To friends, old and new,' he said.

Kylie clinked her glass into the middle, wondering what it would be like if this really was a date. If Damon really had moved to the district intending to settle, and he and her and the Krausses were really a group of friends enjoying a midweek catch-up at their favourite pub.

Damon's eyes met hers, just for a second, and then moved away.

Tom asked Damon how he was getting along with sorting out Frank's belongings and as the conversation veered into stories of other estates Tom had been involved in, and the weird and wonderful things relatives had found stashed in houses, Hannah leant into Kylie.

'You were not joking about the tall, dark and dangerous factor.'

'I know, right?'

'And those *eyes*.'

Kylie fanned herself with a beer coaster as Hannah kept going. 'Am I imagining it, or have we got a good old-fashioned case of URST going on here?'

How the tables had turned. Had it only been a year since Kylie had been having to educate Hannah on the finer points of unresolved sexual tension as her bestie stumbled her way towards happiness with the man now seated opposite her at the pub table?

But that was them. Her own story was turning out a little less happy endy. 'There's a little flutter, sure, but he's not my type,' she said airily.

'He's *exactly* your type.'

'He was my type. Now my type is someone who I can build a life with here in Hanrahan, and who can provide me with a paddock for Trevor and some gumbooted children.'

'Uh-huh.' Which was Hannah's way of saying, *You're kidding yourself.* And also, *Hanrahan has a bloke shortage.* And also, *I'm not telling you anything you don't already know.* Her friend turned to the baby who'd set up a howl loud enough to turn heads.

'I'm just going to pop to the loo,' Kylie said.

'You're not going in there to cry again, are you? Because if you are, I'm going to have to come with you, and I'll have to bring Eva, because this hollering for some Mummy time is only going to get worse judging by the rocks currently living where my boobs used to be, and it'll be quite the performance, wheeling that whacking great pram through all these people and into the ladies'. Just saying.'

'I'm done with the crying, I promise.'

But as she'd clinked glasses and Damon's eyes had met hers, it had struck her that she had indeed been crying and she may look like it. Hannah couldn't be trusted to notice; mascara was a foreign language to that woman. No, Kylie needed a mirror, ASAP.

She weaved through the midweek crowd to get to the central corridor where the main loos were, but then she saw her mother seated in the dining room with a bunch of women who might have been Wendy's sewing group. Kylie froze, then flung her way through the nearest door before she could be spotted. Wendy had a social life?

She ended up on the pub's large wraparound verandah. No matter, there was a smaller bathroom out back and while the latch on the door showed red, she could hear the sound of a loo flushing within. Excellent.

She was waiting beside the heavy door for her turn when a soft voice from beyond a large artificial pot plant said, 'Hello, darling.'

Wendy had spotted her. Of course.

'Excuse me, Mum,' she said, hearing the nicely timed sound of the bathroom door lock disengaging beside her. 'Need the loo.'

Fred, the groundsman at the primary school and one of her car service regulars, emerged and she nearly crashed into him in her hurry to get away from her mother.

'Gettin' busier every bloody week, this place,' he grumbled.

'Hi, Fred. How's that gearbox holding up? I'll check it out for you when you come in for your next service.'

Fred mumbled an answer into his beard, but it wasn't so low that she didn't get the gist: *highway, deal, was going to call, Nigel*.

Suddenly, her need to inspect her running eye makeup and escape her mother didn't feel so urgent. 'What "deal" is this?'

'Er ... shoot,' he mumbled. 'Didn't know how to tell you, love. Fella's had some girl ringing around town, offering his services.'

'What was the offer?'

'First service free for new customers who live in the Hanrahan postcode.' Fred was backing away even as he spoke, the coward. 'And he gives us a car to use while ours is in the shop. Free is free, love; there was no saying no to that.'

'That's true, dear,' Wendy chipped in. 'And such a blessing amid this cost of living crisis we keep hearing about. I'm getting a free service myself, when Autocare can fit me in. Someone from there rang me just the other day and they can fit my car in next month.'

Kylie sucked in a breath. Fred's disloyalty was annoying. But her *mother's*? 'I offer courtesy lifts home,' she said. 'And I give discounts, too, for regulars.' *Plus, I'm not an evil dick.* She hated that she sounded desperate and teary. Desperation sucked. Tears sucked even more. But a free service for locals? *Free?* Nigel was trying to drive her out of business by any means possible and he'd likely succeed with this tactic. There could be no other explanation. She felt like she'd been punched.

'Are you quite all right, darling?' said Wendy.

No. She was not all right. And the fact that her mother couldn't work out why was part of the reason she was so not all right. But pride could be a fierce motivator, so she stopped grinding her teeth long enough to speak. 'I'm totally fine, but also totally busting, Mum, so if you don't mind ...' She looked meaningfully at the now vacant loo.

'Everything all right here?'

Damon. Of course. Just when the evening couldn't get any worse—a witness to her humiliation.

'Everything's fine,' she said. But everything wasn't fine.

Fred took the opportunity to do a runner. Wendy took the opportunity to sigh gently and walk primly off down the corridor back to her sewing group.

'Hannah and Tom had to take off,' Damon said. 'The baby wouldn't stop wailing and they both leapt to their feet like a grenade pin had been pulled.'

Good. Now there was no need to go back into the crowd and pretend she was okay. She'd committed to driving Damon home, but then she could hightail it back to her flat to fall apart in private.

'Kylie?'

She didn't want to look at him, because she very much feared she looked a wreck, and also there was the small matter that she was possibly-maybe-definitely about to have one of those things that other people had but which she didn't believe in: a breakdown. She pushed the door open and disappeared into the loo.

The paper towel from the dispenser was about as soft and comforting as sandpaper, but she rinsed some water over it and held it to her face. Tears could sting. Either that, or her mascara was made of some weird sort of chemical that reacted with tap water to become acid. She was making a sopping mess and her nose was running too, now, and, dear god, why didn't this bathroom stock decent tissues? She reached out blindly for more of the sandpaper and a bundle of it was put into her hand.

Far out, who—?

'What the hell are you doing in here?' she demanded.

Damon had one hip perched against the counter top and was watching her with those dark, dangerous eyes. 'Are you okay?'

'This is a *loo*. For *women*. Who want to be *alone*.'

'You didn't lock the door. Also, this loo is unisex.'

Seriously?

He pulled another square of hand towel out, wet it under the tap, squeezed it out and said, 'You've missed a bit.'

She looked in the mirror and what was looking back at her was not good. Smudged makeup. Pale face and end-of-day hair. Red eyes. Drooping shoulders under a pink blouse that had seemed cheerful when she'd put it on but now looked like puce. She'd more than missed a bit. 'You know, before Hannah decided she was in love with Tom, she'd have been the one in here with me. She'd help me mop up my face then we'd go to my place and binge eat ice-cream until the world felt like a better place.'

'I'm sorry,' he said.

'I'm very happy for her,' she said, eyes welling again despite the fact she had them plugged up with hand towel that resembled papier-mache. 'It's just ... sometimes I do feel a bit alone.' Was this what that meltdown in the vet office had been about? Was she *lonely*?

'I'm standing right here. You want to tell me what that guy said to upset you so much? Or was it the woman?'

'Fred. He's okay, he just ...' Was the straw, perhaps. 'And Wendy. She just ...' Another straw. Which made her, Kylie, the camel. She was making no sense, even to herself.

'He just? She just? Wendy has to be your mother, right?'

It *would* be a relief to blurt all this stuff out. 'My business is struggling,' she said, dabbing at the black marks under her eyes with the soggy paper. 'I've been kidding myself it's because I was a newer business in town, and there are some old-school people here—my mum being leader of that pack—who think women mechanics are a threat to the natural world order. And old-school prejudice may be partly true, but I've suspected for some time that another mechanic was badmouthing my business—I told you how Nigel Woods has been to my workshop, snooping around and so on—but just now is the first time I've learned how far he's prepared to go to see me fail. Fred used to be my customer. Not anymore, apparently. Same with … Wendy.' A betrayal which *cut*.

Damon cleared his throat. 'Yeah. About the Woods bloke …'

She turned her head to stare at him. 'What? He's not had his staff call you, too, has he? Offer you free stuff to get the vineyard's business?'

'No. It's just, before Hannah took off, she told me to warn you that your nemesis was here at the bar. Nigel Woods, I assume.'

Oh, god. She couldn't face him. But maybe she had to. She squared her shoulders, blew her nose and smoothed her hair back into a neater ponytail. She was Kylie Summer and she was not going to be intimidated out of earning her place in the world by some dickhead bloke with a scary spider tattoo.

'I'm going to go find him and tell him what a shit he is.'

'That's one option. You want some advice?'

'No. Yes. Maybe.'

'You never want to tell someone what a shit they are when you're upset.'

'I'm not upset.'

'Sweetheart, you're a terrible liar. Come on, let's get out of here. You can tell me what a shit he is all the way home.'

CHAPTER 17

Damon's one and only friend in Hanrahan did a stellar job of pulling herself together on the way home. He knew, because he got to listen to every word: Kylie was one of those people who resolved stuff by talking it out. As he was more of a stuff-his-personal-drama-into-a-black-hole-and-ignore-it-until-it-turns-into-a-barnacle-in-his-chest type of person, he was a lot more interested in the process than he might otherwise have been.

'It's not as though I've stolen any of his customers. George Juggins—he had the workshop before me—operated in Hanrahan for *years*. Is it my fault old George let business slide after his wife died? Talked about handing the lease over to Nigel but then never got around to it? No.'

Um ... contractually speaking, that would depend on what exactly Nigel and George had talked about and agreed to and in what terms, but Kylie was getting more animated and less sad every minute, so it didn't seem the right time to start with the legal nitpicking.

'Besides, you'd think this town would want a mechanic who is actually a decent person. Who they don't have to drive thirty minutes to get to. Haven't I just been a freaking hero and saved Dave Ryan's paddlewheeler?'

'So true,' he said soothingly. He used the voice he'd use in court when he was leading a witness into a trap with a carrot rather than a stick, which struck him as being woefully insincere. Was this the point Warunya and Sean had been trying to make? That he was insincere in court?

But he did want to calm Kylie. He liked her. Oh, sure, he fancied her too. Who wouldn't? Kylie had a sunshine quality to her that made the world—his world—a whole lot brighter. Kylie made him want to be sincere. Or at least be seen as sincere. He wasn't sure he could actually tell the difference, which probably made him the most shallow person alive.

'That boat can continue to be a Hanrahan icon thanks to me,' she said. She might have even done a bit of a head toss while she said it, which drew his attention to her hair. Still caramel and blonde and streaky. Still delectable. He rested one arm along the back of the ute's bench seat and touched a strand with a finger.

'An icon,' he echoed. Huh. He was getting good at this soothing stuff: less with the pedantic questioning and more with the word echo.

'When visitors flock to town to day trip on the PW *Moana* and then spend up big in the café and the pub and the book and gift shop, I helped make that happen.'

'No question, you saved the town,' he said.

'I have not crawled my way out of my mother's narrow little vision of what my life should be just to crumple because one awful ex-con is trying to put me out—'

She broke off mid-sentence. Before he could ask how she knew Nigel Woods was an ex-con, she was pulling off the road and coming to a stop in a splutter of gravel.

'Did you just say *saved the town*? Are you making fun of me?'

He chuckled. Okay, that last comment had been a little much. 'Not at all. Since I didn't have any ice-cream on hand to binge eat with you, and I have very little experience playing the role of stand-in supportive bestie, I'm still finding my way.'

'Oh.' She reached over and gripped his hand. 'That's actually pretty sweet.'

Sweet wasn't an adjective he was accustomed to being described by, and it made him uncomfortable enough to deflect. 'We both know I'd rather be playing the role of charming city guy having fling with country sweetheart.'

She let go of his hand. 'Well. You were sweet for a moment.'

And then they were barrelling out of town again. Kylie must have felt confidences were over—or that he'd ruined the moment—because she turned the radio up. Without her monologue on the evils of oppressive highway mechanics to occupy them, he grew distracted by the smells wafting up from the two massive double pepperoni and cheese pizzas in the boxes occupying the bench seat between them.

'Am I the only one about to drool over that pizza smell?'

Kylie glanced at him then back to the road. 'Been picking up habits from that great beast of yours, I see.'

Damon lifted the lid of the top box. 'He's not my beast,' he said.

She took the piece of pizza he handed her and drove one-handed while she ate it. 'You sure? He's got to belong to someone. If not you, then your mother.'

Damon had a mouthful of pizza, so articulating how little of an opinion he had on his mother's ability to care for a dog was limited to a grunt.

'Hannah and her brother Josh might be able to find someone who's willing to take on an old dog. You want me to ask? The sooner he gets settled in a new home the better, perhaps.'

For some reason, Damon did not at all want to talk about the difficulties of rehoming an old dog. Alfie loved the lake. He loved sleeping in the patch of sunlight beside Frank's chair in the study. Alfie loved swimming after sticks and rolling in long grass and—

Damon's train of thought was interrupted by Kylie's hand sliding into the pizza box for another piece. He gave it a pat.

'We're nearly home. Why don't we eat the rest on the dock and watch the stars for a bit? Crack a beer, maybe.'

She was silent for a bit. 'You know, considering the business nature of our relationship and everything, maybe we shouldn't be watching stars together on docks.'

'Alfie can be our chaperone to make sure we don't say—or do— anything inappropriate.' His mind instantly filled with images of all the word 'do' could imply.

'Damon,' she said, in a half-laughing, half-exasperated way.

He grinned; she could hear it in his voice. 'Hey, it's your vow, not mine.'

Snowy River Vineyard was just after the next curve and Kylie dropped down a gear to turn the ute into the gravelled drive. 'What did Frank drive?' she said. 'This can't be an easy road in mid-winter after a big snow dump.'

'An abrupt and obvious change of topic, but I'll play along. There's a LandCruiser in the garage. It'd have ten years on it, but it looks well cared for.'

'Lakefront land, a young vineyard he must have set up and planted, all the gear for it and a very nice house. Your uncle must have done okay for himself. I wonder what he did for a crust before he moved out here.'

'My uncle,' Damon said. 'You know, I've not been thinking of him in those terms.'

Kylie looked at him. 'Why not? He's your mother's brother, isn't he?'

'Half. Estranged. No relationship at all.'

'Ouch. If that's the way your mother thought of him, I'm surprised he left her anything in the will, let alone all of it. Modern families are full of halves and steps and de factos.'

Damon leant back in his seat to look at her. His arm was still resting on the bench seat, but he had—somehow or other—moved from touching one strand of hair to having his fingers tangled in her ponytail. He gave one lock a little tug. 'So says the girl who's avoiding her mother.'

Kylie snorted. 'Okay. You've got me there.'

'My mother has so far been very cagey about the whole who-is-Frank and why-was-he-a-stranger thing, but,' he said, 'I might have an answer to the how he earned a living question before he came out here. Tom says he wrote some kids' books years ago that did pretty well. I found a book on his desk, an old one, that was written and illustrated by F.D. Silva. Frank, I presume.'

'F.D. Silva,' said Kylie. 'Why is that ringing a bell?'

'There's an easel and stool and a stack of paints—artist paints, that is—in that little weatherboard boatshed you might have seen near the dock, and there's art upstairs on the landing that's in series, like maybe it was the original artwork for a book. Animals, mostly. Marsupials, dogs, cats. A lot of tractors, now I think about it, which no doubt you would appreciate more than me, and—'

'Tractors?' said Kylie. 'No way.' She started reciting in a singsong voice: '"Noisy little tractor, tries to go faster, hurries down the paddock with his engine saying, 'Roar!'" That was my favourite book as a kid. The beginning of my interest in tractors. It's one of the few memories I have of my dad, him reading it to me at night. Do you think your Uncle Frank could have written my favourite book? That would be something, wouldn't it? Have you got internet service?'

'Uh … three bars.'

'Do a search for F.D. Silva, kids' books. What titles come up?'

Damon typed into his phone. 'Let's see. There's a website but it's defunct. Oh, here's an old bio on a publisher's page. *Much-loved children's author F.D. Silva gains his inspiration for stories and illustrations from the countryside in Victoria near Bendigo where he lived as a child.* Hmm. Mum grew up in country Victoria too, but … I'll jump ahead to the bibliography. Oh, there's heaps. The most popular ones seem to be *The Enormous Dog*—I've seen a copy of that in his study—*A Cautionary Tale About a Gecko Tail, Noisy Little Tractor*—'

'Whoo!' said Kylie. 'That's the one! This is *awesome*! I wonder if Mum still has my copy at home? I mean, it was years ago. It'd have to be out of print now. To think he retired out here to Hanrahan and I never even knew.'

Damon looked up from his phone as Kylie parked the ute by the house. All thoughts of pizza and uncles and kids' books went pfft and his guts and chest cramped.

A nondescript sedan that had not been at the vineyard earlier in the day was now taking up space in front of the garage door, and leaning up against it was a tall streak of a guy with an old felt Akubra pulled low over his face.

'Looks like you've got a visitor,' said Kylie.

'Not for bloody long,' Damon said grimly.

CHAPTER 18

'Damon?' Kylie said. 'What's the matter?'

'Not what,' he said, letting himself out of the ute. 'Who.'

Alfie must have heard the engine noise because he'd settled into a rhythm of big, booming barks, but the dog fell silent when Damon yelled at him to cut it out.

'Hey, brother,' said Nick.

'What are you doing here?'

Nick Johns pulled a folded piece of paper out of his shirt pocket and handed it to Damon. 'Mum asked me to give you this.'

Damon took the paper, unfolded it and read it in the light from the portico above the front door. He shoved it in the back pocket of his jeans like he would a used bus ticket. 'Consider it delivered. Now you can hop back in your car and go back to Melbourne.'

Nick shook his head. 'I was hoping I could stay for a bit.'

'Here? With me?'

'Yeah.'

'You've got to be joking.'

'Damon.' Nick looked across at Kylie, who'd climbed out of the car but now looked as though she wished she hadn't. He dropped his voice and said, 'I'm in a bit of a bind.'

'Shit,' said Damon. From the corner of his eye, and despite the pincer grip his ribs had had on his diaphragm since the moment he'd seen his brother standing there, all casual and yeah-whatevs-man in that fucking annoying way Nick had, Damon could see that Kylie was debating whether or not to escape.

Fair call. If he could've tiptoed away like she was doing, leapt into a ute and done high-speed burnouts all the way back to the main road, he'd have done it, too. More fool him for being the loser with the DUI disqualification.

The thoughts plastered across her face were so easy to read he would have laughed if he hadn't been feeling so breathlessly murderous: *Your brother's famous? I so want to stay and witness the drama but good manners dictate I go. And OMG, why all the aggro? I thought my family was dysfunctional but this is next level!*

'I'd better sort this out,' he said to her. And by sort, he meant run his brother off the property, at the end of a pitchfork if that's what it took.

Assault, bodily harm, manslaughter: take your pick, they'll all get you arrested. A timely reminder from Dr Gloom.

'I'll get the groceries out of the ute,' he said, instead of running for a pitchfork. 'What say we split the six pack and the pizza?' He'd have liked to ask her for a raincheck on the sitting-on-the-dock thing—he had really, *really* wanted to sit on the dock with Kylie, and look at stars and play with her ponytail a little longer, but—

'Did someone say pizza?' said Nick. His brother straightened from his slouched pose against the sedan—very much a studied, Nick Johns manoeuvre—then prowled over to the ute and pulled open the passenger door. 'Two pizzas. Three people. Six beers. I love it when a maths problem has a serendipitous ending. I think we can make this work.'

Shoot me now, thought Damon.

'Where shall we eat?' Nick said jovially, either immune to the atmosphere or acting immune to the atmosphere—Damon didn't care enough to spend time figuring out which—then pulled the boxes out of the ute. He balanced them on one hand like he'd grown up in a pizzeria and could juggle them just as easily if he chose.

Freaking show-off.

Kylie, Damon noted sourly, had that dazzled look that women got around Nick. He blamed the schmooze factor. The charm. The height and the chiselled jaw and the mellifluous voice.

'Er ...' she said, her car keys dangling in her hand. Yep, dazzled.

'I insist we all eat together,' said Nick. 'Lead the way, Damo. And—' He tucked his spare arm under Kylie's and his eyes, damn them, were probably twinkling. It was too dark now to be sure, but Damon would have bet money on it. 'Who might *you* be?'

Kylie looked at Damon with raised eyebrows, but didn't, he noticed, make any effort at all to get out of Nick's clutches. 'I'm Damon's mechanic,' she said. 'But I should probably leave you boys to sort your, um ... selves. I've got vengeance to plan, anyway, which is best planned alone. You keep both pizzas,' she added, which was a more noble gesture than Damon could ever recall his brother making. 'I probably have a tin of soup or something at home that might still be within its use by date ...'

Okay, not totally noble, but her words did at least take the sharper edges off his mood. And his barnacles. 'That is so tragic, Kylie.'

She looked at him, and there were more questions in her face than he could count. 'I know, right?'

Maybe having Kylie as witness would keep him from committing one of Dr Gloom's crimes for as long as it took to send Nick on his way. But if she stayed, he wanted her on his arm, not on bloody Nick's.

The dog emitted a howl loud enough to shatter glass.

'Alfie!' he yelled. 'Cut it out.'

'Wait,' said Nick. 'Wait, wait, wait. First: there's a dog here? Second: his *mechanic*? And third: vengeance against whom? Too much information all at the same time. Hellooo, Kylie,' he said. Actually, he drawled it like he was on an episode of *The Bachelor*. 'Nick Johns. I am so pleased to meet *you*.'

'Give it a rest, Nick,' said Damon.

Kylie had finally pulled her arm free. 'You know what, guys, I'm picking up on a whole lot of family vibes that maybe don't need a witness. I'm going to take off.'

'But we just met,' said Nick, deploying sad face. One of his many, many faces.

Damon sighed and did what he absolutely hated doing: he let it go. All this frigging arguing meant dinner was going cold, the beer was going warm, and Alfie's voice box was about to get a repetitive strain injury. 'Come have some pizza, Kylie.' Not quite in the way he'd been planning on the drive out of town, of course.

He unlocked the front door and led them through the passageway to the family room at the back of the house. He opened the French doors, to the delight of the malodorous fur bomb waiting there. Nick hung back to check out the sofas, the view, the fireplace, the everything.

'Wow. This is so *fabulous*.'

'For god's sake, do us all a favour and don't break into song,' Damon said.

Kylie gave a snort of laughter beside him and he threw her a wink. To his surprise, he heard a chuckle emerge from his brother. Hmm. He'd have to try harder with the insults next time.

The weathered old picnic table where the scones were served on picnic day was clean and dry, so he flicked on the switch that lit the garden with a zig-zag of fairy lights, then headed that way. 'The fridge has water and long-life oat milk if anyone's not in the mood for a beer.'

'I'll find serviettes or something,' Kylie said, and disappeared into the pantry, leaving him alone with his brother. What a traitor.

Damon sat on one side of the picnic table and Nick on the other, the pizza boxes between them like no man's land in a war zone.

'Why are you here?' Damon said. He could have prettied the words up, but what was the point? He and Nick didn't have a relationship, any more than, it seemed, Frank and Deirdre. When Nick became a teen idol and moved to Melbourne for his 'career', they grew apart.

That was the short story, anyway.

Nick glanced towards the house, where Kylie could be seen pottering about behind the kitchen windows. 'It's family business.' His brother, oblivious as ever to anything that didn't involve the spotlight shining right on him, had no clue that Damon might actually have issues of his own to resolve and didn't need Nick and his dramas parachuting in.

Damon nodded. 'You know what, Nick? I met Kylie about a week and a half ago, and already I know her—and like her—about a thousand times better than I know and like you. Whatever private things you have to say, maybe you need to bugger off and tell them to someone who's actually part of your life.' Harsh. But also true.

Nick didn't budge from the bench. Either he had his head so far up his own arse he hadn't heard Damon or he just didn't care.

'I'm in trouble, mate. I need someplace to stay for a while and Mum said you could do with a hand here.'

'I've got everything sorted.' He had barely anything sorted, but what he really, really didn't need was his head getting messed up even more by having his brother in eyesight every day.

'I might need a lawyer.'

Damon sat back. He put his hand on his chest and breathed in cautiously. No sharp edges, no dizziness. So far, so good, he could risk a comment, maybe. 'You're in the entertainment business,' he said. 'You must have a fleet of lawyers. And I know you've not been around to witness any of the achievements in *my* life, but just to give you the super quick version, I'm a barrister, so strictly speaking I don't give legal advice to random walk-ins off the street.'

'I'm not saying I do need one. I just might. And if I do, then I'll want you to help me. You're the best.'

Damon's chest tightened. And then tightened some more. Not too long ago, he would have nodded and said, 'Yeah, I am,' or something equally as cocky, but now …

He looked out over the ink-dark water, imagining swimming his way into calmness. Push the arms out, a sweep of water, a kick of the legs, repeat … After a while, he said, 'What's this legal problem, then?'

Nick shook his head. 'Do you not follow my career at all?'

'Um, no.'

'Oh. I thought maybe you hadn't heard because you've been away from home.'

'Nope.'

'Some sort of work sabbatical, Mum said. She didn't know what for.'

Damon smiled. His shark smile, the one that told opposing counsel to be very, very worried. 'For having no conscience, apparently. So, whatever it is you think you're wanting from me, Nick, you've picked the wrong brother to sweet talk.'

Nick sighed. 'I've picked my only brother.'

The tinkling of glass and ice cubes broke the silence—Kylie was inbound. She'd found a tray and filled it with a jug of iced water, coloured glass tumblers and a few of the serviettes from the pantry, which, strictly speaking, belonged to Picnic in a Vineyard Pty Ltd. Alfie trotted by her side wearing his angelic look, but with a suspicious collection of breadcrumbs clinging to his whiskers. If that dog had been in Damon's recently bought groceries, there was going to be trouble.

'Your friend,' Nick said, sotto voce. 'Is she the type to be making a quick buck selling stories to the gossip mags?'

'No,' said Damon, not at all confident how he knew the answer. 'But you can tell me the rest later.' Or not. Damon so did not care.

Nick waited until Kylie had set the tray down on the picnic table, then pulled open the pizza boxes. 'Pepperoni,' he said. 'My favourite. Can I hand you a piece, Kylie? And then you can tell me all about you.'

'Sure,' she said, flashing Damon a look.

He flashed her a look back. If she was counting on him to get the conversation rolling, she was going to be disappointed.

Kylie stepped into the breach. 'But let's talk about you, first. *The* Nick Johns, right here in Hanrahan. I was disappointed when you gave up on the singing.'

Nick had a mouthful of double cheese and pepperoni, but he could still manage an idol-winning smile. 'You and me both, sweetheart.'

'Her name's Kylie,' Damon said. Announced, really. Like an idiot.

Both of them looked at him in faint surprise. Yeah, okay, so he was feeling territorial. Maybe that's what happened when you became a de facto dog carer: your animal instincts rose to the surface. He'd be peeing on shrubs and eating a sock next, just watch.

Alfie made a low, warbling noise just to remind everyone that he was ready and willing to take on the job of eating the crusts that were going spare. Kylie poured herself a glass of iced water. She'd put leaves in the jug, Damon noticed, something fragrant (and hopefully edible) from Frank's kitchen plants.

'So why give it up?' she said, when it was clear they had all chosen to ignore Damon's churlish mood.

Nick shrugged. 'Recording songs takes more than a willing singer. I needed a record label to get behind me, and it just didn't happen after that first single, so I ... diversified.'

This was the first Damon had heard of Nick's career being anything but a light-hearted skip from one awesome opportunity to the next. But then, his source of information about his brother was Deirdre. The brief glance into the real Nick gave him a stab of nostalgia. When had he last felt like he had a *brother*? Before Nick auditioned for that talent show, certainly. Back when the two of them had been regular kids, in a regular neighbourhood, doing regular things like wrestling over the TV remote, chucking the footy in the street out front, banging on the bathroom door to tell the other one to hurry up and pee already, they were gonna be late for school. Back when Nick had still been Damon's idol and not the country's.

'I loved that show you did last year, the documentary on old theatres,' said Kylie. 'Hanrahan has some lovely old Federation buildings but no old theatre, sadly. Cooma has the Savoy, but it was built in the fifties so it's not as charming as some of the ones your show visited.'

'I'd love to see Hanrahan's old buildings. Maybe you could show them to me.' Nick was all focused interest now, the rat.

'Um ... well. I've got work, which keeps me pretty busy.'

'Work as a mechanic? Or work driving my brother around at sunset with pizza and beer?'

Kylie blushed. No question. Sure, the fairy lights weren't bright, and the tiny moths and other insects fluttering about each bulb in a death-wish frenzy were dimming them even more, but she definitely blushed.

'Kylie restores vintage tractors,' Damon said, unsure if her reaction was because Nick had implied she and Damon were involved—he wished—or because she was offended. The tractor comment came out of nowhere, but it did the trick.

'No way.' Nick deployed surprise-face and reared theatrically backwards on the bench. 'I was master of ceremonies one year for the Golden Oldies Truck, Tractor and Quilt Show in Dubbo. I love that stuff.'

Yay. His brother was flirting with his not date. And—worse—was his not date flirting back?

'I went to the tractor pull in Wombat back when I was a kid. My dad took me. It was awesome.'

'I bet it was. What made you pick being a mechanic as a career?'

Kylie was glowing. Why hadn't Damon thought to ask questions like these? *Because you always think it's about you*, he could hear Sean and Warunya saying. *You're a show pony who loves being the centre of attention.*

'Oh, I always liked tinkering with gadgets, and I have a methodical brain,' she said. 'It's a good fit.'

No mention of the disapproving mother, Damon noted. Perhaps Kylie didn't tell just anyone about her problems—a boundary he could respect. He didn't tell just anyone about his problems. One of them being the brother sitting opposite, hogging most of the pizza and all of the attention.

'Damon?'

Kylie and Nick were looking at him expectantly. Shoot, what had he missed?

Kylie pointed to the side of the house. 'Should the dog have that?'

He followed the direction of her outstretched finger to where Alfie was busy tugging a sack out of the weatherboard shack by the old dock. Crap. He'd opened the place up this morning when he was on his asset-register tour of the property, but hadn't got much further than noticing the easel and paints set up inside. Clearly he'd left the door off the latch, if the dog was now helping himself to whatever was in reach.

He rose to his feet. 'Alfie, that's not for you.' Fertiliser with blood and bone? The dog was capable of eating the whole of it, sack, contents and all. Tulip bulbs? Bark mulch? None of it sounded ideal if it ended up wedged in a canine digestive tract.

The dog's face was in the sack up to his eyebrows by the time Damon made it over. He read the words on the sack—high nitrogen fish meal—and grimaced. 'Alfie,' he said, sharply. The dog looked up, managing to look saintly and innocent, pellets stuck to the drool on his lower lip. 'Get out of here, go on.'

The dog heaved a sigh and dragged himself from the shack. Damon looked around for somewhere to store the sack out of reach and moved into the shadowy corner at the back, behind the artist setup he'd noticed earlier. A tarp hung across the back corner and he went to shift it, but something hard and metal rammed into his shin. 'Huh,' he grunted, and lifted the rest of the tarpaulin out of the way.

A silver motorbike sat neatly askew on its kickstand. It was small, retro looking, and its tyres were flat, even a city slicker like him could work that out. But the metal body had no dings or dust or rust.

'Frank,' he said admiringly. Forget that hideous orange tractor—*this* was a find.

He stuck his head out of the shed. Kylie needed more business, hadn't she been telling him that the whole way home from the pub? 'Kylie, come check this out,' he called.

She hopped up. 'What am I checking out? Oh,' she said, a moment later when she'd reached his side. 'A motorbike.'

He frowned. 'We find a tractor and it's like Christmas came early. We find something that's actually cool and you're like, *meh*.'

She grinned. 'The heart wants what it wants, Damon, even when it makes no rational sense. It is cool, though.' She wandered closer. 'A Honda Supercub? No, it's a Littlecub 50. Fourteen inch wheels rather than seventeen inch. A 2010 model, I think? Fuel injected, electronic or kickstart. I like the vintage look, of course. Is that a forest green metallic sheen I'm seeing under the dust? Finding parts is probably not too much of a challenge; this was a popular machine in its day. Frank loved his toys.'

'It's not Frank's anymore.' He couldn't believe how he'd just said that; like a seagull who'd pounced on a dropped chip at Circular Quay.

'Right. Your mother a bikie chick, is she? Leathers, bald blokes with bushranger beards, attitude?'

He laughed. 'Deirdre? Hell, no. You reckon you can get it working?'

Kylie ran a hand over the faded leather of the seat. 'Sure. Parts might need to be ordered in, but yeah, I could get it working. I won't know if it's a small or big job until I start tinkering.'

'I'm booking you in.'

'Seriously?'

'Chauffeur, only friend in town, real mechanic. It's a lot to juggle, I know. Think you can handle it?'

She grinned. 'Turns out, since my nemesis has started trash talking me to the few customers I have managed to acquire, I have some openings in my service calendar. When do you want me to start?'

'Whenever you like.'

'Pity I'm all gussied up,' she said, 'or we could have found an old plank and wheeled it into the ute now.' She cast a glance down at her outfit, which was unfortunate, as it made him do the same. The blouse skimmed over curves that his agile imagination had no trouble fleshing out, and her jeans clung pretty much everywhere.

'Yeah,' he said. 'Too bad you're not in your overalls.'

She laughed. 'That's something I don't hear too often.'

Had she edged closer to him? Either she had or his sense of smell had grown more acute, because over the shack smells of fertiliser sacks and turpentine and dried-out citronella garden torches, he was getting a waft of pure Kylie.

'Yeah?' he said. 'Those morons you're meeting on your country dating app must have very poor taste.'

'Moron, singular,' she said. 'Blokes are thin on the ground out here.'

Somehow or other he'd edged a little closer to her, too, and the moths dancing around the fairy lights must have invited all their friends to dance with them, because the light spilling into the shack was dim. Moody. Secretive.

'They are?' He was losing the conversational thread.

'In the last twelve months, I've met up with exactly one moron from my dating app. I told you about him. The tax guy?'

'Oh, yes. The broad-toothed rat. Was he a good kisser?'

She was grinning and very, very close. 'I'm not sure how that is germane to this conversation.'

'I find it's always good to establish a base line: Crap, Okay, Good, Better, Best. I'm wondering where our ratty friend landed on that scale.'

'I don't kiss everyone I go on dates with.'

'What about everyone you have taken a vow to not go on dates with?'

She stopped laughing. 'Damon. We talked about this.'

'I'm very forgetful.'

She snorted. 'I think you have a mind like a steel trap, Damon.'

'Whatever kind of trap my mind is, it's a trap that's forgotten all the really great reasons we listed about not capitalising on this awesome—truly awesome—chemistry we've got going here.'

'I knew it,' she said, apparently to herself. 'Tall, dark and dangerous. The reasons haven't changed.' Was she telling him? Or herself?

'Perhaps we need a new arrangement,' he said.

She frowned. 'I'm not getting your meaning.'

What a liar. 'It sure feels like you're getting my meaning, Kylie Summer.'

The corner of her mouth quirked in that way he knew meant she was enjoying this as much as he was, despite her vows to the contrary. 'That wasn't quite what I meant.'

No-one had ever accused Damon of being risk averse and he wasn't about to change his spots now. He ran a hand up Kylie's arm from elbow to shoulder, letting the heat from those firm biceps of hers fill his grip. She let out a little sigh, and if he was a sighing kind of bloke, he'd have let one out of his own.

He didn't. He seized her other arm, drew her up against him until those bloused curves, those snugly filled jeans, were pressed against him from chest to calf, and he fastened his lips to hers.

Damon had kissed plenty of women. He enjoyed it. He loved it, in fact; he'd been a living-in-the-moment, kissing-all-the-girls kind of guy ever since he'd worked out that girls thought he was easy on the eye. But he was now quickly working out one very salient fact about kissing, and that was that he'd not kissed Kylie before.

She was an inferno when he'd expected warm. She was comfort when he'd expected casual. Most wonderful of all? She was in his arms.

'Wait,' she muttered against his mouth when he was past the point of thinking in any words, even one-syllable ones.

He did as she asked, leaning his forehead against hers. 'I think my libido just exploded.'

He felt her chuckle against him before she pulled away. 'Yeah. Wow. Maybe that wasn't such a great idea.'

'It was the best idea I've had in years.'

'Be serious for a second. For two people who are determined to mean nothing to each other, you and me are sure getting complicated.'

A cocky response was all he had. 'Complicated is how I roll.'

'But that's not how I roll,' Kylie said. 'Not anymore.'

A cough from the doorway stopped him from saying anything further. Nick. Of course.

'If you two are finished hooking up in here, there's pizza going cold and I'm losing the battle against eating more than my share.'

Kylie found her voice before Damon did. 'We're, um, just working out how we're going to get this motorbike loaded into the back of my ute.'

'Easy,' said Nick. It was too dark to know for certain, but Damon would have bet ten bucks his brother had just deployed bloke-who-sorts-all face. 'Where will I find a plank, Damo? I can roll it up, no problem.'

'A good singer *and* smart,' said Kylie. 'It's a winning combination, Nick.'

'So they tell me.'

'I'll bring the ute round,' said Kylie, leaving the hut. Couldn't get out of the shack fast enough, in fact. 'Someone better make sure I don't hit the dog. There's no telling what damage that great lump would do to my bullbar.'

Damon followed her out and watched her walk away, unaware of his brother's eyes on him until he turned and saw the look on Nick's face. 'What?' he said.

'You sure you've only known this chick a week? The roof looked like it was about to melt when I came in.'

'Do something useful, will you, and find a plank. You want my help with your legal problem? The first rule is going to be to stay out of my personal life.'

Nick's chest rose and fell. Dramatic flair or actual relief? It was hard to tell. 'You're really open to helping me?'

Of course he was. It had just taken him a few moments and a good long kissing bout to realise he didn't always have to behave like the wounded cocky shit. 'The second rule is to stay away from Kylie.'

CHAPTER
19

If Tall, Dark and Dangerous had turned out to be a crap kisser—to use his own scale—then Kylie could have enjoyed his company, fixed his motorbike, admired his tractor, driven him around for the short time that he was here and then waved farewell with barely a twinge.

Problem was, he was *so* not a crap kisser.

'Wait,' said Hannah, who had suggested a pre-work coffee to debrief on their interrupted pub drink and was now seated across from her at The Billy Button Café. 'You kissed Damon, in an old *shack* of all places, and this is the first I'm hearing about it?' Hannah's voice would have woken the dead. It certainly got the attention of the grey nomads enjoying their lumberjack cake dessert at the next table. 'You should have texted me *immediately*.'

'Hannah! You want to go and hire a megaphone and announce it in the town park? I don't think the kid working the desk at the bus depot heard you.'

Her friend grinned. 'Sorry. You took me by surprise, that's all. This man drought of yours has been going on so long, I thought you'd hung up your girdle.'

Kylie didn't feel like grinning. At all. But how to explain that to Hannah? She sidestepped the question by looking at the fig toast on Hannah's plate and wondering how dough and fruit and a cooking process could produce something so alluring. Giving in to temptation, she helped herself and smothered it with the butter Vera and Graeme bought from the little dairy down near Dalgety.

'Girlfriend,' she said, in a fair estimation of her used-to-be cheerful self. 'I don't even know what a girdle is, exactly.'

'Me either. I bet Wendy would know.'

'I bet Wendy still owns six of them, all in sensible beige.'

'Did you see her last night at the pub? She was in the dining room.'

'I threw myself out through a verandah door to avoid a confrontation. Fruitlessly, as it turned out. She found me in the corridor.' Found her and delivered the news that Wendy, like Fred, had zero interest in supporting her business.

'You know, she's not always pursed lips and judgement, Kylie. She saw me when we were leaving and came over to say hello. I suspect Eva is having a new pram blanket stitched even now.'

'She saves her judgement for me.'

Hannah squeezed her hand. 'I'm sorry.'

'It's not that I don't want a man and kids and family, Han. It's just ... that's not *all* I want. Why can't I want more? Why shouldn't I want to *be* someone? Have a profitable career that I'm interested in, a mother who doesn't guilt trip me all the time, and a nice ordinary farmer who likes me for me, not for my ability to dish up slippers and meatloaf?'

'An interesting sounding dish, Kyles.'

'The slippers wouldn't be on a plate, idiot.'

'Just checking—culinary skills aren't my forte. And you *are* someone. An awesome someone. It sucks that your mum doesn't understand that. But, Kylie, your mother might *never* understand why you switched out your curling wand for a torque wrench. Guilt tripping you wouldn't work if you let go of the guilt.'

'You're beginning to sound a lot like Marigold, Hannah. One bossy wise owl in this town is enough.'

Hannah chuckled. 'Sorry.'

'You know, Mum being angry with me and tut-tutting my every decision was easier than this new tactic of hers. Lately, I keep getting the sad eyes. Like she did her best but I went and effed up my life anyway. I hope this isn't a precursor to the depression of last time. But you know, I can't remember what she was like before last time.'

'That's because you were a teenager, Kylie, not a psychologist.'

'I suppose you're right.'

'I'm always right, which is why you should listen when I tell you nothing is effed up about your life,' Hannah said firmly. 'And I'm an expert in effing things up, as we both know, so you can believe me. You know what your mother's problem is?'

Kylie had a pretty fair idea, but she wasn't averse to having her idea confirmed. 'What?'

'She tried so hard to give you the life *she* wanted. To be a housewife, to own six beige girdles, to run those slippers to the door when the man of the house came home from his breadwinning and then dish up apricot chicken or meatloaf or whatever—the whole old-fashioned deal. She's so stuck on being miserable about the life she wanted but didn't get, I don't think she knows how to help you to have the life *you* want.'

Kylie nodded. 'I blame my father.'

Hannah raised her eyebrows. 'That's a bit tough, isn't it? The poor bloke's been in the Hanrahan cemetery since you were, what, six?'

'Exactly. If he'd had the common sense to hang around, maybe Mum would have worked out that marriage and dependence haven't been in vogue for decades. Instead, she's put Dad in some shrine because she was forced to take in ironing to make ends meet, and she won't be satisfied until I'm worshipping all that he stood for—sorry, all that she *says* he stood for—right alongside of her. I mean, why couldn't she have turned her ironing hustle into a business? Started a laundromat? Done something other than wring her hands for the last twenty-five years?'

'She's not like you, Kylie. She's not dynamic. You know what she needs?'

Kylie snorted. 'A reality check?'

'No. She needs a man.'

'*Mum?*'

'Yeah. Think about it. What better reality check than having a relationship with an actual man as opposed to a shrine? One who does annoying things like leaves the loo seat up and cuts his nasal hair over the sink and leaves the gunky bits for someone else to clean up.'

Kylie narrowed her eyes at these alarming details. 'Don't tell me there's trouble in paradise already.'

Hannah chuckled. 'Oh, I wasn't talking about Tom. You know he's perfect.'

'Hmm. I used to like you a lot more when you weren't so smug.'

'I know, right?'

Kylie inspected the fig toast crumbs that had fallen onto her saucer. 'That'd be fate giving me the finger, wouldn't it?'

'Your mum hooking up with a bloke before you?'

It had sounded bad in her head but it sounded way worse out loud. She needed a change of subject. 'Should we schedule another women in business meeting? Janine is keen for us to hold one at the library.'

Hannah could switch gears in an instant, thankfully. 'If it's going to be in library opening hours we'll need to give everyone a little more notice so they can organise their work shifts. How did the flyer project go? Any takers?'

'One taker so far. A retro-styled motorbike. It's in my workshop now, waiting for me to start work on it.'

'Who had one of those tucked away needing to be done up?'

Kylie smiled. 'The kisser.'

'This conversation just keeps circling back, doesn't it?'

Vera materialised by their table, clad in a chocolate brown apron and carrying a plate of tiny, glossy tarts. 'You two got room here for me?'

'There's definitely room for that plate of goodies,' Hannah said, sweeping their coffee cups to the side and helping herself to a tart.

'I've been experimenting with my lemon curd,' Vera said. 'This is a taste test, which of course makes them calorie free, so eat up and give me your opinions.'

Hannah was on to her second. 'Pretty sure calories don't work that way, but I like your thinking. My opinion? They're awesome.'

Vera took one herself. 'Graeme gave this batch the thumbs up and you know how picky he can be.'

'The thumbs up? That man was toying with you—they're way better than that. They're amazing. Almost as amazing as the kissing story Kylie has been telling me.'

Kylie rolled her eyes. 'Hannah.'

'Kissing? Who?' said Vera, agog.

If the kissing in the shack had meant nothing, Kylie would have loved nothing better than turning it into a fun story. Girl talk. Instead, she deflected. 'It doesn't matter who, Vera. He wasn't a keeper. And I'm at the stage of life where I'm done with fooling around with anyone who doesn't fit in with the promises I've made to myself about the sort of life I want.'

'I wonder …' said Hannah. 'I wonder if you've become as rigid in your own thinking as Wendy has in hers.'

'What's that supposed to mean?'

'Don't get stroppy, Kylie, but you might need to ask yourself if this promise of yours might be doing more harm than good.'

Vera nodded. 'I agree, and I don't even know what we're talking about. Change isn't always a bad thing, Kylie.'

They didn't understand, either of them, and she *never* got stroppy. Well, not often.

'The only change I need to work on right now is my business plan. Especially now the highway mechanic is offering a free first service to new customers who live in this postcode.'

'Ouch,' said Vera, taking her hand. 'I heard that on a radio advert. Tough to compete against free. I think Maureen was onto something the other day when she said you need to find what your point of difference is and lean into it. Why is having a car serviced by you different from having it serviced down on the highway by Nigel?'

'I'm not a total dick,' said Kylie. 'That's the difference. Not sure I can lean into that.'

Hannah took her other hand. 'You don't have a dick at all,' she said.

CHAPTER
20

Try as he might—and he'd tried pretty hard, for days now—shifting Nick out of Frank's house was proving difficult.

His brother spent the first few days acting evasive and wounded. Nick's high spirits on meeting Kylie had evaporated on her departure and he'd been going for long, unexplained drives in the daylight hours, and moping about the house in the evenings ever since. Whether the high spirits had been an act or the mopiness was—or both—who knew? And where was he driving? And would it kill him to bring home a fresh loaf of bread? When he returned in the early evenings, he'd tinker with the old timber rowboat lying in the long grass by the lake and take it for long, sunset paddles.

Damon spent the days alternately brooding and wondering if it was too soon to call Kylie for another road trip. He could visit the workshop to see how the motorbike was doing, but that could be handled just as easily over the phone. He could make up any number of reasons to go and see the lawyer on estate business, but again … that pesky form of communication, the phone …

The brothers settled into a pattern of avoidance: Damon packed clothes into garbage bags and filled the skip bin he'd hired with old newspapers and broken shade umbrellas and the like, and Nick made himself scarce. On about the fourth day of Nick's stay, he finally made himself useful by starting the ride-on mower (despite Maureen's dire predictions) and tidying up the lawn.

One day his brother happened to be at the vineyard when the paddlewheeler arrived and triggered a break in the stand-off. The scones, the tourists, the prettiness of the boat ... Nick had been agog. He'd not been in celebrity mode, thank god—he'd worn his hat and his glasses and lurked on the periphery—but he'd been interested. The café crew bustled in and out of the back door and down to the picnic area and the smell of scones filled the house, and the place felt, well, *cheery*.

'I love that boat.'

'Yep.'

'So weird to see it here, on a lake, and not on the Murray.'

'So weird.'

'You know its history?'

'Nope.'

'Pity. It'd make a great documentary: *Australia's Historic Waterways, with Nick Johns.*'

Silence, and Damon felt guilt tripped into choking down his first response—*It's not all about you, Nick*—and saying, instead, 'Frank helped restore it. There's some community group in Hanrahan that has its records. He might've even been planning a kids' book on it—I told you he was an author. You should check out his folio. It's on an easel in the shack down by the dock.'

'The snogging shack?'

Damon sighed and it was back to silence again. The café crew had left six scones on a paper plate on the kitchen table with a little note saying *With compliments, from Vera and Graeme. Come say hello at The Billy Button Café.* Nick ate four of them. Not that Damon was counting.

He was absolutely counting.

Nick quit the long drives soon after that and hung around more, and Damon's efforts to send him on his way back to Melbourne became stymied by Nick combating Damon's tactics with tactics of his own.

'Don't you have a home of your own? Why aren't you in it?' Damon would say. 'Frank's house is about to go on the market.'

'Because I'm here, licking my wounds,' Nick would reply. 'Don't *you* have a home of your own? Why aren't you in *it*? And why isn't Frank's house already on the market?'

Good question. One Damon was avoiding reflecting upon because he'd managed to convince himself he had more pressing matters on which to reflect. Namely, the grapes. The bulging, growing, dark-hued grapes, about which he had yet to make a decision. Also, the cupboards. Also, the dog, who was now competing with Damon's shadow to see which could be closest to him at all times.

His inventory of vineyard assets was complete, and he'd emailed it to the realtor, who was now pressing him to fix a date for a photographer, stylist, drone footage, all the other steps that would show he really was doing what he was supposed to be doing, which was selling the vineyard and banking a big fat cheque into his mother's bank account and freeing himself up to return to his actual life in Sydney.

The one he ought to be missing like a phantom limb.

'So. Uncle Frank,' said Nick one morning at the kitchen table. 'You ever hear much about him?'

'Nope. You?'

'No. Makes you wonder what else Mum's never told us.'

'Like … about what?'

'About Dad.'

Johnnie Johns had married their mother, divorced her, then moved to Thailand, where he'd married a Thai woman, had another three kids and pretty much forgotten about his first family other than child support, which had arrived like clockwork until they'd each turned eighteen, then stopped. That's where that story ended.

'We've been adults a long time. Plenty of time for Dad to reach out if he wanted to. It's not as though either of us would be hard to find,' Damon said. 'Especially you.'

'Yeah. True. Still.'

Did Nick *miss* him? Damon barely remembered Johnnie. The person he'd looked up to growing up had been his older brother Nick, and look where that had ended.

'This legal problem,' Nick said, as he hogged the last piece of bread from the freezer and slung it in the toaster. 'The thing that's getting me down and about which you have shown no interest at all.'

This was a grenade if ever Damon had heard one. And the thing Nick didn't know was that Damon's defences were currently at an unprecedented low. He took an experimental breath in, wondering if his lungworm was about to start playing up. All was … clear. For now. Hoping he wasn't shortly to regret the words, he said: 'Let's hear it.'

'You know, this has been written up in the media. You could have tuned in to the fact that your brother was in a state of distress and looked it up at any time.'

Could it be the case that one person already in a state of distress—himself—became blind to another's, in this case Nick's? He waited for some expert commentary to leap forth from Dr Gloom, who was normally only too happy to spring uninvited into any conversation.

Nothing.

So Damon responded the way he'd responded to Nick for years. Dismissively. 'Yeah, I could've, if hearsay and opinion columns actually mattered. Why don't you tell me what's going on?'

Nick sighed. 'There was a sacking on set. It's caused some problems for me.'

Hmm. Damon considered this for a moment, wondering if he should—if he *could*—get involved. He was on time out, after all. Burnt out, possibly nuts, riddled with lung drama. But … the one thing he had reflected on about the law during his early morning swims in the stillness of the lake, was that he'd begun this career with more than a commitment to being the best. He'd begun it with a commitment to making the world a better place. And sitting at a kitchen table gathering information over toast crumbs was not how cases were won. He went to the study and collected a few items, then came back. He laid out a yellow A4 notepad that he'd had in his briefcase and a quite splendid ink pen from Frank's desk drawer. Alfie followed him to the study, stood patiently while he gathered his stuff, then trotted loyally back to the kitchen at Damon's heels. He wedged himself under the table where, no doubt, he would soon be snoring thunderously, while slowly depriving Damon's feet of all feeling.

So far so good. 'What was the show?'

'*I'll Take It From Here.*'

'Never heard of it.' Unsurprisingly. Damon read the news on his phone, avoided the radio and only watched TV when he was desperate. Pub trivia night on pop culture? He'd be scoring a big fat zero. Having a TV teen idol brother did that to a guy.

'It's new. We filmed the pilot last year, then the production team had to shop it around the stations to see who'd pick it up, and the first season started filming a month ago. It's a comedy show. The show regulars perform skits and a special guest, wearing some sort of superhero garb, will fling open a door at a pivotal moment in the skit and announce, "I'll take it from here." From there it's all ad lib and heroic hyperbole, hilarity ensues, et cetera, et cetera.'

Nick said that with zero hilarity. The show itself sounded like an idea that had been done before, but whatever. The bare facts were all Damon needed to give his brother some idea of what he was in for; he didn't need to get dragged into the minutiae. 'What's your role on set and who did you sack?'

'You mean, what *was* my role. And I'm the one who was sacked.'

Damon frowned. 'Wait. *You* are the complainant?'

'If by complainant, you mean the injured party, then yeah. I thought you might've picked that up from my general air of moody introspection, humiliation and defeat.'

'Mate, you have more general airs than a hot air balloon. I ignore them.'

'Like you've been ignoring the fact I told you I need to stay here, and yet you keep trying to get me to leave?'

'I thought you were grandstanding. Besides, you've got a house in Mount Martha.'

'It's currently rented out to an English business coach and his author wife and their three absurdly tall children. I was supposed to be in paid accommodation in Docklands for six months, so renting it out was … prudent.'

All the hassle of putting your stuff in storage and letting out your house for six months? There had to be a reason for that, and the only one Damon could think of wasn't prudence. It was desperation.

'Right,' he said. 'Prudence. So, you're on set filming scenes of hilarity and so forth. What next?' Damon knew he was delivering these questions like they were coming out of a nail gun, but time was money in the legal world. Usually it'd be a solicitor briefing him, they'd run through the facts and contentious issues around a boardroom table or over a phone, Sean would take notes and type them up for the case file, along with links to relevant statutes and case law, and that was when Damon's work really started. Finding an angle, justifying it, then delivering it in court so that anyone with clout—the judge, the jury—agreed with his version of events.

'I was sacked.'

Yeah, that part he understood. 'What were the grounds?'

'For the prudence?'

Man, this was like conversing with a toddler. He was so not cut out to do solicitor grunt work. 'No. For the dismissal.'

'Oh. About midway through filming the first episode, the producers decided they wanted someone who'd appeal to a younger audience.'

Ouch. That must have burned the one-time teen idol.

Nick read his expression. 'I don't care about that. What I do care about is the fact that I had a six-month employment contract, with accommodation, and now I've got no income and nowhere to live until my tenants move out.'

'But you've got savings. You've got the rent money coming in.'

'The mortgage gets the rent money. And savings? Mate, I'm in the entertainment industry. I live from job to job. That's why I was over with Mum in New Zealand—it was somewhere to stay that's a whole lot more comfortable than my car. But you know Mum … she's exhausting. When you rang to let her know you were finding this place a lot of work, I figured why not come over? Lend you a hand with whatever needs doing here, and maybe you can give me advice about this whole sacking thing. Like, was it fair.'

Damon had resented turning up here and discovering the little favour he was doing for his mother was actually a house, a vineyard, a picnic business, a dog. Now—and yes, he knew how contrary it was—he felt unreasonably ticked off at being asked to share. But hang on. Nick *was* a drama queen. His face, even now, was in full woe-is-me deployment; who could trust anything he said?

'Just how broke are you?' Damon said.

'I'm not broke. I just don't have an income for the time being.' Proud face. Maybe even a little bit of pissed-off face.

Damon dug a little deeper to where his empathy—if he still had any—might lurk. 'I'm sorry, Nick.' And he almost meant it. 'Let's start with the employment contract. Do you have a copy? And I can see if I've got any contacts with experience in wrongful dismissal cases.'

'I suppose now might be a good time to mention that the woman who fired me …'

'Yes?' Damon said. There was always a complication, and here it came. 'Just spit it out, Nick. What about her?'

Nick cleared his throat. 'We hooked up a few times. Nothing serious.'

'You mean, *you* thought it was nothing serious.' She'd clearly thought it serious enough to give Nick the boot when he pissed her off. 'I'll need details. Text messages between the two of you, emails, both business and private.'

'That could get ugly.'

'Welcome to the legal world. Ugly is how cases are won, Nick: by dredging up all the little details and knitting them tighter than an ugly Christmas jumper. Ugly is my special skill.' A thought he might need to reflect on later.

His brother sighed. 'Okay.'

'Was it possible she thought there was something serious going on between the two of you?'

'You've got it the wrong way about, Damon. I wanted us to be serious. She's the one who just wanted to fool around.'

'Ouch. You in love with her?' Damon wasn't sure why he'd asked that question. It had just ... popped out. Like the law cared about trivial things like actual *love*. Jealousy, sure. Vengeance, hatred, spurned affections were common motives for crime. But *love*?

And ... why had he been so quick to assume his brother had been the bad guy in the relationship drama?

Nick shrugged.

The silence in the kitchen went on so long even the dog paused his snores. Damon started to realise how very unprepared he was to help his brother. How very unresolved was all his past bitterness about being left behind. Nick was unhappy and all Damon could do was write out banal comments like *age discrimination* on a yellow notepad.

The problem between him and Nick had started when Nick had won the competition. He'd needed to move to Melbourne and their mother wanted to move with him. Damon had said he wanted to stay in Sydney, and they'd just said ... okay. They hadn't even tried to talk him into keeping the family together.

In the end, Deirdre moved to Melbourne with Nick, which was just what Damon had said he wanted. But *had* he wanted it? Sometimes, he reflected, having a smart mouth and a knack for persuasion was as much a burden as it was a gift. He'd been miserable and lost and alone and A) they hadn't even noticed and B) he'd felt obligated to prove to himself and to them that he would never need them ever again.

It took Damon a second to switch out of the movie reel he'd had playing in his head to the present. 'So, you don't know if you were in love or not.' A classic courtroom tactic—echo the witness statement as a rhetorical question, and bloody useful for those moments where you'd drifted off into your own personal baggage and couldn't remember where in heck the conversation was at. 'Wasn't your first song a remake of something sentimental and trite like "Love Is in the Air"?'

'You know, put-down comments like that are always more about the person who utters them than they are about the person who has to listen to them for the five thousandth time.'

Damon sat back in his chair.

Nick wasn't finished. 'You're not the only one who got messed up by the whole teen idol thing. I don't know, all right? Love is complicated. Especially when you grew up in a household where it was thin on the ground.'

The furball compromising Damon's blood supply grunted in agreement, but Damon had no opinion on the matter that he was willing to voice. *A household where love was thin on the ground.* Yeah, he'd thought Dr Gloom would want to file that away for later use.

'I'm right, though, aren't I?' his brother said. 'You can't just terminate someone's employment contract because a viewer survey reckons an actor's not young and hipster enough for a role.'

'Not without compensation, I would have thought, but it will depend on the contract you signed. You may have already agreed to being dumped without notice. I do know that age, disability and injury are not grounds on which an employee can be dismissed. Research will inform us whether or not you have a case.'

'Us?'

'Me and my clerk, Sean. He's a genius on a keyboa—' Crap. Was Sean off limits? The terms of Damon's time out had not been given a framework. 'I'll have to get back to you on that.'

'Okay.'

Okay? Nick's career was at stake and that's all he had to say? Maybe he needed more detail. 'Damages is where the big money is, of course. If they've broken the law, but don't want the bad publicity, then a damages settlement out of court can be the way to go.'

'Whatever you think.'

Damon frowned. It wasn't about what he thought. 'If you're out of pocket, then you should be compensated.'

'A little cash would be welcome. I don't suppose the estate could swing me a few bucks for helping out, could it? I've got experience on the land. And I did just mow the grounds.'

'You've done farm labouring?' The entertainment industry must really suck.

'Yeah. Two seasons on *Celebrity Paddock to Plate*. I can milk a cow, wring a chook neck and braise a coq au vin with crème caramel afters that'd bring tears to your eyes. Made the semifinals.'

'Riight,' said Damon. His bad. The word 'experience' clearly meant something entirely different to his brother. But the crème caramel thing was giving him an idea. 'Did you by any chance bake any scones while you were plating up chook carcasses and harassing the dairy cows?'

'No, but how hard could they be to a man who's mastered the art of cooking custard while smiling winsomely into a television camera?' Smug face again, but this time Damon could see the joke in it. 'Why?'

His inner warning bell was telling him he was probably going to regret this, but ... 'If you fancied a bit of cash, the estate is currently paying a local café to run the picnic business that you saw in action. Some business deal that Frank was involved with that can't be messed with, allegedly. The *Moana* fronts up four afternoons a week, two dozen people alight and expect to eat two or three scones each and be served endless cups of tea or vile instant coffee. They wander about the gardens and the vineyard for an hour or so, then they reboard the vessel and paddlewheel their way into the sunset. The estate could hire you instead.'

'How much cash are we talking?'

Damon plucked a random figure from the air. Four afternoons, ingredients, set up, pack down, whatever. 'A thousand a week.' Generous, perhaps, but it was a nice round number and Deirdre A) wouldn't care and B) was in no place to cavil, since she was the one who had sent Nick here.

'Do we have a food service licence? We needed a food service licence when I played a junkie on the run who slept rough in back of a fish and chip shop. Now I think about it, we probably needed the picture of one not an actual licence.'

'No idea.' But an excellent question, and one which might be the exact leverage Damon needed to dissolve the arrangement with Hanrahan Trekkers. Trap Alfie in the kitchen for an hour or two and the dog hair alone would create an environmental hazard.

'I can do it. When's my first gig?'

Damon chuckled. 'It's scones, jam and cream, mate, every Wednesday, Friday, Saturday and Sunday at two o'clock. I don't think you need to overthink this into a "gig".'

'You've got a lot to learn about stagecraft, Damon. I'll need to inspect the pantry and find a supermarket. How long do you think this paddlewheel deal might last?'

'The contract expires at the end of the Easter school holidays, so that's the worst case scenario. Earlier, if we get an offer on this place and I need to get heavy handed with Hanrahan Trekkers and their contract.'

'If I could live here until Easter, help out, keep the afternoon teas on schedule, that'd be just about long enough to get me out of trouble.'

'I'm not following.'

'My tenants. Their six months will be up in April. I'll have my home back, and it gives me a couple of months to find some work. My legal problem is no longer so urgent.'

'What about the unfair dismissal? The ageism? The girlfriend who signed you up and shagged you senseless and then gave you the flick without a moment's regret?' Damon had to force himself to shut up. Why did he care? Why didn't his *brother*?

Nick shrugged. 'The publicity. For a celebrity fringe dweller like me, bad publicity—dobbing on my own—might mean I never get another job. You've offered me an alternative, which is a happier outcome all round.'

'Mate, a thousand bucks a week for a few piddly weeks is not an alternative to suing a production company. You'd be winning the full terms of the contract. And damages. And—of even greater value—an apology.'

'Apologies don't pay the mortgage.'

They sure as shit don't hurt, though.

'Does pride mean nothing to you, Nick?'

His brother deflected the question. 'Does happiness mean nothing to you, Damon?'

CHAPTER 21

Australia Day sees tractor enthusiasts from all over the country converge on the town of Wombat, in southeastern New South Wales, for the annual tractor pulling competition. Enthusiast and owner Chris says he's found many a treasure in a farm shed which today forms part of his hundred plus collection of vintage tractors. His ride in this year's competition? A Chamberlain Super 90.

Australian Vintage Tractors Digest, *February 2024*

Kylie knew she'd read an article about a Chamberlain tractor recently, and she found it in the second magazine she plucked at random from her coffee table. The starring tractor in the article was not quite the same model as the one living at Snowy River Vineyard, but it hailed from a similar era. The Super 90s weren't in production until 1962, four years after the first Champion 9G trundled off the production line, but both of them were, in her rose-tinted opinion, excellent tractors. Both of them were sturdy. Loyal. Dependable.

She'd almost—almost—invited herself back to the vineyard for a more thorough inspection of Frank's tractor, but that, she'd decided, would have been courting trouble. Even she knew that the Chamberlain wouldn't have been the real reason for her visit.

Tractor magazines had been occupying a lot of her spare time lately. They were her go to in times of stress, and the long overdue talk that Kylie needed to have with her mother? Definitely stressful.

She knew what she wanted to say, but she was letting her resolve to say it cure for a few days like it was enamel paint.

Or she was procrastinating. Maybe a little of both.

Losing it in the pub loo could not happen again. How to prevent that? Well, she either managed to explain to her mother the concept of loyalty and support, or she stopped caring what Wendy did or did not do. They were her only choices.

To prepare herself into a suitably calm headspace, she read comforting articles in her magazine collection on her sofa, nobly withstood the lure of ice-cream from the IGA, and she worked on her business plan, trying to come up with an idea so awesome, so brilliant, it would be the jumpstart her business—her *life*—needed.

She also wrote on her business plan, in capital letters and underlined and surrounded by a border of asterisks, the word FOCUS. Focusing wasn't something that came easily to her, so anything that might get in the way of saving her business had to go. All this heartfluttery stuff with Damon?

Delicious but pointless—it had to stop.

The hand-wringing over her mother's disappointment? Hannah had been right when she'd said the guilt tripping wouldn't work if Kylie let go of the guilt. Easier said than done, but that was what the get-together this afternoon with Wendy was all about.

Worrying about what Nigel Woods was or wasn't doing?

She couldn't control him or whatever freebies he offered. She had no desire for vengeance; that had just been foolish knee-jerk talk. Sure, it had made her feel better in the moment, but vengeance wasn't her style.

Finally, she could procrastinate no longer. She paid her long overdue visit to the sensible brown brick bungalow on Hope Street where she had lived for the first twenty-one years of her life.

She gave a little sigh as she rested her hand on the front gate and surveyed the small, fussily tended garden. It didn't take much of a mental leap to realise the attributes she most admired in tractors were those she most admired in people. An even smaller mental leap was needed to work out that loyalty—or lack of it—was at the heart of the deepest rift that existed between her and Wendy. And Wendy's disloyalty *hurt*. How could her mother not see that?

Nothing had changed since her last visit, which had been an inflammatory occasion that now lived in her memory as The Online Dating War of July 6th. That event had ended with a door slam (Wendy's door, Kylie's slam) and a prolonged communication blackout that hadn't resolved itself until Christmas.

Nothing ever changed at 24 Hope Street, not even the flower varieties planted in the garden beds, where snapdragons and begonias and pansies marched in orderly rows. The front path was painted a dark, terracotta red and the little white wrought-iron gate that separated the path from the verge creaked on its hinge as she opened it, the way it had always creaked.

Even the walk from the town square where her flat was to her mother's house made her feel like she was turning back a clock. She'd walked home this way from school and from the salon when she worked there. She'd snuck home after dark this way after a date on the lakeshore with a boy who her mother hadn't approved of, and she'd ridden a bike home this way from the fish and chip and milkshake shop that had been the go-to hangout in town when she and Hannah had been twelve-year-old tomboys, all freckles and tangled hair and skinned knees.

The windows either side of the front door were large enough for her to see inside, and the place was as neat as one of her mother's sewing pins. About as charming as a pin, too, in Kylie's opinion. The window to the right had scalloped lace curtains that reminded her of doilies. To the left was a bedroom window—her mother's room—where the bed was (of course) tightly made, the laundry hamper would have no more than one day's garments in it, and last night's water glass would have been whisked away and washed within minutes of Wendy having started her day.

Kylie's own bedside table? Her mood softened a little as she reflected on the fact the little flat she rented was just how *she* liked it, clutter and chaos and all. Her bedside table was barely visible under its load: half-read books, automotive and tractor magazines, half-a-dozen not-quite-empty water glasses and teacups, tissues (some clean, some not so), a blister pack of contraceptive pills, pens, hair ties, a pottery bowl overflowing with nail polish bottles, dust that she'd get around to cleaning one day …

She knocked on the door. She had a key she could have used, but when your relationship was as problematic as hers and Wendy's was, it seemed odd to be letting herself in unannounced. Besides, arriving in the guise of a visitor rather than a deeply hurt (and pissed-off) daughter might remind her to hold onto her manners.

'Kylie!' her mother said brightly a few seconds later, as though all was well between them. 'What a darling outfit.'

This was all they had in common now. A similarity in looks and a shared love of fashion. The darling outfit had taken about an hour to choose and resulted in pretty much everything Kylie owned now being out of her wardrobe and scattered across her bed and bedroom floor. Wearing overalls would have been seen as an act of war, however, and since she wasn't here to light up the tension between them with a flamethrower, she'd eventually settled on a frock. Wendy loved frocks. Maybe she'd see it as an olive branch.

'Can I come in?'

'Of course. I was just preparing dinner and there's enough for two. Why don't you stay?'

'Perhaps a cup of tea,' Kylie said.

Kylie waited until the tea had been poured and the how-are-you chitchat was out of the way. She could have launched into the whole disloyalty thing then, but instead said, 'I've been doing some work for a customer on the far side of Lake Bogong. There's a property out there being made ready for sale; it was owned by an older man called Frank Silva. Did you know him?'

'I don't think so.'

'He was pretty chummy with Maureen Plover, apparently. And Kev Jones. Anyway, I found out the other day that he wrote kids' books, and guess what?'

'What?'

'You remember *Noisy Little Tractor*? It was my favourite book as a kid. Frank wrote it! And he lived here all this time with none of us knowing.'

'Fancy that.' Wendy had returned to the vegetables on the kitchen table. Two carrots were being sliced into neat little discs with a large knife that had grown thin from repeated sharpening over the years.

'I wondered if it might still be here, my copy. Aren't there boxes in the attic with some old books in them?'

'Oh, I haven't had a handyman up in the attic in a long time, darling. I don't know what's up there.'

'You mind if I have a look?'

'Up a ladder in your nice dress? Don't be silly. Come back one day in those horrid overalls of yours if you want to climb ladders.'

'Mum, they're not horrid, they're practical.'

Wendy sniffed, but didn't answer, and the carrot discs started getting thinner and thinner.

Climbing a handful of ladder rungs into an attic was such an easy little task, and to be told off for wanting to do it ticked Kylie off enough to launch into the real reason she was here.

'Why do you have to disapprove of everything I do, Mum? Why can't you once, just once, say something like, *Gosh, I'm so lucky to have such a practical daughter.*'

The carrots were done and now the celery stalk was beheaded with a sharp snap. She waited for her mother to say something. Anything. Defend her position, tell Kylie she was mistaken, get *angry*. It wasn't as though Wendy couldn't be practical when circumstances warranted. She could change a lightbulb, dig lint out of a dryer, cut and baste and stitch whole *outfits* … but add in any job that a 'man of the house' might do in the imaginary world in which Wendy Summer lived, and you'd think the apocalypse was nigh. Lawnmowing? Outsourced. A leaky loo or a broken fuse? Same.

'I have not been a lucky woman, darling,' her mother finally said.

Lucky had been a poor choice of word. 'Luck' implied that fate was taking a hand with what happened or didn't happen in life, which was so untrue it was laughable. Hard work was what made life happen. Having goals and sticking with them.

'One dead husband is not the end of the world.' Crap, even as the words left her mouth, she was regretting them. The fact she barely remembered her father did not mean he hadn't been the centre of her mother's world. They'd had a life, a relationship, memories before she was alive, and for six years after she was born. 'I'm sorry, Mum, that was—'

Her mother had abandoned the knife and the vegetables and was now leaning over the cutting board and flinching as though she was being whipped.

'That was too harsh, Mum. I *am* sorry.'

But you know who else had been crying recently? Leaning over a sink in a pub loo as though they, too, were being whipped? She had been. Her, Kylie Summer. And where was Wendy's apology for that?

'Something else that has been harsh lately has been me hearing that you are a customer of Nigel Woods. Do you know what that man is doing? Trying to drive me out of business. Do you know how that makes me feel?'

But her mother was doing what she did best: silently weeping. Kylie was so, so over it. If this had been the first time? She'd have been over there flinging her arms around her mother and holding her, stroking her hair, patting her back. But now? The thousandth time? Kylie had nothing left to give.

She left her at the kitchen table crying into the celery and went into the corridor where the trapdoor to the attic was. The pole and hook was where it had always lived, in an umbrella stand beside an old-fashioned timber writing bureau that had been Wendy's mother's, and Kylie had the trapdoor pushed up and the ladder assembly down in the blink of an eye.

She climbed the ladder and pulled the cord on the single bulb so the small space was lit. There was no headroom, just rafters and silver-backed sheets of insulation above, and ply panelling creating the small storage space in the roof cavity. Her dad had built it. He'd been quite the handyman, according to Wendy. Quite the man. Quite the everything.

The boxes were there, as suspected, their cardboard joins protected from dust and insects by fat stripes of tape. Kylie released some of the vicious *shit* she was feeling by ripping the tape up and the nasty, abrasive, tearing sound was like the nasty, tearing abrasions her heart was feeling. She lifted the flap on the top one and—

Let out a breath.

Oh. Childhood. A sweet time from long, long ago that was so buried under recrimination and difficulty that seeing ribbons from when she'd done ballet down in Cooma for a year or two, when she was maybe eight or nine, felt like she was the carrot, and a knife was slicing her into teeny tiny pieces.

School yearbooks were heaped into another box, and stuffed into a corner was a painted green rock with googly eyes stuck on that she assumed had meant something to her at one point if she'd gone to the trouble of keeping it. Or—another knife cut—her mother had gone to the trouble of keeping it. And at the bottom of the box?

A pile of her old books.

Ragged copies of Dr Seuss books were on the top of the pile (she'd loved the one with the dad and the bicycle), then a May Gibbs hardback that looked unread, a copy of *The Binna Binna Man*, and there, at the very bottom, wrapped in crumpled tissue paper that may once have been white but was now sepia like an old-fashioned photograph, was her copy of *Noisy Little Tractor*.

She opened the cover and saw a handwritten message in what she could only assume was her father's handwriting. *To Kylie. Happy Birthday. Love from Dad.*

She swallowed. This book had been her constant companion after her father had died—a workplace accident involving a forklift and a ramp that hadn't been properly secured—and she'd taken it to school with her and slept with it under her pillow. She'd been six when she'd sat in the front row of the church beside her mother and looked at the long, pale box in which she'd been told, perplexingly, that her father would now live. That book had been a comfort at a time when very little in her world had made sense.

She'd memorised the words, because she'd certainly not been a gifted reader when she was little, and she felt a surge of comfort even now as she turned the page. *Sad little tractor, stuck in the mud, rain falling pit-a-pat and all the farm in flood.*

'Kylie? Come down from there. You're making me nervous.'

'On my way,' she said, but she stayed where she was, turning the pages. The tractor illustrations were as adorable as she remembered: large wheels and a sturdy body coloured a cheerful red. Farm animals lurked in the corners of the pages—a cat, a puppy, even a possum with a bushy tail—and someone, presumably her, had added some childish drawings in coloured felt pen that looked more like scribble than art.

'Kylie?'

Her nose was running, damn it, and her eyes felt a sting in them, but surely that was just the dust. She wiped her face with the clod of screwed-up packing tape she'd discarded earlier and then, book in hand, she plinked off the lightbulb and reversed her way down the ladder.

'Found it,' she said. For some reason she couldn't meet her mother's eyes and the need to get out of there, to be in her flat, with her mess and her tractor magazines, and her business plan surrounding her like castle walls, was *urgent*. 'Gosh,' she said brightly, as she used the pole to lift the attic stairs back into the ceiling, then turned briskly for the door, 'did I love this book when I was little.' No mention of the harsh words spoken in the kitchen. No mention of how the box of mementoes had made her feel like the foundation on which she'd built her life now felt shaky.

Her mother's words were said quietly, but they stayed with Kylie long after she'd let herself out the front door into the summer evening and hurried—bolted—to the front gate.

'No. You loved your dad.'

CHAPTER
22

Escaping to her flat was the only thing on Kylie's mind, but her walk home took her past the workshop and she was nearly there when a shadow flickered ahead.

Why it sent a chill down her spine, she didn't know. She was flustered, probably, that was why. She was shaky. Emotional. She'd had a trip into childhood and she'd made her mother cry (again) and this was no time for freaky bloody shadows to be fluttering in the late evening gloom.

She stopped walking. 'It's nothing. A possum on the powerline,' she whispered. 'A moth in the streetlight.' Bogong moths, after which the lake was named, could be as big as her hand when they were on the wing. It was a little early in the season, of course. They didn't fly down from the rocky crevices of the Snowy Mountains until autumn, and the powerlines and streetlights were on the other side of the street ...

But still. Plenty of reasons for shadows to be flickering about in front of her workshop without her going full horror movie over it.

This was Hanrahan. No-one had been attacked walking after dark here in living memory.

'Don't be an idiot, Kylie,' she muttered.

A car engine roared in a back street, something with a V8 and souped-up pipes, and squealing tyre noise followed. *Hoons*, Kylie thought with a faint smile. She could do with a few more of them on her books; hoons loved spending money on their cars. She was close enough to the workshop to see the light she left on in back spilling through the small window beside the roller door. The old fuel bowser, long defunct, loomed, reminding her of the cenotaph in the town park where the names of the young men lost in the world wars were inscribed. Young men who had probably brought their Model A Fords and Buicks to this very bowser.

'Hello, darling,' Kylie said to Trevor as she passed the skeleton tractor. She had her phone's torch app shining so she could see the lock to insert her key, but from the corner of her eye she noted that there was something wrong with Trevor's profile. She swung the beam of light around and couldn't stop a scream from ripping out of her lungs.

A head—a severed freaking *head*—had been left on what was left of the tractor's metal seat.

༄

The copper, Meg King, was sympathetic, but unhopeful. 'Pity you don't have a security camera out here. I'll check with the businesses across the road in the morning in case they've got one that covers the street.'

'What about prints? Can't you dust … that or something?'

'Fingerprints off a pig's head? That'd be a forensic first for the Hanrahan Police Station. In theory I believe it's *possible* to lift prints from skin with some sort of complicated glue and magnetic powder combination, but ...'

Yeah. Chucking a pig's head out of a hoon car probably wasn't even a crime, even though it felt like one. Even though it felt very, very threatening.

'You pissed anyone off lately, Kylie?'

She was three days late on her tyre invoice, but she doubted a national company hired head chuckers. She and her mother had just had a barney, but what was new about that? Besides, the meat in Wendy's refrigerator wasn't likely to be larger than a pork chop or a half-kilo of mince, and Wendy was probably still standing below her attic door, wringing her hands.

There was only one answer. 'Nigel Woods.'

'The mechanic down on the highway?'

'I've no proof. None at all. But he's mouthed off at me a time or two in the pub on a Friday night. Stealing his customers, he reckons. He's conveniently forgotten I took over the lease here from a mechanic who'd been in business from this location for sixty years. Before Nigel set up shop by a few decades. Recently I did a job on the paddlewheeler and Nigel was pissed off about that.'

'Mouthing off at the pub is a lot different from leaving a decapitated head on your business premises. I've mouthed off at the pub myself a few times when the pie warmer's empty.'

Kylie tried a faint smile; being a people-pleaser was a hard trait to switch off, even when she'd rather be curled in the foetal position on her bedroom floor, crying. 'We've all been there, Meg. But ...'

'Yes?'

'Nigel was here. The other day, after he found out I'd done some work for Dave Ryan when he was out of town. He was talking a lot of weird stuff in a menacing way.'

'Define weird and menacing.'

'He told me he was in some prison up in Queensland and he showed me a tattoo on his arm. A spider web. He seemed to think it would scare me shitless and he was right. It did.'

'An ex-con. That is interesting. I'll run his details when I get back to the station. Now, why don't we work on the practical stuff and check all the locks. Is there a back door?'

'Nope. Just this glass door and then the roller door.'

'Windows?'

'A little one in the bathroom. Louvres that have been there since the moon landing, probably. A kid could probably climb in if the louvres were smashed, but not an adult. Definitely not anyone old enough to drive a V8.'

'Why do you mention a V8?'

'Crap, sorry. I was walking home from Mum's place—she's on Hope Street—and so the workshop was on my way. When I was maybe … there?' Kylie pointed. 'On the corner? I heard a muscle car revving up and taking off at speed. Squealing tyres, the works. I didn't think anything of it, but the timing works. That—head—wasn't there when I left at four, and I was back just after half past six.'

Kylie unlocked the door and spent a minute switching on every light in the place. The vineyard motorbike was where she'd left it, its disassembled engine parts laid out in order on a tarp. Workbench was untouched, as were the little nook where she had a bench seat and magazines, the old dresser up back with the kettle and bar fridge and the tiny office with its backless swivel chair and cheap printer. She inspected every wall, every surface, every inch of which she was bloody proud.

'Am I reading too much into this?' she asked. 'Because I'm feeling quite threatened, Meg. Quite a lot freaked out.'

Meg sighed. 'Look, it could be some random prank. It might not even be directed at you. Doesn't your nephew work here after school?'

'Braydon. He's more of a cousin somewhere along the family tree. He's a sweetheart.'

'Yeah, that's what I mean. Do the girls at school think he's a sweetheart? Because high school girls can get pretty malicious.'

'Not with a pig's head, surely?'

Meg snorted. 'I don't get called out to the high school very often, but when I do, it's usually girls squabbling over a boy. Keyed cars, graffiti, the odd punch-up.'

'But sitting it on Trevor—'

'On *who*?'

'Trevor. The 1955 Massey Ferguson TEF 20.' At Meg's continued look of confusion, Kylie added, 'The tractor. Sitting it on Trevor makes it very personal. I love that thing. It's on my business card, on the signage painted above the roller door. The pig's head was meant for me.'

'I'll go for a drive down to the highway workshop now, see if anything looks out of place, or if it has a car with a V8 and an empty butcher shop bag on the front seat, and I'll drop in tomorrow for a chat with Nigel. But I strongly counsel you to keep your suspicions to yourself and your nearest and dearest at this time—we don't want to escalate whatever problem he has with you.'

'Okay. Thanks.'

'That's your ute parked out front, isn't it? Why don't you drive it home rather than walk. I'll follow you. Maybe you could call someone to stay with you tonight. After a scare like this is no time to be alone.'

'Thanks. I'd appreciate it.'

No way was she calling anyone. Hannah and Tom would be tucked up with baby Eva at Ironbark Station. Hannah's brother Josh would be on daddy duty if Vera was working tonight at the café. Graeme would be with his partner, Alex, her apprentice-cousin Braydon would be with his guinea pig and not even a pig's head scare was enough to drive her to call her mother. *Those overalls have brought nothing but trouble into your life.*

No, what Kylie needed to ensure a good night's sleep was what every single woman over a certain age needed: a dog. Preferably a loan dog, however, because she was pretty sure her flat had a no-pet policy written into the tenancy agreement.

Jane Doe, Josh and Vera's ancient brown labrador? No. Jane was besotted with Josh and would chew through a leash—or Kylie's flat door—to return to him.

Maybe Hannah had a client on holiday who'd be happy to let Kylie dog sit for a night or two ... just until her heart rate settled back into a normal rhythm. Although not much chance of organising that tonight.

After Meg had seen her indoors and proceeded to freak her out even more by looking in cupboards and under beds and out on the minuscule balcony before telling her to lock her door and keep her phone by the bed, Kylie sat by the window, looking down at the empty street below.

'You're being an idiot,' she told herself. She was up a flight of stairs. Hanrahan's cop was a phone call away ... although didn't Meg switch her phone through to the larger station at Cooma when she was off duty? Forty long minutes' drive away?

She looked at her phone. Mental to call him. Ridiculous. Especially since she'd sworn off the heartfluttery stuff and had to focus from now on. But hadn't he said the dog would need a new home?

Stuck out there on the other side of Lake Bogong was no way for Alfie to meet potential new owners. But in town, having a sleepover or two with her? Walking along the foreshore, supervising the workshop? This was the opportunity Alfie needed to help find his forever home.

She tapped on the most recent contact she'd added to her phone before she could overthink it.

'Well, hello, driver.'

That *voice*. Her innards warmed before she could remind them they had no business warming in that useless way.

'Hi.' Her brain had stalled. Ringing had seemed a good idea, but now it just seemed very ... forward.

'How's my motorbike coming along?'

'Er ... good. Listen, I have a favour to ask.' No, that wasn't the way a businesswoman would speak. It certainly wasn't the way Dave Ryan would speak. 'I mean,' she said, starting again, 'I've had a great idea to help you solve one of your problems.'

'A favour or a problem. Which is it really?' he said, sounding amused.

That was the trouble with Damon. He got stuff. On the instant.

'All right, I need a favour. Actually, I need Alfie,' she said in a rush.

'You need the dog?' If eyebrows rising upwards had a sound, then that sound came through the phone.

'I've had ... an incident. At the workshop.'

'Someone spilled a tub of butter and you need Alfie to slurp it up?'

'I wish. No. Um—look, this is going to sound silly, I know, but someone left a pig's head at the workshop and I'm worried that it's a threat to make me close down my business.'

'Bloody hell.' The amused, bantering tone had gone. Damon was brisk. A little hoarse. Intense. 'You called the cops, right? Wait. Does Hanrahan even have cops?'

'Of course we have cops. Well. One cop. Meg King, she's awesome. Only, there was no way to identify who left it, and of course it might be some random prank thing, but ...'

'But you're worried.'

'Yeah. I'd call one of my friends to come stay with me but they've all been incredibly selfish lately and gone and got married and had babies.'

'Those bitches.' It sounded like a forced joke and his voice had a rasp in it she wasn't used to.

In the same spirit, she forced a laugh. 'My thoughts exactly. Anyway … I was thinking, maybe, since looking after Alfie came as a surprise to you and you're looking for a new home for him, maybe he could stay with me for a couple of nights. I can put the word out that he's up for adoption …'

She let the words taper off, aware suddenly that it was now after eight o'clock, that Damon had gone quiet, that she was sharing very personal details—her insecurity and vulnerability, no less—with someone for whom she had complicated feelings but was determined not to act on. At least, not act on again.

'He's on his way,' Damon said.

'But—you can't bring him here, you don't have a licence. I'll come get him.'

'Alone, on this lonely road? After a threat? Women are assaulted every day in this country and the outcome is rarely—'

He broke off, like he was too wound up. Even more wound up than she'd been when she'd seen the abomination befouling Trev. 'Um, Damon?' she said into the silence. 'Are you okay?'

He was quieter now. But firm. 'Nick's still here, hanging around like a bad smell, so he can drive. What's your address?'

She didn't want to be beholden, not really, but oh, the relief. 'Just off the town's park. The flat above the store that sells gifts and books. I'll text the address.'

'Keep yourself safe until we get there.'

CHAPTER 23

Keep yourself safe? What was he, a stodgy hero in some old romantic drama?

Damon would have kicked himself if he wasn't already feeling well and truly kicked. *Feeling powerless is a common consequence of trauma. It results in an overwhelming desire to manage situations involving—*

He tuned out Dr Gloom's expert testimony and headed to the guestroom. He wasn't a hero—far from it—but he'd heard need in Kylie's voice, and that had been enough to get himself moving, but even as he rushed to grab the dog and be out the door, a part of his brain was telling him that if he didn't get a hold of his reactions, he'd soon be texting Kylie to only answer the door if she recognised his secret rat-a-tat-tat.

Dial it down, Damon, he told himself. *Not every drama goes from zero to sixty. Not every drama becomes a crisis that ends up with a bad guy being prosecuted in court.* The memories in his head of testimony from cases of sexual assault or harassment or aggravated burglary or even stalking were from the abnormal range of human behaviour, not the normal.

He found a leather holdall in the mudroom that looked rather like the sort of thing retirees might use to carry around their prize set of bowling balls. The initials *F.S.* were painted on it in flashy gold swirls, but it was something to throw a few overnight things in. Then he found Nick in Frank's room, tucked up amid a half-dozen pillows, watching something on his laptop.

Nick pulled the earphones away from his ears as he looked up.

'You know he died in that bed.'

Nick sprang up off the bedspread like he'd been electrocuted. 'You're joking.'

'Of course I'm joking. I have it on good authority Frank died in the vineyard, a pair of secateurs in his hand.'

Nick deployed thoughtful-face.

'What?' said Damon, who was back to feeling in control now he had a plan. Also, he was very much looking forward to seeing Kylie. He manfully resisted the urge to roll his eyes at his brother's face.

'Just thinking ... that sounds like a great name for a stage play. Maybe I've been wasting my talents singing at RSL clubs and compering reality TV shows. I should write something, Damon. Produce it, even.'

Oh, here it came: steely-eyed charm coupled with deep voice deployment.

'And the Logie for best original screenplay goes to Nick Johns, star of stage and screen, for his breakout hit, He Died With a Pair of Secateurs in His Ha—'

'Yeah, yeah, if only I was interested in hearing more. Can you drive me into town?'

'What, now? Take the car, mate.'

'Me and Alfie. You in the driver's seat. Let's go.'

Nick sighed. 'Why can't you drive?'

'Remember that help you wanted from me? And that thousand dollars cash per week? Well, guess what? They're both conditional on you driving me into town. Right now.'

'You're a bit of a prick, Damon. Did anyone ever tell you that?'

Damon smiled his sharkiest smile. 'Mum was right. We *are* getting to know each other. I'll grab the dog's lead and some kibble. See you out front in two minutes or all deals are off.'

'Can you at least tell me why we're in some mad rush to leave this frankly *sumptuously* comfortable house at this hour of night?'

'It's Kylie. She's in trouble.'

'Oh, *Kylie*. The shack kisser. Who means nothing to you, nothing at all, but who I'm not allowed to talk about or get to know.'

All things considered, not a bad interpretation of the status quo. 'Yeah. Her. Now it's one minute, so move your Logie arse.'

༄

Kylie did not fall into his arms, but Alfie fell into hers, and hero by proxy felt pretty good.

Of course, Alfie didn't quite fall. He'd have crushed anyone he fell on, even a great ox like Nick. But the old boy was pretty pooped after the excitement of a night-time car trip wedged in the back seat of a sedan, the thrill of piddling against a power pole while waiting for Kylie to buzz them through the door off the street, and then the effort of lugging himself up a narrow flight of stairs.

He'd also managed to wind the dog lead around and through Damon's legs, so the pair of them were tangled like spaghetti when they reached the door. When Kylie greeted the dog by kneeling to his level and opening her arms wide, Damon had to unclip the dog's collar from the leash so they didn't both fall over. Alfie lurched into Kylie for a full-body embrace and rested his muzzle on her shoulder and Damon could just stand there and feel ... better.

It took him a moment to recall that he wasn't the one needing to be protected.

'Thank you, Alfie,' she said. 'I hope you like Vegemite toast, because the pantry's pretty bare.'

'I brought kibble,' Damon said, holding up a plastic box.

'And ... Alfie's favourite bowling balls?' she said, eyeing the holdall in his other hand.

'That'd be my overnight bag.'

'Why would you need an overnight bag?'

'Alfie felt his skill set in the security business might be a little rusty, so he suggested I come lend him a hand.'

Her eyebrows indicated her alarm. Or was it surprise? Whichever it was, his ego found it quite deflating. 'Um ... thank you, Damon. Really. But the dog's enough. I'm probably just being silly anyway.'

'Too late—Nick's driven off. Is that the couch? I'll sleep there.' Alarm or surprise, he wanted to quash both.

Kylie was looking stressed. And tired. And emotionally done. Ever since his little adventure into the back alley behind the courtroom, he knew what that felt like.

'Alfie prefers a bed,' he continued, 'so I hope you've got one big enough for him and you. His snoring is only slightly very loud.'

'Um,' she said again. This was not like Kylie, to be short on words.

'I'll boil the kettle,' he said. Listen to him, sounding like he knew what mothering was all about. 'You find your pyjamas and then you can take a cup of tea and Alfie off to bed with you. Try to get some sleep.'

'I didn't know you could boil a kettle, Damon.'

She was making a valiant effort to pretend she was okay, and he could appreciate how hard that was. 'My skill set is many and varied,' he said. 'I'm also incredibly nosy, so it will afford me great pleasure to snoop about your flat and find myself a spare blanket and a sheet.'

She stopped arguing then, and disappeared down the short hallway and through a door while he found a tea caddy, shoved four tea bags in a teapot, and plucked a couple of mugs from hooks screwed into the old dresser that took up more than half of the small kitchen nook. Alfie nudged hopefully at a small flip-top rubbish bin in the kitchen until Damon told him to cut it out, at which point the dog mooched off to sulk.

Kylie reappeared a little while later, hair damp and pulled back in a ponytail, covered ankle to neck in a fluffy dressing gown the colour of fairy floss and navy socks on her feet. He'd found a couple of quilts rolled up and stuffed into the old TV stand where a DVD player might once have lived, back when people had such things, tucked in with a Scrabble board and a well-thumbed copy of *Internal Combustion Engine Fundamentals*, and set the quilts out on a shortish L-shaped sofa.

Hmm. Nobly sacrificing a decent bed for sleeping in a boomerang shape on a lumpy sofa. Maybe this time away from court really *was* turning him into a nicer person.

He sat down.

Kylie sat down.

There they were, seated side by side, all alone, and it was ... pretty darned nice, if you ignored the fact that one of them had been harassed with a pig's head and the other of them had abandonment issues and a catalogue of hideous forensic material living in their brain.

'You've eaten, right?' Kylie said after a silence that might've been construed as awkward. If he was interested in construing things with Kylie. Which he totally was, of course, but which he'd—they'd—well, *she'd*—decided against.

'I'm not here to be looked after. I'm all good.'

'Right.'

Another silence.

'You want to talk about it?'

'No,' she said with a shudder, but then proceeded anyway. What was that like, he wondered? Just ... letting go of the need to feel strong, in control, objective. Just blurting stuff out. 'It was awful, Damon. Just sitting there on Trev, dead and fleshy, and for a second or two, you know, it was like my eyes and my brain couldn't communicate with each other to work out what was going on.'

'Non-medical shock. A typical reaction to sudden fear or anxiety. It releases adrenalin into the bloodstream; blood flows into the limbs; you can hyperventilate. It can take a while for the adrenalin to normalise enough for your rational brain to reassert itself.' Listen to him, spouting off facts like he was Dr Gloom himself. Which, actually, he was. Duh.

She was staring at him with raised eyebrows. 'You seem well informed on the subject. You're not a *doctor*, are you?'

'No,' he said, wondering why he wasn't keeping his mouth shut. His plan to keep himself sane by attending to the property sale then getting back to his actual life in Sydney was starting to seem part of a hazy distant past. 'It's a common defence for drivers who flee a hit and run.' Not for all of them, of course; only the ones who turned themselves into the police as soon as their rational brain was in charge once more. Yeah, he *really* needed to steer this conversation onto a new tack.

'No way. You're a *lawyer*? I thought you were an unemployed, suit-wearing bum living off Mummy's apron strings.'

He chuckled. This making Kylie feel better gig was making him feel better, too. 'Guilty on a few of those charges, Your Honour. Yes, I'm a lawyer. Yes, I own suits, and yes, I'm not engaged in any income-producing work right now. But no, I'm not living off anyone's apron strings. For starters, my mother wouldn't be caught dead in an apron.'

'Unlike mine,' Kylie said. 'Wendy thinks of an apron as professional attire on the same level as surgical scrubs or astronaut suits.'

It didn't sound so bad to him, the idea of a mother who thought being a homemaker was a vocation; who thought being an involved parent was a role that should never end. But, as every barrister knew, context was everything. He hadn't had fresh-baked biscuits waiting for him in the kitchen when he came home from school, or even a mother waiting for him, but he hadn't been smothered, either, or made to feel bad about the career he'd chosen.

'Mum self-diagnosed herself with chronic fatigue syndrome when I was at school.'

This was quite a segue from the pig's head, but he assumed Kylie wouldn't have mentioned it if it wasn't on her mind. He had things on his mind himself, so who was he to cavil?

Then he frowned. 'She diagnosed herself?'

'Yeah. Looking back, that was the starting point of everything going wrong between us. She wanted me to look after her and she's my mum—of course I agreed. Also, I'm an idealist. Also, I'm a people-pleaser. I can remember going to see the principal of Hanrahan High to tell her I was dropping out, and Miss Lawson telling me I was making a mistake, but I took off out of her office like I was Florence Nightingale astride a white stallion.'

He could see it. A young Kylie, all freckles and flyaway hair and fervour.

'Was your mum actually unwell?'

'Oh, yes. For sure. But whether it was what she said it was, I don't know. Could have been depression. Could have been dissatisfaction with her lot in life. I haven't a clue, really, but she did stop coping for a while there. She was so low, she couldn't take in ironing, and the family allowance we got from Centrelink didn't go far, so after I quit school, I started working a few hours a day at the hair salon Mum went to. Sweeping up hair, mostly. Us girls at the salon used to do each other's hair and nails and makeup when there were no customers in. After a few months, Mum started caring about getting up again, and getting dressed and living and so on, but it never crossed anyone's mind that I should go back to school. I enrolled in a beauty course that I could do part time while I worked at the salon.'

'Did you miss it? School?'

'A lot. Not that I was the world's best student, far from it. But I missed my friends, who were all doing fun stuff. I missed netball. Hannah reckons I was Mum's crutch.'

Hannah sounded spot on.

'Hannah's not got a lot of time for Mum, which is a little ironic, considering both of them have had their challenges coping with life. Although, lately …'

'Lately?'

Kylie huffed out a breath. 'Hannah suggested the other day that I was being as rigid as Mum in my thinking, which is so not true. Anyway, whatever; despite everything, I did end up finding my way to a career I do love.'

'Against your mother's wishes.'

'Oh, yes, but it was difficult and not without a truckload of guilt. Even now, when she sighs and moans about my life choices, a part of me worries that one day the sighs and moans will turn into more. Like her not getting out of bed again for months.'

'You're not responsible for your mum's choices, Kylie. You're not a health professional. Nor is your mum, for that matter.'

'You know, you dissect a scenario in a very clinical way, Damon. All fact, all head.'

'Is there another way? Facts tell the story. Facts allow us to make decisions.'

'Maybe that's the difference between you and me. I'm an emotional decision maker. Well, mostly. Since I opened up the workshop and realised I had a lot of catching up to do to live the life *I* wanted to be living, I've had to harden my heart a little.'

'Hence the vow.'

'Yes,' she said. 'The vow: a profitable small business, a farmer, little gumboots in a paddock.'

His ego took that as another blow, and he wished he hadn't mentioned it, because now all he was thinking about was what might have happened between them *without* the vow.

He pulled his thoughts back to where they ought to be focused. 'Speaking of facts and scenarios and dissection, we seem to have digressed.' At least, he had. 'You think the pig head was meant to threaten your business?'

'What else could it be?'

Good point. 'Are you going to talk to the guy? The other mechanic?'

'Nigel bloody Woods.' She sighed a bit when she said it, absentmindedly pulling a little of the quilt over her legs. Something— either the proximity of two totally-not-involved human beings, both running at the required thirty-seven degrees, or his suddenly rampant libido—was making him break out into a sweat. Not a lungworm sweat, which was good, but a vow-breaking sweat, which was bad.

'You want me to crush him for you?'

She was surprised into a laugh. 'What, you want to go swaggering into his workshop and start throwing socket wrenches around?'

He grinned. 'Honey, I love that you think I would know what a socket wrench is. I was thinking more along the lines of a ruthless letter. I don't like to brag—' Totally untrue; he loved to brag, '—but I can draft an epically ruthless letter.'

'Really?' Kylie was grinning too, now, and her face had lost its pinched look. She was leaning back in her corner of the couch and looking at him like they were two people who liked each other a whole lot, and he was trying very, very hard not to think about the fact that they were getting all cosy under a quilt.

'Let's see,' he said, trying to encourage some of his blood to return to his brain. 'I'd start with something benign, just to lure him into reading it, you know? Something like, *Dear Nigel, I do hope you're well. Also, financial ruin and prison time are the least of what will happen in your immediate future if you don't desist from leaving butchered animal products at my client's—*'

Kylie held up a finger. 'Not client,' she corrected. 'I can't afford to be some pin stripe suit-owning lawyer's client. I'd accept "mechanic", since your motorbike is currently in a hundred pieces on my workshop floor. Or "chauffeur".'

'*Apologies ... at my chauffeur-slash-mechanic's business premises. Herein notwithstanding ipso factum whereof, thereunder and therefrom—*'

He stopped because Kylie had thrown a cushion at him. His inanity had worked, however: she was laughing. Hopefully the horror-movie macabre of the severed head had been replaced by the just annoyance of a woman whose business was being harassed.

'That reminds me,' he said. 'Alfie and I found something you might like to see.' He reached into the bowling ball bag and pulled out the bulldog-clipped manila folder that he'd thrust in there at the last minute. Legally speaking, it wasn't his to remove from Frank's house, but he was considering this a borrow and not a breach of Frank's will. 'Here, check this out.'

He opened the folder and laid it over the quilt that covered Kylie's knees. Some of the pages were just words, disconnected gibberish mostly, with the odd heavily scored out sentence. *The paddlewheeler loved her new home on the lake, but she missed the push and pull of the tide.* Other pages were numbered, with paragraphs neatly typed, and notes in the margins like, *This verse to be on a double spread*, or *Dark blues, orange contrast, plenty of white space around the pelican.*

The coloured pages were the real find, and as soon as he'd seen them, he'd realised what Frank had been doing with the easel set up so close to the dock: he'd been working on illustrations for a new book.

Kylie turned the pages in silence while he looked on.

Frank's drawings had charm, and he had a knack for giving personalities to the subjects he'd drawn: the pylons of the dock had the faces of weathered boatmen; the *Moana* looked cheerful and plucky; even the currawong watching from the upturned hull of the old rowboat in the wildflowers by the water had a bossy, imperious flourish that reminded Damon forcibly of Maureen.

'Oh, Damon, what a wonderful find. I hope your mother will appreciate this.'

'Frank's writing collection doesn't go to Mum. He's bequeathed it, and any royalties arising, to the community association.'

'Really? What a shame he didn't have time to finish it. I loved the tractor book he wrote when I was little. Which reminds me,' she said, a little darkly considering she'd just been waxing lyrical over the paddlewheeler drawings, 'I went over to Mum's today and found my copy.' She looked as though she was getting weepy.

'Um, is everything okay?'

She sighed. 'Not really. Mum and I had a barney. As per usual.'

'I'm sorry,' he said.

'Life seemed a lot simpler, once. Back then, I mean, when picture books were important. Childhood. When all you had to worry about was having to eat your carrots and the malicious pranks in your life were limited to the boys at school pulling your plaits.'

She fell silent and he would have liked to have put his arms around her and given her a hug but there was that vow sitting there on the couch between them, very much in the way. Instead, he glanced at the time on the fussy gilt clock hanging above Kylie's kitchen bench and said, 'You know what? I think you need to go to bed.'

He gave her leg a brisk, no-vow-broken pat that was, he thought, as noble and self-sacrificing a thing as he'd ever done. 'A night's sleep will help put everything in perspective.' A maxim that had certainly never worked for him, but he'd said it now, and maybe Kylie would believe it even if he didn't.

She nodded. 'Okay.' She rose to her feet and went a little down the corridor to the bedroom, from where the not-so-faint sounds of Alfie's snores were rumbling like thunder over the Snowies. 'Damon?'

'Yeah?'

'Thanks for being here. I did need a friend tonight. I'm glad it was you.'

An old clock ticked in the courtroom and, behind him, the small group of family members and court reporters were talking sotto voce while the complainant took a seat and was sworn in again.

'Silence please,' called the court officer.

Damon got to his feet. The kid was barely old enough to have his case heard in the adult courts and he'd been crying for most of the morning.

Well, there'd be more of that to come. It was Damon's duty to test the details—the minute details—of the beatings, of the fear, of the intimidation. Why? Because people lied. Had this kid lied? The balance of probabilities was no; the kid had no power, and in Damon's experience, the power imbalance between a bullish personality and a vulnerable one was what enabled the beatings and the fear and the intimidation.

But the law didn't work on probabilities.

'We'll start with the incident which you allege occurred on the morning of eleven October, and I present as Exhibit 410-C a diagram showing the placement of rooms on the eight-floor college accommodation block, with Mr Ravell's room marked and Mr Salander's room marked. I also present Exhibit 410-D, being a police incident report dated eleven October, and Exhibit 410-E, being a series of X-ray images of the complainant's clavicle taken on the same date.'

The medical evidence was the turning point. If Damon had been on the prosecution, it'd be his ace card. In fact, without it, this case probably wouldn't have made it to court, because sexual assault cases were way too common and the DPP had to spread its thin resources where they would have the most impact.

But Damon wasn't with the DPP. He was engaged by the alleged assaulter, who'd borrowed money to fund his defence, because if he lost, he'd be deported. Which made it Damon's job to discredit the medical evidence. Discredit the complainant. Poke holes in his account, suggest a motive of malice, infer unreliability, culpability, drug use, bring up every foolish moment of the kid's short life ... Basically, to make him cry.

He'd certainly achieved that; so far so good. 'Now, Mr Ravell, in your own words, please tell the court what occurred when you returned to your room.'

But actually ... so far, not so good. Because now Damon was the one in the room on the eighth floor of the student accommodation block. Damon was the one being pinned to the wall by a large and fleshy elbow. Damon was hearing his own collarbone crack, and then he was in a black, hot, airless space where the only thing he knew was that if he didn't stop panicking, he would die.

He woke on a giant suck-in of air, every rib straining, every muscle in his diaphragm cramped taut. A hand was on his cheek—not a bullish one, but a nice one. A *lovely* hand, and the contrast between where he'd been just a moment ago and who he was with now was too much.

He kept his eyes closed tight and worked to breathe in a normal way, not a panicked way. That case had no resonance with his life; none. So why was he having to dream it? *Why?*

'Sorry to wake you,' a voice whispered close to his ear. 'I'm going to dawn yoga then to the workshop and I'm taking Alfie with me. Go back to sleep.'

A kiss may have landed on his forehead and then a heavy, furry, slightly stinky snout snuffled at his cheek and ear before turning away. Dog nails clicked over a hardwood floor, but it was a faint, restful sort of sound, and then he heard the snick of the lock as the door closed behind them.

Damon turned his head deeper into the pillow because he didn't want anyone, ever, even the delectable and practical Kylie, to see him as raw as he was this minute. He waited until he'd heard the thud of Kylie's feet going down the stairs to the street level, then he rolled onto his back on the too-short sofa and looked up at the peeling but still ornate plasterwork in the ceiling and considered the three facts which would govern his next decisions.

A) His avoidance strategy wasn't working.

B) He needed to read the articles Sean had emailed him.

C) It was time to call Sean and Warunya and admit that he might have to rethink his commitment to being the best of the best. He was, honest to god, burnt out.

CHAPTER 24

As Kylie rounded the corner and the vista of foreshore and lake in the soft gleam of dawn spread out before her, she realised she was late for yoga. The regulars were already in position on their mats and they reminded her of the sort of art installation you might see in a public park in Melbourne: *Twisted Limbs in Bronze*.

Twisted nosy limbs, she amended a bare minute later, when Val demanded to know if word on the street was true: Kylie had been spotted leaving the Hanrahan Pub with a bloke and did this mean her updated RuRo profile had borne fruit?

She smiled blandly. 'No such luck.'

Marigold was giving her The Look, so Kylie handed Alfie's leash to Kev then dropped down onto her mat and started stretching. 'Still single, still looking,' she said, trying not to dwell on the fact there was, this very second, a sleepy male body taking up space on her sofa.

'Maybe that's your tagline for this week,' said Kev. He winked when she looked up at him, then looked meaningfully at Alfie. Of course he'd know who the dog belonged to; he'd been out there running Irrigation 101 classes, hadn't he? Today Kev was sporting a sheepskin-lined, mustard-coloured corduroy jacket over his shirt that had to have been living in his wardrobe since the 1970s. '*Still single, still looking, still the sweetest girl Hanrahan has to offer.*'

'Thanks, Kev. That makes me sound desperate.'

'Angle crescent lunge,' barked Marigold. Was that even a position? Marigold seemed to be making up her own moves now. The usual soundtrack of cracking ankles and grunts and squeaks of yoga mat rubber accompanied the transition, and Kylie felt the tendons in her legs complain as she twisted over. Marigold hadn't mentioned the pig's head, so hopefully that story wasn't yet doing the rounds. By lunch it would be all over town. *Someone* would have seen the police car pull up outside her workshop and stickybeaked long enough to see the filthy great head despoiling Trevor.

Disinfectant, she thought, as the tendon in her shoulder went twang. *A wire brush. Maybe a full-on blast from the high-pressure hose and a coat of fresh paint on its metal seat would restore Trevor's dignity.* If she was a better daughter, she'd call Wendy, too. And later, after coffee, she might be ready to think about the fact that her growing feelings for Damon felt more worrisome than the pig's head and her fight with Wendy combined.

She blew her hair out of her eyes and focused on the person on the mat closest to the lake. Tall, buff, Royal Australia Navy tracky daks. Just the change in direction her thoughts needed. 'Tom? Is that you?'

'Don't make me talk, Kylie, or I'll fall over. But yes.'

'Since when did you do dawn yoga?'

'Since forever,' said Marigold. 'If you graced us with your presence more than twice a week, Kylie Summer, you'd know that.'

'It's good for my back,' said Tom.

Oh, yes. Tom had spent most of a year with a bit of steel from an oil tanker wedged dangerously close to his spine. Thankfully a closed chapter now.

'The man at the pub, Kylie. He wouldn't happen to be Damon Johns?' Marigold said, long practice allowing her to interrogate her yoga participants while maintaining rigid control over a pose that resembled a clump of spaghetti. 'Don't think I don't recognise that animal.'

'Settle down, Marigold. Yes, but only because I'm doing some work for him.'

'Hmm. You know my opinion and you've chosen to ignore it. I think you and I need to have a chat in my office later, Kylie. About life choices.'

'I didn't know you had an office, Marigold,' Tom said.

'She means the ladies' loo at the Billy Button,' Kylie said. 'That's where she likes to deliver tough love to us lucky ladies.' Although what tough love Marigold thought she needed that she wasn't already getting, Kylie wasn't sure.

'Eagle pose, everyone! Focusing!' Marigold wasn't being lenient today with chitchat.

Cowed, Kylie concentrated on moving through the forms, and before long, Marigold was instructing everyone to baddha konasana. She now sat amidst them, serene, knees out and feet together, which was apparently totally easy for her despite being seventy-something, but was making Kylie think her pelvis was about to break in two.

'Breathing. In, hold, out. In ... hold ... out.'

Kylie did as she was bid, and it was on the long hold, when she'd finally managed to clear the bad clutter from the fight with her mum and the pig's head out of her mind, and allowed some of the good clutter some room—a cosy evening under a quilt with a kind, complicated man—that she had an idea.

A brilliant freaking idea!

Vera—or was it Maureen?—had suggested at their business meeting that Kylie needed to 'lean into' her difference, or words to that effect. The difference being that she, unlike Nigel Woods, was female.

She didn't know why she hadn't had the idea before, because now, this minute, as it took hold, she could see immediately that this was the idea all her list making and brainstorming and worry had been working towards.

She was going to rebrand her business as The Hanrahan Lady Mechanic.

And forget the staid old colours she'd been using on her business cards and on the sign painted above the roller door because those were the colours George Juggins had used when he ran the workshop. She was going pink. Her favourite pink: bright, warm and very, very loud.

What were the negatives? It'd cost her in paint, and she'd need a new teardrop banner to lash to Trev's wheel rims so it could fling about in the Snowy Mountain breeze, but all of those were low-cost items. Doable, if she was frugal, and staggered the purchasing over the next couple of weeks before she staged a big reveal.

Would the pink colour alienate male customers? Only the stodgy ones, surely. Besides, hadn't she read somewhere (possibly on the RuRo app, but whatever) that there were more women in Australia than men?

Business cards were cheap(ish) if she took a trip down to Cooma and had them printed through the stationery store, and Braydon could recolour the flyers he'd designed. She had a vision of the cool girls from the musical *Grease* strutting along in their pink jackets and it put a smile on her face, which must have pleased Marigold, because she uttered one of her rare-as-hen's-teeth compliments: 'Lovely pose, Kylie. Excellent. Now, everyone, last move, you know what to do.'

Marigold's face was turned up to salute the sun, which had now risen over the town's Federation buildings and was burnishing the lake like aged steel. Everyone followed her lead, until her posture relaxed, which was the signal for yoga coming to an end.

'Now,' said Marigold, 'before you all rush off to start your day, if anyone here knows a good architect or draftsman, can you let me know.'

'Are you renovating, Marigold?' said Mrs Northam.

'Heavens, no. It's not for us, it's for the community hall, so an architect or draftsman willing to do voluntary work would be ideal.'

'Why do you need an architect for the community hall?' Kylie said. 'I thought Josh renovated it already for you.'

'It's the archives, pet,' said Kev. 'We've had a few bequests, lately, historical documents and whatnot. From this dog's owner, for one.'

'Did you know Frank wrote books as F.D. Silva?' said Kylie. 'I was amazed when I found out. I still have one from when I was a kid.'

Marigold perked up at this. 'A well-known author, you think?'

'Well, you'd have to check with the librarians, but yes, I think so.'

'I see a fundraising opportunity in our near future, Kevvy,' said Marigold to her husband. 'A literary display. Add that to the bright ideas box when we get home.'

'Hold your horses, pet,' he said. 'We haven't room for the *Moana* records in the hall yet, let alone whatever's coming our way from Frank's collection.'

'And it's been a busy funeral season,' mused Marigold, who, besides yoga, craft nights and her presidency of the Hanrahan and District Community Association, also acted as a celebrant for weddings and funerals. 'Old darlings dropping off the perch willy-nilly. Who knows what other relics from Hanrahan's past will be bequeathed to us?'

'The town hall might need to allocate some space to these archives, Marigold,' said Tom.

'Ugh,' she replied. 'Entrust our precious records to Barry O'Malley? Not in a pink fit, Tom. No, it's up to us. With all this material coming in, we're definitely going to need a fundraiser. A big one. One that will fund a display area so tourists can pop in and see Hanrahan's treasures. Any ideas, people?'

'A long lunch in the grounds of the community hall?' said Kylie. 'The "long" is the length of the table, so you might need to hire some trestles. The high school had one for parents last year and I rigged up a rotisserie for a—' *pig*, she almost said, before realising that it was way too soon to be thinking about pig parts. Luckily the suggestions were rolling in so fast, nobody noticed.

'A craft stall,' said Julianne, who was one of the Wednesday night crafters.

'We can run another trivia night at the pub,' said Tom. 'Hannah and I'll throw in a keg, and Ironbark Station can put up a meat tray for a raffle.'

'A lamington drive,' said Kev. 'We haven't had a lamington drive since the 1980s, my love.'

'Boring,' said Marigold, rolling her not inconsiderable bulk effortlessly to her feet. The sun had been saluted, the chitchat had been had. 'I want to do something different,' she announced as everyone coiled up their mats and prepared to go their separate ways. 'Something glorious. Memorable. *Fun*. Everyone go away and report back to me with a new idea. Off you go, my yoga lovelies:

namaste, chop chop, a new day awaits. Kylie? My office. Don't forget. Make it soon.'

From yoga, Kylie went straight to work, where she kept her eyes averted from Trevor as she unlocked the door. Thank heavens Meg had bagged and tagged the head and taken it away last night. She found a bowl of water and a slice of cheese for the dog, then left him guarding the workshop while she showered in the coffin-sized cubicle in the bathroom. She had a stash of overalls at work, so she changed into a set then hit the greasy green button that lifted the clunky old roller door. The morning sun sauntered in, a welcome visitor.

By seven, she'd said g'day to the first—but hopefully not only—customer. Sandy, the vet clinic nurse, needed an annual service and a wheel alignment on her ten-year-old SUV. By half-past, Kylie had worked out that, happily for Sandy but unhappily for her, there was nothing wrong with the vehicle requiring an immediate and expensive repair.

By eight, she was done with Sandy's car and onto her second cup of instant coffee, starting to wonder if she could scrounge enough coinage from the petty cash tin to pay for a takeaway latte made by the magic hands of Graeme. Too soon, perhaps. More effort was required before she could reward herself with proper coffee, and besides, all this work and efficiency was settling her mood. Normalising things. Well, work life things, anyway.

Why had she kissed Damon on the forehead as she'd left this morning? A dumb move, because now she couldn't stop thinking about it.

Chores, she reminded herself. Plans to pinkify her business. And, as much as she was itching to call Meg King to see if any progress had been made in locating where the pig's head had come from, she decided instead to check her bank account. If any funds had come in, she could start putting her rebrand into motion.

She clicked her way in past the log-in and password only to stare at the screen. What the …?

She wondered if there was a leak in the cylinder she used for welding; perhaps being high on argon caused hallucinations.

She closed her eyes, told herself not to be an idiot—good things *could* happen—then opened them again. The four-figure deposit sitting smack in the good column of her bank account balance was really, truly there. Dave Ryan had paid his bill for the time she'd spent on the PW *Moana*.

She could do more than work on her rebrand. She could get some of the bills rammed onto the spike on her workbench *paid*. Braydon's wages first. He was saving for wheels of his own and he deserved a bonus for those flyers he'd made. The kid was okay, and nothing said, 'Kid, you're okay,' like a little extra something in his pay. Plus, she'd be needing him to pink up her flyer design for a new print run.

Monthly hoist repayment: done. Rent on the workshop: done. Part payment on tyres and the bank balance was back down to a level that meant she'd be on three star mince and carrots for another week, but what did that matter? She loved mince and carrots.

Okay, a total lie. What she did love was not wasting money on frivolous stuff while everything was so precarious.

Sandy was back just after nine to collect her car, which Kylie had washed and vacuumed to ensure the repeat work. Sandy made a fuss over Alfie, who, it turned out, was a Cody and Cody Vet Clinic regular.

'Looks like a new car all over again,' Sandy said. 'I'd forgotten what a treat that was. Thank you.'

'It'll stay that way a little longer if you encourage the boys to not wedge half-eaten pieces of toast into the seat cracks.'

'Oh, crap. Sorry. I thought I'd got the worst of it out.'

Kylie grinned. 'The month-old toast was easy, but there's no getting rid of that teenage-boy-just-played-footy smell.'

'Agreed. You should smell our laundry hamper. It's eye watering.'

'I can imagine.' She wanted to drop the service rate down a little—Sandy was probably only marginally more flush with funds than Kylie was, and she was bringing up three boys on her own since her exes (or Dickhead No.1 and Dickhead No.2, as Sandy liked to call them after a few drinks) took off.

But she'd taken a lot of trouble setting her fees, so why undercut herself? Would Dave Ryan, the most successful business operator in Hanrahan, offer a discount on a lake cruise just because someone was a single mother of three boys?

Hell, no.

After Sandy left, Kylie pulled the remaining bills off the spike. How to order them? By age? By amount? By necessity? Without oil and fuel filters and batteries, she couldn't operate, but was that fair to all the tradespeople who'd extended her credit?

Nope. By age it was. 'Please let none of them be over sixty days,' she muttered.

'Talking to yourself?'

She jumped. Not with fear, but with ... gosh. Something that was totally inappropriate for a woman who'd made a vow the way she had made a vow.

This Kylie–Damon thing, it was unsettling.

But it shouldn't be, so she decided her jump was just an ordinary surprised sort of jump. Nothing to get het up about. No reason at all to be feeling all breathy and tingly and *flushed*.

'Damon,' she said. Did her voice sound weird? It certainly sounded weird to her. 'Hi.' Big breath in, big breath out, just like at yoga, and start again. This was her workspace. She was The Hanrahan Lady Mechanic. 'Come to check on your motorbike and your dog, I see,' she said. Hah! Now that should put the kibosh on this breathy nonsense. Maybe she should pull out her invoice book and charge him for an exhaust manifold or something.

'Sure,' he said, but he hadn't even looked at the disassembled motorbike or paid any attention to Alfie, who was cavorting by his feet, winsomely. He seemed … not his usual cocky self.

'Pretty keen to lay my eyes on you again, too, for reasons that are a little less clear.'

If she'd been drinking water she would have choked. Dancing around their mutual attraction like they had been she was (sort of) cool with, but a direct comment like that? An invoice was in no way going to kibosh this. She grabbed the latest Bridgestone catalogue and fanned herself. She'd have liked to do it surreptitiously, but, turns out, there's no surreptitious way to fan oneself with a hefty, multi-paged tyre catalogue.

Get a hold of yourself, Kylie. He's a bloke, nothing more. An unsuitable bloke.

The hotness, the bad-boyness—*the kindness*, her contrary brain reminded her; he had, after all, come to her rescue last night—all of that was outweighed by the fact *he was not sticking around*.

A little burn seared her heart the way splatter from a weld might burn her cheek if she didn't cover up enough before she lit the torch. Damon was throwing off sparks and she needed to suit up to stay safe.

'You're not supposed to be saying things like that, Mr Johns.'

'I know. Blame your sofa.'

She blinked. 'Um … how is my sofa to blame?'

'Sleeping on a woman's sofa blurs the social lines.'

'Gotta admit, I've not slept on many women's sofas.'

'Me either.' A statement which could be interpreted in a multitude of ways. 'Loving those overalls, by the way.' He grinned, back to his old self, in that way which made her hormones curl into crisps.

She looked down. Her King Gees were utilitarian, grey, spattered with substances that a forensic team would need a week to decode and as shapely as a sack of flour. 'I'm beginning to think you have a fetish.'

'Me too,' he said.

She leant back on her desk chair, crossed her steel cap–booted feet and looked up at him. He was a long streak of handsome and he'd wandered into her life and was now throwing flirty lines her way and it was so not what she'd budgeted for. Just look at her desk planner. Nowhere, not anywhere, did it say, *Waste time flirting with charming out-of-towner.*

'Damon, can I ask you something?'

'Sure,' he said.

'Why are you hanging out with me?'

He looked at her for a long moment and, yep, more welding sparks. More hormone crisps.

'You want the real answer or the socially appropriate answer?'

She watched him leaning casually against the hoist that was ten per cent hers and ninety per cent her bank's and wondered why it was that conversations with Damon always felt so ... dangerous. So ... shifting sand. How many of his previous answers in their many conversations had just been 'socially appropriate', whatever that meant.

'Let's go with the real answer this time.'

'Okay.'

The way he looked at her was definitely part of the danger. He had a way of looking that made a girl feel like she was the centre of all that mattered. Which couldn't, obviously, be true. Ha ha, they'd just met; he was out of her budget. But if it *was* true? Man oh man, that would be something.

Her vow, she reminded herself. She was playing for keeps now, not for fun, and Damon wasn't sticking around, so it was pointless wasting time obsessing about the way he looked at her.

'I guess,' he said slowly, 'part of me—a lot of me, if not all of me, but definitely the shallow part of me, which may be all there *is* of me—finds you very attractive and is thinking why not have a fling with the sexy mechanic chick while I'm killing time in this rural dead end? Because I'd like to. Have a fling. With you.'

She sucked in a breath. Sure, that's what she'd thought he was doing, but hearing it spelled out like that? All bald and charmless and *dead*? Was kind of awful.

'And ... the rest of you? What do you mean you don't know if there's a part of you that's *not*—to use your word—shallow?'

He took his time answering. Alfie, who'd been sniffing around the perimeter of the workshop with keen interest, appeared invested in the answer too, because he sat on his haunches beside Kylie and looked up at Damon, his tail thumping on the concrete floor to mark the breathless seconds between question and answer.

'A week or so ago, I would have said no.'

'And today? What would you say today?'

'Today I'd say it's all getting a little complicated.'

He smiled, but it wasn't a cocky smile this time; it was a little sheepish and a whole lot adorable and Kylie felt her innards go all woozy and warm.

'Basically,' he added, 'I haven't a clue.'

Honesty. Not a currency a people-pleaser like her traded in very often with people who weren't her nearest and dearest. By the sounds of it, honesty wasn't a currency Damon traded in very often, either. Also, he wasn't wrong about the sofa ... it *had* changed their dynamic. She'd worked that out the moment she'd found herself kissing him goodbye before she left. The moment she'd smoothed the dream frown from his forehead.

She needed a minute. She needed a latte. She needed to find coins in her petty cash tin.

'You need a ride home?' she said instead. These revelations required some quiet time. Some reflection. Possibly some tough love from Marigold in the café loo.

'I'm going to drop in to the publican lawyer and see if he's got time for a consult about a few things. Are you right to have Alfie here on guard duty?'

'Sure. If I get a callout, he'll have to come with me. And I forgot to give him his kibble this morning so he's only had snacks from the kitchenette here. He's probably starving.'

Damon cleared his throat. 'Um, maybe not. Was it you who got up in the middle of the night and ate the half-loaf of bread that was on your kitchen counter and shredded the bakery bag into wet slobbery confetti?'

She laughed, then tried to frown as she looked down. 'Oh, Alfie! Naughty dog. Kylie is very, very angry with you.'

'You know, that would almost sound menacing if you weren't stroking his ears while you said it.'

'Well, it *is* hard to be cross with a dog like Alfie. Look at the way he's staring up at me like I'm the love of his life.'

'If you say so. I'm not exactly an expert on the subject.'

'On dogs? Or love?' *Dangerous man, dangerous ground, dangerous question.* The honesty of before must have messed with her. Why else had she asked *that*?

He said goodbye instead of answering. 'I'll see you soon, then? And if you have time later, I'd love that ride home.'

She spread her hands to indicate the empty workshop. 'I have nothing but time.'

He left, and she stood in the sunshine, which no longer seemed enough to counteract all her worries. How had she let this happen? Her feelings for Damon were now ... something.

A big something.

A big, worrisome, needy something that didn't bode well for either her vow or her future.

CHAPTER
25

Stress and perfectionism can create a perfect storm for wellbeing in barristers. On the one hand, the body may react to constant stress and the perceived need for perfection with a panic attack. On the other hand, the mind may react by disconnecting from emotions too difficult to bear. In some cases, a barrister may experience both physical and mental reactions to a heavy and stressful case load and the resolution can only be to reduce that workload and regain some life balance that embraces the world outside of the courtroom.

Anonymous, Barrister 10+ years, www.survivingthebar.dpp.au

A world outside of the courtroom. That sentence alone would have made no sense to Damon a month ago. A year ago. But now? Now he was forced to ask himself what did he even have in his life that was outside a courtroom.

In Sydney? Nothing. Sean and Runya, his closest friends, were both tied up with his court work.

Here in Hanrahan? The place he'd resented coming to but which had somehow burrowed under this skin? Well, he had Alfie to look after. He was caretaker of a few hectares of vines currently burgeoning with grapes and chores. He had a fulsome crush on the local mechanic and, probably the most surprising, he had his brother. Who had asked him a question while they were having their stand-off at the kitchen table that had cut right to the heart of what was wrong: *Does happiness mean nothing to you, Damon?*

Maybe it meant everything to him, and he just didn't know it. Maybe that was his problem.

Tom Krauss opened the side door of the Hanrahan Pub—where a discreet brass plaque announced the office of Tom Krauss, Solicitor, LLB—with a pub apron slung around his neck and a look of harassment on his face.

'Damon! I was hoping for a plumber, but come in. What do you know about leaky loos with thirty-year-old cisterns?'

'Um ... bugger all?'

'Yeah, me too. There's water all over the floor in the men's room and the manager isn't onsite until later. I've turned the water off, so as long as your visit doesn't require me to turn a tap on, we're good to go. Come into my office.'

Once they'd taken a chair each and were face to face over a desk which was as orderly as any Damon had seen, he launched in with the reason for his unannounced visit.

'I wanted your advice on something.'

'Trouble at the vineyard?'

'On another matter. My brother,' Damon said reluctantly, 'is a minor celebrity.'

'Yeah? Which sport?'

Damon grinned. He also relaxed; Tom was his sort of person. 'No, not that sort of celebrity. I wish. Nick won a reality TV singing competition back when he was nineteen and he's carved a career out for himself ever since on stage and screen. A bit of singing, a bit of acting, a bit of hosting. Reality shows, mostly. On an up day he'd swagger on in here and tell you he was a national icon.'

'And on a down day?'

Damon blinked. Tom had done nothing more than turn his words back at him, but, for some reason that would require an introspection he wasn't willing to indulge in, he didn't have an answer.

Fortuitously, Tom filled the gap. 'His surname. Same as yours?'

'Yes. Nick Johns.'

'Never heard of him. But I lived offshore for more than a decade, and reality shows aren't really my thing.'

Yeah. Snap to that.

'So, what's the issue? Is he thinking part of Frank's estate should have gone to him?'

'Nothing like that. He's turned up saying he needs somewhere to live for a bit because the project he was working on terminated his contract prematurely when it was decided he was too old for the viewer demographic.'

'Rough.'

'Not just rough. Illegal. The Equal Opportunities Act, Victoria's Charter of Human Rights, the—'

Damon was breathing too fast. Talking too fast, but Tom, thankfully, didn't notice. Instead, he laughed. 'Mate, you don't need to convince me. So what happened?'

'Nick was sacked. He's in a financial hole because of it, but he's worried if he makes a lot of noise it'll turn the industry against him. Also, there was some shagging involved.'

'Isn't there always? He's probably right about getting the industry offside. No-one likes a dobber.'

A shot across the bows from the ex-naval officer? Damon shot one back. 'An attitude which contributes to the exploitation of Australian workers.'

Tom grinned. 'Steady on, mate. We're not in court now.'

Damon took a breath. 'Sorry. Being argumentative can become a habit.' Along with, apparently, emotional disconnection and panic responses. And in chambers, he and Runya and Sean often worked out the angles of a case by taking turns playing attack or defence. A variation of the six thinking hats system they'd used a hundred years ago when the three of them ruled the Sydney secondary schools' debating competition for twelve golden months before—to use the most accurate summation of all that had gone wrong in the Johns' household—shit got real.

'A useful habit, though. Is that why you're here? To talk the case—or lack of case—over?'

Damon eyed Tom, the country solicitor working out of a pub, who'd apparently spent his morning wrestling with a wrench and a plunger, with renewed respect. Hanrahan kept offering up one surprise after another.

Or—an unwelcome thought—maybe Damon was offering up one biased thought after another. 'Among other things, yes,' he said.

'Litigation gets messy, that's all I'm saying,' said Tom. 'Although why I'm telling a barrister that, I don't know.'

Damon nodded. Tom wasn't wrong, and Nick wasn't wrong, either, to weigh up the pros and cons now he had another income stream and somewhere to pitch his swag.

'Nick's ambivalent about taking it any further, but I think he should understand his legal choices. Have you been involved in any age discrimination in the workplace cases?'

'Age discrimination? No. I have been involved in two unfair dismissal cases, though. An apple picker on a working visa who was turned off for questioning why they weren't being paid superannuation, and a bus driver who was sacked for being grumpy.'

'Grumpy? That's a new one.'

'That's what his termination letter said. "Grumpy with tourists who asked for advice, which has dragged the business down via one-star ratings online", or words to that effect. A sternly phrased letter with a couple of paragraphs of the relevant bit of law they were breaking and the fines attached thereto—'

Damon chuckled. 'Thereto?'

Tom smiled. 'This is the country. Clients love a little legal lingo; it's seen as value. Anyway, the letters did the trick. The grumpy driver got his job back after he agreed to do a workplace behaviour course paid for by the bus company. The apple picker was offered four weeks' pay in lieu of notice, which she was delighted to receive, all outstanding super was paid, and she disappeared up north to make mojitos on Hamilton Island until her visa ran out.'

'Sounds like two happy outcomes.'

Tom smiled. 'Being a country lawyer has its upside. Happy outcomes weren't a regular occurrence in my last job.'

'Yeah? Where were you stationed?'

'Bahrain. The details are classified.'

Damon digested that. If he'd known Tom better, he might have said something, because surely the military had its own share of workplace stress—particularly those in the military who now limped due to a shrapnel injury. But he didn't know Tom better, and the habit of never speaking about any topic without maximum confidence and minimum care was not an easy one to break.

He turned back to Nick's problem. 'Let's say I draft a stern letter but the production company isn't as amenable as your bus company and your apple farm. If they want to argue the matter, court costs can break a person.'

'Well, sure, but only if they're awarded to the complainant. Do you think your brother's making a vexatious claim and would have to pay costs?'

'Not at all. But justice isn't always served in the courtroom, is it?'

'A cynical view for a barrister.'

'A realistic view from someone who—' *plays fast and loose with manipulating juries.* 'A realistic view,' he repeated.

Tom said nothing, but that pen of his went click-click-click in his hand.

Time to end this subject and move on to another. 'I'll talk it over with Nick some more,' he said. 'Try and convince him he needs to stand up for himself.'

Tom put his pen down. 'Sounds to me like you might be missing your day job, mate.'

When he first arrived in Hanrahan, Damon would have had no hesitation in agreeing with Tom on that one. And he did miss his work, but the thought of turning up at court in Sydney and disgracing himself in front of a judge? A jury? A client?

No way. Not before he had found some way to reassure himself he was okay.

Life balance, he could hear Sean and Runya saying to him with their know-it-all faces on.

Okay, so they weren't always wrong.

He turned to the second of his reasons for stopping by. 'On another matter, I notice there's a lot of fruit on the vines. Frank's books show he's harvested in previous years anywhere from the end of February through to the end of April, and transported the grapes to a local winery for pressing and fermenting and bottling. If the property's not sold by then, I'll be needing to organise pickers. Trucks. Packing boxes …' He shrugged to indicate all the other many things he might need to organise but didn't have a clue as to what those other things might be.

Again with the pen clicking. It seemed to be a thinking thing. 'Remind me, when are the *Moana* picnic cruises scheduled to wind up?'

'End of the Easter school holidays, so assuming that means New South Wales school holidays, that'll be the third week of April.'

'Looks like you'll definitely be harvesting, then, doesn't it? That is, if a buyer doesn't come forward. Colin from Elders tells me you've been dragging the chain about getting the sale photos taken.'

Damon made a mental note to scratch Colin from the list of realtors he was willing to sign with. His three-month time out had seemed a life sentence when he'd flounced out of Sydney. Now? Well, time was passing, he no longer found the country quite so oppressive, and he had—stuff—going on that he wasn't ready to say goodbye to. *Like,* he thought with a faint smile, *the owner of one uncomfortable, boomerang-shaped sofa.*

'I wonder …' said Tom.

Damon raised his eyebrows.

'Your mother. How important is the value of this grape harvest to her?'

Damon shrugged. 'Not at all important. She has no idea what Frank's setup is here, and she has no interest in finding out. My mother,' he added, 'is very involved in the Wellington theatre scene. Her life revolves around going to see plays, lunching with the who's who, and mahjong. She's not short of a buck, and neither is her current husband, and she's not a fan of rural life.'

'I've had an idea that might solve your harvest problem.'

'I'm all ears.'

'I was at yoga this morning—'

'With Kylie?'

Tom said nothing, but he said it in a very speaking way. And, damn, if Damon didn't feel a flush running up under his collar. There was that pen again—*clickety click click*—before Tom carried on as though Damon had said nothing at all.

'—at yoga this morning and there was talk of a fundraiser being required for an extension to the community hall. You know the building?'

'I know nothing. About community halls or fundraising or what this has to do with my harvest.'

'Hear me out. The hall is the home of the Hanrahan and District Community Association. It's used for functions, and it houses the town's historical collection, and it's the town's oldest surviving building. It's at the southern end of town, in the park between the esplanade and the lake.'

'Uh-huh.' If the dots were there to be connected, Damon wasn't spotting them.

'The other noteworthy thing about the community hall is that it's run by a woman called Marigold Jones.'

'Large woman? Bossy? Likes to drop in unannounced to people's houses and switch kettles on?'

Tom grinned. 'Oh, yes. Marigold is a tyrant. Indomitable. An organisational powerhouse and indefatigable in her pursuit of greatness for the town of Hanrahan.'

'Lucky Hanrahan,' Damon said drily. 'Her husband Kev has been helping me with the irrigation at the vineyard. Him, I can deal with.'

'Marigold would be able to organise pickers for your grapes and transport of the harvest to whatever winery Frank has used in the past for processing in the blink of an eye.'

Well, this was sounding promising. Why all the community hall talk, Damon wasn't sure, but—

'*If*,' said Tom.

Oh. The publican lawyer had an agenda.

'If?' echoed Damon. He already had one manipulative female in his life—his mother. Did he really need to embroil himself with another?

'If you let her turn the harvest into a fundraiser.'

'So you're suggesting your town tyrant comes out to Snowy River Vineyard with a team to pick the fruit, the fruit is driven away and sold, and she keeps the proceeds for her hall?' That sounded absolutely fine with him. Fruit problem solved. Now all he had to do was keep the vines alive until the harvest, and Kev was already onboard for that. 'Done.'

'Excellent. But … I think she'll be expecting to dress it up with a little more finesse than a truck and a handful of pickers.'

'She can dress the harvest up as much as she likes. If the fruit's picked and gone by the time the picnic business winds up, I don't care what she does.'

Tom was smiling. 'So, we have a verbal contract? I know you hold power of attorney for your mother so can act on her behalf. I can tell Marigold the harvest is hers, to do with as she will, and you don't care how she runs it?'

Damon nodded. 'So long as the grapes leave the premises and the harvest team leave the land neat and tidy for any prospective buyer, then we do, indeed, have a verbal contract.'

'You're being very community minded, Damon.' Tom looked pleased with himself.

'Huh,' said Damon, standing up and shaking Tom's hand. 'That doesn't sound like me.'

CHAPTER 26

Later that day, when Kylie saw Damon returning to the workshop, he was carrying two takeaway coffees and a brown paper sack that, even from this distance, she could tell was from The Billy Button Café. The good news: the man, the cups and the contents of the sack. The bad news? He was not alone.

A woman was walking beside him, one Kylie had last seen standing below an attic trap door, only in a different outfit. Today's was a stiff, smartly ironed, cotton A-line skirt, a scoop necked T-shirt in a colour that could only be described as fuchsia and strappy little sandals that were the polar opposite (footwear speaking) of the steel-capped boots adorning Kylie's feet.

Her mother. Twice in two days. And there was that punch of guilt again, straight to the ribs.

Unfortunately, pretending to be away on a callout was not an option because the roller door was up and she had tools scattered all over the broken concrete pad out front of the workshop. Restoring the sanctity of Trevor's seat had so far involved several buckets of diluted, industrial-strength cleaning solution and an orbital sander to erode whatever pig head vibe might still lurk thereafter. She was now employed in buffing what was left of his old metal with car wax.

Damon and Wendy were chatting. Damon must have said something funny, because her mum laughed coquettishly and tapped him on the arm. As they approached, Kylie could hear the last words of their conversation.

'This is my stop. Nice chatting with you, young man.'

'This is my stop, too.'

He looked straight at Kylie when he said this and gave her a wink, which Wendy Summer—unfortunately—saw. Kylie could imagine the wheels turning in her mother's head: *handsome young man, two cups of coffee, destination* Kylie?

'Hello, darling,' said her mum, walking forward and presenting her powdered cheek so Kylie could kiss it. It seems Wendy had decided yesterday's row had never happened. Surprise, surprise.

'I see you've met Damon.'

'*This* is the man you were telling me about? And you were with him at the pub the other night, too.'

When had she mentioned Damon to her mother? Oh, yes, on the phone, when she'd lied. 'The online pervert. Yes, this is him.'

'Steady on,' said Damon.

'*Kylie*,' hissed her mother. 'Please. I'm so sorry, Damon. Kylie likes to make fun of my old-fashioned ways. When did you move to the district? I don't think I've seen you in town before—'

'Mum, Damon's a customer. That's all. The one related to Frank Silva, the author.'

'Oh. Of course. Well, I'll leave you two to chat.'

'Did you want something, Mum?' Because Wendy was looking a little paler than usual.

Her mother cleared her throat, hesitated, looked around at the scatter of tools on the cracked concrete and the open roller door and—no doubt—her daughter's sweaty face and grubby overalls and general air of harassment, and said, 'It can wait.'

Kylie watched as her mother swished off back in the direction of town, her back ramrod straight, her hair so coiffed and lacquered even the brisk breeze off the lake couldn't shift it, then headed back into the gloom of the indoor workshop. Alfie lifted his nose from the old car footwell mat she'd found for him to lie on as she turned the angle light on above the workbench.

'Does your mother always put such a cranky expression on your face?'

Kylie sighed. 'The answer, of course, is yes. I expect that makes me a bad person. Being charming doesn't come as easily to me as it does to you.'

'Charm isn't my only virtue. I also excel at bringing coffee to cranky mechanics. Latte, no sugar, skim milk, is that right?'

'How did you—? Oh. Graeme.'

'Yes, Graeme. He's quite something, isn't he?'

She accepted the coffee and took a grateful sip. 'He's not the only one who's quite something.' She blinked. 'Sorry. That came out before I could edit it. You're right, that sofa has messed things up.' She rocked herself side to side a little on her wheeled stool. Was this where she 'fessed up? Where she admitted to him (and herself) that her vow was buckling under the strain?

She'd almost forgotten what it felt like to feel wonderful, not worried. Loved, not loveless. Happy. Even fleetingly.

And at the moment, the challenges were heaped so impossibly high, that fleeting happiness seemed more important than all the boundaries she'd placed around herself.

He cocked his head to the side. 'Why the thinking face?'

'I was just thinking about boundaries. My vow, you know. My commitment to this place …' She lifted her hands to encompass the workshop, which represented years of effort and determination and self-belief in the face of a not-small amount of opposition. 'Hannah asked me the other day if I'd become as rigid in my thinking as my mother, just in a different way. Have I—am I—making good decisions or bad ones?'

He didn't seem to have moved, but suddenly he was a whole lot closer. His stubble was rough and uneven after a night on her couch, but his hair had a ruthless part dragged into it. He looked half-city, half-country. It was a look she very much liked.

He held out a hand and she put hers in it, dragging in a quick breath as he dragged her to her feet. 'I can assure you that I am a bad decision,' he said. 'But if your vow is wavering …'

'You know I want a farmer,' she said.

'I own one plaid shirt and don't plan on buying another.'

'Someone nice and ordinary.'

'I'm rarely nice and I doubt I'm ordinary.'

She was going to care about those things, deeply, again and very soon, no doubt. Like within minutes. But not, it seemed, at this very moment.

'I'm tired of thinking about everything I want but don't have. I'm tired of thinking about problems that need solving.'

'You know I'm one of those problems,' he said gently.

'Agreed,' she said. 'I knew that the second I laid eyes on you looking all sulky and flustered in that apron.'

He didn't seem to be listening. Instead, he pulled her close and did some delectable nibble thing in the space between her sensible, fire-retardant work collar and the skin below her ear.

Her last thought, before she clamped her oil-stained hands around Damon's dark and dangerously attractive face, and found his lips with hers, was that she was breaking her vow to herself.

Having a man in her life wasn't the be-all and end-all, the one-way trip to lifelong happiness ... Wasn't that the life lesson her mother had never learned? That no matter how personable or charming or handsome a bloke was, none of that made him suitable? None of that made him reason enough to treat your own dreams and aspirations as less important?

Only, wrapped in Damon's arms, sinking deeper and deeper into the heat, he really did feel like the be-all and end-all.

He felt like love itself.

Which was *crazy*.

She pulled herself away from Damon's hot mouth. 'Wait,' she said.

Damon rubbed a hand through his hair, ruffling that neat city part. 'I was wondering when you'd remember this was a bad idea. If you were waiting for me to remember, sorry—I can't even remember my name at this minute.'

Damon had his back to the workbench and he pulled her into his arms again but left his head resting on the top of hers. She lost her train of thought while she tried to remember what, exactly, had been the handbrake moment. He was rubbing her back, little there-there pats that soothed rather than heated, and her cheek rested on his chest. His heartbeat made her feel teary, suddenly.

What was it about humans—ones like her, anyway—that made them need so deeply?

'Damon?'

'Yes?'

'I think I'm in over my head with this. If we—if this—goes any further, then I'm going to be very, very sad when you go back to Sydney and I never see you again. I hope you can understand that.'

The there-there pats slowed, then stilled. She was being embraced. Gently. Like she was priceless and valuable and important. Oh, he was Mr Charming all right. And he smelled amazing. And she felt like she never wanted to move.

So she did. She pushed away a little and looked up at him. 'You're a complication, Damon.'

He gave that cocky little grin, the one that made her want to climb onto his lap and take up residence.

She eyed him. 'How sure are you that you want to go back to Sydney when all this vineyard stuff is over and done with? That is a question that needs a real answer, not a socially appropriate one.'

'I'm sure,' he said in a low voice. 'Resuming my work in court—it's important. Vital, even. Maybe now more than ever.'

All right, then. Asked and answered. She'd known all this, he'd told her all this time and again, so why the feeling of doom and gloom?

Because you let him get to you. Because you make bad decisions. Because you've got a great big feeling lurking in your heart that you're too scared to put a name to.

She told her inner voice to shut the hell up. This conversation had gone too deep, too quick, and she, for one, was at risk of drowning if she didn't find something light to cling on to. Time to put pathetic, needy Kylie away and remind herself who she was. Kylie Summer. The Hanrahan Lady Mechanic, no less.

She cleared her throat and smoothed her ponytail. 'I've got some orders I need to put in to suppliers, then I can drive you home if you're ready to go. Since we're agreed snogging is the path down which we shall not go, why don't you do something useful and bring my tools back inside,' she said. 'I'll get online and do my orders.'

'Actually, I thought I might catch a ride home on the *Moana*,' Damon said, 'since it's picnic day. Only if you're keen to have Alfie another night, of course. I doubt he'd be welcome aboard.'

'Sure. Whatever.' Was this him giving her space? Or giving her the brush-off? 'Never mind the tools, I can bring those in.'

'I've got it.'

She opened up her battered laptop and started sending emails for oil and air filters and engine mounts. His shoulder bumped hers from time to time as he brought in the bits and pieces she had scattered on the forecourt and asked her where they lived, but the pool of light shining down over her workbench was, she was happy to note, not at all romantic like lamplight, but utterly utilitarian, coming as it did from a double row of fluorescent tubes.

Damon finished his task and prowled around her workshop, stopping when he reached his bike. She glanced at her watch. The *Moana* wasn't due to depart for another half-hour or so, and the dock on this side of the lake was barely five minutes' walk away.

'How do you know how to put it back together?'

She typed *Fuses* into the search bar, chose the ones she needed, then hit *Order*. 'I'm the one who pulled it apart, which is the way I'll remember. Plus, Braydon got some specs off a website for me.'

'Braydon?'

'My cousin's son. Seventeen years old, brimming over with goodwill and hormones. He works here as part of his vocational ed course at school.'

Damon had a hold of the clipboard she'd left in the middle of his disassembled motorbike. 'What's this?'

'Oh, parts. The bike's in great condition, but some things don't last, no matter how carefully they've been stored. Rubber perishes, gauges stick. The filters will all need to be replaced as a starting point, then we work out from there. The tyres have about as much traction left as a baby's bottom, so they have to go.'

'Uh-huh. And you buy these, you rebuild the bike, then you bill the customer?'

'Yep.'

'Seems it might take a long time to earn money that way.'

'Tell me about it,' she said.

'Maybe you should get people to pay you a retainer?'

'A retainer?' She swung around on her chair. 'Like I'm a lawyer? Yeah, that's not the way things are done in Hanrahan.'

He smiled, one of those slow-burn versions that had her heart rate galloping way more than a person who was trying to pay bills had any need for. 'That,' she said, pointing at him, 'that is exactly the sort of look that can't continue.' She turned back to her computer, then jumped when he leant in behind her and rested his cheek against hers.

'I don't want you to be sad, Kylie, when I leave.'

Why, *why*, did he have to smell so good? Why did he have to be some random city guy who was going to blow through town and leave her behind?

She dragged in a lungful of Damon smell and held it for a long second.

'Then stop snuggling up against my cheek, Damon.'

He gave an exaggerated sigh, but moved away. 'Okay, then. But listen, why don't you write me up an invoice for the parts you're ordering and the time you've spent so far disassembling the bike. I like to pay as I go.'

She turned her face so she could see his eyes, the muddy dark blue of them, so close to hers. His lashes were all dark and intense. Thunderstormy.

Since when was she comparing eyelashes to the bloody weather? She took a breath. This—whatever this was that was steaming up the metal fittings in her workshop—needed to come to an end before she lost her grip on what was important and what was just another chapter in the long story of not-quite-right Kylie romances.

The conversation, she reminded herself. *The business transaction.* 'You seriously want to pay as you go?' she said after a long moment.

He smiled, and the crinkles at the corner of his eyes turned him from dangerous to ... nice. Which, somehow, made her heart hurt a little more. 'Seriously.'

'This is not some pity move, is it? Helping out the broke girl from the country who's gotten herself in a little over her head with the flash guy from the city? Because I do not need your pity, Damon.'

'Hey, you're the woman with your own awesome business and a driver's licence. I'm the loser here.'

She chuckled, and if it wasn't totally genuine, it wasn't totally not. A guy less like a loser it was hard to imagine.

'Well, that is true,' she said.

This was better: joking, banter, light-hearted chitchat like when she'd just been the mechanic off the paddlewheeler and he'd just been the hottie stranger in the crumpled suit.

It was false, of course. But it was *better*.

CHAPTER
27

The PW *Moana*'s tickets for the two o'clock departure were sold out, but the skipper gave Damon a wave when he saw him haggling at the ticket office and welcomed him aboard. He found a seat behind the bridge on the upper deck, on the *Crew Only* side of a roped-off area: a varnished timber storage box. He was glad of the sun once the boat pulled away from the dock. The breeze had some chill in it, but the cabin at the back blocked most of it. Over the stern rail, Hanrahan's buildings lost their definition as the paddlewheeler moved away from the gentler curves of the eastern shore and approached the more rugged, mountainous shore on the far side.

'Welcome to the *Moana*,' said the skipper's voice through a speaker lashed to a flagpole. 'And welcome to Lake Bogong. On today's journey, we'll be sharing with you a little history, a little geography and geology, but don't worry, there'll be plenty of time for relaxing and enjoying the scenery. Our cruise to the Snowy

River Vineyard, where we'll be having afternoon tea, will take us just over an hour and, birdspotters, you are in for a treat. Now, I know a lot of you are wondering what a Murray River paddle-wheeler such as the PW *Moana* is doing on a small, landlocked lake up here in the Snowy Mountains, so let me tell you a little bit about this boat. A few years ago, she was a wreck, and—'

Damon tuned out the skipper's voice and turned his face into the breeze. He knew the story by now and he knew that Lake Bogong was the largest of the natural lakes in the region, not manmade like Lake Eucumbene. Rather, it was an old glacial lake, connected to both the Moonbah River and the Snowy River. His late night reading in Frank's study had taught him about the platypus downstream in the Moonbah, and the pelicans and thornbills who called the lake home. He knew about trout, and how snowmelt lifted the water levels each spring. And he knew that endangered mountain pygmy possums nested above the snowline on the western shore.

For a guy from the city who had had no interest in anything beyond city life and his career when he turned up in Frank's driveway, he'd somehow acquired more than a few bits of local knowledge.

And—interesting thought—could it be that all this new knowledge might act as a counterweight to the years and years of expert testimony on difficult subject matter that he'd filed away in his head?

The brain is capable of retaining a great deal of knowledge, consciously and subconsciously.

Okay, he agreed cautiously. No argument there.

For instance, knowledge might be how to differentiate between the blood spatter pattern from a bullet from a handgun fired at close range, versus the blood spatter pattern from a rifle at a range of forty metres.

Not a memory he needed to recall, so he dug a little deeper …

Or, knowledge might be that in a period of drought, it is best to prune all but one cluster of fruit from a vine stem, to ensure one quality bunch rather than three or four bunches lacking in juice, flavour and aroma.

That was better. That was a memory he *liked*. Dr Gloom didn't always have to be so ... *dark*. Could it really be as simple as that? Replace the bad memories with good? Was this what all those articles meant when they talked about life balance?

He closed his eyes and the sun and the movement of the boat and his tiredness from very little sleep lulled him. So many conundrums. So easy to let the steady thrum of the engine and the plish-plash of the giant paddlewheels just ease the conundrums away ...

Instead, he dug his phone out of his pocket and clicked on the meeting link he'd set up. One ring ... two ... and then Sean and Warunya were onscreen, and he realised how much he'd missed them.

'Where on earth are you?' said Warunya. 'In a wind tunnel?'

'Hang on,' he said. He tucked himself into a corner between the upper deck cabin and the storage box. 'Better?'

'A little,' said Sean. 'Did I just see a flagpole? Are you on a boat? I thought you were selling a vineyard.'

'Yes, I'm on a boat. A hundred-year-old paddlewheeler, to be precise. And yes, I'm selling a vineyard.'

'We are *agog*, Damo. Details, please.'

'I'm near a little town called Hanrahan in the Snowy Mountains. It's west of Cooma.'

'Would you call that wine country, Runya?' asked Sean. Warunya considered herself an expert.

'Cool climate grapes, perhaps. I've visited a winery at Tumbarumba, but that's on the other side of the Snowies from memory—'

None of this was germane. 'I have something to talk over with you both,' he said.

'It's fine. Come back,' said Sean. 'We miss you. Also, we miss your income.'

'That's so heartwarming,' Damon said drily. He took a breath. Talking stuff out was so not his natural go-to, but he'd learned a thing or two on the occasions when Kylie was venting about her nemesis and her mother. She'd been upset, she'd talked it out, and then she'd seen her problem from a more considered perspective.

That's what Damon needed. Perspective.

'I read your emails, Sean.'

'What emails were these?' said Warunya.

Damon could see Sean shush her.

'I've also been doing a little research online. There's a few websites—Wellbeing at the Bar is one of them. It's a UK site but the stories on there make compelling reading and I think you guys were right. I was heading for a fall. What you don't know is that I had an episode—a panic attack, I think you'd call it—in the back alley behind the courts, and Judge McMary witnessed it.'

'Crikey,' Sean said. 'What did she say?'

'Nothing. I didn't give her the opportunity to.'

'I'm so sorry, Damon,' said Warunya. 'How are you feeling now?'

'Good. Great, in fact. But I had a dream last night that I was in court, and it didn't end well. The stuff I'm reading suggests that the next steps if I don't want my career to blow itself up into smithereens are to get a little help dealing with stress, and to take longer breaks between cases.'

'You reckon you can do that, Damon?' said Sean. 'You kind of get a bit manic when you're in court. Like your ego and the adrenalin rush and the madness of it all is a drug to you.'

Yeah. That, he'd have to agree with. But ... he'd recently discovered he had something motivating him to try. Someone. But what if it wasn't possible? He needed to know that his idea for change was workable before he clued Kylie in on what he was thinking. She might be able to fool other people with that fun and friendly persona she was always wearing, but he was an expert in reading people. She was as committed to her business and to Hanrahan as he had been to his career in Sydney. He could say nothing to her. Not yet. She was stressed enough already without him adding what-ifs into her life. She'd as good as made him promise not to break her heart.

He couldn't recall ever feeling a responsibility so overwhelming.

'I think you're being very mature about this,' said Warunya. Something she had never accused him of being, ever, in all the years he'd known her.

'It does stink a bit of failure,' he admitted.

'No way. Think of all the times we've read in the law society journals about barristers and lawyers getting arrested for cocaine possession, or for running pyramid schemes, or driving over a traffic island after woofing into a litre of merlot over lunch. I hate to say it, Damon, but that might have been you.'

A hideous thought.

'There's a few inherent problems though.'

'Like what?'

'Work. Life. I've got a mortgage that'd make your eyes water if I told you how big it was. And ... I'm thinking I might like to work remotely when I'm not in court.'

'From the spare bedroom in your terrace house? You'll go mad in there, Damon,' said Sean. 'You love company. You love talking. You're like a show pony who wants to be the centre of attention.'

He chuckled. All that was true, but ... 'I'm going to come back to Sydney to see my bank manager and think about a new plan.

One that works for everyone.' And by everyone, he mostly meant for him, for Kylie, and for Alfie. 'Like, we maybe invite some other barrister to help pay for our chambers, Runya.'

'Wow. This sounds like a lot of change, Damo.'

Yeah, it did. But the biggest change wasn't the bricks and mortar stuff, it was him. Changing his goals. Just a little while ago he'd been all about measuring success by how awesome a barrister he was and how 'fees earned' was looking. Now he'd added another criteria, one that outweighed fees and even his own awesomeness.

Nick had opened his eyes to the concept, but his brother hadn't been wrong. Damon wanted to be happy.

He could see the other side of the lake coming closer, and the old dock was no longer a smudge of charcoal and chocolate; he could see the pylons. The garden. The house that felt like a home. Alfie wouldn't be there for once, since he was still in guard dog mode over in Hanrahan, but Damon decided he didn't totally hate the idea of walking into the house and finding Nick in the kitchen, neck deep in flour.

He was being sentimental, he knew it, but the sun and the steady churn of those paddles ... it was so easy to find himself living in a daydream—actually, it was so easy to find himself living in *Kylie's* daydream—and picturing a tractor trundling through the rows of vines up on the nearby hill, kids in gumboots, Kylie tinkering with a whippersnipper motor on the wooden steps of the snogging shack.

Crazy. But *what if*?

CHAPTER 28

When Kylie needed someone to tell her what to do, and where she'd gone wrong, and why she was so incapable of making a promise to herself and keeping it, she had two choices. One was Marigold Jones. Sure, there was an age gap of more than forty years, but Marigold was blessed with a nosy disposition, a kind heart and, above all, confidence. If you wanted to be told what to do, then a sesh in Marigold's office would most likely sort you out and send you on your way with your life choices for the next decade mapped out for you in technicolour.

But Kylie didn't need a map outlining her next decade; she had that already. What she needed now was someone who understood that, sometimes, your map went rogue; while she'd been distracted by Tall, Dark and Dangerous, her subconscious had gone and added gullies and cliff edges, crocodiles and creeks, and all the signposts that had been so clear and legible were suddenly, inexplicably, missing.

She needed tough love. Emphasis on the love.

Of course, it was nearly eight at night by the time she'd worked this out, so she didn't ring Hannah, she texted.

You still awake?

Depends. If you need me? I'm awake. If a meteor is imminent and life as we know it is about to end? I don't care, I just need sleep.

Need not meteor. Are you in the town apartment or up at Ironbark tonight?

Ironbark.

On my way.

Wait ... before you hit the road, give me a clue. Am I hauling out an ice-cream tub and two spoons? Tissues? Sharpened stakes? A preggie test?

Kylie sniffed. Hannah truly was the best.

A cup of tea and tissues will do.

Sorry my darling. See you soon xx.

Ironbark Station, where the Krauss family had bred stockhorses for more than fifty years, was not an easy drive in winter, but in summer, after a dry spell, the winding mountain road could be traversed in a little over half an hour, and when the scrub and gums abutting the gravel started to thin in the higher elevation, the stars lit the night sky in a way that would have been beautiful, if Kylie had been of a mind to be noticing beautiful things.

Hannah must have been keeping watch for her headlights, because she was coming down the stairs and reaching out to open the driver's door of the ute before Kylie could even get the engine turned off.

'Thank you for waiting up, Han. You're the best.'

'Through thick and thin, my friend. Come on in.'

The homestead where Hannah lived was a lovely old building with wide verandahs and leadlight windows blinking on either side of the open front door. There was more than a whiff of cattle and horse hanging in the air, which Alfie must have noticed, too, because he had his muzzle raised and was taking huge, whuffy snorts of air in. Lights in the distance marked the start of stables and work sheds.

'Let's sit in the kitchen,' Hannah said, leading the way down the central hall and into a huge room out the back. 'The station cook always has goodies in the fridge that we can pilfer. There'll be nothing for you, Alfie, however. Where are your ribs? Where is your waist?' Alfie made no effort to look sheepish.

Kylie sat, then all it took was for Hannah, her best friend since the two of them had matching pigtails and missing front teeth, to flip the switch on the kettle and pick up two floral mugs from the draining board cluttered by baby-feeding paraphernalia, to get the tears rolling.

'Kylie!' Hannah abandoned the teapot prep and wrapped her in a hug.

Kylie pressed her face into her friend's neck and sniffled. There was no point prevaricating. 'I'm pretty confident I'm about to get my heart broken.'

Hannah's hand, patting her back, hesitated before it resumed its comforting rhythm. 'Tall, Dark and Dangerous, I presume.'

'Who else is there in Hanrahan to get heartbroken over?' Kylie said thickly.

'And what does Damon think about this?'

'I haven't told *him*. Jeez, Han. But he's going to leave town any day and I'll never see him again and all my mother's prophecies will come true and I will wither up into an old maid down there on the shores of Lake Bogong.'

Hannah's hand kept patting. 'Not quite a maid, Kylie.'

She sniffed. True. But: 'Small comfort, Hannah.'

'Okay. So tell me all about everything.'

'I knew I liked him. I mean, what's not to like? And yes, the kissing—whatever—is wonderful. But I put the brakes on. A little harmless flirting, and I was clear with Damon that my life plan could not include him because of course I'm saving myself for my farmer and my little gumboot kiddies, but then, boom.'

'Boom? Define "boom".'

'Damon brought Alfie over to keep me company after Trevor was assaulted with the pig's head. That was the start of it. Then today, in the workshop, things got a little—heated.'

'Heated? Wait. A. Minute. So much there to unpack. First a garden shack and now canoodling in a workshop?'

'Does it matter where? Focus, Hannah. Anyway, somewhere in between me first giving Damon the go-ahead, and then telling Damon that all this fooling around had to stop, I knew. It was like I'd just dropped my big spanner on my foot. I *knew.*'

'Interesting. Let's hear more about the pig's head.'

'Hannah. I am in *love*. With a man who is *leaving*. And I am behaving *badly*.'

'Yes, but I've known about that since I saw the two of you making gooey eyes at each other at the Hanrahan Pub. This, however, is the first I'm hearing about Trevor's assault.'

How this was relevant now she had an actual crisis to deal with, Kylie had no clue, but she gave Hannah the speed version. 'Nigel Woods came over to bully me into shutting up shop. I refused. A few days later, I found a pig's head on Trevor.'

'Far out. Did you call the police? Why didn't you tell me?'

'I didn't want to give dickface the satisfaction of knowing that he'd got to me, so I kept it quiet. Meg came over and took the head away. She's making discreet enquiries, or whatever it is police do when they've got no proof about who did what.'

'Right. So, you didn't call me, but you must have called Damon, if he looked after you.'

'I wanted to borrow Alfie. You know, as a security dog.'

They looked at the sprawling beast.

Kylie broke first. 'You're right, of course. Alfie couldn't chase a criminal three feet. I called Damon because … because …'

'Because you've got feelings for him. Wow, it's lucky you came over,' said Hannah. 'It's like I'm the authority figure now on guys and love and relationships.'

Despite her general misery, Kylie found herself snorting. 'Oh, please. You catch yourself one heart-throb and you're the expert?'

'I'm a Tom expert. That's all I'll ever need to be.' Hannah reached over and held Kylie's hands. 'I don't really know how to advise you here, Kylie, other than to be honest with yourself. And honest with Damon. You called Damon after the pig-head incident because you have feelings for him. Ask yourself this: Why did he come over? Could it be that he has feelings for you?'

'Lusty ones, sure,' she said. 'But beyond that?' Kylie let out a sigh. 'I don't know. He's actually quite cagey about his personal feelings. He said to me the other day when I asked him a question, "Do you want a real answer or a socially appropriate answer?"'

'Hmm. That sounds like a big red flag, Kylie.'

'Yes, I know, but he's also got these really watchful eyes that sometimes seem so very sad, but he never opens up about why. And Alfie's got his number—the pair of them seem inseparable. He's funny. He's sweet. He's a little outrageous, you know—he'll say stuff and you think, *What? No-one says that stuff out loud.* He asks a lot of questions and likes to play around with the answers you give him. It's … exhilarating.'

'And what about his life when he's not in Hanrahan? Who's he being funny and sweet and outspoken with then?'

Kylie shrugged. 'I'm not sure.'

'You've been kissing guys in shacks without knowing anything about them?'

'Hey, we can't all fall in love with our older brother's best friend who we've known since infancy.'

'Sorry. I stand corrected.'

'Besides. He has told me a few things about himself. For instance, I know his driver's licence has been suspended for three months after a driving under the influence charge.'

'My. That's quite a recommendation.'

'And I know he's got some sort of work issue, which is why he had time to come up here and sell Snowy River Vineyard for his mother. He's a lawyer.'

'Do a search online. If he's out of work because he's stolen money from a charity and pushed it all through the pokies, you'll find it.'

'I don't know. That seems a little ... stalkerish, doesn't it? He seems keen to get back to his career in Sydney. Like he's got something to prove. He got all, I don't know, intense when he was talking about it. His job means the world to him, Hannah. It certainly means more to him than one semi-broke lady mechanic living in the foothills of the Snowy Mountains.'

'I'm sorry, Kylie.'

Yeah. So was she. 'Oh, and his brother is Nick Johns. Remember him?'

'Get out. "Love Is in the Air" Nick Johns? *Celebrity Bake Off* Nick Johns?'

'Yep. They seem to have some friction between them. Again, I don't know why.'

Hannah reached across the table and placed a hand on her forehead. 'You don't feel like you're deranged with fever. But, Kylie, I've got to tell you, you are sounding deranged.'

Kylie narrowed her eyes at her friend. 'Han, you're missing the point here.'

'Well, clue me in, because so far, all I know is that the guy you've suddenly decided is "the one" sounds not just unsuitable, but also like a bit of a loser.'

'Yeah. That's what he said.'

'Hmm. Pity he's not leaving sooner than Easter.'

'He might do. Depends how quickly he sells the place, I guess.'

'Oh, you are behind on the news. Marigold has concocted some scheme to run a harvest festival around the vineyard's grapes. A fundraiser, where people pick grapes, have a long lunch, listen to music and so on. She wants me to organise a baby animal petting zoo, can you believe. Tom brokered the deal and Damon agreed.'

Kylie blinked. Damon agreed? 'A festival at the vineyard? That does not sound like Damon.'

'Well, we both know Marigold. Do you imagine he had much say in the matter?'

Kylie took a sip of the tea that had been plonked in front of her. 'Maybe my rebrand will bring more work in, then I won't feel obliged to say yes if Damon asks me to chauffeur him again. Alone time together in the ute ... it'll make me weak, Hannah. It makes me lust after dangerous men who aren't farmers and I really, *really*, need to protect my heart from this guy.'

'Okay, you ban all lusty ute time, and you will not be weak. I can text you every day to remind you. Wait, what rebrand is this?'

'You remember how you told me I didn't have a dick?'

Hannah laughed. 'Did I? Well, I wasn't wrong, was I?'

'It inspired me to make a change. I'm going to rebrand my business as The Hanrahan Lady Mechanic, and go full pink. I'm just getting all the bits and pieces as I can afford them, and then when I have everything assembled ... ta-da!'

'Nice. I like it. Only, Kylie ...'

'What?'

'I wouldn't be too sure that more customers will get you out of temptation time with Tall, Dark and Dangerous.'

'Oh? Why is that?'

'I didn't tell you everything Marigold has planned. Kev thinks the festival should include a tractor pull. He's nominated you to organise it.'

CHAPTER 29

Damon could not recall when he'd agreed, exactly, to spending a week tramping around the vineyard with Marigold Jones, but that is precisely how he did spend the next week, which upended his plan for a flying visit to Sydney to reboot his life. Kev was often with them, chattering about impellers and ag pipe, pounds per square inch and water storage, and consequently the vines were getting water and the grapes were getting bigger at almost the same pace as Marigold's harvest festival plans. Kev was also the one to deliver the news that harvesting the grapes didn't mean the work was over: after the harvest, the pruning. 'A month's work for a bloke on his own, son.'

Crikey.

Of Kylie and his dog, nothing was seen for days. He drafted a few text messages, some funny, some profound, but deleted them all before sending. She'd been very clear that she didn't want to be sad, and he was working on being a person who was connected with his emotions, and his emotions were telling him that he needed to respect her wishes.

Nothing in his future at this point in time was definite. He had planning and thinking and therapy to do. Risk Kylie having even one sad moment because of him?

Nope.

Besides, just because he'd rethought his need to be the best and busiest barrister ever born, didn't mean he'd lost any of his competitive edge. When he had something definite to tell Kylie about how he hoped his future would look, he was going to win her back. No question.

One day when he returned from a testing couple of hours in the garden hanging a few kilometres of fairy lights, he headed for the kitchen to report his progress to Marigold, and discovered that while he'd been up a tree at the behest of the bossiest woman in town, gathering scratches and abrasions, Kylie had not only brought Alfie home, she'd also returned the motorbike in full working order.

'She didn't stay?' he said. Unnecessarily. The only ones in the room were him, Nick, Marigold, Kev and one very happy dog.

'I invited her to stay for a meal of grilled cheese on toast followed by my celebrity bake–winning crème caramel, but even that couldn't tempt her,' said Nick. There was just enough pity in his voice to make Damon want to say something cutting about celebrity crème caramel, but his heart wasn't in it. Also, Damon thought, he rated his own charms just a little higher than grilled cheese.

'Sit down, love, and I'll pop the kettle on,' said Marigold. 'Kevvy, pass the scones.'

Nick coughed. 'They're for the paddlewheeler.'

He wanted to say something even more cutting about it being inconvenient and maybe later, but Marigold stared him down and within a couple of minutes tea had been made, scones had been buttered, and they were all sitting around the kitchen table. Damon hunted for a conversational opener that didn't involve him and his disappointment at not being granted a hectic ride through the vineyard on the back of a retro motorbike, his arms firmly wrapped around his mechanic.

'You'll need to send me an invoice for the time you've spent training me on irrigation,' he said to Kev, finally hitting on a suitably boring topic.

'Return the favour sometime,' Kev said.

'Sometime may never come, Kev,' he answered. 'The place is being sold.' He said it like the mantra it had become. He'd already received an off-market offer from some grazier in Queensland who was looking to retire on a few acres a long way away from the punishing Queensland sun. The offer was sitting on the desk in Frank's study, along with the agreement he was yet to sign with the realtor. And was contemplating never signing.

'Return the favour to someone else then.'

'Now, boys,' interrupted Marigold, who had finished her tea and left a half-moon of violent orange lipstick on the rim of the teacup, and was now inspecting a clipboard into which she had various papers wedged. 'This is a perfect opportunity for a little meeting since we're all here.'

This sounded ominous.

'I've drawn up plans for the picnic area by the lake to become the lunch venue. We'll be seating a hundred at long trestle tables.'

Damon nearly lost his mouthful of tea over the table. 'A *hundred*?'

Marigold ignored him. 'I've borrowed a small flatbed truck to take crates of grapes to the winery over at Berridale, and the winery is lending us their crates. They hold about ten kilos of grapes each and they're stackable, so quite easy to manage, and they protect the grapes. I've ordered two cool rooms from the party supply people in Cooma. One for the grapes—they like to be kept cold after they're picked apparently—and one for the lunch supplies.'

Tom hadn't been kidding when he'd said Marigold would be able to organise his harvest in a heartbeat. 'How much are you charging people to come and work here for a day?'

'Darling heart, they're not working. They're having an experience. Grape picking, a lunch of salads and grilled meats and roast vegetables, a wine tasting. *Entertainment*. They're getting an absolute bargain for a hundred dollars a head.'

A *hundred* ... That was ten thousand dollars. Less food costs, of course, which would be considerable, but still. A hefty profit for the community association. 'You really think you'll sell a hundred tickets?'

'I expect to sell out in a few days, Damon. Especially when everybody hears I've managed to secure actor and TV personality Nick Johns to be the MC.'

Damon looked at Nick, who gave him a wink. Not a surprise to anyone at the table but him, apparently.

'He's also agreed to let me put his name on every piece of advertising I can dream up. Which is plenty, as it happens,' Marigold said smugly.

'I thought you were lying low,' Damon said. 'Licking your wounds. Planning vengeance best served cold and all that other stageworthy stuff.'

'I'm seizing the day, Damon. Pivoting with change, going where the fair winds take me, enjoying the moment. You should try that some time.'

Ouch.

Nick grinned. 'Also, Marigold reckons the local journos might come up and do a segment on the festival. You know me, always fishing to get my face on the telly.'

'It'll be a day to remember,' Marigold said with relish. 'The *Moana* is going to moor at the dock with a string quartet playing music from its back deck, portaloos—glam ones, pet—have been ordered, and I thought I'd pop them in behind the big shed. You'll need to get the tractor out of the way of course, but it'll need to be out anyway for the tractor pull.'

'What tractor pull is this?'

'Frank's Chamberlain against a tractor from Dalgety. Fastest tractor to pull a pallet of grape crates over a short distance takes home the Inaugural Snowy River Vineyard Harvest Festival and Tractor Pull winner's trophy.'

He had to chuckle. Really, this woman was quite something. 'You say that as though there's going to be more such festivals, Marigold.'

Now she was winking at him. 'You know, pet, I wasn't sure about you when I first met you, but you're winning me over.'

'Gosh, that's a relief,' he said drily.

'If you get sarcastic with me, I'll just like you even more, Damon. Now, what else is there? Oh yes, I thought we'd open up the boatshed by the dock for people as a space to view Frank's artwork. The festival is the perfect day to celebrate Frank's former career as a much-loved children's author and illustrator. I think we can leverage that to our advantage, and a little birdie told me this is where he kept his paints and easel.'

A little birdie being her new bestie Nick, Damon assumed. She wasn't wrong, though. There was space enough for whatever Marigold had planned, and in the middle of the day, with the old wooden double doors flung open to the sun, the place was quite charming.

'Nick tells me Frank seems to have been working on a new book about the paddlewheeler.'

'Yes. The pages are in the study, waiting to be parcelled up for your community association.'

She tapped a finger against her lips. 'I wonder,' she said.

'You've had an idea,' said Kev complacently. 'Let's hear it, love.'

'I wonder if this might be just the thing to get you back into Maureen's good books, Damon.'

'I'm quite relaxed about being in her bad books, Marigold.' Especially since Nick had taken over the picnic duties.

'Now, don't be churlish. I think you should ask Maureen if she could curate this exhibition space.'

He manfully kept his eyes from rolling. 'Exhibition space' was a very exalted term for the dusty, spider-rich weatherboard shack. 'And you think that'll cheer her up, do you?'

'That, and the opportunity to finish this masterpiece that Frank was working on. We hold the rights, you know, to posthumous works.'

Funnily enough, he did know, what with having read the will and all.

'Once we have Maureen involved with the festival, she'll write us up a ripper of an article in The Hanrahan Chatter, and that, young man, is what we in this town call good publicity.'

Damon sighed. 'All right. Leave it to me. What date is this shindig happening?'

'The last Sunday in March.'

'Better mention the other thing,' Kev said, inclining his head in Damon's direction.

'There's more?' he said. 'A circus tent with trapeze artists? A waterskiing exhibition? Fireworks?'

Marigold rested her hand on his where it lay on the table. 'Kylie's in charge of the tractor pull. She'll need to come out and measure up a suitable space for the event.'

He blinked. 'Great. Awesome. She can come any time. Why all the long faces?'

Her fingers gave his a squeeze, and then: 'She has a condition. She'd prefer it if you weren't here when she comes by.'

Oh. *Oh.*

Marigold nodded, and then she said nothing, but she said it in a very speaking way.

'That sour face of yours is turning my milk into buttermilk,' said Nick as he measured out ingredients.

Damon frowned, then stood up. 'You're hogging the pantry,' he said, which was churlish but easier than answering. 'I need to get into the freezer.'

'Frozen dinner again?'

'Is that a problem?' He wasn't sure why he was feeling so combative all of a sudden. But he was.

Nick shouldered in beside him. 'You want lasagne or beef massaman curry?' Their stash of frozen Billy Button Café meals was diminished, but by no means spent. Thankfully.

'Curry,' he said. Then, after a pause: 'Thanks.'

While the microwave did its thing, Damon sat on one side of the kitchen table with a notebook that he was pretending to write useful things in but was actually just doodling in, while his brother stood on the far side, surrounded by baking paraphernalia. Alfie lay under the table between them.

'What even is buttermilk, anyway?' Nick said after a while. 'I mean, I've seen it in stores, but is it butter? Is it milk? It's a conundrum.'

'Google it,' said Damon unhelpfully. And, it has to be said, snarkily. 'I've got conundrums of my own. The realtor is badgering me, and this festival is turning into such a circus we may never get the place tidied up. Alfie, old man, quit drooling on my ankle.'

The dog yawned, showing him an impressive display of yellowed and ageing teeth, then flopped across the door to the pantry to scratch wistfully at the kibble tin.

Nick dusted flour off his hands and went to the huge oven. 'What about a date variety?' he was muttering to himself. 'Or a savoury cheese scone? And there's always someone asking why we don't cater to the gluten intolerant. Am I overthinking this, Damon?'

'Sounds like a you problem. I'd rather be in court facing a hostile judge than worrying about baking.'

'I'd rather be baking scones than be on stage, worried about being pelted by empty beer cans,' said Nick. 'Or worse, full ones.'

Damon caught his brother's eye and was surprised how easily the snark slipped away as he grinned. When was the last time he'd shared a joke with his big brother? Not for years. Not for nearly two decades. That was a lot of rocky ground right there.

Damon finally got around to working on his Jobs To Do list while he ate. Frank's clothing had been packed up into boxes for the vintage store in town, and was now piled in the garage. The skip he'd ordered was full from decluttering the various sheds and he'd need to get it taken away. Nick had proven to be not totally useless and had mowed and whipper-snipped the vineyard into order, and—

He looked up. Nick had started singing to himself, something about the boys from the bush. Damon had forgotten that, the way Nick sang to himself anywhere, any time. In the car, in the shower, in the bunk bed below him when they'd shared a bedroom as little kids.

'You still do any singing professionally?' he said.

Nick stopped, looked up, then did a fake stagger backwards. His fingers were covered in butter and he had flour all over his shirt. 'Did you just ask me about my *life*, Damon?'

Surely he had asked other questions. He was a nosy, questioning sort of a guy. Although ... perhaps shutting Nick out was part of his whole shutting-out-emotion-to-deal-with-cases mode. His disconnection and his apathy.

'I did,' he said. 'Feel free not to answer.' Possibly not an improvement on disassociation, but old habits and all that.

Nick rolled his eyes. 'Let's see, do I sing professionally? Not often. I scribble down a few lyrics now and then. When I was doing that travel doco about country pubs, I sometimes hopped up on a stool. The whole trip really opened my eyes to country music.'

It was Damon's turn to roll his eyes. 'Everything is a song in country music. "Look, honey, I dropped a mug". That's a song. "I shoulda waited for the steak to cook before I ate it". That's a song.'

Nick opened the utensil drawer. '"I beat my brother with a wooden spoon until he showed some respect". Maybe that could be the title of my next song.'

'You've got to admit, country music does love to be literal. "Home Among the Gumtrees", "Leaving on a Jet Plane".'

Nick grinned. 'Oh, there's way more fun titles than that. I heard one once when I was in Nashville, "You Stuck My Heart in an Old Tin Can and Shot It Off a Log".'

'You're kidding me.'

'I am not. But the point you're missing is that country music loves its literal titles, because they're just a cover to hide the deeper subtext.'

'Like a wooden spoon has subtext.'

'What about being a kid and licking cake batter from a wooden spoon? Don't you wish we could have been those sorts of kids? With that sort of a mum, instead of one who went to work all the time when we were kids and couldn't put us in daycare fast enough?'

Damon frowned. The silence got a little longer and uglier than he'd expected.

Nick scattered flour on the tabletop and upended his bowl onto it. 'Just say it, Damon. Whatever it is you want to say, the reason you've hated me for the last twenty years. The reason you never ask me how I'm doing and never call.'

Damon had a glib comment right there, ready to rip out, as much for laughs as to deflect Nick from the truth, but then Alfie sat on his foot, nearly crushing it. He looked down at the calmly panting face of the big black beast. Words—his go-to, his favourite friends—were not coming.

'You know, I could never work out which it was that you were jealous about: me winning the competition, or Mum coming with me to Melbourne and you being left in Sydney.'

'I wasn't jealous.'

'That is such bullshit. You know how competitive we were about anything and everything growing up. You thought I won Mum when I won that singing contest, and you got vicious about it.'

'Mum's not such a great prize.'

'Well, sure, we know that now, because we're adults. But when we were kids, we didn't exactly have another parent to compare her with, did we?'

'True.'

'Also, just so you know, in case our whole lives are still a competition to you, a career in entertainment isn't anything to be jealous about. It's hard and the self-doubt is crushing, and there's this perception that glory is enough of a reward and gosh darn, you want to be paid *as well*? And—'

'It wasn't the bloody singing contest.'

He hadn't meant to raise his voice. This was the scene in the Thai restaurant all over again, when Sean and Runya were trying to talk to him but there'd been a barnacle in his chest that he just couldn't get out.

There was no barnacle now, thankfully. He realised he could get pissed off with his brother without having some sort of lung-crushing, life-altering event. Good to know for next time.

'It was the move to Melbourne,' he said, but quietly. 'Specifically, it was me not wanting you to go, but you going anyway.'

'No-one was stopping you coming with us. In fact, we begged you to come with us. *I* begged you. You were insistent that you could fend for yourself.'

'Yeah, but you didn't have to agree so easily, did you?'

CHAPTER
30

'She's here.'

Kylie jumped and closed the *Snowy River Star*. Her mind had been a million miles away from the imminent danger of morning tea with Wendy Summer, which she had agreed to in a spirit of pessimism that life couldn't get any worse so why not just get it over and done with. Thankfully, she had a women in business meeting scheduled for lunchtime today in the café's back room (Topic: Goals Aren't Just for Sport) so the day wasn't going to be a total washout.

Graeme gave her shoulder a squeeze. 'I'll bring you an extra big piece of cake, darling.'

Kylie looked up at the café door. Wendy was standing under the awning to get out of the light rain that had been falling since midway through this morning's yoga sesh and she looked ready to host a bridal shower, wearing a peach twinset (that Kylie only felt slightly envious of) with a gathered cotton Liberty print skirt. If

Kylie moved fast, she could be out through the kitchen door and into the back alley before her mum reached the table ... but what would that prove?

Nothing but cowardice, that's what.

Two weeks had passed since Kylie had discovered the miserable truth that she had fallen in love with the handsome stranger she had been determined not to fall in love with, and she'd spent a considerable amount of time in the days since staring listlessly at what she had to show for her life's endeavours to date. She had Trevor. She had her beloved classic tractor magazines. She had friends, she had her business support group, and she had an online dating bio that had attracted not one blip or swipe or ding in months.

No, wait—she was supposed to be listing the things she could feel good about, not the things most likely to make her weep in front of her mother. And there *were* good things. Dave's payment had allowed her to loosen the purse strings a little, she had her rebrand plans pretty much sorted and, whacko, no-one had thrown part of a butchered animal at her workshop recently.

The café was bubbling over with morning patrons, as it pretty much always was. A birthday breakfast was going off in the back room, families—happy ones—sharing platters of Vera's raisin and oat cookies, and helium balloons bobbed about with *Happy 60th* stamped on their sides. Marigold and Kev were up at the counter waiting for a harassed-looking Josh to box up slices of cake. Kylie suspected Josh had been roped in to work by his wife.

So many people. *Her* people. Hanrahan people. And they had worries and squabbles and financial pressures of their own, but they'd managed to put them aside for long enough to enjoy a cup of coffee. How long had it been since Wendy and Kylie had come together and actually *enjoyed* themselves?

Months. A couple of years, probably.

It made her sad. But it also made her tired. And their last argument? About loyalty and betrayal? It had been one of those moments that split families irrevocably.

Wendy was at the table.

'Hi, Mum,' she said.

'Hello, darling,' Wendy said. Her look travelled from Kylie's hair, down her arm to the wristband of her overalls and across her overall-clad chest to her other arm. Yes, Kylie hadn't bothered to change. No, she didn't care that her mother would disapprove. 'I'm so pleased you agreed to meet; I've been just *sick* since we had that little disagreement. Have you ordered?'

'Not yet.' Her mum might feel sick, but not so sick that she was willing to alienate café staff by taking too long to order. Manners before family, no surprise there. Kylie reconsidered the cake she had thought she wasn't going to eat, no matter how delicious a slice Graeme gave her. Four hundred calories of fat and sugar she did not need, but they'd taste great.

Wendy was either avoiding the nitty-gritty or saving it for last. 'That man I met outside your workshop, Kylie! He was adorable. I take back everything I said about that horrible online dating place. The right age, sensible clothes, none of that man-bun nonsense like that last one you were seeing. This one could be a keeper, Kylie. And just in the nick of time, too.'

This was how it always began. Even if her mum meant well, she just said the wrong thing. Always. 'Thirty-one is the new twenty, Mum,' Kylie said. 'Every magazine at every hair salon and lady mechanic's workshop in the Snowy Monaro district says so, so it must be true.'

Her mother's brow creased, and she held out her hands so Kylie could reluctantly rest hers in them. Oh, boy.

'My time with your father was too short, Kylie.'

'I know, Mum.'

'I think, if only he'd been spared a few years longer, you'd have seen …'

Heavens above, was that a tear? 'What would I have seen, Mum?'

'What a family home should truly be like. Maybe then you wouldn't have given up everything we'd worked so hard for to become obsessed with engines by that horrid place. It's driven such a wedge between us, darling. I can't stand it.'

'That horrid place you're talking about was TAFE, Mum. The same place where I did my Statement of Attainment in Lash and Brow Treatments. Which you signed me up for. I like engines. I'm good with engines. What I'm no good at is pretending to be someone I'm not just so you can be happy. What about *my* happiness, Mum?'

It was like her mother was wilfully hard of hearing. 'Our little girl, a mechanic.' Said the way another mother might say, *Our little girl, sentenced to life imprisonment.* Any more of this and Kylie was going to order two donuts as well as cake. Four. A dozen.

Her mother let out a sigh and dabbed the napkin to her eyes like a funeral attendee, and that did it. That totally did it.

'You know, Mum, one day it would be nice to hear you tell me I'm doing something right for a change.'

'Oh, honey,' her mum said. 'I've been looking forward to that day too. That's why—'

'Good morning, darling ones.'

Before Kylie could excuse herself and remember some incredibly important thing she needed to be doing, like stabbing herself in the eyeball with a fork, Graeme was putting coffees they hadn't even ordered on the table. He blew her a kiss as he whisked off back to the counter. Why couldn't Graeme be her mother? They could do DIY projects on weekends in matching tool belts, then paint each other's nails while drinking prosecco and looking up Henry Cavill photos online.

'You finished with this, then?' said a gruff voice near them. A hand—a large, meaty hand, attached to a large, meaty forearm—landed on the copy of the *Snowy River Star* that Kylie had been reading. On the forearm was a spider web that looked horribly, creepily familiar.

'Nigel Woods,' Kylie said, leaning back in her chair a little so she could look up at him, and wishing he wasn't standing quite so close. Annoying to see him in her favourite café, but she'd seen him here before. It was Graeme's fault, probably, for making such excellent coffee. Or Vera's, for baking such delectable treats. 'How incredibly not lovely to see you again.'

'How's business? Can't be too good if you're sittin' here eatin' cake.'

'It's awesome, thanks for asking.'

'I hope you've thought some more about my offer.'

'Your threat, I think you mean.'

'Kylie?' This was Wendy, who'd finally clued into the fact that she wasn't the only one who wished Kylie wasn't The Hanrahan Lady Mechanic. 'Who is this man?'

'No-one important,' Kylie said, refusing to let her eyes drop from Nigel's. They were having some sort of stare-off, which felt very schoolyard and silly, but at the same time felt very life and death. Like, if she dropped her eyes first, he'd have won and could just saunter up the road and take over her workshop whenever he chose.

Stuff that. And stuff him. And stuff being too scared to speak up.

She pushed her chair back and stood. 'Actually, since you are here, Nigel, I have a couple of things I want to say.'

'Yeah? What's that?'

'I know you've been badmouthing me all over town and I'm done with it. I'm done with you coming over to my workshop and getting all in-my-face with your creepy spiderweb bullshit.'

'Pretty brave here in this café, aren't you, girl? We'll see how—'

'Yeah. We will see. Because the other thing I want to say to you is that I've had a lawyer friend of mine do a little research on illegal business practices.'

'Illegal? That's bullshit, and—'

'If I hear of you talking down my business or poaching my customers, you'll be hearing from my solicitor. Tom Krauss.' Tom wasn't the one who'd put this idea in her head; Damon was the one who'd rattled off some jokey letter. But a real letter might actually be a great idea. 'He's right here in town if you want to come spin your spiderweb stories to him, too.'

'Now, there's no need to be like that, Kylie.'

'No, there isn't. There is plenty of room in this district for both our workshops and I don't care how badly you compete with me—I just want you to compete fair.'

'A woman running a workshop is never going to be competition to Autocare,' said Nigel.

Wendy gasped. 'Is this—?'

Kylie ignored her. 'Really? Then prove it. Try to be a better mechanic, not a bigger arsehole.'

Her hands were shaking as she sat back in her seat. The café, she realised, had become as hushed as a theatre at the end of a particularly dramatic scene. Tears were blinding her eyes, but they weren't sad tears. They were tears of freaking *ladypower*.

'Darling,' her mother said in hushed tones.

She couldn't stay and listen to whatever homily her mother felt called on to deliver, so she stood up again, slugged down the rest of her coffee, and picked up her keys.

'Mum,' she said. 'That is an example of the sort of rubbish I have to deal with. It would be so nice if I didn't have to deal with it from you, too. Now, I'm sorry to cut this short, but I have a business to run and my business requires me to make an urgent purchase.'

Her mum was still gaping like a fish. 'What purchase is that?'

'Paint.'

Three hours later, Kylie had two ladders and a trestle set up in front of the roller door, tarps everywhere weighed down with the heaviest tools she owned, and eight litres of the brightest, pinkest paint the hardware store in Cooma could mix for her. Thinking, planning and worrying about what would or would not work was over: assembling her plans was over and her rebrand started today.

She was trying to decide whether to start with Trev or the sign above the roller door when she heard a cooee from down the road. She looked up, and there was Hannah in her vet scrubs, carrying a paintbrush in one hand and a bottle of wine in the other, baby Eva strapped to her front.

'It's a bit early for plonk, isn't it?' Kylie said.

'Graeme called. Said you'd got into a barney at the café. Then—can you believe it—your *mum* called me, Kylie. Said she was worried about you and would I check up on you. And then, because apparently you are the only show in town today, Sandy said she saw you setting up painting trestles when she drove by to take the bloods down to the pathology lab in Cooma, so as soon as I'd finished wrestling a tumour out of a savage little Maltese terrier and feeding my little angel, I did the noble thing. I told Josh he was in charge of all my afternoon cases, and I am here to help.'

'That is so lovely,' Kylie said, giving Hannah and the baby a hug. 'But what about the business lunch? I'll have to give it a miss today, because I'm currently filled with rage and I'm channelling it into action, but—'

'We've rescheduled, and Vera's going to come here once the lunch rush dies down. She says she's got a very expensive pastry brush that she is prepared to sacrifice if that's what's required.'

'You guys,' said Kylie. 'You're the best.'

'Yes. Yes, we are. Now, give me a job.'

'Can you cover the edges of the roller door with masking tape with a baby strapped to your chest?'

'I'm a woman. I can do anything.'

That was what Kylie needed to hear. She was a woman, too, which meant she could do anything. Even survive a broken heart. In her head, Damon and her business had become opposite weights on a pendulum somehow, a kind of either/or scenario, the logic of which was telling her that she would survive Damon leaving if, but only if, her business survived.

So that's what had to happen.

Ready. Set. Paint.

CHAPTER
31

The bedroom Damon slept in at Uncle Frank's house was quiet and dark and the thudding of rain on the roof overhead was a lullaby. Dawn hadn't bothered turning up yet and Damon would know, he'd been awake for hours, listening to the patter of rain become a drumroll as his watch ticked away the hours. He'd tried to divert himself from a sleepless night of reflection in every way possible. Chamomile tea had been a nope. Sudoku on his phone also a nope. He'd spent a couple of hours reading a well-thumbed copy of *The Small Scale Vintner's Handbook* and it lay beside him now on the bed, splayed pages down like a dead bird, while lines of it now lived in his head.

> *In a humid environment, trim the stems of your vine so that air can circulate freely around the grape clusters. In a hot, dry environment, encourage the stems to form an umbrella shape cascading up and over the fruit to provide shade and shelter.*

According to the handbook, he ought to be getting out of bed, anyway. The rain overnight had chased his irrigation worries away, but, according to the dog ear he'd bent on page 46, he had mulch to turn and fertiliser to spread. He also had weeds to pull and growth to snip, according to the dog ears at pages 53 and 87. Maybe the rain would ease soon, and if he spent the day wearing himself out in the vineyard he'd be able to put the image of Kylie's sad face out of his mind.

He considered texting. Something fun. Or profound. Or nothing. Should he? *Shouldn't he?* Damn it. He grabbed his phone and typed in a message.

Heya. Alfie says thanks for having him to stay. Also, please come over anytime for the tractor-pull stuff. And for any reason. I promise no hugging. I can make myself scarce too if you want :(Damon.

Friendly but not too friendly. Sad but not too sad.

He lay on his back looking up at the decorative plasterwork that surrounded the light fixture, and thought about how much self-reflection sucked. After he'd exhausted all interest in plaster rosettes, he sat up and brought his feet around so they thumped on the floor, and waited for the comatose labrador, who now apparently shared his bed, to notice.

The dog let out a groan, curved his back and stretched his four legs, which Damon had learned was part of Alfie's morning routine. 'Big stretch,' he said automatically. It was a dog ownership thing, apparently. Who knew?

'How about a walk, mate? Or a swim in the rain?'

Alfie flopped onto the floor and came around the bed to sit and look lovingly up at him, and the churn in Damon's stomach from wondering how on earth he was going to reboot his career in a part-time, fly-in, fly-out way and still be able to afford the home he wanted, melted. Dogs. If he'd known how useful they were at soaking up negative emotion, he'd have gone with a different career. Dog sled driver. Sniffer-dog trainer. Pet groomer.

'Lake? Or hill in the vineyard?'

Alfie woofed.

'Both? Okay, then. Let's do the lake first.'

He snagged an old anorak from a hook downstairs, then left the kitchen door open behind him and set off across the cold, wet lawn down to the lake. He ignored the dock and stepped instead onto the pebbled scree of the shoreline, heading east. Ahead and above were the mountains, but there was too much cloud cover and barely any light in the sky by which to see them. The rain had eased to a sprinkle, and to his right, across the lake, he could just see twinkling lights dotting the low dark line of land. Hanrahan.

Alfie zigzagged ahead of him, shoving his muzzle into puddles and driftwood and then barking hysterically when a pelican, roused from sleep, clacked his beak at him before swooping off out of sight over the water. Mist hung low, lit by the fingers of dawn creeping over the mountains. Fish plopped, crabs scuttled and Damon's gumboots crunched as he walked. He was a long way from the snarl of traffic in inner-city Sydney.

He felt a long way from the person he had been there, too. He felt ... calmer. Less driven by the need to fill every waking second with case work or social footy or a dinner with some passing fancy. His memory felt a little more balanced now he had other stuff in there besides courtroom stuff. He smiled a little to himself. Who would have thought he'd lose his head so bad over a chick in overalls that now he was having to rethink every angle of how he was living his life? Rejoice in knowing how to turn on a pump and unblock an irrigation spigot?

He came to a halt as Alfie dropped a large stick on his boot.

'No way are we taking that home.'

Alfie put a paw on it, then looked up and tilted his head.

'You want me to chuck it? Do you even know how to run, Alf?'

The dog wagged his tail, so Damon reached down for the stick, then sent it spinning into the water. He laughed as Alfie launched himself into the lake like an old tugboat skidding and sliding its way down a ramp.

'That's gotta be cold, buddy.'

Alfie circled around, the stick in his mouth, and motored back in to the shoreline. For a dog with all the grace of an overgrown wombat on land, the old boy swam like a dolphin.

'You shake on me and I won't be sharing my toast.' Not that it would matter. Damon was already wet from the mist and mizzle.

The dog ignored the threat. Damon, in the same spirit, ignored the shower of dog hair and freezing water that rained over him, picked up the stick and threw it back in the lake.

He'd had a rocky night. No question. But things were starting out okay this morning.

He played stick until Alfie started to tire, then went up through the lines of vines to the top of Frank's property. Up here, he'd decided, was his favourite spot. The view, when the sun was up and when the clouds weren't low and full of precipitation, was incredible, and so was the quiet.

Funny how he'd grown used to that, too.

He'd grown used to a lot of things. Even his brother, who he'd finally worked out was a gentle, easygoing soul. A good brother, but also a good man, who was not to blame for Damon's teenage experience of feeling abandoned by his family.

Emotional abandonment. He'd had it dissected in court by experts often enough, by some shrink psychoanalysing the motives of victim or the accused. And, like most issues of the head and heart, there was therapy available.

Nick was a sweet bloke under all that swagger. Totally unfit to run his career unassisted, as evidenced by this current unfair dismissal case that he was on-again off-again about pursuing, but sweet.

Maybe Damon was the same, only in reverse: totally able to run his career, but unable to be a nice guy unassisted.

'What do you think, old man?'

Alfie grunted. He'd puffed and panted to get up the hill after Damon, but he'd kept at it. Loyal, that's what Alfie was. The word made Damon's eyes hurt. Which was stupid, *stupid*.

'What if Damon has to give you away?' he said.

He'd googled it. Organisations existed to help rehome dogs. It was totally doable, even for old dogs with special needs and butter and sock addictions. But then of course the internet had also spat up horror stories of dogs sold into dog fighting, dogs left in squalor. One dog he'd read about had been abandoned with a load of old furniture on a highway, and had grown into skin and bone while waiting in never-failing hope for its owners to return. Another video had shown a fluffy pup in a too-tight collar abandoned in a cage under a bridge. A fucking *cage*.

He cleared his throat and rubbed his hands over his rough, unshaven face. Thank heaven he'd never had to aggressively cross-examine a dog in court; his panic attack habit might've kicked in a whole lot earlier.

Alfie sat on his foot, rested the bulk of his back and neck and head along Damon's leg, and looked up at him with total trust. Damn it. The dog was right. Damon could no sooner give Alfie away than he could give away his career. Which was a conundrum.

Because he didn't want to give Kylie up, either.

But he was an individual with flaws and he needed to sort them out before he could start thinking about sharing his life with dogs and women. Well, one dog and one woman.

Alfie heaved a mournful sigh and looked hopefully in the direction of the house, where the food lived.

'There are bigger problems in life than getting the lid off a tin of kibble, mate.'

He nudged the dog off his gumboots then started walking down the hill. By the time he'd walked back to the house, he'd made a decision. Several decisions.

Marigold and Kev were going to have to cope without his assistance for the rest of the Harvest Festival preparation. He would call the op shop in Cooma as soon as it opened and tell them the secondhand clothing was ready for collection, and he'd let the skip bin people know they could retrieve their skip. He couldn't spend any more days lying in bed thinking about doing something to help himself. He had to *actually* do something, or how else would he ever know what his life could look like if he embraced a world beyond the law? Measured his own worth on a scale beyond cross examination and forensic minutiae and blood lividity in autopsy photographs?

All of which brought him to the same conclusion: he had to go back to Sydney. Nick could drive him to Cooma in time for the bus to Canberra, one quick flight, and he'd be there.

Organising an appointment with Judge McMary might take some time and finessing, but he had a gut feeling she was the right person to advise him on what his life—his new life—could look like.

'Alfie,' he said to the dog as he scooped out a careful measure of kibble. 'The honeymoon is over, my man, so eat up. Today is going to be a busy day.'

Maureen's house was a lowset brick bungalow that looked cosy if not stylish. A mustard orange Datsun with some age on it sat in a carport and despite it being almost noon the lights were on inside the house as the sun had barely made it through the cloud cover today. Damon patted his pocket to check the letter he'd penned earlier was still there.

Maureen was in the garden in front of her house, a little damp from the weather and surrounded by plant pots and soil, and the malodourous stink of blood-and-bone fertiliser hung in the air. She looked at the white envelope for a long minute before removing her gardening gloves and taking it from him. 'This is from *whom*?'

He cleared his throat. 'You know, no-one's said "whom" to me for quite some time. And I live in a world where legal letters abound. Please, Maureen. Please read it.'

Maureen still wasn't opening it.

'Is there a problem?'

'It's just—'

He waited.

'—if you're going to be nice, I'm going to feel guilty about leaving you in the lurch with all those scones.'

'No,' said Damon. 'You've been grieving. No guilt necessary. Come on, you want me to read it for you?'

Maureen dabbed a corner of a hideously decorated handkerchief to the corner of her eye. 'I can still *read*, young man; I'm not totally decrepit.'

He waited as Maureen's eyes moved over the page. They widened, and then she chuckled. By the time the tears had pooled for the second time, he knew his letter had done its thing.

'Well?' he said.

Her eyes were shining. 'Oh, this is marvellous news!'

'It's a secret. You cannot tell *anyone*. Promise me.'

'Oh, I promise.' She chuckled again, looking down. As well she should. The letter, if he said so himself, was quite something.

Dear Maureen,

No-one feeds me here. Day after day, I stuff my lovely wet nose into the crotch of the new bloke—the nitwit in the suit—and he barks at me to cut it out. There is no love in his voice. Worse, there are never any slices of cheese or ham in his hands for me to help myself to.

Please come back. I promise to try and shed my fur all over the new bloke's bathmat instead of on your trousers. I promise not to drool on your feet as you bake delicious treats in the oven. I implore you, with my big, sad, dog eyes, which you will see for yourself if you ever come back to visit, to return.

The new bloke implores you, too. He drew up the contract which is attached to this letter. I don't understand what it means, but he says it has something to do with giving you all his mum's shares in the picnic business and a right-of-use over the lakeshore from your house to the dock because of some legal mumbo jumbo that my doggie brain has no interest in understanding.

Please, come back and feed me soon.

~~I love your food.~~

~~I love food more than you.~~

I love you.

Alfie x

Maureen's hand, damp hanky clutched within, was poised at the neckline of her flowery shirt, no doubt on the search for a handy bra strap, when she grew still.

'Oh dear,' she said.

Damon was in no mood for pessimism, so he didn't pay much attention. Marigold would be pleased he'd offered Maureen an olive branch, and he had an old-fashioned bowling ball bag packed and ready with his handful of clothes from Penny's Boutique for his return to Sydney.

'I'm sure we can iron out any details,' he said soothingly. Like … could she mind Alfie for a few days since he was about to peel off and Nick had heard about some job? 'Details are my special skill.'

'No,' she said impatiently. The phrase 'nincompoop' hung, unspoken, in the air. 'My gardening gloves. Where is the other one?'

Oh, crap. Damon turned to the dog, who had grown very quiet. 'Alfie. Show me what is in your mouth.'

Alfie grunted. Then he made a noise—a hideous noise, not one of his usual warbling groans—and his massive rib cage lurched out and in and out. Damon dropped to his knees into a puddle and jerked the dog's jaw as wide open as he could. Rubber, just a green and floral finger of it, was wedged so low down in Alfie's throat that Damon couldn't reach it.

Asphyxiation occurs when the airway is blocked for a period of time between four and five minutes.

A useless fact about a human. Damon shunted it away.

The vets do callouts. Josh and Hannah. Lovely people and you don't need to guilt trip them to get them here.

Now there was a useful fact. Thank you, brain. No time for a callout, however, the dog needed saving now. 'Do you have a car, Maureen?'

'There. The carport. It's unlocked.'

'I'll put the dog in and call the vet.'

'I'll grab the keys.'

CHAPTER 32

Pink paint worked! Either that, or an article Maureen wrote in The Chatter about the new women in business group that met in the café had touched a nerve among the locals in Hanrahan. Job number one for the day had been a customer she'd never seen before, who'd needed a new battery and had booked a service in for the following month. She was thrilled to add them to her customer database.

Job number two was a lawnmower—a spark plug job that took about half a second—but a job was a job and the owner took a fridge magnet with her new logo on, so she considered that a win.

When the bell at the open door to the workshop tinkled a few moments later, she looked up to see Kev Jones standing there, a set of keys dangling in his hand.

'Got me a little tyre trouble,' he said. 'Darn thing keeps going flat. Wondered if you'd take a look.'

'How old are your tyres?'

'Not as old as me, but old enough for me to have no idea when I last changed them.'

She grinned. 'Let's take a look. How's Marigold? I've been a little slack on the yoga front lately and I keep expecting to find her on my doorstep, ready to take me in hand.'

'Full of pep as always, and busy over at the vineyard most days. She given you your orders yet about the Harvest Festival?'

'Her orders? I heard it was you who put me in charge of the tractor pull.'

Kev looked smug. 'I do have the odd fabulous idea, pet.'

'Yes,' she said. 'Funny how they always involve other people giving up their time to your community hall.'

He grinned. 'You know you'll love it. Pity the old boy outside isn't up to competing. Don't know about that colour, though.'

Kylie turned to look at Trev, who was now as pink as her sign and her roller door. Not a traditional Massey Ferguson colour, but perhaps pink was the new hi-vis orange. 'It's my rebrand, Kev. I have a new business name, too: The Hanrahan Lady Mechanic.'

'I love it. Now, I've found you a competitor for the tractor pull. Some bloke at Crackenback Marigold knows—I think she buried his wife last year—has a vintage tractor in working order. He says if we front up the funds to hire him a decent flatbed trailer, he can tow it up to the vineyard.'

'What's his tractor?'

Kev winced. 'Now, I knew you'd ask me that. Marigold didn't tell me, pet. But you leave it with me. He's asked for some details about the course and the load and whatever coupling mechanism would be used, so I said you'd go over to the vineyard and come up with a plan for him in the next day or two.'

'Oh, did you now?' Kylie said. She'd warned Marigold, in an as don't-ask-me-why a way as possible, that she was feeling touchy about seeing Damon again. She liked to think she was keeping her heart safe. But she would be keen to be involved in a tractor event …

'Might be a bit of business for you in it,' said Kev. 'A fellow who loves his tractors is going to need a like-minded mechanic.'

Mmm. A fellow who loved his tractors was most likely also very much into tinkering with his own engines, but it was a nice thought.

Kev drove away half an hour later with four shiny new tyres on his car and Kylie stroked the neat stash of actual cash she had tucked into her lock box. All in all, The Hanrahan Lady Mechanic was having a positive morning. Maybe she'd pick up a takeaway coffee after lunch.

In fact, she was feeling so happy, so motivated, maybe she was feeling brave enough to hang her OUT ON A JOB sign over Trev and go visit a tractor on the far side of the lake this afternoon. Her heart, surely, had grown some resilience.

But before she could make plans to take off, the rain started to bullet down and the idea of tramping around a wet field to plan a tractor-pull competition course lost its appeal. She had jobs enough to keep her busy in the workshop, but as the day grew even dimmer and the rain began to thrash against the tin roof, a call came in.

'Is that the mechanic?' yelled a quavery voice into her ear.

'Yes, this is Kylie. How can I help?'

'It came outta nowhere, a bloody kangaroo, and now my car's stuffed.'

'Are *you* okay?'

'Yeah, I'm fine but my radiator's totally busted.'

'Is there a lot of steam?'

'Like my old woman's kettle, love.'

A tow job, for sure. 'I'm on my way,' said Kylie. 'Put your hazard lights on and stay with your car. I'll see you in ten.'

It was more like twenty minutes when she got there, though, and she was soaked by the time she'd reassured the driver—an old-timer who looked like a soft breeze would knock him over—and assessed whether he was up to steering and braking in his vehicle while she towed it with hers. She attached her tow hook to the chassis of his hatchback, lit up his hazard lights (and hers) and checked the tow rope was well within the regulation four metres. Once she had her customer sorted, she turned to the kangaroo who'd caused all this drama. Neck broken, for sure. But …

She knelt beside the body. 'Sorry, old girl.' She stuck her hand into the pouch on the roo's torso, just in case, and was equal parts sad and happy when a little face and two pointed ears popped up within the curve of her arm. 'Well, hello, darling. Things look bad right now, but I know just what to do with you.'

The joey wasn't a newborn, but neither did it look old enough to be hopping off into the scrub on its own without mum. Kylie lifted it free of the pouch and found a calico shopping bag on the passenger seat of her ute. She slipped the joey into it, then undid the top few buttons of her overalls and tucked the little thing in. Body warmth was key at times like this; Hannah had taught her well.

She called the clinic. 'Sandy? Kylie Summer. I'm inbound with a joey from a roadkill incident. Can you contact the wildlife refuge people and let them know?'

'Josh will want to check it out before he hands it over, so I'll call them once he's done his thing. How tiny is it?'

'Almost weaned I'm guessing, but I'm no expert.'

'You're keeping it warm? The poor little blighter will be in shock after losing its mum.'

'As warm as I can considering it's pouring down. I'll be there as soon as I can.'

'Woo! Made it,' Kylie announced as she hurried into the Cody and Cody Vet Clinic.

Rain was everywhere: in her hair turning it to frizz; soaked through the calico bag and the joey's fur, making the little thing tremble against her breast; and now she was tracking it in over the floor of the clinic from her boots. Her fire-retardant overalls were streaming water the way snowmelt urged a river into flood, and yet the clouds that had decided to upend themselves over Hanrahan still weren't satisfied. Fat pellets peppered the large glass windows that faced the street, so noisily that while Kylie could see Sandy's lips move, she couldn't hear what the receptionist was saying.

'Josh is expecting me, right?'

She heard something about Josh and a bull stuck in mud and barbed wire, and Hannah being out the back changing into scrubs, and then the brass bell above the door tinkled behind her as someone else arrived.

She turned. And stared.

Kylie had never been so drenched, and a second ago, she would have thought it would be impossible for anyone, ever, to be wetter than she currently was.

She would have been wrong.

'Oh my,' she said. Involuntarily. The man who'd just flung open the door so violently that the inner handle had nearly punched a hole in the plaster wall behind was a sight to behold.

Damon. But not just the usual tall, dark and dangerous Damon. This was *wet* Damon. Wet, white-shirted, Mr Darcy-climbing-out-of-the-lake Damon. And in his arms was a bedraggled and groaning dog that could, to the uninitiated eye, have been mistaken for an elephant seal.

Sandy, who hadn't bothered getting up from her seat behind the front counter for Kylie's emergency—an orphaned native animal, no less, an icon of Australia, no less, who she'd saved from roadside peril and certain death and had thereby ensured the continuation of a species—leapt to her feet. 'Let me help you,' the receptionist said breathlessly. 'Oh my god, is that Alfie? Not another sock?'

It was, indeed, Alfie.

'He's eaten a gardening glove,' said Damon. 'It's wedged in so far he's choking but I can't get it out. I'm pretty sure he's about to die.'

'Hannah!' Sandy could put some lungs into it when required, and her voice rose well above the rain this time. 'Emergency!'

Next minute, Hannah was hurtling around the corner from the direction of the treatment rooms, still adjusting her navy scrubs, but very much in charge. 'What's up?'

'Choking. On a glove.'

'Oh, Alfie,' said Hannah. 'All right, follow me.'

'Um, Han?' This was Sandy.

'What?'

'Parent–teacher interviews. I have to go. Bad timing. I'm so sorry but—'

'Right. Yes. Of course.' Hannah scanned the clinic waiting room, and her eyes landed on Kylie. 'Why are you here?'

Kylie unzipped the top two inches of her overalls. 'I rescued a joey on the highway from the pouch of a dead kangaroo.'

Hannah nodded. 'Right.' She marched over, unzipped Kylie's overalls to the waist and hauled the joey out. 'Sandy, pop this little one into a crate with water and a hot blanket and then you better get to the school. You two—' her finger pointed back and forth to Kylie and Damon, '—Treatment Room 1. Stat.'

Kylie flicked a glance to Damon, who was looking pale, stressed, and yet still, very much Mr Darcy. 'It's this way,' she said, heading into the first treatment room to the left.

'Get the dog onto the table, handsome,' said Hannah.

Damon hefted Alfie onto the stainless steel table, where the idiot mutt kept trying to scrabble onto his feet.

'Is this some canine version of terminal lucidity?' he said.

Kylie blinked. Was that even a thing?

Damon wasn't done, and his words were tripping over each other and stress was rolling off him almost as fast as the rainwater. 'Rallying before death, a pre-mortem surge, it's a sure sign he's about to die, right? Asphyxiation is a four- to six-minute experience for humans and it's been over thirty now. Physiological differences, larynx size, perhaps? Trachea diameter in dog versus human, or—'

Hannah's eyes met Kylie's with an expression that Kylie had no trouble at all in interpreting because she was thinking the same: *What the hell?*

'Forensic data, sorry, it's in my head a lot but I'll shut up now,' Damon said, standing over Alfie like an avenging angel and any intervention would need to be done via him or else. 'I'm here to help.'

There was no way he could help; the guy was a hot mess, and that very fact was giving Kylie a lot to think about but not just this minute.

Hannah snapped on gloves, picked up a set of forceps that looked like they could deliver a nine pound baby out of a hostile birth canal, and looked up at him. 'I don't think so, mate.' Hannah was short, but you didn't mess with her when she was working. 'Step away from the table. That's an order. Kylie? Gloves on. There. Now, Kyles, you hold his head still while I lever these idiot jaws of his open.'

'You're not going to sedate him?' This was Damon, who'd moved back as ordered but was still hovering very close by.

'We can save him, or we can sedate him. My choice is to save him.' Hannah was wrist deep into Alfie's jaw as she spoke, levering those great forceps of hers. 'If you want to be useful, hang on to his butt and make sure he doesn't wriggle.'

Kylie could see the forceps clamping onto the swathe of fabric half in and half out of the dog's throat. The bundle, slowly but inexorably, was levered upwards, and the dog's guts visibly bulged in and out.

'Is he dying? Is that some sort of terminal convulsion?' Damon had his arms around Alfie, and in between panicking—because that was surely what he was doing—he was anchoring the dog's back end on the stainless steel.

'Gag reflex,' said Hannah in a matter-of-fact tone, as she pulled out one floral fabric and green rubber glove and plopped it into a stainless steel kidney dish. The dog gave a great big belch as it came out, shook his head so his ears flapped back and forth, then sat up on the table looking mightily pleased with himself.

'He's *fine*? Just like that?'

Hannah was eyeing Damon like she was considering if he was the one who needed sedating. 'You know, Damon, there's a family resemblance. Frank couldn't handle it when Alfie needed some veterinary intervention, either. Perhaps being a total softie runs in the family.'

Damon had both his hands on Alfie now, and was leaning down to press his face to the dog's head, but even so Kylie could see him frown. 'I am not a softie,' he said defensively.

Hannah chuckled. 'Get out of here, both of you. Sandy can send you an invoice when she's back in tomorrow. Kylie: you stay.'

Dog and Damon left the treatment room as ordered, and Hannah spent a few minutes pulling off her gloves and swilling down the treatment table with some noxious, bleachy-smelling solution, before turning to Kylie with a look that was equal parts sadness and understanding.

'Kyles,' she said.

'Yes. I know. No need to say anything.'

'Too bad. I'm saying something.'

Holy heck. Did Hannah have *tears* in her eyes?

'I take back everything I ever said about Damon being a red flag. When he goes, I just want you to know that I will be here, ready and waiting, to help you put yourself back together. No matter how long that may take.'

CHAPTER 33

Despite the fact she was wet and cold, Kylie went back to her workshop after the dog drama because her workshop was where the busy happened. And busy was good. Busy was what she needed. Busy meant the head was in charge, and not the heart.

She was frowning down at the mangled radiator of the hatchback she'd towed in earlier that afternoon, when she was surprised by a visitor at the door. Two visitors, actually: a wet, soggy Damon, with a wet, soggy dog. 'What are you doing here?' she said. A welcome, it was not.

Damon smiled. Sheepishly. It was adorable, damn him.

'Alfie wanted to let you know that he had a marvellous time visiting your vet friends and he especially wanted to thank you for your role in his rescue.'

'Oh.' Which didn't really answer her question, and yes, she was being churlish. She really was glad Alfie was okay. Unfortunately, *she* wasn't feeling okay, and Damon, even wet and soggy—perhaps especially because he was wet and soggy—was the reason. 'I suppose you need a ride home,' she said. Dumbing down their relationship into driver and passenger was all the defence she had at this point.

'That's not why we're here. We were hoping, Alfie and I, that we could invite you out for a drink. Or dinner. As a thank you. And also, because we—well, me, not Alfie so much, he, understandably, is feeling rather knackered—have some things to say. To you.'

She should definitely be saying no to that. Definitely, absolutely, a big fat no. She had her vow but Damon had said a zillion times that he cared zip for that, and spending time with him was both balm and poison for her heart.

'Please,' he said. 'I don't like it when we're fighting.'

She frowned. 'We're not fighting.'

'It kinda feels like we are, when you're avoiding me.'

'I'm not avoiding you. I'm avoiding getting my heart broken. Which you could try and respect.'

'I do respect it. But I've missed you. Come on, a drink. A pizza. I'd settle for a shared two-day-old sandwich from the servo.'

Her idiot mouth was saying, 'There's a wine bar in town,' before her brain could object.

'How fancy is the wine bar? Only ... wet man, wet dog.'

'I've got a dryer at home,' she said. 'You can chuck your shirt in it while I change, and I can probably rustle up a towel for your glove-eating friend. Let's drive, though, because this rain is here to stay.'

As she started the engine of the ute, with the three of them all squished in and nearly gagging on the aroma of wet dog, she wondered what in hell she thought she was doing. But she'd had a busy, elated, rocky, sad sort of a day. A complicated day. Her feelings were running amok and her vow was feeling ... precarious.

One glass of wine, maybe one slice of pizza ... what could go wrong?

The rain had brought more cars out than usual and she couldn't find a park close by her flat, so by the time the pair of them and Alfie had run down Paterson Street and across Hanrahan's small park and made it upstairs, she was back to being as wet as they were. Her hair was likely as tangled as Alfie's, but she was playing it cool, keeping the conversation light, feeling very proud of herself. Happy face, resilient heart, independent woman.

But then something happened when she unbuttoned her overalls and pushed them down to her waist.

It hadn't been a move, jeez. Being a mechanic was messy work and she was totally covered under the overalls—conventionally covered, even—by a T-shirt that said *Keep Calm and Tractor*, and leggings that she often wore to yoga, and she had a laundry hamper here by the door so she could ditch messy overalls before she got grease all over her furniture. Ditching her messy overalls at the door was routine. Normal. Totally unsexy. Especially when they stunk like wild kangaroo.

Usually.

Not today, it seemed; something about those buttons being undone under the heated gaze of Tall, Dark and Dangerous had raised the temperature in the tiny flat about four hundred degrees. Perhaps she'd left her oven on that morning; that'd account for the scorch she was feeling when Damon locked his eyes to hers.

'Are we getting undressed?' he said. 'Just say the word.'

'Um. No,' she said. Thinking, recklessly: *What if we did?*

He must have read her mind. 'Bad idea. Your vow, remember? My flaws. Your sad face.'

'Totally. Fancying each other is not sufficient reason to indulge in foolish—'

How had he got that close without her noticing? Or was she the one who'd gotten closer to him? She tilted her head a smidge and stubble—the tall, dark and dangerous sort—scraped her collarbone.

Bad decision, her inner self was saying. *Bad, bad, bad* …

Her outer self was taking absolutely no notice because she'd somehow or other managed to lay her hands on Damon's biceps and given them a good old-fashioned gripping and they were *fine*.

'My face isn't sad at the moment,' she said. An inane comment, but it was all she had.

'That is true,' said Damon, his mouth on her throat now and his hands finding entry points to her overalls in places she didn't even know had entry points and very much trying to do some old-fashioned gripping of their own.

She had found skin under his shirt. That wet, Mr-Darcy-out-of-the-lake shirt. Skin, with muscle under, and ribs enough to match her exploring fingers.

'But you remember I'm not a farmer, right?'

'I remember.'

'And your life is in Hanrahan. You're a country mechanic.'

Her back was up against a wall and a rope was clanging—her macrame pot plant holder that had once held a vibrant little fern but now held a pot of dirt.

'Wait. The wet dog. Who was barely alive an hour ago. The glove inhaler.'

'Forget the wet dog. He's on your bed by now, snoring under your nice clean doona, dreaming of his next misadventure with blood-and-bone fertiliser.'

Damon could make anything sound reasonable. The dog forgotten, she had her mouth on his and her hands gripped in his shirt and guess what? Her hands were strong. Country mechanic hands. She had that thing ripped off him in a heartbeat and—

Oh. She'd have liked to have caught every moment, every movement, every everything, but that was the point where some sort of will-they-won't-they threshold was stepped over—cartwheeled over—and the sheer delight of a late-afternoon bonk with a man who had seriously well-honed bonking skills kinda took over.

The wall took several turns as a prop (her back, his back, her back again), the cowhide rug nearly caused a slippage event that had them clinging to each other like lives could have been lost, and the kitchen bench ...

Well. Suffice it to say never had she appreciated her kitchen so much as in those few long feverish heart-stop-start minutes with Damon Johns.

At some point the rain had been lifted by gusts of wind slamming it into the French doors of the tiny balcony, but that had only added to the sense that the two of them were in their own little cocoon and the world—their real lives—was only a muffled other that could be worried about later. Much later. When her heartbeat was back to normal and her insides had stopped tremoring with delight.

Yeah. An *epic* bonking. And when she could speak again, she was going to say so.

Somehow or other, she managed to still have one sock on. Her underwear—grass green today, as were her nails—was across the room somewhere near the television and she rather thought she might have the imprint of a salad server forever marked on her butt.

So worth it. T-shirt and leggings? No idea. Smouldered into ash by the inferno, most probably.

Damon had collapsed to the floor beside her sofa, jocks around one ankle, hair all mussed, glowing and sweaty in the dim light like he'd just run the Main Range Track. She inspected him the way she'd inspected the vintage ag equipment at the Gunnedah Rural Museum: thoroughly.

He had a faint smile on his face. Not surprising, considering. Turns out, a long, dry spell did for her libido what a long drought did for bushfire: from spark to firestorm in seconds.

'You know what Hannah told me the other week?' she said, hoisting herself properly onto the kitchen bench so her feet—one socked and one not—dangled over the edge. She was naked, but she didn't care. Her hair, she imagined, could be mistaken for wallaby grass, her hands were speckled with grease and oil, which meant her face probably was, too, but she didn't care about that, either. She felt ... wonderful. But she also felt like soon, very soon, she was going to be wondering how much damage she'd just done to her self-esteem. Was her vow to herself really so easily broken?

Damon was putting on his jocks and rising to his feet, looking around as though wondering where his clothes might be. The place looked as though a cyclone had just torn through it.

'What?'

'That maybe I was too rigid in my ideas. You know, about needing a farmer in my life, and little kids in gumboots running through sunny paddocks. But I told you this already, right?'

He'd abandoned his attempt at finding clothing and was now standing in front of her, his arms looped around her waist, his forehead pressed up against hers.

'Have I told you how much I like Hannah?'

Unfortunately, her inner self had started to reassert itself over all the bits of her that were within arm's reach of Damon. This banter, this flirty talk ... she loved that stuff. She loved it so much that, if it kept up, she was going to lose her head completely and then where would they be?

'Maybe I am too rigid. But I also know what I want my future to look like. It's complicated when you're with me.'

'I know. I'm sorry. I wish I had a solution. I've been trying to come up with one. I may even have one, which is what I wanted to talk to you about, but ... I'm anxious. Which is not something I am accustomed to saying. I've had my career goals set in stone for years now and unsetting them? I'm not sure if it's even possible.'

Later, Kylie was going to wish she hadn't steamrolled over this, but she did. 'I think I'm starting to lose my grasp of what's important. I guess ... I'm not sure where all this—' she waved a hand around at the flat, their naked selves, the cyclone, '—leaves us. This ... relationship we seem to be having even though we can't have a relationship?'

He found a sock and pulled it on. 'Have *you* tried to come up with a solution, Kylie? About you and me? About what a future might look like when one of us only wants a farmer and the other of us needs a career in the law?'

She blinked. What did he mean by that? Was he asking her to compromise? So this didn't have to be a bad decision? Or was he just offering advice? If she wasn't such a chicken, she'd ask straight out.

Instead, she said: 'You and me, Damon. It's been more than just fun, hasn't it?'

'It certainly has.' His eyes were serious, but his answer could mean nothing or everything or anything at all; he was good at that.

And she was really good at not finding out.

'Let's have that drink,' she said. 'But not out. I have a bottle of cheap red and a packet of barbecue chips. Are you happy with that?'

'Totally happy.' But his words didn't quite match his expression. Was it the wine he didn't like? The barbecue chips? Or the conversation?

Kylie found two glasses, unscrewed the lid of the wine bottle so she could pour out two serves, and handed a glass over to Damon.

'To Uncle Frank,' he said. 'Without whom we wouldn't have met.'

Was she imagining it, or did that sound a little … romantic? To remind herself where true romance lay, she said firmly, 'To books about tractors.'

He smiled. Clinked his glass against hers. 'To change. And solutions.'

She took a breath. 'What change, specifically, are you referring to?'

'Mine. Yours. Everything.'

'Cryptic, but okay. To change and solutions.'

They each took a sip. She didn't grimace—she was used to cheap plonk—but Damon made a face.

'What?' she said. 'This is where you're supposed to tell me that my wine is excellent.'

He grinned. 'You took the words out of my mouth.' He swilled his glass, laid it on an angle and sniffed the contents, then held it to the light. 'Hmm. Tones of rich, cool earth. A vibrancy that can only have come from rain deluges growling their way across the Snowy Mountains. A robustness that holds an echo of the heavy thud of Alfie's paws along the shore of Lake Bogong …'

'Idiot,' said Kylie. 'It's one paw thud away from being vinegar.'

'I've grown very fond of paw thuds.'

She laughed. 'Maybe a beer would've been safer.'

He set his glass down. That face—the totally happy but not at all face—was back in place. 'We need to talk.'

She blinked. 'Okay.'

'I have to go back to Sydney. It's important.'

'Oh.' *Oh.*

'Do you think you could take care of Alfie?'

'Why can't Nick mind him?'

'His agent has lined up a short-term radio gig in Orbost and he's really excited about it. Work has been patchy lately.'

Hmm. That, she understood. But ... 'Are you leaving for good? For a day, a week, a year?'

'For as long as it takes. I know that sounds cryptic, but I won't know until I've set up some meetings.'

'An unknown length of time, during which I need to be sneaking your giant furball into my no-dogs-allowed apartment. I don't know how I got away with it last time.'

'I had an idea about that. I wondered if I could talk you into staying at the vineyard.'

'At the *vineyard*?' This was out of the blue.

'There's plenty of room. A tractor to play with. Maureen may be there now she's consented to play nice again ... you might like it.'

There was subtext here but she was too flustered to read freaking subtext. *Stay at the vineyard?* 'I'll mind Alfie,' she said, because this was an easy yes. 'I'll give some thought to where we sleep. When are you heading off?' This was the difficult bit. How difficult, she didn't want to consider.

'Today was the plan, but—'

'You were leaving *today*?' Without telling her? And somehow had managed to end his day in her flat? Naked? This was not good. This was awful. She took a sip of the hideous wine because it was a whole lot less hideous than what was going on in her heart.

'Yeah, Alfie's gardening glove messed up my plans. Next flight out is tomorrow, but Nick's not around tomorrow so ... I'm hoping I can pay this driver I know to take me to Cooma in time for the bus to Canberra Airport.'

She wanted to say no way. She actually would have preferred to scream it. But then he'd know how cut up she was, and pride—especially in a crisis moment like this, when it was brought home to you that pride was the *only* thing you had—mattered.

'What will you be doing in Sydney?' What she meant was, *This trip to Sydney better be of earth-shattering bloody importance to be happening now. After this. After everything.*

'Making amends,' he said. 'I was not in a good place before I left, if I'm honest, and I've been giving it plenty of thought while I've been here. It's time to go see what my future could look like. You remember that toast we made to change?'

'I remember,' she said. She had to dig deep then, deep down into that pride she'd spent all these years building. 'I hope it all works out. I probably won't miss you at all.'

CHAPTER 34

A suit-clad Damon—ironed, she noticed, and the creases were almost up to Wendy standard—wasn't the only one waiting when she pulled into the sweeping driveway in front of the house the next morning. Alfie was beside him, a cheerful red bandana tied about his neck, a food bowl and his dented food tin by his side. No visible signs of trauma from the gardening glove incident were in evidence. On the contrary: Alfie looked ready for adventure.

Perhaps Alfie hadn't yet worked out that he, like Kylie, formed no part of today's plans.

'He's prepared for every eventuality when it comes to where he sleeps tonight. You want him in the tray or at my feet?'

'It's your call.'

Alfie made his own mind up by lifting his front paws up to the floor of the passenger seat of Kylie's ute, then looked expectantly up at her.

'Jump,' said Damon.

Alfie's tongue lolled from his mouth. If dog faces could speak, his said, 'Don't be daft.'

Damon sighed, picked the dog up and shoved him bodily into the footwell. It was a squish, like one of those fancy paintings in art books, where noses and bum cheeks and elbows all collided.

'I was hoping to spend the flight *not* picking dog hair off my suit,' said Damon.

Kylie sat in silence, waiting until he had wedged the small leather holdall she'd seen before into the space between the passenger seat and the back of the ute cab, where her jack and bungee cords and raincoat and lolly wrappers lived.

'Damon, I—'

'Kylie, I—'

She turned to look at him. 'You go first.'

'I hope you're not regretting yesterday.' His usual cocky expression was well and truly missing. He was looking … thoughtful. Was that the word?

Pride only allowed one answer. 'I'm not.'

'Me either,' he said. 'Can I ask you something?'

Kylie put the ute into gear and turned towards the highway. 'Sure.'

The rain that had thrown itself down upon Hanrahan yesterday had stopped but the cloud cover was so low the road was dim under the trees. The verge on either side of the small road around the lake was a muddy rubble.

'Your independence means a lot to you, right?'

'It means everything. I wouldn't be busting my arse trying to make my business work if it didn't.'

'And you've lived alone now for some years, I gather.'

'Thanks for the reminder. Yes, I've lived alone. Why the interrogation?'

He chuckled. 'Just fact gathering. You know that's how I make decisions.'

Damon didn't seem in any hurry to say anything more, and Kylie was not feeling inclined to press for details, because maintaining her people-pleasing happy face today was taking all of her concentration. She drove in silence.

On the highway, they passed the Autocare Fuel and Truckstop, and she pictured Nigel Woods in there, scratching his balls and saying *ka-ching* every time someone popped in to buy a hundred litres of diesel and a pie.

Damon started talking while her mind was still caught on Nigel's three-bay workshop, which had appeared to be not only full but backed up with cars and utes and trucks waiting their turn, so she missed the first sentence or two. Maureen's article may have created a ripple of work in her direction, but that ripple was a long way from being the torrent Nigel Woods had flooding in every day.

'I'm sorry,' she said. 'Say that again? I can't send evil glances at my nemesis and listen at the same time.'

His hand stroked her braid where it fell across her shoulder, just for a second. 'I said, if you're interested, I could tell you why it is I left Sydney in the first place.'

'Because you were in a bad way, I think you said. Sure, let's hear it.'

'You know I'm a barrister.'

'Yep.'

'I share chambers with my friend Warunya, who's also a barrister. Our friend Sean is our law clerk. He does our research, runs our court diaries and so on. He did law with us, but he's got some stick up his bum about practising, despite the fact he's smarter than the two of us put together, so he runs our lives instead.'

'You've been friends for a long time, I take it,' she said, thawing in spite of herself. She wasn't mad at Damon, she just needed to protect herself. And after wanting to know more about him all this time, she should be happy he was opening up.

'Oh, yes. We went to school together. Sean and Runya were the year ahead of me but we were in the same debating team.'

'And that was considered cool, was it? Among your classmates?' The only thing considered cool by the kids at Hanrahan High had been sport. And short skirts, now that she thought about it. And hers had been very, *very* short, once she'd got to school and switched out of the Wendy-approved school skirt she wore from home, to the secondhand one she'd bought with her pocket money from the rack out front of the uniform shop and had to wash at home on the sly.

Damon grinned. 'When you're the winning team in the New South Wales Secondary Schools' Debating Union, it is.'

'Did you hear that, Alfie?' she said. 'That was a humble brag. Only low on the humble and heavy on the brag.'

Another tug on her plait. 'Sean and Runya put me in time out.'

She glanced at him to see if he was joking, but he was staring out the window at the rain that was streaking across the glass.

'Time out? Like a toddler who's had too much sugar?'

He snorted. 'I'm pretty sure they'd say that was an excellent analogy. They suggested I take three months away to think about my life choices. I'd just finished a case, earlier than expected, so I didn't have any court appearances booked. And ... well. I had a panic attack.'

She took her eyes off the road long enough to look at him. '*You?*'

'Yeah, me.'

'But you're so ... confident.'

'Yeah, well. The brasher we are, the harder we fall, apparently, us high-achiever, high-stress types.'

Kylie was silent for a couple of kilometres, trying to reconcile what she knew about the man sitting beside her with the man he was describing. Cocky, yes, but in that way that let you know he knew he was poking fun at himself as well as at everyone else. Confident? She thought back to that look of mild terror on his face when she'd first seen him, strapped into an apron. The tension when his brother had turned up out of the blue. That episode yesterday in the clinic with the recitation of medical disaster scenarios that had seemed, not to beat about the bush, rather unhinged. She sighed. Being aloof and upset with Damon was difficult. 'It was quite a fall, I'm guessing.'

'Sean and Runya sent me off to do some thinking, but I'm pretty good at avoiding thinking. And when I set my mind to being good at something, I generally ace it. What I didn't factor in, though, was being out here.'

'Stuck in the country,' she said, remembering that first day they'd met. A thought struck her. 'It's not been three months yet. I thought you were banished for three months.'

'Yes. But this opportunity for resurrecting my career in a less ... panic-inducing ... way that I told you about. I need to talk it over with them.'

Damon might've been going to say more, but they were pulling in front of the bus depot in Cooma. She had so many questions, including why he'd left it so late to tell her all this. Was he—a horrid thought—excusing himself for his role in their fling yesterday? *I wasn't a rat, shagging you senseless and letting you break your vow, I have issues?*

She decided she was feeling a little unwell.

The rain was pouring so hard she had to flick her wipers onto their noisiest setting, which had the effect of stripping the cab of any intimacy it might otherwise have had.

'Here's my card,' said Damon. 'You've got my mobile, but this has my work numbers and email on it in case you need to contact me. I've paid the driver fee already into the same account I used for the motorbike. You will … call me, won't you?'

They stared at each other awkwardly, the wipers going *thwack, thwack, thwack* so loud it was like the ute was under attack.

'If I need you,' she said. Which she would. Every minute and every hour. Which was why she would be tearing that card up into little pieces and then torching it into ash with her oxy-acetylene welder.

For a second, she wondered if he was going to kiss her. Then Damon gave her his almost-a-smile smile.

'I guess this is goodbye.'

'I liked our hello better,' she said. 'Life seemed a lot simpler then.'

'I know. Stay at the vineyard. Please. For me.'

She frowned, but there was just time for a last tug on her plait, a last pat on the dog's head, and then Damon was hauling his carry-all from the car and jogging through the rain into the depot.

She looked at the embossed card he'd pressed into her hand. *Damon Johns, Barrister, Johns & Wickramasinghe Chambers, Macquarie Street, Sydney.* Reading it emphasised the distance between them, which felt a whole lot wider than one rain-drenched gutter and a dreary country bus depot.

She dropped the card into the nook in front of the gearstick where things like coins and keys lived. There'd be plenty of time to think about how foolish she had been later on, when it was just her and Alfie eating ice-cream together on her sofa.

CHAPTER 35

Kylie had become such a devotee of yoga lately that Marigold was starting to take pity on her by allowing her to chitter chat without being forced into punishing yoga poses. Routine, turns out, was a balm for unhappy people who'd let themselves down and only had themselves to blame. Especially unhappy people who felt obliged to pretend to the rest of the world—and by 'the world', she meant Hanrahan—that they were fine.

Take today, for instance. Three and a half weeks had passed since she'd driven Damon to Cooma and realised that their goodbye needed to be exactly that: goodbye.

She trudged along the lakeshore, acknowledging it had been a hard decision. Especially for her, because she wasn't a person who usually added up facts to make her decisions; she used emotions. But this time, her emotions had led her astray, so she'd added up what needed to be added (he'd been very honest about only wanting a fling; she'd been the one who'd been so dumb as to fall in love) and now she was going to stick to her promise to herself no matter what.

Go her.

Kev had acknowledged yoga's cooler mornings by wrapping a scarf the colour of a plum around his neck. He also wore one of his corduroy caps in a faded version of the same colour and had buried himself in a dark puffer coat. He looked like a bush turkey in full wattle. The crossword page was open on his lap and he had a pen in his hand, but he looked up to say g'day when Kylie and Alfie arrived. 'Got a corker for you today, love,' he said.

'Let's hear it,' she said brightly as she threw her yoga mat on the grass. That was the tone she was using these days when out and about: bright. Brittle, but bright. Especially when the topic circled around to anything remotely related to the fellow she'd been seen around town with but who was now gone, gone, gone, though not before he'd ditched his dog with her. What a charmer.

'Darling girl seeks lonely man who can recite lines like this under a moonlit sky by the shores of Lake Bogong: *We would be together and have our books and at night be warm in bed together with the windows open and the stars bright.*'

Marigold, who had been pointing and hands-on-hipping and snapping out directions as to where yoga mats ought to be positioned to the Hanrahan locals who had dragged themselves along, looked up. As well she might.

Even Alfie had been startled by this poetic contribution to the ongoing work in progress that was Kylie's profile on RuRo. This was a far cry from her own recent musings: *Lady mechanic seeks decent bloke for happily ever after. Blow-in dickheads from Sydney need not apply.*

'Ernest Hemingway,' Marigold said, blowing a kiss to Kev. 'They're the lines you recited to me when we first met.'

Kev cleared his throat. 'I know, pet. And it worked, didn't it? Thought our Kylie might need a bit of our luck rubbed off on her.

We've got a little luck we can spare, you and I. Sixty happy years, it's been.'

'Oh, you guys,' said Kylie. 'Stop it or you're going to make *me* cry. Marigold, I thought you were made of tougher stuff.'

'You're going to make me cry in a minute,' said Tom, behind her. 'And I'm a decorated naval officer with balls of steel.'

Decorated, Kylie could believe, but Tom had a mushy core. His twenty-year unrequited love affair with Hannah was testament to that. But that was their story and, sadly, her own story was not shaping up to have a happy ending. Or even a happy chapter.

'I was thinking of something simple this week,' said Kylie. 'Like: *Hanrahan's most desperate single is taking a break from RuRo for the foreseeable future.*'

'Oh, don't give up, Kylie!'

'But we love working on your bio, Kylie! It's the only reason Wally and I come to yoga.'

'Hang in there, Kyles.'

The chorus of well-wishers grew silent as Marigold stopped exchanging fond glances with her husband and barked out an instruction. Kylie handed Alfie's leash to Kev and dropped to her mat. Tom's was beside hers, and while Marigold was distracted by a particularly slovenly outstretched leg being perpetrated on the far side of the group, he leant in close.

'Keep it up on the RuRo another week, Kyles.'

She frowned at him, then wondered if he was interpreting it as a smile, given her head was hanging upside down. 'What's the point?'

'I have a feeling. That's all. One more week, promise me.'

She sighed, but Tom and Hannah had been nothing but supportive over the past month. Hannah had tried to take Alfie off her hands and when Kylie refused, she'd insisted on bringing over dog food and liver treats and Alfie's flea and tick treatment. All from vet supplies that were cluttering up her storage room, Hannah had maintained, as though Kylie would fall for that. But still, she'd been grateful. Dog ownership was expensive.

And Tom had smoothed over the dog-on-premises issue, finding some new tenancy rule that favoured dogs as necessary companions. He'd been vague when she'd suggested tartly he'd do better finding some new animal abandonment rule and dragging Damon Johns' sorry arse into a courtroom to be flung into prison for an indefinite but gruelling sentence involving a stint in a labour camp. Tom had muttered words like *confidentiality* and *unfortunately* and *legally constrained* until she'd wanted to smack him.

One more week would bring them to the Harvest Festival. She had tried every which way to get out of organising the tractor pull, but Marigold had held her ground, so she'd forced herself to do her duty.

The place had sold, of course. When Damon had disappeared, so had his brother, Nick, and a SOLD OFF MARKET sign the size of a billboard had appeared on the road out front of Frank's property. Not that Kylie had done any drive-by stalking of course. Well, not *much* drive-by stalking.

She'd had to endure a little commentary in town. 'Haven't seen your fancy friend around.' 'Lost yourself another one, have you, Kyles?' That sort of thing. She'd not cared about it for herself. As if! But she'd kept her hands clamped firmly over Alfie's ears whenever the subject of the unsuitable bloke came up.

Abandoning her was one thing—and, yes, she did remember all the many, many times Damon had warned her he didn't want to be relied upon—but abandoning *Alfie*?

Unforgivable.

Which was why she'd blocked his number on her phone.

Damon was gone and good riddance and she did not care *at all* so ha-di-bloody-ha.

After yoga, Kylie marched across to her workshop, the not-quite-so-fat Alfie in her wake, lifted the lid on her laptop, logged into RuRo and stared at her profile for a while. No messages awaited her. Big surprise. Last week's tagline blinked away at her and she couldn't be bothered thinking up a new one. Upbeat, optimistic phrases were hard work to come up with at the moment. Worse than hard work.

One week. Maybe Tom was thinking the Harvest Festival would bring in some people from the community within driving distance of Hanrahan—Dalgety, Crackenback, Moonbah, Jindabyne—and that was what he was hoping for her. Someone new. A tractor lover. A fresh start.

Like she could be bothered. Love was hard work and it had left her broken, and why would she want any more of that?

She had a new vow: Kylie was doing things for *Kylie* from now on.

Mother–daughter relationships were under the same broken umbrella as love was, and so what if Wendy had tried to call her a hundred times in the last few weeks?

Alfie, below the desk, gave a little sigh and licked her foot, reminding her that his love was, actually, of value.

She sighed. Bitterness was so not her, but look at her now. Falling in love and having her heart broken had turned her, a sunny, happy, friendly person into … into …

This.

Hannah's words of a few weeks ago tiptoed through her mind: *Are you as rigid in your thinking as your mother, Kylie? Just about different things?* And He Who Must Not Be Named had echoed them in the toast he'd made on their last night together: *To change and solutions*. Even Vera—lovely, soft, beautiful Vera—had said something of the sort. *Was* Kylie as rigid as Wendy in her thinking?

Another thought tiptoed through her mind. An equally unwelcome thought. Had a broken heart been the trigger that had turned Wendy into the hand-wringing, purse-lipped mother she'd become? Her mum had loved her dad, no question. And her dad had done worse than bugger off to Sydney (if that were possible) ... he'd *died*.

In an industrial accident. A forklift had been involved, yes, not a car hoist or a towing strap or a tractor, but definitely an overall-wearing occasion—

Alfie gave his little someone's-arriving-imminently warning woof, and she looked up just as Braydon stuck his head in the door.

'Hello, honey,' she said, immediately forgetting her new vow. Kylie being all about Kylie wasn't who she wanted to be. And maybe Wendy being all about Wendy wasn't who her mother wanted to be, either, but had she, Kylie, ever asked Wendy what she wanted out of life?

No. She hadn't. Hannah, damn her, had been right.

'Aren't you due in tomorrow?'

'Um, school let me off for an hour. Something came up and the principal wanted me to come over and talk to you.'

He looked serious, which was so much the opposite of his usual face that she tapped the stool beside her and gave him a get-yourself-over-here-to-be-hugged wave.

'Are you all right?' she said. 'Because if you've been expelled, yes, I know it seems like the end of the world now, but it isn't. You *will* be okay. Okay?'

'I've not been expelled, Kylie, it's—'

'Oh my god, it's Peanut, isn't it? Alfie didn't mean to bark at him so loudly the other day when you brought him in. Hannah's got him on a diet; he must've thought Peanut was a naughty snack that needed disciplining before he ate it. I *knew* dogs could frighten guinea pigs to death and I didn't even *think*. I'm so sorry, Braydon. I'm an idiot.'

Braydon was laughing. 'No. Kylie! *Listen.*' He grabbed the ten inch wrench and held it aloft. 'This is the talking stick. Like in *Lord of the Flies*. I'm holding it, so I get to speak now, okay?'

Huh. A Year Ten English book. Even she had been at school long enough to read that one. Dull as dishwater, only with a load of smelly boys and a—

Holy shit. And a pig's head.

'Speak,' Kylie said, nodding at the wrench.

Braydon pulled at his collar. Scratched the zit on his neck. Cleared his throat. 'So, um, somebody left a pig's head in my locker at school the other day.'

'That is very interesting,' she said. 'Were you ... alarmed by this?' *Freaked out? Scared witless? So upset you had to call the police and cry on your sofa and rethink every life choice you'd ever made?*

'Well. I was grossed out. I mean, its neck juice ruined by physics book. Anyway, Talia, that's my girlfriend, saw Lucy, who I used to go with last term, put it in my locker, and she told Mrs Manning, and Mrs Manning told Mr Chang, and Mr Chang called me and Talia and Lucy into his office and he went apeshit at us, and—'

'Apeshit. Gosh.'

'Anyway then Lucy started crying and said she shouldn't have done it but how else would I learn how evil I was to dump her and start going out with Talia if she didn't send a clear message, and we'd been studying *Lord of the Flies*, so she had a brainstorm because her brother works at the piggery down near Dalgety, and pigs' heads were the symbol of evil, at least that's what the teacher reckoned but she hadn't really finished the book and the movie was too boring to watch, and she was sorry about both of the pigs' heads, and Mr Chang was like, "Wait, this isn't an isolated incident? Where's the other pig's head, Lucy?" And she was like, "You know. At Braydon's work". Which I knew about, but I didn't know it was Lucy. Not back then.'

He stopped talking. Then he handed Kylie the wrench. Quite hesitantly, too. Perhaps he thought she was going to brain him with it.

'I never told you about the pig's head that I found here on Trevor. I didn't want to creep you out.'

He shrugged. 'Everyone knows about it. The story went round town like lice. People reckon it was Mr Woods, on account of you being a chick and everything and him being a misogynist. Which is so not okay, Kylie.'

That was certainly what she had thought. It was certainly what she'd told the police.

'This Lucy sounds like a nutcase.'

He shrugged. A little too smugly. 'Driven mad by rejection, I guess. It's gotta hurt.'

Hmm. As much as she would have liked to shake some of that smugness out of him, she figured life would do that before too long, without any need for her to get involved. Life had a habit of doing that.

'Thanks for letting me know. I'm going to have to speak to Sergeant King about this, since I already reported the first pig's head.'

'Mr Chang said he was going to tell the police, too. Lucy's shitting her pants.'

'Lucy's older brother is the one who ought to be shitting his pants. I'm guessing he's the one who owns the hot rod car I heard the night I was lucky enough to be targeted.'

'Sorry, Kylie. You can ruffle my hair if you have to, and I won't even complain about it to management.'

She laughed. 'Go back to school, you great idiot. I'll see you for your shift. Try not to dump any more nutcases while you're working for me, okay? Or at least learn how to dump them nicely.'

When he'd gone, she stared at the ancient landline stuck to the wall of the workshop. Bakelite, curly cord, rotary dial ... too bad the landlord owned it, as it was probably worth a few bucks to a collector. Should she call Nigel? Apologise for reporting him for a crime he didn't commit?

Nah. Stuff him.

Wendy turned up at the workshop just as Kylie was lowering the roller door that afternoon.

Perhaps fate was taking a hand in Kylie's life now that she had proved to be so inept at running it herself; she'd been thinking about Wendy, and now here she was.

She took her finger off the button so the door stopped a few feet above the ground and ducked under it. She rested a hand on Trev to remember that she did have virtues like patience and tolerance, and now was a good time to employ some, and to remember that while her mother had booked her car into Autocare to be serviced (betrayal), wasn't it also true that Wendy had asked Hannah to check on her after that scene at the café (thoughtful)?

Wendy was carrying a parcel and she was looking quite chuffed with herself. 'Hello, darling,' she said. 'Can I come in?'

'Er, sure. Let me get this door up again.' Had her mother ever been within the four walls of her workshop? She'd been to the door, certainly. She'd stood out front and held her hands to her cheeks and shaken her head with gentle regret. But had she actually set foot on the stained concrete within? Kylie didn't think so.

Once the roller door had clanked and clanged its way up into the rafters, she beckoned her mother in. 'I have bottled water in the fridge, Mum, if you'd like one. Or I could make you a cup of tea.'

Her mother was walking carefully between the tower of tyres and the ride-on mower Kylie was working on. Grease-stained rags were in an old bucket near the little fridge and a packet of biscuits she'd forgotten to put away lay open on the small bench beside the kettle and the rack of upended mugs.

To her mother's fastidious eye, the place probably looked like the bowels of hell, but to Kylie, the place looked pretty much like it always looked, only, for once, the spike of unpaid bills was empty, the cash tin was gratifyingly heavy and the whiteboard on the wall where she listed jobs was full enough for her to not need to worry about next month's rent or hoist finance payment.

'I'd love a cup of tea.'

Crap. Now she'd have to confess her milk was past its best by date. If she had any. She opened the fridge and looked at the empty container, which had been put back into the fridge rather than into the bin. Her bad. Or Braydon's, maybe. Milk etiquette wasn't something either of them cared about.

'Sorry, I'm out of milk. I have ginger tea. Will that do?'

'Perfect. I love ginger tea.'

Hmm. Wendy's voice sounded off. It sounded very like the bright, sunny tone Kylie was so good at employing herself when she was in her people-pleasing, hidden-hurt, nothing-to-see-here mode.

Kylie normally would have ignored that, but ... there was that word again. Change.

'Is something wrong, Mum?' she said, flipping the switch on the kettle and pulling two freebie mugs off the dishrack: a Burson Autoparts one for her and Kincrome for Wendy. If, as she now suspected, she and her mother had more in common than she'd spent the last few years believing, then if there was something wrong with Wendy, maybe there was also something wrong with her.

'Oh, Kylie. Here. Just open this, will you?'

Her mum shoved the parcel at her and Kylie gave up trying to untangle tea bag strings from the caddy of assorted flavours and turned her attention to it.

The parcel was heavy and fluoro yellow and plastic, and it was addressed to her mother, not to her. She tore it open and blinked at the barrage of hot pink inside. Her favourite colour. Wendy favoured pastels, like peach and apricot and lemon. An internet clothing buy her mother couldn't return? Kylie pushed aside the inner packaging and felt the fabric. Rough. Denim, only not denim. The fabric felt very like the fire-retardant overalls she was wearing.

'No way,' she said.

Her mother smiled a little. Shrugged. 'It's my way of saying sorry, Kylie. I didn't like seeing that man treating you so harshly, and it made me think about my own behaviour. I've been very ... thoughtless.'

'Oh, Mum.'

'This gift is an olive branch I hope you will accept.'

Overalls. The pink so hotly perfect and so exactly matched to her favourite nail polish that she sighed. She held them up and realised there wasn't one pair, but three. On the pair in her hand, *Kylie* had been embroidered on the breast pocket, in navy in a small but subtle font. She turned them over to inspect the back and laughed. In a font that was not at all subtle were the words THE HANRAHAN LADY MECHANIC: *Cars, Tractors, Anything.*

She didn't, she realised, deserve them. She *had* been rigid. She *had* been bitter. She had been as unswervingly impatient with her mother as her mother had been as unswervingly resistant to Kylie's career.

'Do you like them?'

She sniffled a little bit and mopped at her face with a wad of fluoro yellow plastic. 'Oh, Mum,' she said again. 'These are fantastic.'

'They're not all for you.'

'What?' Kylie hung the first set over a stool and pulled out the second. *Braydon*, read the name on the pocket. She snorted. 'Oh, he is so going to wear these. Even if I have to use a block and tackle to get him into them.'

'It's the last pair I think you need to see.'

Kylie placed the Braydon set on top of the Kylie set and pulled the last pair out of the parcel. The tears were plopping out so fast there wasn't enough fluoro yellow plastic in the world that would cope. The writing on the pocket was *Wendy*.

'Oh, Mum.' It was like those were the only two words in her vocabulary now.

'And I'm even going to wear them,' her mother said with a touch of belligerence.

Kylie leant forward and pulled her mother in for a hug. 'I love them. I love you, Mum. And … I think maybe I'm the one who needs to be finding an olive branch online to buy for you.'

Her mum held her so tight it was like Kylie was a kid again, and her life was simple and happy, and every night ended with a little tractor who found ways to be happy despite the mud or the rain. 'I love you, Kylie. I'm sorry I've been such a selfish parent.'

'I'm sorry I've been such a selfish child.'

Life wasn't simple. Life wasn't always happy. But maybe it could be, sometimes. If you and the people you loved weren't too damaged or stubborn to embrace change.

CHAPTER 36

*You are invited to Snowy River Vineyard's
Harvest Festival & Antique Tractor Pull
Tickets include:
A morning of grape picking
Supervised by Berridale Cellar Door vintner and
wine industry legend Chris Farmer*

*A long lunch
Catered by The Billy Button Café with a wine tasting
curated by Graeme Sharpe*

A book launch for The Paddlewheeler and the Pelican
*A collaboration between beloved children's author Frank Silva
and Hanrahan local Maureen Plover*

*A 50-yard dash
A tractor-pull competition between Snowy River Vineyard's
Chamberlain 90 and a rival from Dalgety,*

a Massey Ferguson 35 owned and restored by Dale Emmett. Quickest tow of a trailer stacked with crates of fresh-plucked grapes over a 50-yard distance

Master of Ceremonies of the Harvest Festival is none other than television personality Nick Johns!

Tickets on sale now.
Kids welcome, plenty of parking and the Hanrahan Pub is putting on a courtesy shuttle bus that'll run all day between the vineyard and Hanrahan.

Funds raised will go towards the Hanrahan and District Community Association for the preservation of our local history

Damon had walked the lanes of the vineyard where families were filling buckets with grapes. He'd forced his way between the cello player and the violinist on the deck of the PW *Moana* and insisted on checking the engine hatch to make sure she wasn't in there, fiddling with a piston or something. He'd checked the shack where they'd kissed, the marquee where a crew from the café in town was bustling about with more stainless steel caterers' dishes and bain-maries and hotplates than he'd ever seen gathered in one space, and he'd done a grid search of the flat ground near the lakeside, where a petting zoo was in full kick, a tea and coffee station was set up, a bar was pumping, and where three long tables stretched out like cricket stumps under garlands of fairy lights and crepe paper and greenery.

In the kitchen, he ran across a kid who looked vaguely familiar. 'Do I know you?' he said.

'I'm Braydon. I'm Kylie's apprentice. I'm her cousin, too, so I can be trusted with whatever secrets you might wish to tell me.'

Damon blinked. 'No secrets to impart at this time. What are you doing here?'

'Marigold Jones roped me in. She's not even paying me, can you believe that? Says volunteering is the heart of the community and it's about time I did my bit. She told me to wash dishes, fill tea urns and butter up the old ladies. I mean, that's sexist, right? Hey, you're a barrister, aren't you? Maybe you could go remind her about wage theft. And gendered work instructions to underage vulnerable workers—'

Damon held up a hand and, thank god, the kid shut up. 'Where's Kylie?'

Braydon shrugged. 'Dunno. Not here. Last I saw, she was in her workshop, eating her way through a six pack of donuts. She didn't even share them. I mean—'

Damon left the room before he could get roped into starting a class action on food-sharing practices within the secondary school vocational educational system. He found Nick in the study, having his shirt collar rearranged by a fussing Marigold.

'It's not even ten o'clock and the grapes are halfway picked,' Marigold was saying. 'We need to slow them down. I want you to walk through the pickers being charming and chatty, do you understand? Tell stories and let Kevvy take some videos on his new smartphone. The local news people promised to be here so keep an eye out and do your best to get on camera.'

'Charming and chatty,' said Nick. 'Hog the camera lenses. Got it.'

'If you had bothered arriving a little earlier than last night, Damon, we could have had a run-through and given you a proper job, too.'

Nick sent a wink in Damon's direction, who had cadged a ride with Sean and Warunya. His friends had insisted on attending the Harvest Festival.

'Eleven o'clock, we're launching *The Paddlewheeler and the Pelican*, but we can expect that to be of most interest to the families here with kids, so we'll do that near the petting zoo. Someone better remind me to give the chamber orchestra a break so we can hear you over the loudspeaker. Has anyone seen Maureen?'

Kev Jones, irrigation expert and world's calmest man, was crumpling up raffle tickets and sticking them into an ornate silver wine bucket that looked rather like the one that usually lived in the kitchen. Whatever. Damon didn't care. All he did care about was finding Kylie. And Alfie, of course. But first, Kylie.

'When's the tractor pull?' he said.

'Not until this afternoon. It's last up, when everyone's relaxed and had a beer or two.'

She'd have to be here by then—she was the organiser. Maybe even the driver. At least, she had been four weeks ago, when they'd last spoken.

Kylie had ghosted him. And it kinda hurt.

Damon looked up as Sean and Warunya entered the room. 'Hey, guys, meet Marigold and Kev. Marigold, these are my friends from Sydney. They're very keen to volunteer.'

'Oh, I don't think we are—' began Warunya, but it was too late.

'Come with me,' said Marigold, sweeping them off in the direction of the garden.

'Thought you might have persuaded your mother to come along, boys,' said Kev.

'We invited her,' said Nick. 'She said she'd absolutely love to come, but then of course didn't. It's probably just as well. This place is so nice, I expect she'd have got the pip with Damon for buying it off her.'

'I paid her for it. Well, me and the bank that now owns my soul. Fortunately my terrace house in Sydney is worth more now than when I bought it.'

'Why don't we go have a glass of champagne instead of standing here arguing?'

'Sparkling chardonnay,' Damon said, distracted. 'And no thanks.'

'Listen to you,' said Nick. 'Boasting like a true vintner just because you own a few rows of grapes.'

Damon narrowed his eyes. 'You know, I think I did see Maureen outside earlier, taking preorders for the book. She was looking for the fellow who was all hair, no wit. I think she might have meant you, brother.'

Nick chuckled. 'You've got me there, mate. Why are you looking so cranky, anyway? I thought you'd be on bended knee in front of Kylie by now.'

Jesus wept.

Kev looked up from his raffle tickets, his face as bedecked with interest as the pergola on the lawn was with fairy lights. 'Good on you, son.'

'What I am going to do or not do is entirely my business, Kev.'

He gave them all a glare, then turned on his heel and went back outside. He'd walk the cars. All of them. All the way out to the main road, if that's what it took; if her ute was here, she'd be here, and that would help ease this awful knot he had in his guts.

He'd left her, but he was back. And even when he left, he'd known he would be back. He just hadn't thought it would take so much time to think through all the things that needed to be thought, and organise everything that needed to be organised.

He also hadn't thought she'd refuse to answer her phone when he called.

He was almost at the road when a 4WD rolled in over the cattle grid and parked up in some long grass. Tom Krauss and Hannah Cody got out. Hannah came forward to greet Damon as Tom turned his attention to the back seat to start wrangling their offspring.

'Did you give her my letter?' he said.

Hannah reached into the pocket of her jeans and brought out three or four scraps of paper that had been whole when he'd given them to her last night under cover of darkness at the vet clinic's back door.

He'd thought he was making a gesture. The torn paper in his hand told him he'd been wrong.

Maybe she hadn't even read it. 'Did she …' He looked up at Hannah.

'Read it all? Yes. I'm sorry, Damon. She's really unhappy. I wish you'd let me tell her that you were the one paying for Alfie's food. She thinks you buggered off, not caring about anything you'd left behind.'

He sighed. 'I was hoping she'd come here and we could sneak off and I could explain to her why I've had to take some time before coming back.'

'You want my advice?'

'Sure.' Advice was one of the things he'd needed some time to learn how to take. Advice, help, therapy. All help welcome.

'Go find her. She'll either be in her workshop staring mournfully at Trevor or taking that great mutt of yours to the lake to throw sticks in the water.'

'I can't drive. I lost my licence a while back and three months is nearly up, but not quite.'

'No need to look like the world's about to end. Tom?'

Tom was stuffing something—possibly a swaddled baby, but it could have been a pumpkin for all that was visible from here—into a pram that he'd taken out of the boot, but he looked up. 'Yes?'

'Give me the kid. Be a lamb and drive Damon into Hanrahan, will you? He needs to see Kylie.'

Tom didn't hesitate. 'Jump in.'

Kylie was on her back under the chassis of a HiLux ute when Damon walked up the driveway to the workshop's open roller door. Music was playing from a speaker—something bluesy and earnest and raw—and she didn't hear him approach.

Alfie did. The great lump had been sitting by her feet as though he'd taken on an apprentice role and was ready to pass an oil filter or a spanner at any moment, but he heaved himself up and trotted over to Damon as though Damon was the sun and he was a new day looking for dawn.

Dogs. So bloody awesome.

'Hello, old friend,' Damon said, giving Alfie a rub. 'You're looking very handsome and well.'

Alfie gave one of his groan-moan-rumbles and then tottered off to the browned grass past Trevor to pee happily at the base of an old fuel bowser.

'Kylie,' Damon said.

No answer. Maybe the music was louder in there than out here. He could go tap her on the boot, but she'd be likely to bang her head in surprise.

He took a seat on Trevor and waited.

And waited some more.

And decided he wasn't the right personality type to wait patiently for anything.

Tom's last words to him as they'd driven to town circled around in his brain and he decided they had some merit. He pulled out his phone, tapped around a bit until he was satisfied, then hit send.

Damon heard the ping from inside the workshop; her phone must be bluetoothed to whatever speaker was playing the music. Her boots twitched and he pictured her under the ute, bolting a new exhaust into place (or whatever it was mechanics did under utes) then pulling out her phone to check its screen.

He checked his own.

Hey from RuRo: You've sent a message! Good luck!

He clicked into the message he'd sent: *Hi there. Saw your profile and wondered if we'd be a good match. Thoughts?*

His phone gave a gentle buzz and an answering message flicked up. Huh. He wouldn't have thought there would be room under the chassis of a ute to be texting, but Kylie was pretty small.

Thoughts? What sort of an open-ended question is that? Also, your profile is quite vague, FIFO.

Yeah, that'd be because he'd typed it in three seconds flat and matched it to a poor-resolution photo of him looking as nondescript as possible, wearing a navy shirt and a hat pulled low, standing against a dark wall. Unlike his brother Nick, Damon wasn't in the habit of taking selfies every six seconds and brag posting them online with fatuous hashtags like *#livingthelife* or *#thankful*.

His bio said: *Lonely, reliable FIFO worker living at the foothills of the Snowy Mountains seeks practical and independent lady who doesn't mind being alone when he's away working.*

Nothing for a minute or so, and then:

Sorry, mate. I've been meaning to take my profile down. I'm not good company at the moment, but thanks for reaching out.

Alfie gave a little whiffle as though to agree. 'I'm glad you've been with her, Alfie. I've been a total arse, I know that, but I'm here to keep saying sorry and to explain and to show her I can be better, in the hope that she'll forgive me.'

Sorry to hear that, he typed. *Why aren't you good company? Did something happen?*

The usual story. A broken heart. May not recover. Blah blah blah.

Maybe a pizza would make you feel better. On a dock over the lake but no drama queen brother interruptions this time. I know the perfect place.

Damon heard a thunk under the ute. Either Kylie had hit her head hard enough to be concussed or she'd dropped a wrench. A message flicked upon his phone.

Tell me your real name.

You want full disclosure? Here's a few facts about me, then, to get started. A) You know my name. B) I miss my dog. Also, he's lost weight, well done. C) It is not okay for me to have a profile up on a dating app, either, because my heart belongs to another. D) I'm dead serious about the FIFO. I think I can make it work, but it can only work with someone as strong and independent as you, Kylie. I can do my research and prep work in Hanrahan and court work in Sydney. This list is becoming an alphabet, but I have a fair bit of atonement to get through, so, E) I need to work less or risk going completely berko, but I have a stinking great mortgage so I'm counting on you being a totally successful business owner to help us make ends meet and, finally, F) Trevor needs a new seat. This pink metal thing is doing irreparable damage to my very fine arse (which I've seen you ogling in the past, so no point trying to hide the fact you fancy it). Please forgive me for being away so long. Even though I had to leave you so I could get my personal shit together. Also ghosting me was HARSH.

Never had a wheeled mechanic's dolly gone from zero to full speed so quickly. Kylie practically fell off it in her hurry to roll over onto her hands and knees and spring to her feet, but then she was upright and racing for the wide open roller door, and for a millisecond it seemed like she was going to launch herself into his arms and he was going to get to have his arms wrapped around her so tight she would *know* he was never going to let her go again, without him even having to say anything, and everything was going to be beautifully, simply, wonderfully perfect—

But she didn't. She just stared at him. Cried a bit. And he felt like the scummiest piece of crud that had ever walked into a Snowy Mountains town and ruined someone's life.

'Nice overalls,' he said. Because they were hot pink and because he was an emotional fuckwit. *Why is it so hard to just say, I'm sorry, I'm an emotional fuckwit, I love you?* he thought savagely.

'They were from Mum.'

'No way. That sounds like a story I definitely want to hear at some other, much later time.'

Silence, then: 'Alfie missed you.'

'I'm sorry. I missed him.' Man, this was going to be a long road to forgiveness if they both had to express their emotions via the proxy of a forty kilogram furball. 'I missed you,' he said. 'Desperately.'

'Really,' she said. Her tone was redolent of disbelief.

'Really, truly, cross my heart. I was hoping you'd come out to the vineyard today. It's my home now. Well, a small part of it is mine and a very large part of it is the bank's.'

She said nothing and her face was hard to read. Even for him, an expert in reading faces. This was not going as he had hoped.

He waited for Dr Gloom to weigh in with some shrinky facts about emotional hurt and forgiveness but … nothing.

He was on his own here. Thinking, speaking, for himself.

They stared at each other for a while longer and then he said, to warm up this chilly mood more than anything, 'Hannah tells me you've been moping.'

She raised her eyebrows. 'Hannah? You and Hannah have been chatting?'

He cleared his throat. 'I've been paying her to send dog food over for Alfie each week. We've, um, bonded.'

'You've *bonded*?'

'Well, I've bonded. She's delivered monologues on the idiocy of men in general and me in particular. She's the one who sent me here today.'

'I. Will. Kill. Her. With. My. Bare. Hands,' Kylie said.

'Will you let me explain? Why I went away and why I had to stay away, and why I've come back?' He held his breath. Everything was riding on her answer. Everything.

She sighed and rubbed her face with her hands, leaving an adorable trace of grease from eyebrow to chin. 'I'll listen.'

And Damon told her. About the downside of having a memory that never let him forget anything. About the judge he'd been to see, to talk about his first panic attack. About putting his Sydney home on the market and organising a bridging loan, about persuading his mother to let him buy the vineyard. About rearranging his expectations about his career. About the rift between the brothers after Nick moved to Melbourne. About Deirdre, the mother who was not overly awesome at mothering.

Most of all, she listened to him talk about his doubt. And how he should have gotten help way before now but he'd been too proud, or full of himself, or he-didn't-know-what-but-something, that he'd always resisted asking for help.

And she held him. At first, just his hand. Then she crawled into his lap and held his face. Then they hugged and, okay, they snogged a bit, and Alfie tried to wedge his way between them. But since he was obese and stank vaguely of dead lakebirds, he broke them apart.

'I'm hoping we could start again,' Damon said. 'I can be the newcomer to town, but this time I'm planning on staying, not leaving. You can be the single lady mechanic looking for her happy ever after. I can't promise to love tractors. But I can promise to love you.'

Kylie nodded. 'It's a start.'

'A *start*? Kylie, that was a declaration of love. A beautiful one, considering I felt I needed to weave the word "tractor" into it. Do you know how many romantic poems have involved the word tractor? None. Zero. Zilch.'

'It's the farmer thing. It might be a deal breaker.'

'Look, I know grapes aren't as fluffy as sheep or as eggy as chickens, but what about little kiddies in gumboots running through a sunny vineyard? Do you think *you* could compromise now? Just a little?'

She grinned. 'You're winning me round. But hold that thought, because I am about to be very late for my first ever tractor-pull event. Let's hit the road.'

CHAPTER 37

Damon and Kylie missed the tractor pull, which sucked, because Uncle Frank's—actually, make that Damon's—Chamberlain 90 won. They missed the long lunch and the reading of *The Paddle-wheeler and the Pelican*. They missed the departure of the PW *Moana*, too, which was a shame, because Kylie had been hoping for an opportunity to chat with Dave Ryan and remind him what an excellent mechanic she was.

They didn't, however, miss the washing up.

When they finally made it back to Snowy River Vineyard, the kitchen was a flurry of suds and temperamental, overtired volunteers, who were sent on their way rather tactfully by Damon, who pointed out that since he'd been absent for the best part of the Harvest Festival, it was only fair that he sorted out the rest of the mess. Maureen handed him an apron, winked at him, and took off out the back door.

Two hours later, six exhausted humans and one naughty dog—who'd abandoned his diet to take advantage of the food dropped by kids all over the lawn—sprawled on a picnic rug in the grass beneath the fairy lights, watching the moonlight catch the ripples on the lake.

'I thought they'd never leave,' said Nick. 'All afternoon hiding in a kitchen, washing teacups? Never again.'

'To be fair, I did most of the washing, Nick. You spent about thirty minutes checking your reflection in the glass door of the microwave.' Braydon's wide-eyed look of incredulity at being in the presence of an actual television personality had worn off. And ... why was Braydon even still here? Kylie was very much hoping she wasn't supposed to be driving him home, because she had no intention of leaving any time soon.

Nick pulled a tea towel from his back pocket and mock-whipped Braydon's leg with it. 'Hey, appliance management is a workplace health and safety issue. I was checking that glass for dangerous cracks.'

'Speaking of workplaces and responsibilities, how are you getting home, Braydon?' said Kylie.

'Um ... dunno.'

'He can sleep with Alfie. In the pantry,' said Damon.

Alfie's tail thumped on the grass, indicating his willingness to go along with any plan that included him.

'I can drive him,' said Nick.

Damon was tickling Kylie's ear with a strand of grass he'd plucked. 'What a great idea. Why don't you drive Braydon home and pick us up some pizza? Take Sean and Runya for a drive while you're at it. They'd love to see Hanrahan. Go the long way.'

Oh, yes, that sounded good. Then it would just be him and her, lazing the evening away without a care in the world.

'Soon,' said Nick, in a tone that sounded like he was in no hurry to move. 'Hey, I had a great idea today. For a reality show. The idea came to me at the tractor pull. Seeing all those people come along to see the old machinery—people love a bit of history and a bit of adventure.'

Any other time, Kylie might have cared, but not at this precise moment.

Sean did seem to care. Or he was being polite. 'You are so right, Nick.'

'You know Burke and Wills? Two explorers, tromping through Indigenous country without consulting elders, et cetera, and dropping dead at the end of it? I'm thinking of re-enacting their journey on motorbike. On the Littlecub, actually. And along the way, calling into the towns of outback Australia and talking about how distance and roads have impacted the towns, and checking out any historic vehicles the towns may have tucked away in garages and whatever.'

'Sounds cool,' said Braydon. 'What about you broaden your demographic? Have a teenage sidekick? I bet I look great on camera.'

'Somebody throw a pillow at that kid's head,' said Damon.

'I was thinking maybe you could come with me,' said Nick.

'*Me?*' said Damon. 'Sorry, mate. I'm already straddling life in two places—the Sydney courts and in Hanrahan with Kylie. I don't think I can split myself three ways without coming undone.'

'I meant Kylie.'

Damon narrowed his eyes. 'You want to go on the road with *my* girlfriend?'

Nick laughed. 'Well, she is the only one here who knows anything at all about motorbikes and vintage tractors.'

Kylie smiled. The offer was flattering. Validating, even. But she was happy just where she was. She put her hand into Damon's and gave it a squeeze.

'I'm not going anywhere, Nick. Sorry. Me and your brother have vows to break.'

ACKNOWLEDGEMENTS

My tractor knowledge would struggle to fill a postage stamp (remember them?) so I owe a debt of gratitude to the book *Going Round the Bend in Search of Old Tractors* by Ian M. Johnston, which is not only an informative read but a fun and conversational one.

This book had a tight deadline and I have to thank the HarperCollins editorial team of Julia, Kylie and Annabel who each went above and beyond to help me get the manuscript completed on time.

My sister-in-law Trish and author mate Penelope Janu both gave me advice about the legal world, and if I've got the details right, we can thank them. If I've made some ludicrous legal stuff up, then we can point the finger at me. I spent a most instructive few days watching a murder trial in the Queensland Supreme Court and discovered that a lifelong passion for crime shows had left me with a very skewed idea of the reality of courtroom etiquette and procedure. My tradie sister Liz came through with marine diesel engine advice, and I spent some happy days touring vineyards while I plotted out the lifecycle of Uncle Frank's cool-climate grapes.

The PW *Moana* was inspired by the PW *Mayflower*, currently operating on the Mannum River in South Australia. The *Moana*'s journey from the Murray River via flatbed truck to Lake Bogong was inspired by the *Pride of the Murray*'s long (but ill-fated) journey to the Thomson River in Longreach, Queensland.

Damon's panic attacks were informed by stories shared by members of the bar and I gained insight from, among other sources, the website www.wellbeingatthebar.org.uk.

Alfie's addiction to butter and socks was an easy write. I'd like to thank my labradors (sadly only one still with us), Roly, Rosie and Angus for their commitment to gluttony, bread, socks, stuffed toys, underwire bras, pool noodles, breaking into food tins, and boundless love.

Returning to my Snowy River town Hanrahan was a delight, as always, and if you enjoyed this book, then you might like to read Josh Cody's story in *The Vet from Snowy River*, Hannah Cody's story in *A Home Among the Snow Gums*, or vet clinic receptionist Sandy's story in *A Cattle Dog for Christmas*.

For informal book chat and news about upcoming projects, please follow me on Instagram or Facebook @stella.quinn.author

Regards,
Stella

talk about it

Let's talk about books.

Join the conversation:

@harlequinaustralia

@hqanz

@harlequinaus

harpercollins.com.au/hq

If you love reading and want to know about our authors and titles, then let's talk about it.